Grimes' Redux

An Only Die Twice Novel

Written By

H.A.L. Wagner

Published by

Grimes' Redux: You Only Die Twice Novel © 2023

H.A.L. WAGNER ISBN: 9781942657132

The Grimes Collection:

Grimes' Punishment A Blood, Sex and Brawls Novel

Grimes' Retribution A Debt Paid in Full Novel

Grimes' Reckoning A Waking the Dead Novel

Grimes' Redux An Only Die Twice Novel

Thank you for reading Grimes Redux. Grimes has gone through a lot as a character and Redux, being part four in the series helps to wrap things up for him, but his story isn't over. There will be more Grimes novels.

The first book, Punishment, was an introduction to a young fresh face in the anti-hero genre. A thief, wanting out of the criminal life is pulled back in because he can't turn a blind eye to the horrific nature of men. The effects on Grimes are both physical and emotional. Still, he *endeavors to persevere.*

If you haven't read Punishment, you may want to go back to that first.

As always, if you liked it, tell a friend.

Thank you,

H.A.L. Wagner

Preamble

You've had that one conversation, a story of a wrong that needs righted and when you hear it, you wish you knew a guy like me. The guy to call when court orders don't work, and time served isn't justice served. I'm the friend of a friend, never your friend. The guy you tell people you know but have never met. If you had my number, you'd never make the call because the consequences overtake you with fear. And I'm the guy you never want to see waiting for you.

The mouth of the Gatorade bottle was large enough to fit the two Alka Seltzer tablets in without breaking them. The daytime cold medicine offered a citrus flavor and a little hop to keep me awake. The fizzing slowed. I chugged half the bottle down and came up feeling my eyes begin to open. I burped that heavy feeling out of my stomach then took a deep breath and finished the bottle.

The pain in my head subsided as I sat in my truck parked across the street from Tara Polk's apartment. It was a fourplex with a small yard on a street lined with 100-year-old craftsman homes. Several had been converted to multi-dwellings over the decades. The file Monique emailed stated Tara was a twenty-six-year-old single mother of one, who was having trouble with a stalker.

Monique handed over the case last week, my third case this month. Taking care of a stalker wasn't a challenge so I tacked it on with the substitute teacher taking pictures of his third graders and a serial rapist who didn't let two previous convictions persuade his cravings. Last I heard the rapist slit his wrists after he healed from what I did to him.

To say I was a private investigator was misleading but on nights like this, sitting in a parked car at 1:07 am, having that license, kept the local PD off my ass.

I resumed the game on my phone. A way to pass the time, a simple single player runs and must jump obstacles and collect coins. I never got very far, usually dying in under a minute, but it passed time. When I lived in a duplex years ago, a neighbor kid I sometimes babysat, got me to download it because he played it too. He would text me before his bedtime to see if I was playing, he said we could play at the same time, like we were playing together. His last text was still in my phone. I had ignored it then, now I sit playing the game, wondering if he is too.

A silver Chevy pickup crept past from behind. I slouched in the bench seat. The driver wasn't paying attention to me, his eyes fixed on the apartment. He parked and got out. DJ Hudson, mid-thirties, about 5'10'', crossed the street towards Tara's apartment as carefree as if he were walking home.

I slipped out of the white Ford F-150 and walked in a crouch, keeping my eyes just over the tops of cars until I got to his truck. A neoprene face mask rolled down from the top of my head, the kind motorcyclists use to keep bugs out of their teeth. I laid down flat so I could watch his feet on the asphalt. His tennis shoes went up the curb and across the small lawn of the four-unit complex.

DJ tried the door, jiggling the knob. Things were escalating. Last week he just tapped on the window, then ran off. The locked door stopped him this time. I couldn't let it go another week. He went around to the window. Sorry, Tara, you'll have to see him exposed once more.

Her scream filled the quiet street. His feet swiftly

covered the road back to his truck. I watched him move around the front and scurried myself to the back of the truck. The cab light popped on, my signal to pounce.

My forearm smashed into the base of his neck, bending back his head, slamming it into the door jamb of the cab. With swear words coming out, he tried to turn but I hooked my right arm through his right armpit and palmed the back of his head. With a hand full of his brown hair, I smashed his face into the jamb twice more. His knees gave out as his sight blurred. I let him fall into the gutter.

My size twelve Vans pressed down on the middle of his back.

"Leave the girl alone. She's got enough trouble in her life without having to look at your little prick."

A soft laugh lifted out of the gutter. My shoe slid up his back to his neck and I pressed letting gravity use more of my 200-pounds. His laughter turned to a wheezy cough. I let up.

As I started to walk away, I heard him say, "See ya around."

I turned to find him sitting up, a whistle carried the tune of a broken nose. I took two steps towards him and kicked his head into the open truck door. He slumped over.

"Better not." I said and went back to my truck.

I sat in the cab of my own truck. My eyes drifted to the light in Tara's window. The round silhouette of her face looked in my direction. She gave a little wave then disappeared behind the curtain. The light went out. I doubted she could see in the cab, still, I kept the mask on while I punched out an email to Monique. DJ wouldn't be back to bother Tara or anyone else.

That was it. The violence for the night was over. I could go back to the apartment I had above my friend's automotive shop and try to sleep.

Chapter 1

There's been a break in.- Text message from Willis Sanford, my employer.

At 3 am my brain was dough and my head a bag of cement. The blurred vision cleared, as the text messages came into focus. No, I wasn't dreaming. Slowly a heard of buffalo stampeded over my chest as my heart felt like it was going to break loose and vibrate out of my throat. Vomit. I leaned over putting my hands on my knees, *just throw up and get it over with.* Nothing surfaced. I stumbled from my couch to a pair of jeans on the floor. Once they were on, I slipped over a black hoodie, then headed out the door.

Red and blue flashing lights met me at the parking lot of the CBR building and the push of vomit trapped in my throat again. An ambulance had the back door open, and a plump, curly haired middle-aged woman dressed in white and blue polyester security uniform sat talking with her hands while an EMT held an ice pack on her head. A plain clothes cop with a big gut stood with one foot on the bumper while jotting notes as the guard recounted her tale of assault.

Her wide eyes caught me, and she waved. Her story must have included something about me because the detective rolled dull eyes over me as she went on talking. He jotted notes down, turning his attention to her again. She was a sweet lady and seeing her injured was getting me angry.

"How many of them did you get, before they got you?" I said letting a smile curl in the corner of my mouth.

Barb's head flung back in a cackle, causing the EMT to

lose the cold compress. "Oh, I wish I'd got them all, but they hit me from behind." Her arm swung up as if dropping a mallet on her curly head. "Sorry I let them break in, Roger."

"You did your best," I said.

"Roger Grimes?" The detective dropped his foot from the bumper.

I nodded.

"I'll let the other detectives know you're on your way up." He grabbed a small radio and sent out a call.

I still had to show my ID to two different officers who had to call and talk to someone before I cleared the elevators to the seventh floor of the building. I ducked under the yellow crime tape and went in. Monique's desk had every drawer pulled, the contents on the floor. Sanford's inner office door was open. I paused to listen to muffled voices of more cops inside.

Sanford stood wearing black slacks and a white button-down tucked in with the top three buttons undone exposing a white undershirt and the sleeves rolled up. I couldn't see his face as he looked out the window with sounds of a police camera clicking around the room. Detectives and officers meander about, leaving tracks in the thick gold-colored carpet. One detective would point and the one with the camera would shoot a photo. They stepped on folders, and overturned chairs, poking at anything out of place with pens as they meandered around the office. Pairs of eyes looking at the walls, ceiling and every corner but never doing much except nodding to one another.

Sanford's forearm pressed against the glass for support as he looked west. It was his old neighbourhood, one with slouched roofs on pre-war wood clapped houses. Black rectangles marked the overgrown empty lots where houses burned or were torn down. To his left was the ocean, lined with high-rise condos and massive million-dollar homes.

From this corner office he straddled two worlds, and he sent me out to work in both.

Sanford pulled his gaze from Daytona Beach below to look at me. His hands shoved in his pockets. He knew what I wanted to ask but couldn't because of all the uniforms standing about.

A short man with dark hair, wearing a dress shirt, no tie, held out his card. Sanford took it without looking at it and tossed it on the desk into the pile of miscellaneous papers that had been strewn about during the robbery.

"Grimes, you want the detective to walk you through it?" Sanford said.

I shook my head no. The cop smirked letting me know it wasn't going to happen anyway.

The detective watched Sanford's actions then said, "Call us if you can think of anyone who may have done this."

Sanford looked at me then the detective, "That's why I have him."

The detective shrugged, "Have it your way. We're done here." He waved the rest of the crime scene investigators and uniformed officers out of the office.

"Eager to serve." I said looking around at the mess, wondering what the cops hoped to find in the pictures they took. The thermostat was cranked up making me sweat more than the cops did. I found a turned over chair, a chair with red and gold paisley upholstery. The chair used to be gold but two years ago I sat bleeding in it. After that he had it reupholstered. I sat across from Sanford's large mahogany desk to build some familiar structure to chaos in the office.

"Friends of Detective Waycross I assume." Sanford said wagging his eyebrows.

"What gave it away? Their lack of concern or the way they photographed every document instead of the scene as a whole," I said. Waycross had been a copycat vigilante who was out for profit not Hammurabi's Code. Sometimes I took more than an eye, sometimes I took the whole head. Waycross wanted cash not revenge. He shook down drug dealers and pimps. I exposed him for the crimes he committed, the local newspaper labelled him the town's most wanted Vigilante. He didn't last long in prison. Some on the force still idolized him for what he did and hated me for what I did.

The heat kicked on once more and we listened to a whirl escape the vents. He sat in silence; his usual machinegun mouth was out of bullets. Slowly he sorted papers into piles without any order. The silence was uncomfortable even for me.

On the carpet lay a bottle of cognac. I set it on the marble countertop. The minifridge was feet from the wall and on its side. What was ice was just a puddle now, so I poured three fingers of cognac straight.

The lawyer collapsed back into his leather chair and rested drooping red eyes on the drink then sipped. "Thanks, my friend." He tapped his long brown fingers on the desk as his brain went back to work. Sanford leaned back, taking his fingers off the desk and tapped together tip to tip. He took a deep breath and exhaled.

"They got our files." Sanford stood up from behind the heavy mahogany desk, "They got the list, they got everything." He downed his drink then went to the bar to refill. I followed him.

"That's why you told the cops they got nothing." I said, feeling more confident in my boss but less confident in my own security. The list was something we had been working on from the beginning. Years ago I burned down a poolhall that was fronting an underage sex trafficking ring. I managed to get a list of names of clients. Sanford went to work figuring out who they were and I spent my time making them pay. We had to be slow, methodical. Just popping off rounds into high end imports would be stupid. We played the long game, sometimes Sanford dropped evidence off with friendly prosecutors. Sometimes it was with divorce lawyers that would expose them in court.

He nodded, raised his glass then took a gulp.

Sanford said, "The files are encrypted. Hopefully, I got my money's worth."

"We never finished it," I said.

"The list? Nah, we didn't. We got close and we made a lot of them suckers pay." Sanford looked at the mess and the opened safe door, "They tossed it pretty good." Sanford said then took another sip.

"Camera's catch anything?"

"Two men, masks, all in black. Looked like pros, knew just what to do." Sanford pulled a laptop computer near him. He plugged in a flash drive, then turned it around so I could see. We sat silently while he pulled up the video.

The video was grey from night vision. The first thief in a black ski mask came out of the mailroom, reached up and spray painted the lens of the security camera. It was small and held two large drop boxes for UPS and FedEx on adjacent walls. I assumed thief one simply hid in there among a stack of outgoing boxes for pick-up the next day.

Sanford clicked on the computer and the screen switched to the camera down the hall. The camera was at an angle so we couldn't see the whole hallway, but I could infer the small black figure was bypassing the security on the back door. Moments later a taller black figure came in.

The camera covering the lobby showed Barb, the security guard, hear something and leave the desk to investigate. The blacked-out camera didn't show the security guard get thumped and locked in the mail room. The thieves made their way to Sanford's office, spray painted the camera and that was that.

I stood quiet for a moment, envisioning how they went about locating the safe and cracking it. No drill holes. The face of the door looked smooth and free from scratches until I got to the bottom right of the door near the hinge. I looked on the inside of the door. A red button sat just above the tiny scratch. I closed the safe. It locked.

"What's the code?"

Sanford hesitated to tell me instead moved near to do it himself but stopped.

"9 9 8 1 7."

I punched the number, but it didn't unlock. He came at the safe in a hurry. Punching the keys himself he got the same red light indicating it was the wrong code.

"I don't get it."

"The thief reset your code," I said. Then went out to Monique's desk and found a long nail file. I bent it at a ninety-degree angle and slipped it between the safe door and frame, sliding it until I hit the reset code button. It beeped and I punched in 11111. It opened.

"I told you to upgrade that thing." I said and sat down.

Sanford stood there looking at the little red button that might have cost us our freedom and maybe our lives.

"You did. I'll get it switched out."

"I'm not sure why they worked together. It was an easy one-man job. The short one was the lock pick, safe cracker. The short one didn't need the tall guy. It was the tall guy's job, he wanted to come. He wanted in, wanted assurance it was done right and was scared to death of a double cross."

"Your professional experience tells you that?" Sanford said referring to my past life as a thief.

"Why'd you keep files anyway? What are they, trophies?" I asked getting back on track with the break-in.

"No, nothing like that Grimes. In this game of chess with the criminal underworld it's more than busting skulls and setting fires. It's about strategy and part of that is knowing what they have done to guess what they will do next." Sanford moved papers into stacks.

Sanford and his chess games. I felt like a pawn from the start of this thing though he always called me his White Knight. The joke wasn't lost on me, a white PI working for a powerful black attorney. Peel back a layer and uncertainty kept a vigil over Sanford's belief in me. Maybe I was only doubting myself being a white knight, because the work was leaving me with a black soul.

He shoved papers in a folder, and said, "I'm sorry Grimes. I really am."

I believed him. He had done his best and I would have to do mine before that information made it to the police or in the hands of the syndicate we were silently at war with.

The yellow carbon copy of the guard's handwritten report was on the desk. She described how the click of a door latch got her up to investigate. In the dark of a mail room, she was struck on the head. They bound the door with rope. Her description was vague; white guys, black masks, one tall one short. That was it.

"Do you have any contacts still in this *business*?" He said that last part like saying an ex-girlfriend's name that had done him wrong.

"No, Billy might."

"I wish we could find Smitty, he could help." Sanford said.

I shrugged, "He hasn't returned any of my calls. Billy's neither." I picked at my fingernail thinking where he might be. The last few years he had been checking in with Billy or I once a month. Sometimes it was to present us with a job, if we wanted back in, other times it was just to shoot the shit. For the past two months I just kept thinking tomorrow he would call. He hasn't.

We set about getting the office cleaned up. The sun was about to rise as we put the last papers in their proper spots. Though the office was not fully back together, Sanford urged me to go home.

"Go get some sleep and come back at nine. We have a meeting at 9:00." Sanford said shaking my hand.

"Okay," I said. Sleep deprived I didn't ask the topic. That came back to haunt me as I got back to my apartment. The old couch screamed out as I laid down exhausted, but rest never came.

Chapter 2

At seven am, I stared at the curvy patterns of the plywood ceiling. After three sets of pushups and pullups, I showered and changed into a pair of khaki Dickies, t-shirt and slipped into a blue mechanic's style jacket. The weather outside was grey and balmy. A little humid for the jacket but experience told me it would rain and afterward would be cool and dry.

With time on my side, I drove along A1A, stopping at a beach approach to watch the surf. The sky was more pink than grey now and filled with silhouettes of birds skimming the rolling waves. The beach walkers were out taking full swinging steps. So too were a few surf fishermen, with nine-foot surf rods in poles anchored in the sand.

A decade ago, Smitty had a twenty-two-foot Grady White with the cuddy cabin. He kept the boat at Halifax Marina in the center of town. After telling Smitty I didn't fish, he said he didn't trust a man who couldn't feed himself. Being young and stupid, I lifted my shirt so he could see the black grip of a pistol. I told him I fed myself just fine.

He shook his head and said cast off was at six. I didn't make it until six-thirty. Passing mangrove covered islands in the river we would cruise to Ponce Inlet then out to the Atlantic Ocean. Once far enough out off the coast he would cut the engines sending us into silence, just the lapping of water against the hull. We baited our hooks and cast out into the deep green waters of the Gulf Stream.

Smitty would tell tales of growing up in Ft. Lauderdale in the early sixties. Catching bait and fishing in canals. He hunted in the glades, living off the land over long weekends. Stories repeated every time we were out, but he enjoyed telling them. His blue eyes would fade out into the Atlantic as his mind filled with simpler sunny days and humid nights. Back before dog racing, the Mob, before Daytona Beach and racketeering and debt collecting.

I brushed the memory aside and drove on to the CBR building for my morning meeting.

Inside the office, the yellow tape was gone, and Monique was standing at a filing cabinet dressed in a pale grey suit that smoothly painted over every rise and fall of her perfect hourglass figure. The top two buttons of a purple blouse were undone leaving the others struggling to hold back her ample chest. Either she hadn't left for court yet or had already returned.

A nod was the only greeting I gave Monique and the only I got in return. For two years I've only ever got ice from her. Together, Sanford, Monique and I, took on the worst Daytona Beach had to offer. Busting up drug labs, sex traffickers and child pornographers were our specialties. Most of it was outside the law. Occasionally we kicked cases over to the local PD. She was there for all of it.

Sitting with one tight thigh on the desk and one dangling loosely over the edge was Alysa. Her blonde hair pulled back tight in a ponytail. She wore a plaid button down open to a white tank top, jeans and flipflops. Her green eyes danced as she talked with her hands. Her story cut short as I walked in.

"Oh, hey Grimes." Alysa said with a quick smile and short wave.

"Hey," was all I could muster. I wanted to hug her or touch her arm. She didn't offer either, so I just stood there.

Both women stared in silence, waiting for me to move or say something.

"Did you get my email, the Polk case?"

"Yeah," Monique said, "I already replied."

I nodded once more and escaped the awkwardness to

Sanford's inner office.

Sunken in the thick gold carpet was Willis Sanford's heavy mahogany desk. All the scattered papers had now found a folder. In front of the desk, the twin antique Victorian chairs were once again upright. Everything in the office had found its place, erasing the nightmare that was last night.

Sanford stood holding the back of his overstuffed burgundy leather chair as he pointed to the earbud in his ear.

His smile was for whoever was on the phone, "That sounds great. Yep…yep, okay take care." Sanford tapped the screen of his cell on the desk, hanging up the call. Taking out the earbuds he said, "Want a drink?"

"Coke."

My order caused him to stutter step as he made his way to the marble covered wet bar cut into the wood panel wall. He didn't question my choice and went about popping a can. There was a bottle of bourbon on the counter. It had been his habit to pour me a glass. Since the crack in my skull courtesy a band of millennial bikers, I hadn't had the taste for the stuff. The routine was still there, the memory of instantly calming my nerves kept me thirsty. Willful moderation was the first step in a long journey to feeling better body and spirit. Feeling better mentally was still a challenge, in my head a cobweb continued to capture too much clutter, never letting anything go.

"Sorry, it's a little warm." He said handing me the can.

The coke fizzed as I sucked it down. Sanford sat at his desk with his own self-medication concoction of Remy Martin cognac and Champaign. Each sip brought a broader smile to his face showing off perfectly shaped white teeth.

"What's up with you and the girl?" he said, pointing to the door.

"That's what our meeting is about?"

"I hear them talking sometimes."

"What are they saying?" I asked leaning forward in my chair.

"Like you say, that's not what the meeting is about." Sanford smiled. Then the smile faded, "We have a pro bono job." His personal wealth and standing in the community made him a beacon in the community to champion the cause for those who didn't have the resources. David fighting Goliath, only Sanford was a Goliath in his own right. What he lacked in paid underlings doing his busy work he made up for with wit and cunning. And he never lost in court. My pro bono work were jobs like last night that filled the stolen files. Not a single hour of my time had been billed to a client in months.

"An off the books job." I grumbled. We were supposed to be phasing those types of jobs out. The avenging vigilante died months ago. My body was suffering the effects of beating in skulls and my mind was slowly disintegrating with every trigger I pulled in the dark. The bad guys just kept popping up no matter how brutally the last one went down.

"It has to do with our first case." Sanford stood up, "Come on, let's go for a ride."

"Shit." I grumbled again as I got to my feet.

Chapter 3

Sanford drove a 2014 Cadillac. The amount of money in his account said he could afford a new one but this one he paid off and with the tuning Billy performed, made it faster than any new one. Sanford was enjoying the deeper exhaust and quicker throttle response as we whipped around a corner onto Beach Street. After a few blocks of being pulled into my seat we turned on to US 1 and headed south until pulling into a diner. The white Dodge Charger with blacked out windows tipped me we would be meeting law enforcement.

The standalone diner was white with blue trim. A cartoonish yellow chic was on the sign. The overall shape of the building made me think it once was once a Taco Bell. Making our way through the small restaurant, I spotted a table with two middle aged white guys in suits with loose ties seated next to each other.

"Camp isn't in on this one." Sanford whispered over his shoulder to me as if reading my mind.

I recognized the two suits. The balding, thinner man was State's Attorney Newstrom from the 7th Circuit Court. He talked tough and made a show of things but when it came time to act, politics and optics got in the way. Special Agent Gibson sat next to him, who had a thick neck and cheap suit, was from the Florida Department of Law Enforcement (FDLE). He was Johnny Law through and through. Together they made an uneasy odd couple. They were handling the prosecution of the perverts I uncovered in a human trafficking ring here in Daytona, but the case had tentacles all the way to the state capital. Those tentacles were buried deep, which made breaking this case difficult. I was glad my part was over.

Sanford greeted everyone by name as we took the open seats across the small table. Both men nodded with Gibson pushing the bronze-colored carafe of coffee my way. I thanked him and filled my cup, leaving it black.

Newstrom's fingers drummed on the file folder until he said, "We're waiting for one more."

I sipped coffee and felt the warmth spill into my empty stomach.

"I appreciate all the hard work you two have been doing on this case. Your testimony, Roger, has been fantastic." Newstrom's tone was confident, but his hand still covered the file.

I leaned back folding my arms which prompted a look from Gibson, even when his stare was fixed ahead or to the other side, his peripheral vision was always on me. All the depositions and cooperation from Sanford and I, and Gibson still radiated his distrust. Proof he was a good cop, he knew a crook when he saw one, reformed or not. If I wasn't sure about being reformed myself, then why should he?

"But *Newsome*, here, isn't holding his breath on convictions." Sanford said then sat back in his seat, folding his arms. Proof, evidence, confessions, none of it would be enough to get to the powerful. Heads of corporations, political elite, or family lineage all seemed to be enough to shake off whatever implications the state or media made.

Newstrom's eyes narrowed as the tapping on the folder stopped. "This isn't some TV drama that can be wrapped up in an hour."

"We're having a problem with witnesses. They wind up dead." Gibson said then sipped his coffee. His eyes fixed on me through the steam from the mug.

"Just what do you want from us?" Sanford said then removed his steal framed glasses and rubbed his eyes.

Newstrom released his grip on the folder.

I looked around at three sets of eyes filled with eager anticipation while simultaneously back lit by dread. I pulled the lid off pandoras box and looked inside.

The top few pages were documents with state seals stamped on them. Skimming, it was all things I had read before. Then the glossy eight by ten-inch photos. Two dimensional scenes of things I saw in 3D, the cold bodies of kidnappers and pedophiles, some with eyes open gazing up into nothing, others clinched tight fearing the punishment I gave. Bodies stuck in eternal poses like mannequins splattered in ketchup. An emptiness to their faces that made their appearance unreal. I had worked hard to forget that scene, made by my gun and my hands. The faces had all been blurred and buried in my mind, especially one. Her photo made it all fresh again, shiny blonde hair caked with strawberry syrup, blue eyes looking up but not seeing. I never blamed her for what she did. She made a choice leaving me without one.

The coffee sloshed in my stomach as their screams filled my ears and gun smoke filled my nose. Swallowing didn't help my need to puke.

"You haven't seen these before, I take it." Newstrom said more as a statement than a question. "They're, well, hard to look at." Both Newstrom and Gibson were staring at me. Sanford was staring out the window watching cars, birds, anything but my reaction.

"No," I said truthfully. These pictures were new to me, but the images I had seen before. I was there, I put the bodies there on the floor. The pictures continued to another crime scene. A pimp beat to death and left in a tub wrapped in a shower curtain. His door man's face was in pink bits along a sidewalk, stomped repeatedly. Pictures of three burnt corpses from a house fire. I went into it all that night so fast and so blind. Death was not on my lips, or in my thoughts, but the rage I found inside me when I looked into the eyes of Joss, a fifteen-year-old prostitute changed everything for them and for me. These people in the photos, these predators, I killed them. The proof it wasn't all a bad dream was staring back at me.

Gibson sighed with warm coffee breath breezing into my already nauseated face. He thought less of me for letting some crime scene photos turn my stomach. He checked one more mental box that I was no killer. It only helped my cause to let him think that, so I didn't try to withhold my disgust.

He reached out and grabbed the last photograph; one I hadn't seen yet. "This is what we're after." He turned the picture sideways and slide it closer to me. A pistol, a 9mm, one I recognized from that night. It was in a teenager's dead hand named Jinky, and I had put it there while he was alive. And he used it to right his wrongs. A young punk who got the raw end of life handed to him too early, so he made sure to give it back to other young kids. Only he learned something about himself that night, he started towards forgiveness by accepting he was a victim in an endless cycle of abuse. Rage brought him there that night same as me.

"What about it," I said.

"It's a stolen gun." Newstrom leaned further over the table.

Gibson's eyes were crawling all over me, reading the word *criminal* like it was on my forehead. I couldn't escape it. No matter the good I did or the justice I delivered, I was a crook, a thug, gutter trash that these two law enforcers would like to see dead on a poolhall floor with the rest of them.

"Sure, it's stolen, these are criminals. Get to the point," I said.

"The human trafficking is proving to be more of a well, dead end." Newsome looked to Gibson who was sitting still while looking me in the eye. My eyes pinched as I fixated a stare on the folder.

"This case is huge." Sanford said, "Why aren't the Feds all over this one?"

Newstrom leaned across the table. He slipped out a photo of the pool hall. Dead lay where I dropped them. "See the white guy? He's a Russian national. The Feds got his counterpart to flip, and he got immunity. They lost interest in our *little backwater town.* But with things stalling, they're sending an agent to assist."

"One agent?" Sanford said. To which Newstrom nodded.

"What about the others, none of the people you've arrested over this has flipped?" I said with my eyes drifting back to the picture of the blonde. The lavender and vanilla of her hair returned to me, the feel of her skin and the night we spent together all came back in a wave that left an acid burn in my chest. Pressure built in my forehead and my eyes felt like they were about to rocket out of their sockets. Sweaty palms wiped over my thighs.

"Low hanging fruit. We need to break through to the top." Gibson looked over at Newstrom then back at me, "One, we had one." Gibson said.

"Had?" Sanford coughed out a laugh.

"What are you saying? Everything I did was for nothing?" I said with a voice full of gravel.

"No, no one is saying that." Newstrom began, "Our strongest witness was about to flip, but he's gone off the radar this week. Just when we needed his testimony."

"He's been missing 48 hours." Gibson said.

"We're scrambling here to catch up." Newstrom said leaning in on the table. His hands began to rub together.

"What's this got to do with me?"

"We think there's a connection between this gun and the

witness. If we get him back, he might lead us to whoever killed these people." Newstrom said.

My palms covered over my face as I took a deep breath. Sanford drummed his fingers on the table. There was a connection between the gun and who killed them. The gun came from my pocket.

"Why are you looking for a trigger man, when more heinous criminals are still out there?" I said.

"We get this *trigger man*; we get who ordered it." Newstrom said.

"I gave you all I have." I said then stood up looking at the exit. Gibson's hands came off the table. He was ready to grab me, and I welcomed it. The pressure inside of me wanted out and what better than to slam this cop's face on the table. I turned to Gibson letting my right leg slide the chair away from me. If he were really going to lay his hands on me, I would return the favor fivefold.

"Now wait Roger." Newstrom used words to try and restrain me, Gibson was silently on his feet with his hands at the ready. "This *is* your problem. Whoever wacked this guy will be coming for you next. Don't you see that? They're cleaning up loose ends. Your office was hit."

"The Russians?" Sanford said.

Newstrom waved his question off, "No, they're experts at cutting ties and covering their tracks. It's not them. I believe they were looking to find out what you know. If you could just share the copies of those files with us—"

Sanford's hands went up, "Not going to happen. But" he lowered the hands, "I will draft up something to fill you all in." Sanford finished by looking at me. My eyes were on the saltshaker. The only way to keep from showing my hand.

Gibson waited for me to take my seat. Then he sat. Sanford gave me the eye and I eased my shoulders. More coffee gave me something to with my hands.

"What about all Hines's friends?" Sanford said to the two law men across from us. When they didn't respond in time he said, "I gave you names, and I don't see any of them in this file. Ricardo Delgado, Barbara Lumino and Peter Danzig."

Newstrom cleared his throat and lowered his head. "Do you realize who you're talking about? They are Daytona Beach, hell, Florida royalty. I'll tell you what I told you two years ago, evidence. Get something more substantial than being seen at social gatherings with Hines. Hell, there must have been three hundred people attending those parties."

"Not the same parties we're talking about." Sanford growled. Fear was not something Sanford understood or tolerated. The man had been through a lot in his life. From running the streets with the wrong crowd to a young boxer with high prospects, the man kept moving all the way through law school and a multi-million-dollar firm. Pride I had in my boss, but more importantly confidence.

After the poolhall shoot out and Gregg Hines's suicide I retreated into myself and put distance between Sanford and his mission. The thrills came through reckless gambling that got me into more trouble. I should have been out hunting, searching for the rest of the people that sat at the poker table with Hines. Newstrom was right, the elite were hard to get to. Some of the low hanging fruit were plucked, none gave up the top names. The official FDLE investigation was hot, and it looked like they would be hauling people in any day. By the time I was back working for Sanford much of the case was cold. We moved on to our own low hanging fruit.

"Sorry I'm late." A friendly voice came from over my shoulder. I turned to see a tall man in a tight light grey suit. His white shirt had no tie. His hair was black and perfectly styled in a fade with the top slicked over to the side leaving a perfect part. His jaw square and his build solid. He looked like a Hispanic Ken Doll.

"Special Agent Alvarez, FBI." He said and extended his hand. A firm grip. He went about shaking hands and repeating his title and name to everyone, so there would be no forgetting it.

He swung a chair from an empty table and sat at the head of ours. Gibson and I looked each other over then each took our seats.

"Our federal support." Newstrom said then thanked Alverez for meeting us, but his smile faded too quickly to be sincere. He didn't like the watching eyes of the FBI on his investigation. His reputation on the line, Newstrom reached the bottom of the barrel and asked me for help. It was entertaining enough so I stayed for the show.

Alvarez flipped through the folder. His smile from the introduction never faded as he got to the last picture. "A real blood bath." Then he closed the folder and let the smile fade.

"Harry Muncy." Newstrom said then poured himself some more coffee. Newstrom reached down to a satchel and retrieved another file, "Harry Muncy is a career criminal, had his hands in all sorts of rackets. He started out a thief and gradually expanded out, forming ties with various criminal organizations." Newstrom slid the folder over to me. I didn't bother looking at it. My earlier rage was subsiding into a quiet nothingness, a skill to get me through situations like this. Remain calm, straight faced, and focused on breathing. I just had to get through it and soon I'd be out.

When I refused to open the file, Newstom continued, "Muncy was something of a conman and managed to work his way in with Gregory Hines and the others at the *card games* and island vacations. He knew all the players."

Whether Newstrom knew it or not, he was talking code. My investigation uncovered these 'card games' where hell was realized for the kids that got pulled into the underworld of trafficking. And the island vacations are where they ended up. It was no secret who was at the games and the vacations, but power bought silence on every level, from Tallahassee to the media refusing to cover the story. Sanford had compiled a list of players, but we were waiting on the federal government to step in and take them down.

"So where is this Muncy?" Alvarez said.

"Missing, presumed dead." Gibson said.

"He's in the wind. We approached him with full immunity. He waffled. After we balked at witness protection he disappeared." Newstrom said.

"You'd need a federal prosecutor for that." Alvarez said with a return of that smile. Newstrom nodded in agreement but rolled his eyes a little.

Sanford took the file. A man who was never silent unless a judge told him to be, hadn't spoken much this morning. The break-in and now back into this case of child trafficking had put a cork in his bottle.

"Again, what does this have to do with us?" I said.

"We need you to look back into the case, go back through your contacts that got you to the pool hall that night. Find us something we missed." Gibson said looking at Sanford with narrowed eyes.

The victims had their justice that night, the night I killed all those involved. Someone had escaped justice that night, Harry Muncy, a onetime thief, just like I once was. Evidently, he decided to stay in the underworld while I tried to get out.

"Fine." I said and stood up causing everyone else to rise.

"Special Agent Alvarez is here to help with your-" Newstrom said softly.

"No." I started to walk off. Gibson lifted his hand

inching us towards that dance we've wanted since meeting months ago.

"Hold it." Sanford snapped in a heated whisper. "Grimes cool it. And you," he pointed a long finger at Gibson, "Back your ass up." He tugged on the white collar around his neck. "We're gonna look into it and get back to you." Sanford gathered up the file.

Agent Alvarez held a soft smirk. That was all my nerves could take. Newstrom's protests faded, and Gibson's face grew red with frustration or maybe it was the castration Sanford delivered.

Outside, I leaned on the Cadillac and looked back at the four men through the diner window. Sanford stood nodding his head then he wagged his finger at the state cops. This went on for a few seconds until Sanford shook hands and came out with the folder under his arm.

Alvarez was right behind him. I checked the door handle, it was locked.

"Hey, Mr. Grimes, I'm sorry about that back there. This was all just dropped in my lap, and I flew in this morning and…obviously you have a history with those two." Alvarez smiled with all his teeth showing. The sun was bright, his hand went up along his brow to shade yellow-brown eyes.

"Yeah," was all I offered.

"Well, I look forward to working with you. I've read through the files, and you really stepped in something deep."

"Seems like it," I said.

"Special Agent Alvarez," Sanford said from the other side of the car, "We'll be in touch when we have something."

The locks popped. I slipped into the warm leather of the Cadillac. Alvarez grabbed the door.

"Sure thing. Looking forward to working with you

Roger." Alvarez said and shut the door.

He stood there watching us drive away.

Down the road Sanford slapped me in the chest with the folder. "What the hell was that back there?"

I kept quiet as my hands shook the last of the adrenaline out.

"Did you even get to the other file? Go on take a look."

"I don't need to look, I was there, remember."

"Just because you want it over, don't make it over Grimes. Go on and look at that damn file." Sanford cussed for a second time this morning. He never cussed, not even after last night's break in.

I sifted through photos of Harry Muncy. In his fifties, grey hair, thick middle gut with tattoos on one arm. I didn't recognize his face. My time as a thief and burglar hadn't crossed with his. Then I got to another face, this time familiar and of someone still alive, I hoped. He was about seventy years old with precious metal streaks of gold and silver hair and wore a bright blue polo shirt. If he were smiling in the photo, I'd see his gold tooth but instead his face folded around the edges with concern for whatever it was he was doing. He stood on a dock beside a tide up cabin cruiser.

Smitty, the man with no first or last name. The man responsible for elevating my criminal career. I had known him since I was a teenager. A friend of my parents in a way. He hung out at the restaurant my mom served at. After class I would walk past looking through the window to see if he was at his usual back-corner booth with high padded sides. If he was in there alone, I would go in, and he made sure I had a meal. If there were men at the table with him, I knew to keep walking. He got word I started stealing cars and robbing banks with my best friend Billy Horseblood. Once Smitty got involved we started training for bigger heists, stuff that required security training. He sent us to private security training, the kind of classes taught by former Navy Seals and Secret Service. We had to know how they operated to use it against them. Most of our classmates got plucked by contractors and foreign governments. Billy and I went back to stealing.

"I said we needed to find Smitty. Didn't I say that? For two weeks. Now FDLE wants to talk to him, got him tied up in this somehow. When Gibson said, 'look at your contacts' this is who he was talking about." Sanford unleashed a barrage of words on me, built up after being so silent in the meeting.

"How much do they know about Smitty and me?"

"If you'd have just kept calm in there, we could have found out how involved he is." He turned to me, "Happy now? Hot head." He said punching the gas, zipping the sedan through traffic.

My eyes drifted out the window to the passing street. The bums and prostitutes continued to shuffle along Ridgewood Avenue. They never seem to go away, day or night, cold front or summer heat, up and down, back and forth they paced like old zoo animals locked in cages. They had given up, the wild that once made them fierce was gone. Their only cage was their life with bars made from choices.

"This shit just won't go away." I mumbled.

"Cases like this can take years. Newstrom is doing the best he can, he has to cover everything he does in triplicate to make sure it sticks against anyone he throws it at." Sanford went on talking in legal terms about the case and how things worked. Then in mid-sentence he stopped.

"But that's not what you meant." Sanford glanced over then back to the road ahead as we neared his office. He knew me well. From the look in my eye to my half a statement.

"Nightmares, PTSD, stuff like that? Monique can get you more Xanax or whatever you need. I know a therapist, just don't ah, you know, spill everything that's bothering you."

"Just shut up a minute." I said with bitterness at first than a smile broke across my face as he began his 'yes massa' routine in jest to ease my tension. He got away with that kind of humor because he lived under segregation in the south, and experienced things I only read about and watched portrayals of in movies.

"I've worked hard blocking out images from that night. Those two cops have me relive it moment by moment with endless statements and depositions, except I have to give the edited, PG, version where I witnessed it all from my truck outside. Always careful to keep the *big lie* that I was the one squeezing the trigger and ending all those lives." I said closing my eyes and seeing the face of a beautiful blond mother that had been the first woman in a while to give me butterflies. I killed her leaving her son an orphan.

"I can't even imagine it, Roger. But think of the young lives saved and changed by what you have done. You dismantled that child trafficking ring. You alone did that."

"You know I used to babysit her son. I hated it then, but now looking back it wasn't that bad. He was a good kid and just wanted a father figure. He'd sit and ask me questions, random shit, never really waiting for my answer. I would try and just get him to play a video game to shut him up. Then he would want me to play too, and I suck at that stuff." My knee bounced and that rope around my chest slipped into a knot once more. I thought it had gone, I thought all of that was over. It's never really over.

"I'm sorry son. I didn't know you knew her boy. Look at it like this; you saved the boy from a possible nightmare of a life."

"In what way? I killed his grandfather too. I mean he really is an orphan and has no idea why."

"Hey now, you didn't kill Hines. He took his own life and he started on that path years ago." Sanford pulled the car into the parking garage taking us out of the bright morning sun.

"I might as well have. I went there to kill him." I wanted to crawl out of my skin and into someone else, and wake up reborn, someplace else with a new life. Anything to get distance between me and what I had done.

Sanford put the car in park, shut it down and exhaled while looking straight ahead at the concrete wall of the parking garage. "Look man, you can't live in the past with the dead. Live for the living. Looks like the cops haven't found Smitty, so he's still off their radar. Our priority is to find out how Smitty's connected to this Muncy fella. He's too old for that stuff." He wasn't looking at me when he smiled. His hand gently patted the steering wheel. "He means too much to you." He said then got out.

I took another second to myself, then followed him out of the car.

Back in the office, Monique handed Sanford a stack of papers he needed to review, and sign then went on to catch him up on what she had been working on. It was nothing that concerned me, so I stood silently. She finished and walked out to her desk.

"When you get a chance, can you email me the surveillance video of the break-in?"

Sanford looked up from the stack of paperwork, "There isn't much to see, but I'll send it."

His eyes went back to the work before him, "Did you want anything else?"

"Nah," I shook my head, "Guess not."

"Don't worry Grimes. The way I have those files encoded, they're useless to whoever has them. I could however use them myself. We need to get back on the trail we had two years ago. I'm not even sure where to start." Sanford looked at me with eyes wanting to read a road sign.

I gave him a nod then closed his office door behind me.

Sitting cross legged at her desk, Monique looked up and gave me a little smile. Despite the small size, I enjoyed it. The little things, often unspoken, kept us tight. We understood distance didn't mean a lack of caring.

I walked past her then stopped and went up to her desk. "Can you look into something for me?"

She stayed focused on the computer screen, "Isn't that your job around here?" she said then looked up to meet my eyes. Something was on my face she read quickly.

"What is it you need Grimes?" She said with her penciled brow pulled together by real concern.

I grabbed a pen and scribbled down a name. "Let me know he's in a good place." I handed her the note and left.

Chapter 4

Smitty's folder was spread out over my bed. I stared down at the surveillance photos of him on a dock talking to Muncy. In another photo he was looking right into the lens. The old guy was good. Sanford still believed Smitty was just mixed up in his old mobster ways, but I was beginning to doubt there was any accident to Smitty being involved in Muncy's disappearance. My biggest question was why. He knew how tied to this case I was and how much I wanted these bad guys to serve time or worse for their crimes.

Downstairs Billy was using every tool in his shop. Grinders, sanders, pneumatic drills, all of it was giving me a headache. Special Agent Alvarez had already called thirteen times since leaving the diner, his next stop would be the shop. I just needed someplace quiet to rethink finding Smitty.

I sat in the back parking lot of Coopers Irish Bar. It wasn't yet eleven a.m. The back door was propped open for a delivery when I walked in.

"We aren't open yet." Yelled a voice from somewhere I couldn't see.

"It's me, Roger." I said stopping in the long dark wood paneled hall lit by neon beer signs.

"Oh, hey Roger." The voice I now recognized as Wayne the owner of Coopers. "C'mon in. Chastity is here somewhere."

"I'm here." Chastity yelled with her familiar rasp from behind the bar. She stood there holding the remote scrolling through the guide, setting each TV to a different channel.

Chastity had her burlesque body squeezed in a Kelly-green tank top with the Coopers logo screened on it and khaki shorts. She was tall with smooth caramel colored skin and kinky hair dyed blonde with a few red streaks. She was older than the rest of the waitstaff at Coopers by ten years.

"Anything you want to watch?" she said pointing the remote at me as if I could reach twenty feet or so and grab it.

I shook my head no, laying the folder down on the bar, and taking a seat. It was thicker now with records on Smitty I downloaded from the state website. My friend Detective Camp was able to send me what the Sheriff's Office had on both Smitty and Muncy. I recited the paragraphs more than read them. I had been up for four hours already and even more if you don't count the couple of naps between one and five-thirty this morning.

The folder lay open as my eyes wandered off into the light of a big bright morning sun casting golden rays through the front windows of Coopers. Dust particles danced in the air and settled randomly onto the dark polished wood and brass accents of the Irish bar. Somewhere in the folder, between pictures and typed papers, were supposed to be clues to where and how Harry Muncy met his demise. Hope for Smitty to show up with that gold tooth of his gleaming in the sun was disappearing. My elbows on the bar held up my head as I tried to fit pieces of two different puzzles together.

The pictures and notes took me back fifteen years or so to when I was a kid fresh out of high school. My mother had left town, one of her many back-and-forth trips, trying to make a fresh start someplace else but always coming back to Daytona. I was homeless, sleeping in my car or crashing on Billy's couch. Then Smitty showed up with a job offer. His hair was more gold than silver then, but that shiny gold tooth seemed to flash every time he had a plan for a new heist. The burglaries were always in another county or state and always came to us through a broker. The money was good, and he taught me how to spend it, in a smart way not a flashy way that brought the heat down on us. In a twisted way he was the structure and discipline I didn't know I was missing. Now I needed to be there for him.

Chastity dropped two elbows down on the bar with a thud.

"You gonna ask my girl out or what?"

"What?" I said looking up from the folder that still held secrets.

"For real? C'mon Roger." After years of 'hey you' and 'what's up guy' Chastity finally got my name right. The thing was, if she was using my name, then she meant what she said. I liked Coopers more when Alysa worked there. Her face with those smiling eyes that popped against the Kelly-green Cooper's polo was more intoxicating than the liquor. Last year, the bar became my second office. Sometimes my only office after I was kicked out of one for living in it. That and some jerks kicked in the door. The suit wearing tenants didn't like that and out I went.

"She's been busy with her gym and stuff." I said running a hand over my bristly buzz cut. "I think she needs a more normal guy."

"What's normal these days?" Chastity chuckled and went back to opening the bar.

A groan echoed from inside the men's room. Something you normally want to ignore, but since Chastity, me and Wayne were the only people here it got my attention. A soft crash followed by something bouncing around in there got me off the stool. I took a few steps when the door opened, and Wayne came out huffing and brushing the hair from his face.

"Chastity," He carried a plastic trashcan with a dent in the side.

"Yeah boss." The chesty bar tender said holding a pen

up to the cooler door counting beers.

"Who is it, damn it?"

"Who what?" she said getting an attitude with his vagueness.

"Dirty needles again. Someone is dealing out of the bar and junkies are shooting up in the bathroom again." Wayne pulled the translucent plastic bag from the container. Pressed against the side was a needle.

"Welcome to Dirt-Tona Beach." She said and went back to counting. "I worked days all week, boss." She said against the fogged glass of the cooler.

I was standing next to the bar owner now, "How do you know it's drugs?"

He fought rolling his eyes as he turned my direction.

"It's been a *problem*." He said and twisted up the bag and held it out like there was a rabid opossum in it then he went out the back door for the dumpster.

I was back on the stool staring down at the file. Chastity was right, this really was *Dirtona*, I had been shoveling too much dirt these last few years. The years before that, I was part of that dirt.

Chastity dropped a black stout in front of me that I didn't order. The flavor was chocolatey with a hint of nut. Not my usual but I liked it. I pushed it away. One would lead to two and the rest of day spent here at the bar. That was in my past too.

Wayne was behind the bar still complaining about keeping the drug addicts out.

"Chastity, you better tell whoever it is that is letting these junky assholes deal in my bar they better cut it out or else." Wayne said with a finger pointing at her.

The seasoned bar tender shrugged, but when Wayne

refused to lower his pointer finger, she nodded acceptance of his order. After he went back to his office, she mumbled something under her breath.

"I take it this isn't something new." I said not looking up from the folder.

She sucked in air because whatever she was going to unleash was big, then gave it a second thought and blew it out, saying, "He's big talking. He knows who it is and won't do anything about it."

"Why?" This time I was looking at her. I had known Wayne for a few years now and he always handled everything at Coopers. Though not a large guy, he could toss drunks across the room and bust up cat fights with one hand.

Leaning in close Chastity pressed her ample cleavage over the top of the dark wood bar. "He can't." She whispered then turned quickly going back to her work.

This was Wayne's business, so I went back to my business in the file folder on the bar.

A few minutes later I had a pen in my hand making notes over notes on other notes. There were a lot of question marks in there. Smitty had kept on being a criminal while I supposedly quit to become a PI. He had more underworld connections than the Atlanta Airport had connecting flights. The old guard still held action around town, guys like Reuben and De Carlo. Guys I knew of, but Smitty kept them from knowing me, never bringing me fully into the criminal fold. Lost in thought I never heard the two men until one cleared his throat.

Both white guys, the one to the left was lanky the other chubby all over. The chubby one was shaved smooth all over and the lanky one had something that looked like a beard smudged on his gaunt face. The fat one wore a Tampa Bay Bucs jersey and jogging pants, though I doubted he ever jogged in them. The skinny guy had baggy jeans and a long sleeve t-shirt with sweat stains in the pits. They stood without talking.

Chastity turned from her business behind the bar. "Sorry guys, we don't open for another twenty minutes."

"How come he got a beer?" the chubby man said.

"He's a beer rep trying to sell us a new brew." Chastity said quickly as if rehearsed.

The chubby guy let out some air between his yellow teeth then said, "Sure. We're here to see Wayne anyway."

"Over here." Wayne said from the doorway of his office. The two men followed the sound and went in shutting the door behind them.

It didn't take long for the voices to grow to shouts that penetrated the wall. Coming here early was supposed to give me the quiet time needed to review Smitty's file.

The office door blew open and Wayne was holding the knob shouting for the two men to leave.

As they exited the office, Chubby said, "Watch yo self, old man." Then he slung a shoulder into Wayne as he walked out. Wayne snorted, flaring his nostrils, but he didn't move. Lanky trailed, locking eyes with the bar owner, then he laughed loudly.

Maybe it wasn't Wayne's fight, but it could be mine. I grabbed the pint glass and swallowed down the rest of the stout. After I burped the nutty chocolate after taste, I slipped off the stool and went towards the office.

The two thugs swiveled their heads my way as I walked up.

"Sit back down." Chubby said with Lanky nodding in agreement. I kept walking forcing a look between the pair, then they separated to my left and right.

I stood there. To their right was the hallway and the exit.

They had their way out if they chose to use it.

"Go back to your drink." Chubby said and started towards me, daring me to move in this head-to-head game of chicken.

I dropped my right foot back letting my shoulder follow. Chubby decided not to offer me the same concession and slapped his right shoulder into my chest. I reached behind him and grabbed his left wrist with my left hand and my right hand gripped the back of his neck. With momentum, I drove his face into the wall just missing the neon beer sign. I kicked his knee and he buckled to the floor. Another kick for good measure sent Chubby rolling towards the back door.

Turning around I found Lanky swirling his fist while rocking back and forth. A street fighter who had watched too many YouTube videos. I timed the circling fist and went low, covering my face with my left, I twisted my hips and popped up driving my right into his gut. He wrapped around my arm lifting off his feet for a second before I retracted my arm. He fell to the floor in a fetal position.

I snatched Lanky up by the waist and ran him out the door. Outside, his wiry frame hit the rail and he went over the side spilling onto the asphalt of the parking lot.

I stood in the hallway blocking the exit while Chubby found his feet. A flake of eggshell white paint was stuck to his puffy cheek. His eyes were filled with frustration backed by anger. His feet pressed forward but his shaking knees kept him in place. He backed up then dipped around me, scurrying through the door. In the parking lot he picked his friend up off the asphalt.

"This ain't over. Next time you won't get a cheap shot like that." He shouted with a finger pointed my way, "I wasn't ready!"

As I watched them hobble to their POS Honda Civic, I heard the engine of another car start. A sliver Chevy sedan with blacked out tint rolled from its parking spot. A glimpse through the windshield left me seeing only two hands gripping the wheel. The car was familiar, but not enough to be sure of a memory.

Feet ran up on me from behind. I spun on my heels looking for more of a fight. It was Wayne.

"I could have handled that!" He said sliding a hand over his hair. Then he took long strides back to the office. I spun back around to catch the license plate off the sedan but it was gone.

The office was a long rectangle with a table stretching the length of one wall and another covered in plywood shelves holding things like glasses and company shirts. In the back was a safe and beyond that a door. The door was shut.

Wayne was on a laptop computer and turned slowly towards me. I looked past his shoulder and saw myself on security monitor split into six smaller boxes. Each box held an angle of the bar.

"I appreciate the hand, out there, I just don't want any extra trouble around here. It's bad for business."

"Maybe I could help?"

"I don't want them killed, just the hell outta my bar." Wayne said with a slight grin to keep his nerves in check.

"Me, kill?" I said pointing at myself. "I was just gonna say I could make some calls."

Wayne kicked out a desk chair on wheels my way. I sat.

"And make them *disappear*." He used air quotes.

"You must be confused; I've never killed anyone." I laughed like he was pulling my leg but, I was pulling his.

"The rumors aren't true?" He had disappointment on his face like he just found out his son didn't make the varsity team.

I shook my head no, then shrugged like I had no idea how that rumor started.

"Well, anyway, I don't need a PI to handle the drug dealers. I think they got the point and won't be a problem," he said.

"Do you really believe that?" I said and swiveled side to side in the chair. It squeaked.

He sat up in his seat. "I can take care of it."

"What if their boss doesn't like that?"

Wayne moaned. "Chastity." He slapped the table, not hard but enough to make the laptop jump. "The only thing looser than her mouth…" He cussed a few times.

"I like this place and hate to see it close or worse."

His eyes twitched then looked away, "Don't worry, nothing's going to happen." He stood up, "I've been at this a long time. Thanks for the offer." Wayne stuck out his hand and we shook. His grip was lighter than I had remembered.

I let it go. The man didn't want to talk. I needed to get on with finding Smitty. Once that was done, I could come back and try to persuade him.

Chapter 5

The metal framed chair with thin vinyl seat was cutting off the circulation to my right leg. I shifted once more then back again. My foot went out over the coffee table that was really nothing more than a narrow gangplank, leaving my foot to dangle on the other side and further the fight for circulation. I kicked it out, hitting the edge of the tall counter. To the left a red steal door that led to the bays. Next to it a coffee machine that was never cleaned, above hung a twenty-inch TV, because anything larger would block the door to the bays. On the other side of the TV was the stairway that led to my apartment.

The steel door opened to the wail of an electric guitar as classic grunge blared from the bays. "Where'd you go this morning?" Billy asked shutting the door behind him, returning the rock and roll to a murmur. He poured thick black coffee into a mug as stained as his hands. He took it over to his desk and sat down in a large desk chair with yellow foam coming from tears in the faux leather and leaned back taking a sip.

I shifted in my seat. "You expect customers to wait in this medieval torture device." Pins and needles prickled in my foot.

"I don't expect my customers to wait at all. I'm focusing on custom builds, longer projects like that Mach 1." Billy pulled back on his long black braid that was starting to show silver strands in it. He was about ten years older than me and had that permanent reddish tan due to his three quarters native blood, but he still had that one quarter Florida Cracker. He was proud of both sides of his family tree even if they probably spent a lot of time at war with one another.

He had been my friend for fifteen years and my mentor for ten. When I quit stealing, he quit being my mentor, but he was always my friend.

"Got a new case?" Billy said keeping his attention on his computer monitor shopping for car parts.

I held up the folder and said, "I met with those two from FDLE yesterday."

Billy shook his head. It wasn't that he hated cops, he just didn't like them being so close.

"Yeah, well they want me to look into stolen guns that are tied to the human trafficking from a while back."

"Whoa, who would'a thought Daytona would be such a hot bed of organized crime." Billy said as he spun in his chair for the mini fridge behind him. He pulled out a ball of foil and unwrapped a turkey sandwich. His jaws unhinged, taking a generous bite. He set it down as he chewed, leaving grease smudges on the white bread.

"It gets even more *organized*," I said.

"Smitty." Billy said. He had a longer professional history with the last mobster in Daytona Beach than I. Billy was already taking jobs from Smitty when he brought me in.

The old guy was hesitant at first, giving the impression he didn't want me around. It took some convincing from Billy and a couple of clean heists to tear down the mobster's guard. Once I was in, he treated me like family. Cash was fronted for jobs, guards paid in advance to let us in or look the other way, and we stayed in nice hotels, always at Smitty's expense. When it came time to split the loot, my young age was never a factor in the percentage I received. I thought I had it all and wanted more. Billy convinced me if I branched out on my own or tried another outfit, the jobs and split wouldn't come close. So, I stayed loyal to Smitty up until I quit. As nervous as I was to tell him, he took it without anger. He seemed more disappointed in me than anything.

"So, did you find him?" Billy said with his head cocked to the side, waiting on my reply. I must have gone back into one of my stares.

"No, nothing." I got up and laid the folder open on the counter. Then spread the photos out for Billy to look through. "You know a guy named Harry Muncy?"

He took a bite of his sandwich then wiped his fingers on his jeans before handling the photos. He mumbled a few cuss words as he looked at the dead bodies in the pool hall. What I had done that night became real for him. Then he paused on the one with Smitty on the dock.

"Look familiar?" I said hoping Billy would see something I didn't. Maybe the dock or boat in the distance would spark a memory.

"No."

"This Muncy is the missing star witness." I pointed out the stout thief in one of the photos.

Billy took a bite of his sandwich and leaned back in his chair as he chewed. He mumbled something I couldn't understand. He repeated it then finally after some old coffee he said, "What was Muncy's specialty?"

I flipped through the folder to his rap sheet. "Well, he was picked up a lot. B&E, larceny, and robbery. The guy's specialty are safes, but he's done just about everything. His first arrest was in '77."

"Before my time, but" Billy held the phot up studying it. "He looks familiar. Color his hair and thin him out a little. A little, younger and taller, he could be you." Billy chuckled.

When he saw my frown he said, "He could be the guy from one of my jobs, before you and I became a team."

"When was that?"

He scratched the part in his scalp and said, "Late 90's.

Pre-9-11. If it's the job I'm thinking about because we had to go into Canada and none of us needed passports, then."

"What was the job?"

"A smash and grab at a Montreal Jewelry store. I drove the getaway car right into a parked Semi then drove the Semi over the border. Got paid when I dropped it off. Don't know what they took or what it was worth. It was worth twenty-five G's to me." Billy's smile faded, "Well fifteen after *The Tavolo* took a cut." Billy shook his head then his smile returned, "Ah hell, it was enough to put down on my house."

"Isn't there anyone from those days you could call, ask around about Muncy?"

Billy smirked and shook his head no. "Things are different now. Hell, I had a beeper back then. How would I even find a land line for someone anymore?" Billy looked up from the pictures. He ran a hand down his long black braid. It was his way of thinking. "I worked as part of a crew with no names and the players changed depending on the job. We used code names and shit. I would get a page, an offer to work and a meeting time. If I agreed, I went and the details were discussed, the crew introduced, and we went about planning and so on."

"What about that Tavolo? Does he have a contact number?"

Billy smirked, shook his head, "Not a *he*, a *them*. It's a group."

"Of thieves?"

"No, the Tavolo is a group of thief financers." Billy stood up and looked around the small office. He pulled his cell phone from his pocket and laid it on the desk. I inched to the edge of my chair.

"Legend goes, it was once a single man. He was Italian, Sicilian or some such thing from New York City. Anyway, like all New Yorkers he retired to Florida." Billy chuckled to himself. I was on the edge of my seat hearing his tale.

"The guy organized the groups, put the calls out, set up meetings, things like that."

"So, a crime syndicate." I said going to the fridge and pulling a Mountain Dew. I went back to the chair and plopped down, putting my feet up on the magazine covered table.

"Not exactly. More like a thief headhunter or job board. You could leave your number, but you never had his."

"How'd one man become a group?" I said slurping Dew from the can.

"Long before I came around, the guy was dead or gone. A group had risen to take his place. They expanded things. Like with all growth they also over extended. Hired crews with little experience, started taking large percentages, stuff like that." Billy sat back down in his chair. "I heard the competition came in and wiped them out."

"Is that how you met Smitty?" I said.

Billy nodded.

I slouched back in the uncomfortable chair. "If you, Muncy and Smitty all worked together through the Tavolo, maybe there's a connection there we can try."

"I'm not sure digging up the Tavolo is a good idea. Besides, Smitty can take care of himself," Billy said waiting for me to make eye contact with him. When I did, he looked down at the keyboard and punched away. "Be nice if you got a case that paid some actual money."

"I'm looking into something for Wayne."

"Hopefully not for a bar tab."

"I'm not sure."

Billy grinned and rubbed his thumb and forefinger

together, "Might be a nice feeling, cash in your hand."

"I get it, I get it. I'll get you some rent money today." I said, getting the hint I hadn't paid rent in some time.

"Some money?"

"All the money." I got up and headed out the door. Billy chuckled alone because I didn't think it was funny.

I stopped in the doorway, "While I'm out, try and dig up some contacts of Smitty's I can run down."

He gave me half of a two-finger salute as I left.

When I opened the door on my 1978 Scout II the scent of warm vinyl wafted up my nostrils. From the corner of my eye, I noticed a tiny bubble under the pine green paint on the bottom of the rear fender. My finger softly rolled over it as I fought the urge to pick at it with my pocketknife. The pine green paint was less than a year old and worse yet, I did the prep work, that rust spot was my fault. There is no defense against the damn salty air of living near the beach. Nothing lasts forever.

The 345 ci motor fired as it should. While I let it warm just a moment, a ding from my pocket got my phone out. A text I sent to my favorite part-time drug dealer, James, came in. He was a good kid I persuaded to go back to college by making him a deal. If he stayed in school, I'd ignore the side business.

His text was three-dollar signs. I sent back one and he replied with two. I agreed to our negotiation, and text to meet me on Sea Breeze Avenue.

I crossed the hump of the bridge and looked out at the ripples of the Halifax River. Tucked along the shore were plenty of long docks jutting out with fish holding along the pilings, just waiting for a soft plastic bait to swim by. It had been a cold winter, lingering on into February. It would be another few weeks before my thinned Florida blood would tolerate fishing on the river.

At a drive-up ATM I pulled out enough for rent and to pay James for what he knew. Then went across the street and let the Scout rumble to a stop in front of the 7-Eleven. I killed the motor and flipped the hidden starter switch under the dash. Not the most sophisticated security system but after it was stolen last month, it was the quickest thing I could do. Billy promised to have a more intricate system installed soon.

Inside the convenience store I poured myself a Slurpee and went back to wait in the Scout.

A compact sedan pulled up next to me. On the roof was a Pizza Hut plastic delivery logo. Out of the car came James. He was tall and lean, wearing black denim pants and a tee shirt too large for his frame. He walked around and got into the Scout.

"You got a real job, good for you." I said and sipped my Slurpee.

James laughed, "Glad you think so. I saw that thing lying in the road and had an idea. Why not copy an existing business model."

"So now you're in the drug delivery business." I stabbed my straw into the cup and mixed the remnants of my frozen drink around.

"I'm actually learning something in college." James shrugged, "I've got a business model all written and everything. I get the call and make the delivery. No one knows the wiser. Cops drive right by me no matter what neighborhood, day or night."

There was no arguing,. I had always kept pressure on him to stay in school and make something of himself. When I was his age, I stole cars and robbed banks.

Chitchat was over, I got to the point, "Who deals on Beach Street?"

James was looking down at several unread text messages that had come in. He closed it out and looked up, "It's not like there's painted lines on a map or some shit. I stay clear mostly because of the delivery thing, but from what I hear, whoever it is has protection."

"Like 3rd Street?"

"Nah, nah. 3Rd Street can't protect themselves anymore, not since someone shot half their asses and got away. It's like they're scared now he'll come back." James leaned back so he could look me over anticipating me to react.

I refused to show the warm wash of pride I felt as I thought back on the impact I've had on the criminal element in this town. There was never a plan to become a crime fighter, like some gun toting comic book hero, but circumstances were what they were and avenging a good friend's overdose had made the dent I wanted. I cut at least one snake head from the many. Now another had taken its place and they had backing. Higher up the drug chain. That didn't frighten me. Those types rarely fought. Maybe I could give my hands a rest and finally get the swelling in my knuckles to go down.

"Anyways," James continued disappointed at my refusal to acknowledge knowing about the gangland killings. "It left room for others to expand."

"Like others that aren't afraid because they have protection," I said.

James shrugged.

"What kind of protection?"

James hesitated; he shook his head then followed through with opening the door. "These aren't street thugs or foreigners neither. They just don't seem to be afraid of anything or anyone. Probably white dudes in suits, 'cause they never go to jail."

The hypocrisy was not lost on me. Belief in hope for James kept me out of his business. At some point he would come to his senses and quit before he got busted.

"That's all I know." He sat there looking through the windshield of the Scout and into the 7-Eleven. He swiped through his phone and then looked back at me, waiting for me to say something or to pay him. I pulled two one hundred-dollar bills from my rent money stack and handed them over.

"Damn, what business are you in again?" James said, snatching the two bills I had out for him. He had never asked what my line of work was before now. We just had a simple exchange of information for cash.

"Cool it, I've got bills to pay just like everyone else," I said. The cash went back in my front pocket with no intention of telling him what I did to earn it. James shook his head and folded the bills, putting them in his pocket.

James exhaled loudly as if to say something or get me to say something. Sitting in silence was my specialty. I'd win a gold medal if it were a sport.

"So anyway." James said leaving it hanging in the air between us. He grabbed the handle of the car door. He climbed out of the Scout but hung on to the door.

"What?" I said.

James shrugged, "Nothing, I just thought you going to ask me about something else."

"Like?"

"Word's out on that vigilante dude. They comin' for him."

"What are you talking about?"

"The guy who shot up the poolhall and did some headhunting shit around town these last two years?"

"The cops busted that guy. He was one of their own, a bent cop." I said forcing a smile behind the lie. Detective Waycross had been pinned with the vigilante badge, but he was a copycat, out to shake down criminals for cash. He wasn't the one taking down criminals in the early morning hours while the rest of the beach community slept to the sound of crashing waves.

"Then I guess he's got nothing to worry about." James shut the door.

I wasn't going to let ghetto gossip bother me. The vigilante had been caught and he was dead. It didn't matter if hoods and thugs didn't believe it, the cops did and that's all that mattered. James's information wasn't the quickest two-hundred bucks I've spent but I expected more. It pointed to the suit wearing world, full of power ties and cufflinks was something I only gazed at through a telescope. I didn't have power lunches or board meetings, but I did know a guy who did. So, I called him.

"That was fast, whatcha got for me." Sanford fired off in his usual Tommy Gun fashion.

"More questions. What do you know about Beach Street?"

"Narrow it down."

"Who would have control over it? Like what goes on, who can build or lease a space."

"Three companies."

"Three's company?"

"No. Three companies own nearly all of the street. It's made up of Daytona top brass, former mayor, real estate tycoons, and the like. Ricardo 'Ricky' Delgado, Peter Danzig and Barbara Lumino are at the top of the top. We had them on our radar, but it went nowhere."

"The ones Newstrom failed to go after," I said. Sanford

and I had done some leg work on them as well. Delgado was big in the Florida real estate game. Not just buying and selling, but ownership. Shell companies held tens of thousands of acers in the tens of millions of dollars. Much of it sat barren or lined with pines and occasionally harvesting the trees. A family history in the state dates back over 150 years. Delgado roads avenues and highways travel through three of the surrounding counties. His family line had dwindled to just him. He was in his sixties and had two grown adult daughters who were not living in Florida. I wasn't surprised.

Peter Danzig maintained the political ties. Like Hines, Danzig worked as an insurance lobbyist. With the amount of hurricane damage in Florida and new construction constantly going up, he used millions to persuade elected officials that insurance companies had Florida citizens' best interests and pocketbooks at heart. His mingling in politics started before he was born, before his father was born. Money could bring prestige, but power came through control and the best way to do that was by controlling the lawmakers, the representatives that made the laws we were all supposed to abide.

Barbara Lumino was married to a hotel financier. She had political ambitions. Became mayor of a small town, then county mayor of a neighboring county. After that she kept getting appointed to bureaucratic jobs, places she could peddle her influence. Her husband's influence ended when he passed and took all but one hotel with him. A house of cards, built upon fraudulent time share schemes and Ponzi type investments, when he wasn't there to shuffle all the money around it collapsed. Barbara remained in Daytona Beach managing the only hotel they owned together. This was free and clear and somewhat of a landmark in Daytona Beach, due to its history of hosting the original NASCAR meetings back when they were still racing on the beach.

"They're smart and rich and can take their time. There were other criminals out there we could tackle. You think they're involved in the gun running?" Sanford was growing frustrated by my slow pace. He wanted answers, not questions.

"No, not gun running, something else."

"I'll always trust your instinct, but like Newstrom said, those are big names. They ain't no joke, Grimes. Darn, those missing files. I know we were looking into them early on."

"It was the early days; we didn't know how far or wide this would go."

"We had to much faith in the process."

"If you can get me some information on them, I'd appreciate it."

"Whatever they are involved in, my professional legal advice, tread lightly and anything you dig up, kick it over to Gibson."

"We've got the FBI interested now." I said and hung up. FDLE had dropped the ball. Newstrom wanted to make a name for himself, but he wasn't up to the challenge. The fancy high dollar lawyers shut him down. It would take absolute evidence, red handed, to get them in chains. Partnering with Agent Alvarez was the only way to ensure that.

My next stop was back to Billy's shop. Except for helping me hurt criminals, Billy had stayed on the straight and narrow. The status of his underworld ties was unknown. To keep from back sliding into the criminal world, I cut ties with what few people I knew in it. Getting popped on trumped up charges of buying stolen merchandise got me nine months in the county jail. It was only a couple of power drills, but the judge had seen me in and out of his court room enough to recognize my face and he wanted to hand down a sentence that would stick. What do you know, state funded rehabilitation worked? Nine months locked up was enough to reform me, in a way. At least I quit stealing.

To do that, I became a private investigator and Sanford hired me. Soon he was handing me cases that went beyond the duties of just observing. I became an active participant and the actions I took resulted in a lot of death and destruction. Physical pain should have told me to quit, and the mental pain should have got me to run away, but I took up Sanford's idea of a *white knight* avenging the innocent against the rapists, drug pushers and murderers in our city. Soon I became the blacked-out silhouette of a vigilante. Hunting down criminals and handing out final judgements. The cops wanted me, and the crooks wanted me. Walking the tightrope ended recently. Then James went and dropped a rumor on me. Someone wasn't buying the whole story of that crooked cop. They knew the vigilante was still out there.

A reformed criminal is like a sober drunk. There was no twelve-step program for me to go though. I had to create my own and it was mostly booze and pills to numb my mind and dull the physical pain of countless fights. My hardest fight was to change, to get away from that night stalker and return to the sun shining in my face once more. And I had done it with my last case. The vigilante was done with, only now as I held the photos of several dead in a pool hall two years ago, I can't help but feel that addict claw its way out of my chest as the thirst for justice wanted quenching. My feet were shaky as I got back on that tightrope.

I sat in the office of the shop in a steel chair with two small squares of vinyl wrapped pads that gave no comfort. My knee bounced from the black sludge I poured out of the coffee pot and my gaze was fixed out into nothing.

Billy came in from the bays and hooked a set of keys in the white metal first aid box mounted to the wall. He stood at the counter and wrote a work order. I was still fixed in my stare, somewhere between thinking or not thinking. My brain was connecting dots that led to flashes of faces and places. I bounced around timelines and searched to connect more dots. But the dots floated, never intersecting. The last thing I saw was a dog, then Billy waved a hand and whistled at me.

My eyes peeled from the lids as I broke them loose from their frozen gaze.

"Have a nice trip?"

"Oh, I had to track down a lead and stuff."

"No, I mean just now man. Shit, I've seen thousand-yard stares but not thousand light year stares."

I put a stack of cash on the counter. "Rent."

Billy whistled, then said, "Thanks brother. This helps."

I nodded.

"You want to turn some wrenches? Maybe that will help work out that weird face you're making." Billy laughed and threw a greasy rag at me. My reflexes worked even when I wasn't thinking and caught it.

"I'm going to head upstairs," I said. I should have got back in my truck and set out to find Smitty. He's out there somewhere and if the cops find him before I do, the next time I see him will be during visiting hours at the federal pen.

I stood in my sparsely furnished apartment. That old couch was calling to me with its crushed velvet cushions and sagging springs. Like that ex-girlfriend who calls you in the middle of the night, you say yes because you just want something familiar. Billy, Smitty, hell, the rest of the world would have to wait. I needed sleep.

Chapter 6

Power naps do wonders for the body and the mind. Refreshed, it was time to take a deeper dive into the missing Smitty. He wasn't an island. He had connections and friends. Dead or alive he was physically taking up space somewhere. It was time to find out what they knew, but underworld pros didn't like questions, it brought the smell of bacon in the air. A miss step, stutter or any exposing questions would not only get me in trouble but send a ripple through the criminal pond that would travel faster than I could to get ahead of it.

At the top of the list was The Daytona Beach Racing and Card Club. I went through the doors, picked a program up at the counter. There was no matinee race today, leaving all the handy cappers in the simulcast room screaming at wall-to-wall TV's showing horse racing and dog racing from around the world. The floor was carved up into long rows of desks with small dividers between them and small TVs attached to every other desk. The room was split by a small bar against the back wall and in the middle sat an island with tellers ready to take bets. For those who wanted to place their own action, to my right was a line of self-betting machines.

Smitty knew everyone here, he'd been hanging around the dog track since forever. In the early days, when the mob still controlled the action, young Smitty was a lead out. Lead-outs make sure the greyhound has the right blanket. If the dog is in the fifth position it better have a five on its sides. Smitty had other jobs too. When he wasn't a lead-out, he ran messages. Fearing every phone in the track tapped by the FBI, (which they were), a gangster upstairs would send a message via Smitty to the trainers. This set up which dog would take a dive or win. The tricks to getting a dog to win, I won't mention. Then the tip was relayed to a visiting politician or city official the mob needed paid off. The politician would make the bet and win. At the tax window a switch in the payout was made. By all appearances it was clean money.

From running messages to payouts, the natural jump was to become a bagman. If cash needed to be paid out, he delivered it. When cash needed to be collected, Smitty collected. Rumors, stories friends of friends told, created the reputation of Smitty as a debt collector. As his reputation grew, he got popped. When he refused to roll on anyone, it was ten years in a federal pen. By the time he got out, the mob had moved on from Daytona Beach, his name had not. He was made and lived like it.

Billy started taking me to the dog track after we fenced some goods or got a payout for a stolen car. We would drop some fresh cash and sometimes make more back. He knew all the regulars and I was introduced on professional terms. I quickly became a regular among the cigar-chompers and crumpled up losing tickers strewn along the dingy linoleum floors.

A no smoking sign hung below a wall of 4k Ultra-hi-def TV's, leaving me unsure if any of the regulars were even here anymore. Luck could be on my side as I spotted a teller from years back. She had dark brunette hair pulled back tight, heavy black eye makeup on and if I checked behind her right ear, I'd spot a little blue heart tattoo.

"Hey Gina." I said leaning on the counter.

She smiled. Deep lines formed around her mouth as crow's feet sunk around her eyes. Her memory failed to recognize me. I didn't blame her for not remembering, it'd been over ten years since we really talked. Back then she was hot stuff, probably in her late thirties but she wore it well. Hair was lighter and face tighter and I'd wait in her line even if it meant missing post time laying the bet.

When Smitty had caught us being chummy he pulled me aside and said she was crazy. Billy and I took that to mean he had personally experienced her crazy.

Here she was now, a little grey and few more lines around her eyes, but still looked hot to me.

"How'ya been?" she said remembering enough to know she knew me from some place.

"Good, I'll take Pompano, the three-four, three-four over the six." I said and slid over two dollars.

She punched big keys on the machine and a ticket printed out. She smiled and waited for me to do or say something.

"I used to come here all the time with Smitty." I said and took the ticket.

Her mouth made an O just as the word "Oh," came out. "I remember you now, you were a young'in then, I guess we all were." She laughed and showed me her yellow chain-smoking teeth. I used to watch her take a smoke break, down by the kennels where Smitty and other old timers hung out waiting on a tip from the trainers. She'd laugh and blow smoke with all the old men doing the same. They banned smoking on the property and all those old guys died anyway.

"You seen Smitty around?" I asked as casually as I could while taking the ticket. A guy got in line behind me. He was slapping the racing form against his leg while his eyes flicked from us to the post time counting down on one of the many TV's.

"No." was all she said and then she tapped a key on the machine again getting it ready to take another bet. The guy behind me pushed forward as I stepped off to the side. He started mumbling numbers off as she typed.

"Dang," I said, "I was hoping to catch him here."

She shrugged then sat back on her stool and studied her

own racing program.

The race at Pompano was about to start so I mixed in with the rest of the crowd, necks bent up, watching the TV.

And they're off! I became like the rest of the gambling junkies, slapping programs, screaming numbers at TV's, all in a rhythmic chant, *C'mon, c'mon*, smack-smack, *go-go!* My heart was thumping in cadence as my dogs rounded the final turn and sprinted into the stretch. Holding my breath along with the rest of them. And then the inevitable cheer of victory or sigh of defeat. Back to the program, back to the plan to make a quick buck. My heart slowed as I crumpled the ticket and laughed off the two-dollar loss.

There was a guy ahead of me in her line. She punched out the rest of the guy's bets and then said to me, "What'll it be?"

"I don't want to bet." I said to which she sighed.

"Try Ruben, he's up there in his usual seat." She pointed to a row of six-foot tables with small partitions set up between them and tiny televisions attached by a swing arm.

Ruben Rotstein was balding with thick glasses that had once been transition lenses but now were stuck somewhere between day and night. His silver mustache only had about three days growth on it, but the hair coming out of his ears had at least a week. If he were standing, he'd be a bowling pin, big head, long neck, flat chest and heavy around the middle tapering off to legs somewhere. His cream polo had two blue strips around the chest and a large breast pocket.

Ruben pulled a stack of tickets an inch thick, peeled three off and crumpled them. Then with his hand swept them into the corner of other crumpled tickets.

He had before him three opened programs all marked up in pencil. He picked one up and began to study his own notes scribbled in the margins.

"What?" he said not taking his eyes from the program.

"I don't know if you remember me –"

"I don't give tips, kid."

"I'm not looking for a tip, I'm looking for a guy."

His brown eyes pushed up under heavy strain of bushy eyebrows then he went back to watching the race on the small TV mounted to the desk.

"I'm looking for Smitty." I said leaning down to make sure he could hear me through all the ear hair.

"C'mon! Ah damnit, you stupid son-of-a!" Ruben's swear words trailed off into mumbles as he crumpled up a ticket with string of number combinations longer than my bank account.

He pushed away from the desk, slapped his hands down on large thighs wrapped in brown polyester and said, "Smitty, Smitty, Smitty. Yeah, I'm looking for him too."

Finally, I was getting somewhere. Ruben would point me in the right direction.

I waited. Then waited longer.

"You find him, you tell him Ruben wants his money back." Ruben pushed off the desk to get up from his chair. He was still leaning on the desk hunched like a gorilla then slowly straightened up. That's when I noticed the desk behind him move. It slid out a little but didn't move as much as the King Kong gorilla sitting at it did.

The half-man half-ape stood up, puffed out a pair of pectorals you could crush a walnut between. I don't know how I missed him. I do know a zoo someplace was missing him.

"Now," Ruben said looking me up and down from behind tinted bottle lenses, "Just who the hell are you?"

The big man didn't waste time coming out from behind

the desk, giving him a clear shot at ripping me in half.

"Roger Grimes." I said not giving the big man any attention. The ape wanted me to look up at him and feel small. Instead, I kept my eye on Ruben, letting the man in charge know if the ape made a move, I'd break the old man's windpipe first.

Maybe it was my name or maybe it was the look on my face, but the old man looked to the ape and gave him a half grin. The big man dropped his shoulders.

"Yeah," he said then took his finger and thumb to wipe out the corners of his mouth. "Yeah, okay, I remember you. You've gained some weight, Roger." He shrugged, "Smitty ain't been around. Just what do you want with him?"

"I need to check in with him."

Ruben studied my face. His thumbs went into his waist, then he hiked them up to his belly button.

"Check in about what?" He pinched the bulb at the end of his nose, felt something stick to his finger and wiped it on his pant leg.

"Do you know where he is or not?"

Ruben crossed his fury arms over the rut cut by the waistline of his pants. "I aint seen you around in how long? Remind me, I'm old."

"Smitty and I go back a while, a decade at least." My knee twitched, I wanted to kick the information out of this old guy, but that isn't how things are done. Though Ruben's power wasn't what it once was, he wanted things done as they always had been. With me standing here asking for help reinvigorated his stature and Ruben wanted to milk it for what little it was worth.

Ruben laughed then wiped the corners of his mouth. The ape smiled but didn't laugh.

"Times that decade by five and maybe, just maybe we're even." His pale brown eyes narrowed. A once dead fire from years of irrelevance was stoked. He wanted me to fan the flame into a blaze. If I pushed him on this, he wasn't going to physically handle me, but he would order his big man to.

Kiss the ring and all that crap. The old mafia movie bullshit was over if it ever actually existed except in the heads of guys like Ruben. The knot in my chest was tight and the only way to loosen it would be the take the bodyguard apart in front of Ruben. This wasn't the place or time. The dog track had police officers making rounds. Also, once I found Smitty, he'd give me hell for not playing along. That stuff was in his head too.

"That's why I came to you first Ruben. Smitty and I check in regularly. You know he trusts me; you know our past. I need to find him for his own good." I gave up more than I wanted but there was no other way.

"What is it you want to discuss with him?"

"Just checking in with him. He's old and I worry when he doesn't call me back."

Ruben's arms dropped from his sides as he scoffed. "We're all old now. You sound like my daughter. Calls me from New York threatening to come down here if I don't call her right back. Did you try Tully's?"

"Not yet. I was closer to this side of town. Thank you." I nodded to Ruben.

"Sure-thing Roger. And you see Smitty you tell him he owes me. That tip on Sweet Baby Louie was a bust."

I cracked a smile but Ruben nor the ape smiled back.

I went up to Ormond Beach, to Tully's Tap Room. On the drive I wondered what would have happened if the ape had got a hand on me. My reflexes were better than ever, but lately my fights had been only street fights, scraps with untrained fighters. Most of my moves consisted of dodging eye gouges and holding wrists with long fingernails trying to scratch my face. Big muscles don't make you the best fighter, but if he got me in a submission hold, it was over and tapping out wouldn't end it.

Tully's Tap Room sat on a busy corner just over the bridge on the beachside. It was the oldest continual restaurant around and kept the original appearance of rustic wood beams and white plaster walls mimicking a British Countryside pub. Inside the deep rich wood continued with a bar running down one side and large booths on the other. A scatter of tables settled in between. On the walls hung pictures of Big Ben, Tower Bridge and photos of the English countryside.

The heat was cranked up in the place, drying me out instantly. I stood on creaking wide cut pine boards and looked over the empty room. It was still early even for the retirees that flocked here at 4:30. A tall, thin bar tender with a black mustache and wavy black hair was polishing a glass. His eyes fixed on the glass, double checking for prints then slid it into the holder above the bar. He tugged at the bottom of his maroon vest.

"Can I help you." He said dragging out the, *UUUUU*.

"No." I said walking with direction. The booth I wanted was a large semi-circle with tall wooden sides leaving it very private. It could easily seat eight men comfortably. I couldn't see in but knew from experience whoever was seated could see out.

"Sir," the bar tender called, but I kept going. I had been here plenty of times since I was a teen. My mom had been a server through my high school years. We shared late night meals from Styrofoam containers. Sitting in a stained white button-down shirt, black slacks, just as stained, she would divvy up food that was about to spoil, the stuff the chef was going to toss the next day.

I brushed the memory aside and stopped short of the booth.

Looking back at the bartender, I said, "I'm looking for Smitty."

His pause held knowledge. He grabbed a glass and went back to wiping it. I started for the bar when the sliding of trousers on vinyl, brought me back around to the booth.

"Roger, that you?"

I was looking at a squat man, a turtle in human form. He had a large nose that filled his face and a chin connecting at a forty-five-degree angle to his neck. His skin was tanned, blotched with darker sunspots from over exposure. Gold rimmed sunglasses were pinned on top of a bald head with more sunspots. An unlit cigar waved me over to the booth.

"Hello, Mr. De Carlo." I said to Roman De Carlo. If Smitty was the last of the mob in Daytona Beach, Roman was the last cop. Supposedly he had been a good cop in New York then retired to Florida, finding a second career as a bent cop in Daytona. He made it as high as interim chief but couldn't get the official blessing from the mayor. Eight months after the mayor passed on De Carlo, in a big October Surprise, pictures surfaced of the mayor doing lines of cocaine in the back of a strip club off Ridgewood Avenue. The mayor lost and De Carlo, with revenge served, faded into retirement.

I stood at the round table, one that felt empty without Smitty sitting with me. I had sat here before, sometimes before a job, but never without Smitty. After De Carlo was no longer a cop, he lost some power of intimidation, but earned it back in unspecified ways, keeping his seat at the table.

"Ain't seen you around lately, kid." De Carlo scooted around from the right to the center of the table, putting him to my left. The cigar went into his shirt pocket then he moved his cell phone next to his drink, the only two things on the table.

He waved for me to have a seat. I didn't say anything. I slipped out of my coat and into the booth.

"So, what's new?" He asked leaning his elbows on the table.

Remaining silent, I shrugged.

His fingertips began a rhythmic drumming on the old resin wood table.

Being that it was still early there was no wait staff but the bartender. He came over to the table and took a slight bow asking my order.

I looked at De Carlo's tumbler with melting ice and knew I better order a hard drink. I stretched my neck back to see the shelves of liquor.

"Bourbon and ice."

The bartender nodded. De Carlo lifted a finger signaling another round for himself.

With the bartender back behind the bar I said, "I'm looking for Smitty."

He nodded casually, to say he understood, but not ready to tell me anything.

"Heard you, ah, went straight." De Carlo said reaching for his phone. He clicked the side button to reveal the time as well as a picture on the lock screen of two young kids on the beach. Grandkids I supposed.

"Sorta, yeah."

"What the hell kinda answer is that?" His eyes narrowed under the hanging flaps of skin brought down by age.

"I'm a PI now." I said hoping that bartender would hurry it up with the drinks.

"A scab! Ha! Get your jollies recording cheating spouses, do ya?" He rocked in his seat. The bartender came over and dropped two drinks, taking De Carlo's empty.

"You know," De Carlo lifted his drink, sloshing the ice, but didn't touch it to his lips, "you used to be a damn fine thief. I guess you use them skills to spy on people. Hiding in closets and laundry baskets." He sipped.

"Safe cracking."

"What was that?" De Carlo said putting the drink down on the soggy cardboard coaster.

"I was a safecracker. It's not as hard as people think. Average home safes, one minute, bank vaults, with the right tools, thirty minutes tops." I said then took a sip of bourbon.

His old eyes sparkled with the roundness of youth as he imagined what it was like to pull back on that heavy metal door and behold the treasure before you. Those visions were only ever in his head because he never went on a heist. His role was paying the official to look the other way, but I knew it was because he was scared. Scared of getting caught, scared he didn't have the nerve to sit silently listening to the clicks of dial against the ticks of a clock. He felt safer to be on the other end, kicking in doors, bullying his way through with a badge.

He licked his lips waiting for me to continue.

"Smitty set up a job one time. A real simple B&E of a corporate place. We were hired to take a computer processor. It was debuting at a trade fair."

"These days cyber-chips and crap are worth more than gold. I miss the old days. It was more fun busting a perp in a mask with a crowbar. Now a days the best thieves hide behind computers, stealing shit in the cloud." He shrugged and sucked in a piece of ice from his drink.

I nodded. The tech writing was on the wall. Tangible

valuables were harder to get and harder to sell. Dropping a bill bigger than a twenty automatically raised a red flag. Precious metals and jewels are great but finding someone that can melt it down or cut a stone was getting harder and harder. The pool was drying up. The trades were dying. I just didn't see a future that was prison free.

"It had to do with corporate espionage kind of stuff, patten and IP theft. Smitty got us construction crew ID's. I grabbed a ladder and walked in. I hid out in an A/C duct for eleven hours until Billy radioed with the 'all clear'. Then I went to work. Got the chip, got out and no one was hurt. Speaking of thieves, you know who pulled the CBR Building job the other night?" I swirled my drink and sipped.

The shine left his eyes as they narrowed. His head dipped, becoming heavier on his neck.

"You got a lot of nerve kid coming in here asking your scummy PI questions." De Carlo's voice was low, scraping along windpipes to get out.

"That job has his MO on it, and I need to find out why."

De Carlo raked a palm over his tanned face then sipped his drink. He said, "Seems a good PI should be able to find Smitty. Hell, I didn't know he was missing." He was holding it together. This table had the ability to wield power. Like he said, I had been out of the life for a few years now, my chance at a seat had been given up.

I sipped the bourbon, let the tingle subside and said, "Well, I suck at it, and he is missing. I haven't heard from him in weeks. That's unusual." I put the glass down on a cardboard coaster for a Belgium beer.

De Carlo's stare was blank. He was leaning forward as if listening to me tell an interesting story. I wasn't. It was a ploy to keep me talking, dig a hole he could bury me in.

We sat like that until both our drinks were empty.

"Glad we could have this talk. You should come around more." De Carlo waved a hand like I was going to disappear. I wasn't.

It was my turn to lean in over the table. "Mr. De Carlo," I started giving what little respect I had for the crooked cop, "You know me. My mother used to work here. Back then I sat in that table over there several times a week while guys like you, Smitty and Ruben sat here in the *corner booth*. Later on, I sat here *with* Smitty. I didn't spend a lot of time at this table. Maybe I didn't earn my place before I changed careers, but Smitty did earn it. He headed it, and right now he's missing and I'm going to find him."

I stood up forcing the table into his gut. He leaned back, his eyes going wide. They narrowed quickly. I could feel the eyes of the bartender burning in my back behind me.

I had been everybody's kid this morning from the clowns at FDLE to Ruben and his ape to this bent cop pretending he still had the balls to do something. I'm easy going until I'm not.

"Settle down kid. No need to get loud in here." De Carlo's eyes remained slits as his brain was working to balance rage with insult. He kept a cool head under pressure as he had for thirty-seven years as a cop. His hands went down to slide the table back into place. Then he motioned for me to sit.

I sat.

"We've got rules, Roger." De Carlo said with his hand raised, trying to temper me, but it wasn't going to work.

"I take back what I said about not earning my place. I've fucking earned it over and over, in ways you can't imagine. So, you're gonna give me what you know about Smitty." I said with a finger in the old man's beak.

The wrinkles around the old cop's eyes smoothed then deepened in the opposite direction as he began to laugh. He tried laughing me off, but I wasn't moving.

"Nice job. You gonna offer an ultimatum if I don't give up what I know?" He smirked.

"No."

The smirk faded, "I'd love to see you in action Roger." He leaned back with a grin then shrugged. "You remined me a lot of that old mobster son of a bitch." He chuckled then said, "Smitty's the only guy I know that'd cut my balls off and make me juggle 'em before shooting me through the fucking head. Aw, I love that guy."

De Carlo's smile faded at the corners, "Sorry Roger, I don't know where he is. He hasn't returned any of my calls either. Last I heard he had something cooking down in the Keys. That's it. Do what you want with it." He was done talking and I knew it. I didn't believe he told me everything, but it was enough for now.

"Fine. How about a thief named Harry Muncy?"

"Who?" He said shooting his eyebrows up wrinkling his forehead.

"I won't cut your balls off, De Carlo, but I will shoot you in the head." I said easily.

"Okay, okay wise ass." De Carlo sloshed the seasoned ice around in his glass, his faded brown eyes followed the spiral he churned. He looked up to meet my eyes, "Why the hard-on for Muncy?"

"He was seen with Smitty, last time anyone saw Smitty."

De Carlo's lower lip sucked in, and he frowned. "Yeah, Muncy used to pass through Daytona. I busted him one-time off-loading electronics from the back of a warehouse. That must'a been oh, eighty-eight, eighty-nine."

"I was a little young to remember those days so how about recent history, like last night?" I wasn't here for a trip down memory lane. De Carlo was a man in two worlds, cop *and* robber. Rumor was he would set up the take then move in and bust the thieves. Makes him look great to the city fathers. Except he would bring along a rookie or beat cop with a gambling debt and evidence would get miss placed. The thieves would walk. Reputations on both sides caught up to him and he had to cut it out.

"Last I heard, Muncy was busted in the panhandle and the cops had him tied to some other shit."

"Yeah, he was testifying in a human trafficking case. Now he's gone missing and Smitty was last seen with him."

"So, you want Smitty or Muncy?"

"Both."

"What for?"

"Muncy needs to testify and Smitty needs to retire."

De Carlo's belly began to shake as laughter crawled up his throat and wheezed from his mouth.

"Retire? Never. He retires, he dies. If he dies then he's retired, get it?"

I nodded. I knew my chances of talking Smitty into full retirement were slim to none, but the heat was on and any prison sentence now for the old man was life.

"You just have Smitty call me if he stops by." I got up and headed for the door.

"You got a seat here anytime Roger Grimes." De Carlo waved.

Chapter 7

After leaving Tully's I didn't go far. I spent the rest of my day across the street watching the old tap room. De Carlo left and came back for supper then left just before closing at 10. It felt like a waste of my time, but I had to see if my little dust up at Tully's would bring a meeting at the booth. Nothing happened, the old timers were just that. De Carlo's rant about never retiring only meant he didn't know he already was. The mighty Tavolo wasn't what it used to be.

The next morning had been slept away. The sun pushed high in the sky securing its grip on the day. It had been a welcomed cool dry day for a Florida winter. I didn't want to get off the couch as I lay there thinking about all Smitty's friends. He had many but trusted very few. The old couch springs whaled as I sat up to grab my phone. The contact list held five numbers. I had gone through so many phones in the last year that anyone I hadn't spoken to in any longer than that simply disappeared. There was one man I needed to call; he was the kinda guy you just don't show up to see unannounced.

On my way to Kurt's shop, I stopped off for a Slurpee and a protein bar. Driving down Carswell Drive, I spotted countless classic or custom-built cars, anything from a freshly painted '69 GTX to a late 70's Jeep Commando lifted on mud-terrains. There were shops with modern tuners and next to that a four-wheel drive shop with lifted Jeeps and 4Runners parked out front. Billy would be smart to move his shop on this side of town instead of near the hood where he was at now. But just like with all social strata there would come envy, gossip and rumors which always lead to confrontations and fights among shops. The Ex-NASCAR crew men and third generation speed shop owners wouldn't like a former car thief moving to their block. Billy's cool demeanor stops when it comes to the quality of his work. One out of place comment and I would be breaking up more fights than was ever in.

In a small concrete lot, I swung in and parked the Scout. My Scout always gathered attention even in a car town like Daytona Beach. In hindsight it probably wasn't the best vehicle for a private investigator but at the present it was all I had. There were advantages to driving it, when arriving at a shop that moonlights making gun barrels and suppressors, it's nice when everyone recognizes your ride before they see your face.

I got out and saw a broad-shouldered man about ten years my senior waving to me from the open bay door of a wide but shallow metal building.

"Hey Roger." The big man said. He stood over 6'4" and probably 250 pounds. His name was Duke, named after John Wayne. Kurt named his son Duke because he was born the day John Wayne died. Either by coincidence or growing up idolizing his namesake, Duke took on the persona of John Wayne in the way he walked and a little in the way he talked.

"Is your dad in?"

"He surely is." Duke said hitching a greasy thumb over his shoulder. "Go on back." He nodded then he looked out at my Scout and nodded to it as well. Like I said, this is a car town.

As my eyes adjusted to the darkness of the shop, the years of grease and oil spills on the concrete floor crept into my nose. I passed through to a side door and came around to a separate building. It was much smaller but made of concrete block instead of the metal siding of the driveline shop. I knocked on the white door with permanent stains around the knob. I waited, looked up at the security camera and then knocked again. Finally, the deadbolt slid back, and the door came loose. I pushed and let myself in.

A single yellow bulb cast a cone of light over a deeply scarred wooden workbench. Every groove or chip was filled in with grime from years of petroleum products sprayed or wiped. Stacked shelves flanked either side of the bench. I followed the sound of Kurt's shuffling boots as we went back to the source of the yellow light. The man was big. Nearly as tall as Duke but with stooped shoulders that held thick tanned arms ending in callused hands with knotty fingers. Years of turning wrenches gave a permanent hardness to his muscles. His belly ballooned under equally stained overalls. Pinched on his wide nose were glasses with thick curved lenses. Below that a white bristly mustache, stained light brown from nicotine. He dropped his large frame on a stool and put a custom CZ Shadow 2 down on the bench.

"Good to see ya again Roger." He reached out and picked up a burning cigarette from a small black ashtray. He flicked off the long ash and then sucked in white smoke.

"Sorry to just show up like this, but you never returned my calls."

Kurt juggled his white eyebrows up leaving me unsure if he was okay with it or if I had messed up. The man deserved the respect I could give him. He had been in the firearm business a long time. After serving in Vietnam, he became a gunsmith and firearms instructor. Then he got busted in the 1980's when the ATF set him up on a bogus gun buy. It was entrapment and Kurt's lawyer proved it, but they still got him on some unrelated charges. So, after a quick stint in the pen he decided if the U.S. Government was after him for doing things legal, he might as well start doing them illegal.

"Hadn't seen ya in a while. You were coming around nearly every week for barrel swaps and such."

"I had a busy year last year. Things have, well slowed," I said. My life had become a hectic mess and ending the vigilante was the first step in finding normalcy.

"So, what brings you by?" Kurt blew out silvery smoke then smashed out his cigarette. He turned on his stool and reached out for a mat. On the mat was a Glock 17 fully disassembled. With a small screwdriver in hand, he went about installing a shiny red trigger.

"I'm looking for Smitty."

Kurt slowly put the screwdriver down and turned back to me. He looked over the top of his glasses, "Don't know. Haven't seen him."

His nose whistled at a steadily increasing rate. History between Kurt and Smitty went back a long way. I had my own past with Kurt. Last year I bought enough gun barrels and guns to keep him comfortably retired if he wanted.

"It's important. I need to find him. I know he's still in town."

Kurt shrugged, "Sorry. I don't know, haven't seen him." He pushed his glasses back up and went back to tooling on the Glock.

"Don't know what?" I asked standing there.

He shrugged, "Nothing." He said without bothering to look at me.

"What can you tell me about Harry Muncy."

Kurt went on tooling, no flinch, no looking, not even a drag on the cigarette. I no longer existed.

Stonewalled, I left. By him not speaking, he told me all I needed to know. Pressing Kurt could bring long term side effects like an end to my gun supply or an end to my life.

Passing back through the shop Duke was talking to a young tech, instructing him on a CNC machine. He turned and started walking my way. His smile faded and his eyes thinned as he read an expression on my face that I didn't realize I had.

"Did Pop hook you up?" Duke asked. In all our dealings he had never asked a question that didn't pertain to the weather.

"Yeah, sure." I said, trying to keep it light. The skill these guys had in building the finest guns was unmatched in the state. More than that they were a place to swap out dirty pistols for clean ones. Without them, I would be in prison. Local law would have connected my bullet holes eventually. I couldn't afford to make waves.

"Okay, see ya." He said without confidence, like he really wouldn't see me anymore.

"Have you seen Smitty?" I asked. Normally I wouldn't bring up the nature of my visits here in the shop. Gun talk was only back in the small shop. This was a legitimate business, but I was losing my patience.

"Well," Duke looked up to the metal rafters in the ceiling before spinning a yarn but was cut off when Kurt shouted from the back of the shop.

"Duke, get on back here a sec and help me out." Kurt had his hand in the air waving his son back to him. Then Kurt's eyes fixated on me, and Duke picked up quickly what his father wasn't saying.

"Yeah pop." Duke said and walked off.

I mumbled some cuss words under my breath and headed for my truck.

I fired up the Scout and dropped it in reverse. Then hit the brake hard. Behind me was the outline of a man in a suit.

"Agent Alvarez." I said leaning out of the window. He walked up and rested a hand on the windshield frame. Together we looked towards Kurt and Duke as they went into the shop.

"You're a tough one to track down. But now that I gotcha, lets catch up." He walked around the front of the

Scout keeping an eye on me and then climbed in the passenger's seat.

"Nice Bronco." Alvarez ran his fingers along the dash then inspected the back seat. "Not a Bronco. It's a Scout Two actually. Made by International." I forced a smile. His eyes narrowed and he returned the smile. As if our first meeting wasn't bad enough of a start, now, I wanted to smash his face against the dash and give him my size 12 Vans in the ass.

Alvarez nodded his head, accepting what I said. He looked at the driveline shop. "Having driveshaft issues?"

I gripped the wheel, "Sure," I said.

Alvarez nodded. "Oversized tires. You must take this thing off-roading all the time."

"Not since I had it repainted."

Alvarez popped the vent window open then closed it. "Looking good, looking good."

"I haven't found Smitty yet," I said.

"You would think career criminals would have more contacts, people we could interview, friends who know where he is." He looked back to the machine shop I had just exited.

"Good criminals know how to cover their tracks," I said.

"They all get caught eventually. Sometimes it's just a waiting game. Like duck hunting. Have you ever been duck hunting Grimes?"

He didn't wait long for my response before continuing, "You get all dressed up in camouflage, maybe even paint your face green. You get out on the water or along the bank and put out your decoys. Then you sit back in your blind and wait."

I nodded, not caring to hear his analogy. "A blind is like a hiding spot."

"I know what a blind is."

"Because you've hunted before, but not ducks right. The ducks see the decoy and think it's safe to land. That's when you jump up and BLAST'em!" His smile nearly ripped the corners of his mouth apart.

I sat silently, testing Alvarez's own duck hunting skills. It didn't take long for him to grab the handle and open the steel door. He dropped one leg out then turned back, "Easy peasy." He shut the door, a smile still spread across his face. He started to walk off towards a parking lot across the street.

"Gregg Hines had more friends than Smitty," I said.

Alvarez paused then turned and walked back.

"Delgado, Danzig and the other one, from the meeting. You want to take a run at them?"

"They're involved and no one seems able to touch them."

"We're after Smitty for gun running. What do they have to do with it?"

"You tell me. Look into it."

I fired the V8 and pulled away. Maybe that would get the FBI Agent off my back and on to someone else's. Alvarez's about hunting had me wondering was I the duck, the decoy or the hunter? It didn't matter, Kurt's shortness with me was more pressing. Of all the old timers that wanted respect and procedure, Kurt was the only one that deserved it. I pulled over and called Billy.

"What's up?"

"Dude, what's with Kurt? I asked about Smitty and he practically threw me out. So, I tried asking Duke and he refused to talk." I said in a burst.

"Woah. What'd he say exactly?"

"'Don't know. Haven't seen him.' That was it."

"If anyone would know, it should be Kurt. But then again maybe they don't talk as much as we thought. I mean, what's Smitty need with a gunsmith these days." Billy poised the question without considering the recent events.

"Maybe that's why Kurt didn't want to talk about Smitty. He does know what he is into and wants to stay the hell away from it."

"True, Kurt would never work for organized crime. He's independent all the way."

"Makes sense. Hey, can I borrow the F150? My Scout is just a sore thumb sometimes."

I could hear Billy scratch at his chin through the phone, "Ah, I still gotta do the water pump on it, but don't worry, I'll have something running for you when you get here."

"No rush, I'll be by later this afternoon." I hung up. I wasn't going to let Alvarez get into my mind, but I needed him off my tail for a little while. FBI agent Alvarez was just another cop that could smell criminal on me. Washing in bad guys blood didn't get me clean in his eyes. There was nothing I could do to make my wrongs right.

Wayne needed my help with Coopers, so I sent a text to Alysa asking if it was too late for lunch.

We met at Gina's Restaurant on Ridgewood Avenue, not far from the machine shop. Gina's was your usual restaurant, square tables with four chairs and plastic menus sticking from between the napkin dispenser and the bottle of ketchup. Two waitresses stood around the register. Both wore tight black spandex pants showing every dimple in their backside. They both stopped talking to each other and said hello and for me to seat myself.

I grabbed a table in the back. I was on my second cup of coffee when Alysa stood smiling at me from the front of the restaurant.

"Hey, Grimes." She said taking a seat. "I'm starved." Her green eyes immediately began reading over the menu as I began reading her body. Yoga pants in various shades of purple drew my attention. One baggy, long tank top covered over a tighter top that hung just over the top of the Y of her legs. Her arms were toned and natural tan from days at her gym, but without the bulging veins from overuse. Her blonde hair was pulled back tight, and she wore no makeup. She didn't need it. We had never been more than friends but that never stopped the butterflies in my gut getting into a fist fight.

Those boxing butterflies nearly got me to pass on lunch, but I ordered a burger. Alysa had the Greek salad.

We chatted about movies and music and YouTube channels. Her phone chimed with texts, and she muted them while I told her the story of why my favorite Christmas movie was Home Alone That got her on a list of favorite movies for each holiday. I hadn't seen enough to comment on her list, but I tried. Then the food came. As we shoveled it in our mouths, we managed to force words around the food.

"I was at Cooper's yesterday morning." I said between bites of the burger.

"Starting early?"

"I needed a quiet place to study this new case I have. While I was there, Wayne found some drug paraphilia in the men's room."

"It happens." She said putting her fork down to sip some water.

"He seems to think there's nothing he can do about it, that these dealers are protected."

She didn't say anything, just kept eating.

"I offered my assistance. I thought maybe you could help me out with it."

"And he agreed?"

"Not exactly. I figured we could just take a look into it."

Alysa smiled then her green eyes rolled to the upper corner as she tapped her fingers against her lips. Then she said, "I don't remember ever having trouble with drug dealers when I worked there. But yeah, I can ask some of the servers if they know who they are."

"Thanks. Chastity didn't want to talk about it and if she isn't talking it might be dangerous. So be careful."

"Sure, thing *dad*." She said with a chuckle. Sure, it was a joke to her but not to me. Over a year ago Alysa saw firsthand what *dangerous* was, when she was abducted right out of my hands one early morning outside a diner. It was the end to our only date. She had been a bartender around town for years and I liked to drink so for years naturally our paths crossed. That night I found myself at her bar with a drink in front of me trying to figure out a case. We got to talking and that talk carried over to a diner. On our walk out, the part that should have ended with a kiss, ended when I got knocked out and she was taken.

I got her back, but she saw a side of me I tried to hide from even myself. I killed two men before her eyes. It took a while before we even spoke to each other again. Instead of retreating inside herself to deal with the trauma, she became more of a thrill seeker, 'living her best life' as she put it. Fear was something to be chased away with adrenaline. I had been there myself and knew where it led. After her help with another case, I knew I could trust her.

The bill came and I was the only one who took out a wallet. As we left, she said, "So how do I get paid?"

"They didn't teach you that in your online course?" I laughed. "Just write down your time and I'll bill Wayne."

"Two hundred dollars a day plus expenses, right." She smiled and her green eyes flashed fueling the burn in my chest and it wasn't the lunch. I wanted to touch her, but something in the pit of my stomach was churning, holding me back.

Out of nervousness, I laughed loudly that startled Alysa a bit, then I said, "You watch too much TV. It's twenty-five an hour and that's me being generous."

"Deal." She said and hi-fived me. It wasn't the parting gesture I wanted but I'll take what I can get.

I sat in the Scout letting the engine warm. A rush of circling thoughts from that night I almost lost Alysa rushed in. I tried hard to figure out how I could have done things different so she wouldn't have been kidnapped and witnessed what she did. I saw my hands, bruised, and bloodied, battling my way to her. The rage and fear bursting from my heart, but I couldn't see the look on my own face. Instead, I saw the one on hers that said *I never want to see you like that again*.

A knock on the hollow Scout fender caused me to jump out of my memory and quickly look around. A man in his fifties was walking by a smile on his face as he said, "Just wanted to say nice Scout." And he gave me a thumbs up. I mumbled a *thanks* and returned the thumbs up.

It was time to get a different car.

Chapter 8

Billy's eyes fixed on me while the tobacco burned from red to grey. His long black braid hung over his shoulder. He studied the end, fanning it out like a paintbrush then flipped it back over his shoulder. I sat once more in the vinyl wrapped metal chair, picking at the rubber sole of my Vans.

"I called Duke." He said finally dumping the long grey ash off his cigarette. "He didn't want to say much at first, but I got on to some work I needed from him and then he started talking. He said what his old man does is his business, but he knows the old man and Smitty had a falling out. He don't know what it was over, just that they ain't on good terms."

It wasn't like Smitty to sour relationships. He was more of a bridge builder, a guy who knows a guy, and he was proud of that. You need a few bills to get you to pay day, no problem, oh by the way which jai alai player was on the take. If the tip was good, no need to pay him back.

"Those guys have been friends a long time." I shook my head just trying to make sense of what could possibly be happening that would cause a fracture.

"I can only guess. If Smitty is mixed up in this like them cops say, he must'a asked Kurt for a favor or something. Kurt don't mess around. You ever hear that story about the time that biker gang threatened him if he didn't sell them guns?" Billy sat up at the edge of his office chair. I had heard the story, but I let him tell it anyway. "Kurt went over there with one of those lead filled baseball bats and broke the damn vice presidents jaw and smashed up the place. Then he freakin' waits there 'til the president of the club shows up and he breaks that guys arm." Billy let out a nicotine filled raspy laugh. "That old boy is crazy, quiet guy, but crazy. Just like someone else I know." He sat back in chair.

I smiled and took the compliment. I knew what he meant. On the surface I was a calm ocean on a full moon night, but when the storm came it was a category 5.

"So, where do we look next?" I said needing a better direction than I was on.

"We?"

I smiled, it faded as I realized Billy wasn't smiling. Billy was always wanting in on my cases. Usually, I tried to dissuade him from getting involved. He should be all over this case. Instead, he sat in his desk chair like restoring cars was all he ever cared about.

"Smitty is your friend too. You've known him longer than me," I said.

"That doesn't make Smitty and I friends."

"What the hell are you talking about? All those jobs and all the time we spent together means nothing?" I got up and walked over to the counter and began leaning on it.

"Sure, it meant a job and he was good at getting us jobs with low risk and high yield. He was a business partner. It's like if the kid who delivers auto parts to the shop disappeared, I wouldn't drop everything to find him." Billy shrugged.

"All the times he helped us out and you're seriously turning your back?"

"Hey, I'm not turning my back on anyone." Billy was leaning forward in his chair. He eased back, "Look, you and I don't have the same relationship with Smitty. He took a liking to you, wanted to groom you or some shit. He and I always knew the boundaries of our relationship. It was work. He lined up the score and we got it. Co-workers, man, we hang out at the office party but nothing else." Billy was so casual with his description of a twenty plus year relationship. I never saw either of them that way. To me, we were all close, a kind of family unit.

Billy rolled his chair over to the keyboard and started tapping away, surfing the net for rare auto parts. His nonchalant attitude over Smitty missing and in trouble was making me question our relationship dynamic. There were times just Smitty and I would be out on his boat, fishing or out at dinner. He took an interest in what I wanted to do with my life, as I was only in my early twenties then. Stories of how he started out in his teens, running messages for the mob, would grow into cautionary tales of a life of crime. I didn't see it then, but now I realize he was talking me out of being a criminal.

"Do you still have a car for me to borrow?" I said in a lower tone, unsure if I even wanted any help from Billy now.

"Yeah, brother." He got out of his chair and went to a white metal first aid box on the wall. He pulled a key FOB and tossed it to me.

The key was stamped with a Chevy emblem.

"Listen," Billy said, stopping me before I made it out the door, "I gotta get that Mach 1 out this week and Jose's still out until Monday, so I'm behind, but once I'm caught up, I'll help you find Smitty." He smiled and nodded, wanting the same in return.

I nodded then left.

Chapter 9

In the small gravel side lot of the shop, there were two Chevys to choose from, a 1966 Nova wagon with original paint and a few rusty patina spots that were now sealed under eight coats of clear and the other car, an older 5th generation Camaro. The Camaro was sparkling gold with a black roof that at first glance gave the appearance of a T-top. The fiberglass front bumper was cracked, and the tires were worn in a way that told me the alignment was off. With the modern key, the Camaro should be the obvious choice, but I knew Billy's ability to drop in all modern components on a classic like the Nova, so I was getting excited. Then I pressed the unlock button.

I stood watching the lights flash on the Camaro. Disappointment was the least of what I felt. Driving a unique car was important to me. Woven in the fabric of this town were threads of custom cars. With the giant NASCAR track casting a shadow, it wasn't all Detroit muscle that blew exhaust over these city streets. It could be a '67 Austin Healy or a tuned import with a turbo pumping out more horsepower than should be allowed. Having a custom build with performance in mind was the key to cool. Not something that looked like it should go fast but didn't. The Camaro was not what I hoped but it would do the job of blending in with all the other wanna be racecars in town.

Inside the car stunk of old cigarettes. The steering wheel had a dark film that stuck to my fingers and a layer of dust covered everything. I left the door open for the car to air out as I contemplated just keeping my Scout but then I turned the key.

The V8 came to life but it was the whine of the supercharger that had my ears perked. I grabbed the hood latch. There under the hood was a supercharger sucking air, ready to push that V8 all the way.

I did a burn out as a thank you to Billy for the loaner.

The radio was on a hip-hop station that I turned off in favor of listening to the motor. My drive was a short stint along US 1 to a series of blocks controlled by the 3rd Street gang. They were a street gang that had been around since the 1950's. Even back in Sanford's days hanging out at the boxing gym he had to deal with gang members either trying to recruit him or harass him. I had my run ins with them since high school. That's how I met their current leader, D'Marcus, when he wanted me to steal a car.

I didn't have a number for D'Marcus and there would be no sign pointing me to 3rd Street headquarters. I knew the blocks they held most secure and started to circle them. This was the part of town Sanford looked at from his seventh-floor window every morning. His old neighborhood filled with wood frames and slouched roof tops, built around the Second World War. There was never a time these houses were nice or well kept. Those times he turns east to look out towards the ocean from that same office, he never forgets where he came from.

On the corner of MLK Jr Boulevard and Cherry Street sat a place called The Crab Shop. It was one of three businesses in a single-story block building with a beauty salon next door and an empty front on the end. On my third pass I noticed the same man dressed in a green sweatshirt and matching sweatpants sitting on a milk crate by the back door. On my fourth pass, I caught sight of him and his tiny dreadlocks as he walked out to meet a car that stopped. The man leaned on the passenger side door as the window went down. He reached in and shook hands then put his hand in his pocket. The car pulled away.

I parked in the dirt parking lot of a Pentecostal church across Cherry Street and watched both the front and back door of the Crab Shop. It was about four in the afternoon. From what I could see through the window, there were just a couple employees inside. The dinner rush had not started, if they ever had one at all.

The back door held the action. The metal door full of dents was propped open and a man remained sitting on a milk crate smoking a little cigar.

Another car with black tinted windows drove up slowly and stopped. Just as before, green sweatpants man shook hands with the driver and then went back to his milk crate.

My Glock was left in the car, my pants felt lighter and looser, but not presenting a threat was better for me. The last time I met up with 3rd Street gang members I killed four of them. That kind of thing is not forgotten despite the truce D'Marcus and I had that night. A truce means trust and I had to show D'Marcus I trusted him by leaving my weapons in the car.

Green sweatshirt guy nearly dropped the cellphone in his hand when he saw me walking up. A white guy on this block is either lost or a cop. I was neither. It didn't matter because he knew exactly who I was. He backed up to cover the open door then snatched up his sagging pants.

"Yo, front door is that way." He said in a deep tone and pointed with his cigar.

"I need to see D'Marcus." I said turning my palms out but leaving my hands to my side.

Something in his eyes changed and he didn't hesitate to slide his hand into his waist. He was smart enough to grip his pistol but not show it.

"Get lost cracker, ain't no D'Marcus 'round here." He said jerking his elbow but still not showing his weapon.

"Tell him Roger Grimes is here to talk." I said and closed the distance between us.

He started to sway. He wanted to speak but couldn't do that and pull his piece at the same time.

As I contemplated breaking the man's arm and going into the Crab Shop, a second man came through the door. He was tall and probably in his forties with white hair fighting through the black ones atop his head. He had on jeans, a long sleeve white shirt and an orange fleece vest over it.

"What's this fool want?" Orange vest man said to the other guy.

"He say he's Roger Grimes." Green sweatshirt said.

"I need to talk to D'Marcus. It's important," I said.

"Oh hell no." Orange vest said and started towards me.

I shook my head *no* pausing the man's forward attack, forcing him to second guess his assault. In that second, I drove my fist hard into his chest. He staggered back, tripping over the milk crate, and falling to the ground. As he lay there gasping for breath, I turned my attention to green sweatshirt.

He was just clearing his pistol from his waistband.

"Put that fuck'n thing away." D'Marcus barked from the doorway.

He lowered the pistol then stuck it back in his waist. I took a deep breath and let it out loudly. There was no point in playing stoic, I had been shot before and it hurts.

"Pick him up." D'Marcus pointed at the orange vest guy still on the ground. "C'mon." D'Marcus waved me in.

Inside the linoleum floor was slick with grease and the whole place smelled of Ole Bay seasoning. To the right were the fryers and stove tops that heated large pots boiling various food items they sold. I followed D'Marcus to the left and we went into a small office. He was taller than me and weighed about 230. He was athletic in high school but now in his 30's the muscle had settled into fat. But I never doubted his strength. He sat behind a standard metal framed desk with laminate wood top that bowed in the middle. There was a cash counting machine out and a calculator with black smudges on the buttons from overuse. To his left was a CCTV with four squares showing the front, inside, side and back of the Crab Shop.

"What do you want Grimes?" D'Marcus said getting to the point, annoyed with my being there. I had interrupted his business at the Crab Shop, a business that ran on anonymity. I had created a scene.

"I'm looking for Smitty."

D'Marcus shrugged, "Haven't seen him. Goodbye." He said without looking up from the stack of cash sorting in the counter. A swing and a miss gave me strike two.

"You know, Delroy had a lot more in his desk drawer. And he had a nicer office." I said crinkling my nose at the stench. There was a filmy layer of grease on everything, and I knew I'd need to do laundry to get that smell of seasoning off my clothes. His desk was worn in spots showing the lighter wood beneath. The bright fluorescent lights hummed, exposing every stain and dirt-filled cut in the linoleum floor. This was a far cry from the office Delroy had at the poolhall. Rugs, artwork, TVs, even his drawer full of cash was larger. I remember stealing it.

D'Marcus's smile faded. The hot breath was on my neck again, "Shut the fuck up."

I felt the knife tip poke a kidney. "Don't you ever say that name again. I ever see you outsid'a this hood, and you're dead."

I didn't turn, kept watch on D'Marcus's eyes to let me know if the guy behind me moved. I said, "185 South Oleander. Any time asshole."

D'Marcus chuckled then I heard the guy behind me suck his teeth. I smiled a little because that wasn't my address.

When I heard the knife fold shut, I looked over my shoulder. Orange vest and green sweatshirt stood close behind me, guns at their sides. D'Marcus leaned to look around me then said, "What'd you expect? Ain't like you welcomed at 3rd Street parties."

"Yo," Orange vest said leaning close to my ear, "We should just kill this mutha fucka right now." I held back. I didn't come for a fight; I came to find Smitty and D'Marcus could help with that.

"You *kilt* my boy *Stey-Fon*, man. He 'bout to be a baby daddy, but you wasted him." Orange vest said with damp breath close to my ear.

"They know watch'ya done, Grimes." D'Marcus leaned back in the chair. Though some of the men that night had been 3rd Street gang members, D'Marcus had officially sanctioned me to take them out for the crimes of running an underage sex ring. As leader of 3rd Street, he didn't want any part of it. Drugs, prostitution and stolen merchandise was their game. Child sex slaves was not something a man with his own children whom he loved wanted to be a part of. That was on a different level of crime.

"This is 3rd Street business and I have information that may help you out." I said and stepped back just enough to stop smelling the man's nasty breath. I wouldn't have found fault with Orange Vest if he had shot me right there. He didn't say how tight he was with Stephon, but if someone had shot Billy, I'd want revenge too. The worst part was I didn't know which one was Stephon. Every which way that night could have gone played through my head for months. At the end of every scenario, I came to one conclusion, they all made a choice to be part of a human trafficking business and they all chose to fight me. The only thing I could do was end it the only way I knew.

"What could you possibly know about 3rd Street business, I ain't already know?" D'Marcus said leaning over his stacks of cash.

"That night, a couple of the guns used were traced back to an illegal gun running operation that was tied to the human trafficking Delroy was a part of." I said not bothering with the two who still had pistols pointed at me.

"So." D'Marcus said.

"The cops are on to it. I'm a shitty detective but even I can piece together that some 3rd Street members had those guns others might as well," I said. A slight rattle came from behind me as the one with the gun took a closer look at what he was holding.

"Why do you care?"

"Smitty is involved somehow, and I want to get him out before they catch him."

D'Marcus sat back in the chair with his fingertips pressed to his lips. We both knew Smitty wouldn't talk, it's how he became a made-man with the mob decades ago. These guns could still connect D'Marcus to the poolhall, the heat would be back on him soon.

"Smitty stuck his neck out for you that night, so I guess you owe him a favor. But listen, if it gets back that 3rd Street ratted on the guns, next time I or anyone in this room sees you, you're dead." D'Marcus said clearly without any gansta flare or style for effect. He meant it and I knew it.

"Skin heads."

"What," I said.

"You know them skin heads out off International Boulevard?"

"No."

"C'mon, I know you all hang out and tell racists jokes." D'Marcus laughed then the other two laughed.

"Oh, yeah right after we tag synagogues with swastikas

and burn crosses. What the hell are you talking about?" I said leaning on the desk. The two behind me tensed as they shuffled their feet. They wanted to make good on D'Marcus's threat.

"I don't know the name of the street, but you head out just before the county jail and make a left then down that road. Go until you see the keep out signs. They got a zombie apocalypse compound or some shit in the woods. All stockpiled with weapons."

"You buy guns from skin heads," I said.

"Black or white, it's all about the green." D'Marcus opened a desk drawer and inside were two Ziplock bags. One held cash in several tight rolls and the other stuffed with weed. D'Marcus was doing well for himself and 3rd Street as well. Those that died in the poolhall were headed in a different direction, partnering with heavier criminal organizations. D'Marcus said he let me in there to take out Delroy and the rest because 3rd Street wasn't about pimping little kids. I didn't care why he let me then, but now I think it was a power grab and I took care of the competition for him.

"Just one last thing." I said putting my hands up in front of me, palms out, "Do you know how Delroy got hooked up with Milo?"

I heard feet shuffle behind me. The two were growing tired of having their adrenaline running high, hoping for a fight that wouldn't come.

"Nah, man." D'Marcus leaned back in his chair. His hand came up and stroked his chin. "Actually, yeah. A dealer named Deezee. He's still hustling, but he do his thing beachside." D'Marcus nodded his head and that smile spread.

"Deezee? Can you be more specific?"

"Get the fuck out Grimes. I gave you all you gonna get."

I felt that knife tip again and the other grabbed a hold of

my jacket. The room was small, and I didn't want to get stabbed. I was stabbed a few months ago and it hurts, not as much as a gunshot. "Deezee?" I asked again as the hand holding me moved me towards the door.

"Young white guy. Just peek under them white hoods at your next meeting." He laughed.

I nodded then with the help of the other two I left.

A shove got me moving out the back door of the crab shack.

"Don't give a shit what D'Marcus say, boy. We comin' for ya'h." The knife tip was sharp and so were his words. Threats made me angry, made me push them into existence. This time I was keeping my head. I staggered forward out of reach before turning around.

Green sweats held his hand under his sweatshirt, "Yeah, we know who you is son, and we'll be coming for you."

Chapter 10

I shook off the threat of the 3rd street gangbangers.

Smitty would have to wait unless Billy would help me with the Skin Heads. Though he was Cherokee, something about that made him alright with the Nazis. It might also be that he built the coolest muscle cars in town. Skill and artistry can surpass race. And D'Marcus was right, they respected the green. Money and drugs are the only two things that cross every racial, gender, sexual orientation line there is. It was sickening sweet the way skin heads and gangsters bonded over the green.

Taking back streets, I passed through industrial streets lined by cinderblock buildings with metal roofs. Steam rose from pipes atop a commercial laundry warehouse. Another factory next door advertised canvas sails and awnings. I followed the railroad tracks and saw a worn foot path leading off into a dark tunnel of jungle canopy. It led to another homeless camp, people living on the fringe of society either by choice or because they were kicked out. I had uncovered a few, looking for wrongdoers trying to escape justice. Usually they scatter, some stand and fight, boy do they fight dirty.

A tightness encircled my chest, my head filled with pressure. I drove on, past a dead-end alley, one I knew I could find a dark rust colored stain. A victim of my vigilante nights. Then I moved slowly past the black charred remains of a crack house. The match had been mine.

My heart rate increased with the miles per hour of the Camaro. Straight east, over Ridgewood Avenue and down to the river. I crossed Seabreeze bridge and dead ended at the Atlantic Ocean. I cut north and swung into the first beach approach I could find. Like the Camaro was on fire, I jumped out, leaving the door open and walked to the white sand.

Then I breathed, deep, through my nose and out my mouth as fast and hard as I could, over and over until I thought I might pass out.

The sky was grey, the ocean was grey. Only white caps offered a horizon. The wind kicked sand and salt in my face. I dropped my butt in a dune and just stared out over the chop rolling in. I looked north to the high-rise condos. To the south were houses, large beachfront houses. Just three houses down from where I sat was a smooth white finished concrete house, I had been in. Not all the fires I set were in poor neighborhoods, they weren't all crack houses or meth trailers.

That house belonged to a guy named Donovan. I can't even remember his last name. He was ripping off seniors. When one old World War II vet died because he couldn't get his meds, I went in and stopped it. Puke splattered on the marble floor, echoing throughout the house. The ocean was calm that night, the moon full. A commercial fishing boat lit up like a Christmas tree, floated past the large pane windows. Donovan didn't get to watch. I left him on the floor in his own vomit.

This town was full of those memories. Everywhere I looked there was one. I could spend my whole day revisiting them. A tour guide through hell.

I shook the hate off. The memories and the tightness exited with a deep breath. I repeated, *they did it to themselves*, over and over. No one made them criminals, but I made them stop committing crimes. With those thoughts, I would somehow win the battle against myself. First, I had to deal with the ghetto gossip I was quick to dismiss. James tried to warn me and now the two from 3rd Street confirmed it. The cops miss I identified the vigilante, pinning it on one of their own, but the street knew, and it wanted revenge. The war seemed to never end.

I drove heading to the shop focusing on Smitty and getting him out of trouble. Delroy was dead and Milo,

Delroy's introduction into the human trafficking was dead too. Milo's introduction was Gregg Hines, and he was dead. My introduction to Hines came from Sanford. Now I had a new name, a new connection.

"Watch'a got for me?" Sanford's usual speedy greeting when I called.

"I checked out Smitty's old time friends. None of them have seen him."

"You believe them?" It was a fair question that I had not decided on an answer to.

"Sorta."

"I'm listening." Sanford hated dead air and I was full of it, especially on the phone.

"They haven't seen him, but I think they know what he's up to."

"Follow'em, see where they go."

I took a breath and let it out, "Not that easy. They know me, they know now I'm looking for Smitty. If Smitty doesn't want to be found, it's pointless. I showed my hand too soon because I thought our relationship was enough."

"Yep, sure did." Sanford said filling the dead air.

"So now I need you to do some investigating."

"Okay." He said dragging out the *aaaay*.

"FDLE doesn't have a lot of names in these files on the other pedos. Everyone keeps saying this has gone to the top, rattled Tallahassee but I don't see names attached to any of it. They want me to grab an old thief so they can get his testimony."

Sanford's silence caught me off guard. I expected a quick answer on something I overlooked, or he know to be true.

"Who else was in Gregg's circle?" I said, breaking the silence.

"Let me get back to you on that."

"Okay." This time I dragged out the *aaay*.

"All we had were Threes Company as you called them. Two dots we could never connect."

"How about with a Deezee?"

"What now?"

"A drug dealer named Deezee. He connects the dots between Milo and Delroy so."

"So, he's the missing link." His hand went over the phone as mumbles came through. "Gotta run. Talk at yah later." Sanford hung up.

That knot synched once more. Alysa just went out in search of the dealer on Beach Street on my orders. A deep breath did little ease the knot. My fingers punched out a text to check in with her. It should have been a warning to stop immediately but texts can be confusing even in all caps.

I pulled into the shop. The sun had broken through the mask of grey clouds to push beams of fiery orange between the trees and buildings before settling into the west. I sat in the Camaro looking at my phone. The screen was black, and I stared at nothing, processing our conversation. Sanford brought me Hines to destroy what he had been a part of the human trafficking for his own pleasure and that of his friends. They were all power elites who could not be touched and that remained true. My reach stopped at the county line. Not out of legal jurisdiction, I didn't work within the law. I stopped because I couldn't keep going. After what I saw and did, it was enough. I had walked away from it, from Sanford and from Monique.

My departure left the three of us on shaky ground. Sanford was worried I'd snapped, and Monique was concerned I would spill my guts to the cops, or some shrink. I did neither and came back into the fold, back to help stop the cesspool from growing.

Billy had the phone to his ear, as I poured some black sludge coffee into a stained mug then took a seat.

When he hung up, he wrote down something and then looked up at me brushing away a few wild long strands of hair that got loose from his braid. "If you wanna talk follow me."

Inside the shop, the Mach 1 was six feet in the air, tires dangling from the lift. The driver's side tire was off. Below, the concrete was splattered with brake fluid. More dripped from a disconnected brake line, filling the puddle below.

Billy lit a cigarette then grabbed the wrench off the bench. "This damn thing has a gremlin running around. I swear, I fix one thing and another breaks." He stopped yanking on the wrench and looked at me, "This wasn't broke yesterday, nah, yesterday it was the damn float in the gas tank. I drove around and couldn't tell how much gas was in her, but the fucker stopped great." He shook his head and went back to the brake line.

"Want some help?" I said hoping he would say no.

"Hand me the brake bleeder." He said in a reasonable tone.

I got it off the bench and handed it to him. He went to work bleeding out the fluid that was still very clear. I looked up at the brake lines and followed them up with my eyes to the master cylinder.

"It's all been replaced with a modern electronic braking kit." Billy said saving me from making any useless suggestions as to what the problem could be.

I nodded.

"What is it you wanted to talk about?" He said pausing

to ash his cigarette.

"Skin heads."

"Double fuck."

"What? Why?" I said.

"No and no. Grimes you better stay away from that garbage fire, whatever it is. I don't care if Smitty is the skin head king now and sitting on a mountain of guns and trophy hog heads or whatever they do out there." Billy went back to working.

"So, you've been out there?"

"Ah-huh,"

"Can you –"

"No."

"Okay."

"No." he said again.

"Stop saying no. Look, don't worry about it. I'm white with a shaved head. I'll be fine."

Billy went over to the lift control and waved me out from under the car. The lift clacked as he lowered the car then leaned over the fender and looked down from above at what he was just looking up at. He mumbled some more swear words then stood up.

"I can't drop everything to help you, Grimes. I'm running a shop and Jose has a second job, okay, not on vacation. I can't afford to pay him what he's worth. If I don't get this Mustang out this week, I'll lose money on it and damn it, you aren't exactly paying me rent every month to live upstairs."

"Sorry man, I didn't know. Sanford doesn't pay me much, the money we take –"

"Yeah, I know, goes to charity. How about you go tell

your rich boss up there in his glass tower to support the Billy charity. Huh? Maybe you could keep some of the blood money you take and pay your friend what he's due." He went back to the toolbox and started searching for a tool. He slammed the drawer shut; the steal tools rattled inside. A string of Cherokee words rumbled from taught lips. Then he said in English, "Fuck the straight and narrow life. At least I had money when I was thief." He grunted and threw a wrench. Billy's eyes were wide, and his nostrils flared with increased breath. He hated the truth of his statement more than his situation.

Tens of thousands of dollars in cash moved through my hands as the vigilante. All of it tax free and stolen from criminals who stole it from others. It couldn't get more laundered than that and I gave it all away, to strangers, people like Tara or parents of kidnapped children I never found, not to people who supported me. That was the deal Sanford and I worked out. It was the deal that helped me hate myself less each morning. This wasn't about me anymore.

I walked over and picked up the wrench. I took my keys, cellphone, pocketknife and brass knuckles out and set them on the bench.

"What needs to be done first?" I said and handed him the wrench he had thrown.

He started to wave me off then paused, smiled and said, "This damn Mustang. Get behind the wheel and pump the brakes."

I did as he said, and we went to work in the shop. The radio was on the local classic rock station playing songs from when I was a kid skateboarding up and down A1A. Back then learning to land a heal flip or a combination trick was all that mattered to me. I hadn't learned MMA yet, no security training with firearms and no bank robbing or stealing cars either. It was a time when I had plenty of time. Skateboarding, video games and figuring out how to talk to girls was how I spent my days. Nothing ever felt rushed or important. There was always down time when I would get home. 'Latchkey kid' they called it. I had the house to myself in the evenings while mom was serving at Tully's. During the day she was a clump of dyed blond hair on a pillow. To get her up, I'd clang dishes in the sink, pretending to clean them. It would rouse her, and I could tell her about my day before she went off to work. Then I started actually washing more than the single dish I needed, and cleaning was a good way to free up time with her.

A late night usually meant she was flush with cash, but it wouldn't last long, and neither would she. I realized it wasn't always work she was going to. That's why we didn't have food one week or the power off another. Not long later she faded into the dunes of Daytona Beach. By then I found a new family with Billy and Smitty. All the free time disappeared.

As Billy and I wrenched, I couldn't get the white-haired grinning gangster out of my mind. I coaxed Billy into telling me more about Smitty.

Stories of dishonesty loosened rusty bolts. His mind wandered back to sitting in a cargo van watching seconds tic off a wristwatch while looking out at a dark street for anyone who may be looking back. With each turn of the wrench, he told how Smitty had spent months getting to know the night shift guards at an electronics distributor. Buddied up to the guy then found out his secrets. Billy didn't remember exactly but he knew a prostitute by the name of Cindy played a part in it.

Then he turned it around and asked me about the times Smitty took me fishing on his boat. I thought about the time he took me to Atlantic City, then we shot over to Philadelphia so he could show me where he grew up. Why hadn't Billy come? I wanted to ask him, but we were almost done with the Mustang, story time was coming to a close.

"Alright, I'll take you out there. I have to call ahead." Billy began wiping his hands on a blue shop rag. Getting him to talk about what a great guy Smitty could be, hit something in Billy and he was back in wanting to help.

"How is it you're so friendly with neo-Nazis?"

"They ain't exactly neo-Nazis or skin heads. I mean they want to be, but they're mostly just rednecks and something about me being a *redskin* and First Nations people they like." Billy shrugged again like he wasn't sure but we both knew it was the cars he built. They respected his talent.

Chapter 11

Billy and I had finished our day's work at the shop well into the evening. Like usual, post job, we sat on stools drinking Miller High Life from sweating gold cans. Years ago, we'd be in his basement, on a gold velvet couch he got from his grandmother, counting cash from a bank we knocked off.

"Appreciate the help, bro." Billy lifted his beer and slurped. "Feels like old times."

"It feels exhausting." I nodded. Except there was a better feeling, something that was elevated over the old excitement of getting away clean from a robbery or fanning large stacks of cash in our faces. There was an honesty to this feeling, something I could be proud of and something that I could see done. Cars were fixed today, customers satisfied. Where my knuckles would be bruised and covered in another's blood, tonight they were cut and blackened with grease, but it was not something to hide, I wanted to celebrate it.

"I'll have to set up a meeting with the rednecks tomorrow. That okay with you?" Billy said then tipped back the last of his beer.

I reached across the work bench to my phone and pushed the home button. It was nearly ten pm and there were two texts from Alysa I missed between the impact wrench and the classic rock blaring. I only read the second text, she said she was meeting friends at a local brewery later if I wanted to meet up.

"Sure," I said to Billy then I slipped off the stool and staggered up the wooden stairs to my apartment above the shop.

After a shower, I text Alysa back I could meet her about eleven. She texted back letting me know that would work. So, I set an alarm on my phone and passed out for a twenty-minute power nap.

The brewery was tucked back in a maze of drab brown industrial metal fab buildings that housed a cabinet shop, auto repair and a business that keeps those beach shops stocked with towels and keychains. Behind all that were the railroad tracks. Parking was sparse to begin with, but tonight it was nonexistent. Inside the brewery building had a small bar seating about ten people. Outside, a brick patio was surrounded by leafy elephant ear plants and tall palms pretending it wasn't in an industrial complex and blocked the railroad tracks behind the wooden fence. Strings of lights with antique bulbs lit long wooden tables of beer drinkers and on a small stage stood a guy playing an acoustic guitar. Seated in Adirondack chairs, close to the stage, where three young women excited to see this guy sing. The blonde on the end was the one I came to see.

I grabbed a beer first, a stout with a coffee finish. They made the best in town, and I was not about to pass it up.

Standing just behind the three, I waited for a break in the music. Once the young guy thanked the small crowd for listening, I moved up.

"Hey," I said coming around Alysa's chair.

She looked up with those green eyes and already had a smile on her face. She wore a large tan sweater with a large woven scarf draped over it. I was in a flannel and jeans. The air was cool, but the humidity helped it feel warmer. We all dressed like it was Vermont, Floridians hang on to as much winter as possible. After introducing me to her two friends, whose names I quickly forgot, she got up for another beer. I followed needing another myself.

We chatted in line and ordered at the window then took our pints to the corner of the courtyard away from most of the crowd.

"Whoa were you right about Coopers." Alysa said getting to the point. "Wayne just unloaded on me today, spilling everything that has been going on. I had no idea the whole time I worked there."

"Well, you weren't looking for it either."

"Right, worked my shift and went home. I never hung out with the other servers or stayed after closing to drink like they would. I always had my gym to focus on." She sipped her beer. I said nothing, waiting on her to tell me what she knew.

"He thinks you're gonna kill whoever is behind it." She laughed. Her green eyes lowered to the pint of beer as her smile faded. She looked over to her friends. "I told him that's not what you do."

"Yeah, I tried to tell him that too."

"So anyway," Her smile came back but not as strong, "I guess Wayne's business partner has pressure on him to let drug dealers sell at the bar and also other shady business stuff, like off the books money."

"Money laundering or something?" I said not sure what she was getting at.

"Yeah, he wanted Wayne to take on bad debt then write it off with the bar somehow. He explained it all, I wrote it down." She said then looked back to her friends who were seated once more in front of the stage. One of them was obviously there for the singer by the way she clapped and cheered then made her friend do the same with a high level of excitement.

"I'll let you get back to your friends in a second." I said to which Alysa shrugged letting me know she was in no rush.

"Did you get a name of his partner?"

Alysa opened her phone and looked at the notes.

"No, we got interrupted and when I found time alone with him again, he wasn't in a talkative mood." She said with a shrug.

"I can find him through state records."

"Wayne called him a silent partner."

"Ever meet him or see him around?"

Alysa shrugged, "Don't know but I know a way to find out." A smile parted to one side of her mouth.

"Oh, what do you have in mind?" I said returning a smile.

"A little undercover work. I start bartending tomorrow." She smiled searching for my approval.

"Listen, this can get dangerous, and I need you to play it safe. I can't let what happened before…"

"I won't let that happen again."

"Neither will I." My chest burst into flames as sparks emanated from my brain as her hand slipped into mine. She squeezed softly, pulling me into her.

The music started and she looked over to her friends once more. She pulled me towards their chairs near the stage. I resisted. I wanted to tell her the night wasn't over, and we had more work to do. If the lead is hot, it must be followed. From the outside looking in, people get the idea I just drink at bars and make a few calls and that's the job. There is no clocking out until the case is over.

"I've got to go," I said.

She hugged me with one arm and gave me an extra squeeze before letting go. My desire to be liked overpowered my need to be a boss and I let her go back to her friends. Alysa had been eager to join my investigation business, but like everyone, she needed a night off with friends. In my own way I got my time off this afternoon helping Billy wrench on a classic car. Something about using my hands freed up my mind to drift into spaces and corridors it wouldn't normally go. Memories were dug up, things about Smitty I had never thought much about were picked through like searching for a diamond ring dropped in the trash can, I sifted through chicken bones and coffee grounds, the things you don't want to touch. Now with Wayne's silent partner in the picture a question could finally be asked. Why would two old men seemingly independently wealthy take so much risk? I was looking at it all wrong. I wanted the end point, the now, but I needed the cause. To find that, I needed to first find their motivation.

Back in my apartment, the auto shop below was finally silent. The one window was open letting in the puttering of cars and occasional motorcycle roaring along US 1. I laid on the couch staring at the plywood ceiling. My eyes followed the grain in the wood like water running down a windshield. The wavy grain pattern in the plywood overhead blurred with images of Smitty. Clumps of his blonde hair resisted the encroaching silver strands on his scalp. The hair was longer than normal, and he brushed it off to the side of his forehead. That gruff voice of his was in my ear talking about things like family and loyalty. It was the talk he gave me when I told him I was done being a thief, after he laid a guilt trip on me about all the time and money spent on my training. The word trust was thrown around in that talk.

Smitty said, "All these things I did for you, and now you're ready to walk away." It wasn't a question, just reaffirming statement. He patted his hands together as if they had been dusty then he shook my hand and we never talked about me quitting again.

The springs on the old couch sang out as I sat up. Smitty's voice was gone from my ear, but I understood what he was talking about then. He wasn't laying a guilt trip on me at all, yet now all these years later guilt washed over me, circling down the drain in the middle of my chest.

Splashing cold water on my face cleared my guilty thoughts. Understanding cleared my troubled mind. I stumbled over to my bed and face planted.

Chapter 12

Sleep remained just out of reach. Tossing and turning I left the bed for the couch. With no relief, I typed out and email to Sanford with the information Alysa told me. After an energy drink to push away thought of sleep, I was back cruising up and down Beach Street. Scattered cars and scattered people moved about. One homeless guy sat on plant less planter, staring off into his own world. After a few passes along the quiet street, I parked outside Coopers. Inside the action was just as slow. A few at the bar. No one shooting up in the bathroom. I moved on, back to driving aimlessly. Sleep was needed but not on the schedule. A tiny tingle, a push from the inside out was keeping me going. It felt like the old days when Billy and I were handed a job from Smitty. Casing a place was my favorite part. Cataloging the comings and goings of security and staff. Getting the timing right was my specialty.

A message came through from Monique giving up Delgado, Lumino and Danzig's addresses. It was time to get real answers from the power elite. Their lawyers may have kept them from answering questions from the law, but I wasn't the law. They would answer mine. Twenty minutes later, I was sitting outside Ricky's riverfront home drinking a coffee. Billy would tell me to wait at least three days, learn the habits, the timing and develop a detailed plan. We'd case places for a week or more to develop the plan. After sitting and watching the little intrusions would start. A walk along the sidewalk pausing to tie a shoe. Covered in darkness a walk through the yard, getting close to the house, looking for cameras. Night two would be checking the windows and doors for alarms. Then night three would be the assault. The professional side that knew better would have sat for three days, but I wasn't a thief anymore. But I still had the skills.

There was no moon as I walked three houses to the north sat an empty lot, overgrown with Florida jungle. I passed through the blackness following the sounds of the lapping shore. At the river's edge I found the tide out, so I was able to crouch along the sea walls and stumbled over oyster beds, being careful I didn't fall into the razor edges of the shells. The back of Delgado's house was dark, no porch light or lights from any windows either. The mask rolled over my face, and I held my tool bag tightly as I approached the rear corner of the house. After every step came a pause, listening for a human or worse, a dog. The windows were all wired by an alarm system from the 1990's making my life easy. A glass cutter got my hand to the inside to work the wire jumper and a pair of cutters. Then I flipped the latch and slid open the window.

The 1990's décor matched the alarm system. It was a time capsule. A brown brick kitchen with baby blue and pink floral wallpaper. A large light oak dining table. Passing a coquina rock wall, I took the two steps down into the sunken living room with two large leather sofas and a recliner. The TV was new, but the stereo wasn't. Portrait photos with swirling blue backdrops along the hallway confirmed it was Delgado's house.

A soft carpet runner up the stairs kept my steps muffled. At the top all the doors were closed except one.

No sounds, no glow of a TV or light from under a bathroom door either. Just a spread-eagle lump under the sheets. My heart began to thump then rumble as I neared the bed. A direct link to Hines's secret life of child rape was never made obvious to the law or to me. Doubt crept into my joints as my knees locked and my fingers refused to make a fist. This was just going to be an *enhanced interrogation*, nothing more, I told myself over and over. Intelligence was my goal not vengeance.

My gloved hand pinched the sheet and rolled it back. What I saw shocked me more than it did him.

One eye open stared into me. The other was pinched shut. His mouth was open, tongue bulging out. The slash across his throat was clean and deep. Blood had run out the left side and soaked into the pillow and bed.

With my glove and using the back of my hand, I touched his cheek. Cool but not cold. I was no coroner, but guessed he'd been dead an hour or so. Also, the way his one eye was open and the other pinched with his head tilted slightly, I could envision palming the top of his head, holding his right eye open with my thumb as the blade slipped across his neck. The killer wanted him to see it coming, or he wanted to watch the light in Delgado's eye go out.

I went to work searching the house. Evidence was what I came for and it had to be hidden somewhere. It could come in any shape from a computer to a memento he took from a child. Nothing in the closet, nothing in any of the five bedroom closets. The house was too large, and I was running out of time with the corpse.

As I drove the Camaro away from the murdered Delgado, I pulled my cell from the glove box to get Lumino's address. The five missed calls were just as shocking as Delgado's open eye. The first was from Newstrom, then Sanford, Gibson and finally Alvarez called twice. There were more texts, but I chose to listen to Sanford's voicemail. He said Lumino was found dead, throat slashed and no to talk to the cops. The other four voice mails were breaking the same news expect they ended by asking me to talk to them.

With Alvarez being the only one on the outside, and I hoped more objective, I called him first.

"Grimes, where you been?"

"It's after two in the morning. I've been sleeping. What the hell is going on?"

"Don't you check your texts, voicemails?" He laughed.

"Lumino is dead."

"Not just dead, compadre, but murdered."

"How'd she die?" I asked knowing exactly.

"We're at the crime scene now, if you'd like to come take a look." He said without answering my question. A smart enough investigator to hold back info that might come in handy later.

Sanford would spit words like bullets out of a Gatling gun when he finds out I agreed to go. Curiosity got the better of me. Was the wound like Delgado's? How long until someone found him and reported it. I would rather be in the company of Alvarez and Newstrom then claiming to be home in bed when the news broke.

"What's the address?" I said. Alvarez spit it out then asked if I knew it. *Of course, I didn't.*

"I don't know this town well," the FBI agent said, "But as I remember, that's not far from your apartment."

"See you in ten." I said and hung up. Then I punched the gas. Delgado's place was miles from Lumino's.

Turning onto Limino's street I was turned away by a uniformed cop. With my PI ticket out, I told him I was asked to assist on the investigation. He waved me through, and I parked along the road.

Barbara Lumino's mansion sat high on a dune. Even without the third story you could see over most roof tops in the neighborhood. Her house like several others on the block was a 1920's stucco Mediterranean Revival. The square white walls with centered windows reminded me of Billy's house in Holly Hill except larger, much larger. This was the mother hen that laid the egg that became Billy's house.

I ducked the yellow tape and walked up the winding brick walk to the heavy wooden door complete with rot iron hardware. Inside photographers in grey polos tucked into black cargo pants meandered with their heads and cameras pointed down taking shots throughout the house. The red clay tile floor passed through a curved arch entry and met wooden stairs with painted ceramic tiles on the risers. I wound around the staircase following the flashes popping like fireworks until I found Alvarez, Newstrom and Gibson in the master bedroom.

The room was large with dark wood floors, original to the 1920's home. Painting in heavy wooden frames were on each wall. Double doors were open to a closet. The three men were gathered around a nicely made king bed with flannel pajamas laid out. Newstrom had his arms crossed, his hand holding his chin as he looked over, "Grimes. I didn't expect to see you here."

"I told him to come." Alvarez said relaxing the wrinkles grooving across Gibson's forehead. Newstrom relaxed his arms then waved me to the bathroom. Gibson led the way, Newstrom behind me and Alvarez stayed in the doorway.

The bathroom was large with marble floors and vanity. The walls were tiled white and held a mirror on each of them. A large tub with three steps up to it was under the window. It was the glass shower that was still being photographed. Gibson waved off the crime scene investigator.

"Throat cut. Coroner says it was sometime between midnight and two am, but with the shower having been on, he has to check the stomach contents to be more accurate." Gibson said looking into my eyes, watching me watch death. Just as with the photos, he was looking for tells.

The shower was tucked in the corner with one glass wall and a glass door. Two shower heads and a seat. It was big enough for four but only had one occupant. Laying on her back, legs twisted and both hands still clutching her throat was Barbara Lumino. The hotel heiress had met the same fate as Ricky Delgado on the same night.

"Every see anything like it?" Alvarez asked from behind me.

I shook my head without bothering to turn around. They didn't call me in so I could help solve the crime. They were all waiting for me to react, vomit, run or confess. I was a part of this investigation either way. With Muncy missing or dead, we needed all the witnesses, or rats we could find, and someone was making sure no one was left for Newstrom to flip.

"I gave you her name. Her's and Delgado and Danzig. Has anyone checked on them?"

All three deputized crime fighters looked wide eyed at each other for an answer.

"We'll make some calls." Newstrom said to Gibson. The cop nodded and stepped out of the room.

I moved in on Newstrom, "Sanford and I served her up to you. She was part of Hines's poker parties. She knew something and now she's dead."

"Grimes, she was cleared. Do you have any idea how many *friends* Gregg Hines had? She was an enormously rich hotel owner. Her husband practically built this town. For people like that you need evidence real clear red-handed kind of evidence." Newstrom was foaming at the mouth. He wiped the spittle from his lips and put his hands on his hips.

Gibson stepped back in the room. "Got Danzig on the phone. I sent a unit over anyway. Delgado hasn't answered. His executive secretary is on her way over to his house. I'm heading there now."

"Not me," I said. I already knew what they would find, and I had spent too much time in this mouse trap as it was.

"Why is that?" Gibson said.

"I'm tired and if you didn't care about Delgado when I told you to, then why should I now?"

"Just wait a minute." Gibson held up his hand. "Let me see that knife." A growl rumbled low in my throat. Sanford's assumed advice was correct. I should have never come. Guilty before proven anything else. I wasn't invited because of my investigative skills, but their interest in me as a suspect. I pulled the knife and flipped open the blade. Newstrom stepped back but Gibson remained still. A confident cop sure of his capabilities.

"Okay. We don't need you anymore." Gibson turned and headed for his car.

"Well?" Newstrom asked.

Gibson grumble my blade was serrated. He went on to explain to Newstrom why it didn't match. I was out of ear shot shortly after nearly to my car.

"Lucky." Alvarez said.

"I didn't kill a suspect in a case I want prosecuted."

"Oh, I know you didn't do it. I meant you're lucky you get to go home. I suspect we have a long night ahead of us." Alvarez smiled that perfect Ken doll grin. "Or we could go rouse Danzig. See what he knows."

The agent had a good point.

Chapter 13

Alvarez drove because he had the address. Leaving the bright lights of the Daytona Beachside and headed north to the outskirts of Ormond Beach. The road twisted and wound into the pines that opened to small pastureland with pole barns and cattle scattered somewhere in the darkness. An out of place unmanned guard house shown bright against the country road. An open gate greeted us. We passed easily and wound through black-top streets nearing Danzig's mansion. The deeper into the neighborhood we went the larger the homes grew. The size of the home correlated to the amount of vegetation surrounding the driveway. Until each drive disappeared behind low hanging oaks and big leafy green tropical plants.

Salmon colored sand pavers disappeared into the blackness of the tropical overgrowth. This was the house. We went in on foot under a three-quarter moon bright enough to cast shadows. The moon disappeared once under the green enclosure of the tree canopy above. About 200 yards ahead the bright moonlight guided us to the exit. Emerging from the Florida jungle path we saw a clearing of lush grass. Closer to the house a well-maintained island of palms and other tropical plants were lit up from the ground. More small lights in the ground threw up white semi-circles of light all the way to the apex of the large glass double doors. A six-car garage was to the left with a metal roof and two dormer windows jutting out. To the left smaller, Apex roofs marking each wing of the house. There was nothing modest about the house for the real estate mogul.

Two marked sheriff's cars and an unmarked sedan parked in the semi-circle. One deputy stood at the door eyeing us as we got out.

Alvarez had his badge out as we passed. The ten-foot, frosted glass door was open. My Vans squeaked crossing the white marble floor. We were in a sea of white. Walls, pillars, fireplace and leather couch all white with gold trim. Less inviting than the décor was the faces of the men with guns and one woman in a pantsuit, also had a gun.

The other deputy in his green uniform stood next to Detective Rhoshanda Camp. Her eyes cut me as they slashed towards Alvarez. Past them were two typical merc types. Dressed in tight black t-shirts, and black cargo pants tucked into black boots. Goatees and shaved heads completed the merc ensemble. The balder of the two approached us.

"I.D.'s." He said flipping his hand, stopping short of snapping his fingers.

Alvarez pointed to his hip where he had clipped the shiny badge. The guard looked at it then looked at me. I shrugged.

"C'mon, I.D. please."

"I'm with him." I said pointing at Alvarez.

"He's with me." Alvarez said quickly, "On official business." He turned to the older man sitting on the couch. He was about sixty, brown hair, too brown, probably died. His eyebrows were manicured to the point of nearly being shaved off with pale brown eyes below. A finger tugged at his navy-blue sweater. Crisp blue jeans and brown loafers finished his attire.

"FBI, finally someone takes this seriously." Peter Danzig's voice was wispy with pressure behind it.

"Yes, you're in good hands now." Detective Camp said slapping a note pad against her taught thigh. She walked over and extended her hand to Alvarez. He took it softly and leaned in. I thought he was going to kiss it.

"Special Agent Alvarez."

"Detective Camp. I've got what I need here so I'm happy to turn it over to the feds." Camp was not one to put up with uncooperative victims. Her mood set the tone. Danzig was going to be a handful.

"We're just here to assist. Lieutenant Gibson is in charge of the investigation."

"Darn." She said looking back to Danzig.

He shifted in his leather seat. His eyes found mine, pausing long enough to spin the rolodex in his mind. Leaning forward, he scooted to the edge of the couch and sat straight.

"I appreciate all the law enforcement coming to my aide, but as you can see," He waved a hand at his twin security guards, "I am well protected." His eyes pinched slightly as they settled on me. I wanted to look over at Camp or Alvarez and see their reaction, but I was locked into Danzig and what he was trying to tell me, just me. Not the other law in the room.

"Mr. Danzig, that may be, but someone came here tonight to kill you. Whoever it was may try again." Camp said.I caught the gaze of the security team when I began meandering about the large living room. Moving slowly, stepping softly on the marble. The eyes of the security guards pressed against my back as I wandered further into the mansion. I got as far as the mirrored wet bar, with black marble top. It reminded me of Sanford's, but bigger and with more expensive booze.

"Sir, that's far enough." Mr. Security said wiggling his goatee.

"I already told the sheriffs here, but I might as well tell you. I had just worked out in my gym, over the garage. Went to my room to shower and I hear pounding at my door, and I'm being told to stay put in my room. After several minutes my security team signals all clear." Danzig said his seat.

Alvarez didn't have any questions. He was looking

around the room, at the guards, at Camp. So, I stepped up and said, "What did the cameras catch?"

The guards looked at each other then to Danzig. "The cameras? My system is in the middle of changing over. I'm afraid they weren't rolling. I should have got a backup, but who thinks they will be a victim of a violent crime?"

"You weren't, not yet anyway," I said. Camp squinted my way using her eye lids to close my mouth, but I wasn't done. This pedophile had answers and I needed them. "A couple of friends of yours didn't have their security systems working either."

"Friends?"

"Delgado and Luminos."

Danzig looked around the room searching for someone to make sense of what I said. "They are business associates of mine, but what do they have to do with my attack?"

"They're dead. Both of them were murdered tonight by the same person who tried to get to you." Alvarez said. Camp shook her head as she turned her back to hide that bulldog face she makes. The little I knew about investigating left me wondering had Alvarez made a mistake, but Camp confirmed that. The Special Agent wasn't so special now.

Danzig shook his head then lowered it into his hands. He lifted his head again to stare me down, "Are you saying this was an organized attack on me and my associates?"

"Any reason why someone would go to all that trouble?" I said, stepping closer.

Danzig got to his feet. He wasn't going to face me sitting down.

"If you have an accusation, make it." Danzig said with all his breath. He was a good six inches shorter than me but had large features; head, brow and nose that would fit on a man a foot taller.

"Grimes, let us investigate a little more here before jumping to any conclusions." Camp had shifted her posture too, nearly landing between us.

"It's alright detective. You need to understand Grimes, at my level, I open myself up to being a target. As you can see, I've prepared for that. Now, please, it's late and this news is devastating. Please may I have my leave and go to bed?" He stood up slowly.

"Yes, Mr. Danzig. I'll leave one of my deputies outside for the rest of the night. When you're feeling well enough, please contact me." Detective Camp put her business card on the coffee table. She shook her head once more then left with the other deputy. The guard held the door for us as well.

Camp dismissed one of the deputies then told the other to pull around and get ready to spend the night. She walked over to Alvarez and I standing by his car.

"Thank you, FBI." She said.

"What?" Alvarez smiled flashing his straight teeth. A smile he used on women so often fell flat on Detective Camp.

"The names of the victims have not been released. You go and blab it."

"I thought he should know how serious this is."

"Grimes, what the hell are you doing here anyway?"

"I came with him." I pointed to Alvarez.

Camp patted her straight and flattened hair, careful not to itch the scratch. Her head never seemed to stop shaking. "My shift starts in two hours. I'm going home. I'll call you."

We watched her pull away. Alvarez drove us out of there slowly making sure there was distance between her and us.

The scream of the pneumatic ratchet pierced my ears as I sneered at the sun burning through my blinds. Slapping around the mattress, I found my phone. It was ten minutes to eight. Another round of missed calls and unread texts. Information I already knew, they found Delgado, throat slashed. The last text was from Sanford asking if I was in jail yet. Next, I checked the weather. Florida winters are finicky. Yesterday was cloudy, windy and a damp 61. Today with the sun out it could be 75. My phone said sunny and 73, turning to rain later and dipping into the low 50's.

I called Sanford.

"I hope you kept your mouth shut like I advised you."

"Yes," I said.

"Well? What happened when you got to Peter Danzig's house?"

"Nothing. He has private security."

"And security scared away an intruder." Sanford said as disappointed as I was to say it. Not a normal reaction to hearing someone survived an attack, but the two of us were certain at best, Danzig and the others were child abusing pedophiles.

"Does Newstrom want us trying to find their killer now?"

"It has thrown a wrench into things. I sent him over a summation on why we investigated those three as possible participants in the trafficking and now they're dead. Seems someone is cleaning house."

"Let them eat their own. I have other problems."

"Yep, let me know when you find Smitty." Sanford said good-bye and hung up.

With a flannel shirt on I went downstairs for my morning routine to continue. I slurped steaming black sludge while sitting in a customer chair with my feet on the small coffee table. I stared without thought or want of thought, leaving my brain floating in a fog. It was a nice change of pace, and I didn't want it to end.

It ended when Billy came through the door wiping grease from his hands and said, "Finally, you're up. Let's go."

Two seconds ticked by before I remembered we had a date with some skinheads. "One more cup of coffee." I said now wanting the fog to lift.

"Take it with us, we don't have a big window here. Right now, Ham is out there with just a couple other guys. He's more likely to talk with us when no one is around." Billy put the rag down then went to the white metal medicine cabinet and opened it up to select a key.

"I can drive." I said pouring more coffee into my mug.

Billy turned, "Nah." he said and plucked a set of keys.

Outside I saw what the key went to. A forest green 1985 CJ -8 Jeep Scrambler sitting on 35-inch mud terrains.

"We can just take my Scout if you wanted to impress them." I said smirking at the diss on the old Jeep.

"You don't want them knowing what you drive. This sweet beast is going to auction end of the week, never to be seen again." Billy said jingling the keys.

It was a thirty-minute drive out to the skinhead fort with plenty of waves and thumbs up from other Jeepers and fans of the old 4x4. The ride was nice and the higher stance than my Scout got me thinking about a spring-over axle lift and stuffing some 35's under the IH.

The asphalt road faded into white packed dirt. Gravel crunched and popped as it was flung from the wide mud terrains. The swapped in 350 ci LT1 motor ran smooth with more power than the future owner of the Scrambler would dare use. Billy was after me to do a LT1 swap in my Scout, but I liked the sound of the original 345 ci motor. It was unique and stood out among all other classic V8's.

We turned off the packed dirt to a slippery-sand road that snaked through young pines aligned in perfect rows. A dozen or so 'Keep Out', 'No Trespassing' and "Shoot on Site' signs greeted us as we neared the compound.

Billy stopped the Jeep at a simple steel pole gate with tracks on either side of people who didn't let the gate deter them. Ahead were a few single wide trailers and an open-faced barn that held a stage. On stage were both the Nazi flag and the Confederate Battle flag. Flanking the flags were banners for beer and motorcycles. In front of the stage white smoke casually lifted from the black charred remains of a fire.

Billy tapped the horn lightly. He looked over at me and said, "Don't let any of the shit they say bother you, got it?"

I nodded. There were times I would get heated when people made Indian jokes at Billy's expense or angry customers brought his race into their complaint of the bill to fix their crappy car. White, Black or whatever, some people just like to go there. Billy just smiled or laughed it off. He said back on the reservation they made plenty of white skin jokes so maybe it was just karma. Karma or not, it pissed me off, but if it wasn't going to get Billy mad, I just stayed quiet.

Two men came out of the trailer to the right of us. Both men were over-weight by eighty-five pounds or more and wore tight fitting t-shirts that thought otherwise. The elder of the two had a square beard and camo ball cap on. The other had a sparse mustache with his hair pulled back tight to his scalp. The bearded man waved us in. Billy shouted the gate was locked.

"Ah hell, just drive around it."

Billy backed us up then we dipped down off the road and around the gate. We stopped thirty yards beyond the gate but not yet to the center of the trailers. Getting out, I looked around at the rows of pines surrounding us. A whirling passed through the needles mimicking the sound of traffic, but we were too far from any road for it to be anything but the wind.

As the two men approach, Billy leaned in towards me and said in a mumble, "There's a dude laying a bead on us ten o'clock. Remember, be cool."

I didn't look immediately, instead looked right to make sure we wouldn't end up in a crossfire. That side was clear. After a few steps I looked left, but didn't see what Billy saw, just empty woods. The two grey pit bulls laying in a shallow sandy impression took more of my attention.

With a few feet between us, I could see the stains on their stretched-out tee shirts. Both wore military boots, and both were sweating.

"Now who you look'in for *a-geen*?" The bearded one said from between his overhanging whiskers.

"Smitty." Billy said and pulled a cigarette from a pack and lit it.

The beard was scratched with fingernails that needed cleaning and then the man said, "Ain't seen him."

Billy dragged the toe of his cowboy boot in the sand. I kept quiet. It would be up to him to handle these two.

"C'mon Ham," Billy said suddenly using words less than I did.

Ham looked at his counterpart. The younger one looked back tipping his hand to the shooter Billy had already spotted.

"Now what's gotch y'all spooked." Billy said with his eyes focused on Ham.

"Shit, ain't nothing scares us." Ham said with lots of wind behind his words as he let out the breath he had held since denying Billy his answer to Smitty's whereabouts. In the years Billy and I worked together as thieves, I had never seen him intimidate anyone for information. It was always a *this for that* and the swap would be made. This time he either didn't have anything these guys wanted or just wasn't in the mood.

"Then why you got a guy in the trees laying a bead on us?" Billy flicked ash from his cigarette in the direction of the sniper. "You're scared shitless about something. Now maybe you better let us in on it or tell that punk ass bitch to start shootin'." Billy's eyes were slits now and his jaw clenched but his teeth still flashed from his lips.

Ham looked down at a .357 revolver inches from his round gut. The hammer was back, and Billy's finger was on the trigger.

"He can't get us both." I said with my hand on the grip of my Glock jutting from my waist.

"Ya'll crazy suma-bitches." Ham said then forced a grin.

I looked over at the young guy and he just stood slack jawed.

"Wave your boy off and get to telling us about Smitty so I can put this gun away. My hand's getting cold." Billy smiled.

Ham put up a meaty hand and waved out to his right. A man in a ghillie suit with leafy branches jammed in the stringy netting stood up and waved back. That threat was over, but I still had the feeling there were people in the trailers that would have no problem shooting us.

"Let's go in that trailer and have a beer." Ham said and started to turn.

"Hold it." Billy said. "Just tell us what you know about Smitty so we can get the hell out of here."

Ham stopped. The young one turned around. Then Ham slowly turned. "You got one hell of a way about you *injun*. You think you can come hoopin' and holleran' into my camp and push us around?"

Billy and I said nothing.

Ham put his hands on his hips, "Well, whattaya got to trade?"

Billy leaned back, stretching his lower back. He took a long drag of his cigarette then said, "Him." He jerked his thumb my way.

Ham laughed then the young one, a little confused, laughed as well. Billy wasn't laughing.

"Tell us what we came all this way for, and you won't have to look over your shoulder or sleep with the lights on." Billy pinched off the smoldering end of his cigarette then flicked the butt away.

Ham's smile faded. Billy was talking me up to a standard I might not reach. These days I was avoiding violence, the thought of it was making me ill. There was little chance I would have to make good on his threat. These rednecks weren't the 'off-grid' anti-government rebels they pretended to be. For one, there was a power pole out at the road delivering electricity and two, I guarantee some of them were cashing social security checks. They probably had a few illegal guns and had a stash of weed, but nothing that would get me to come back here and burn the whole 'camp' down.

A glint of light to my right caught my eye as the door to the trailer opened. Two men stepped down the few wooden steps to the pine needle covered ground. They were medium builds in jeans and flannel shirts. Pinched eyes and slits for mouths, they sized us up. The air instantly filled with an odor I was familiar with; it was the smell of a fight coming. I had a switch I needed to flip then the fight could start.

Ham looked back at more of his boys. When he turned, he held a smile once more, but after his eyes rolled over me, he breathed the same air I was breathing and knew I lived for this, and they might not.

"Alright Billy… Shit." Ham waved off the boys. The two backed up to the sagging wooden porch on the trailer. "Smitty was out here a couple days ago. He seemed, well, jumpy. Kinda outta character for the old guy. Made me nervous. He said he needed to go fishing. So, I let'em on through." Ham said with a shrug.

"Take us there," I said.

Ham wrinkled his forehead thinking it over. We all knew what 'going fishing' meant, just like we knew Ham's pond was nothing more than a gator mud hole.

"What for? Ain't nothing out there to be found."

Billy said, "It wasn't a question, Ham."

Ham shifted his heavy frame then nodded to the hefty man next to him. The man waddled off. He came back riding in a side-by-side. It stopped and we all got on.

Down a sandy road lined with Pines and palmettos we went until eventually we came to the water's edge. Tall grass dipped down to the tea-stained water. A few dead logs lined the shore. In the mud were plenty of smooth valleys about a foot wide made by leathery gators as they slid back into the water.

There was another set of tracks as well, made from an ATV. Same tire tread as the side-by-side but the width was less.

I knelt looking at shoe impressions beside the tracks. The one set appeared to be tennis shoes and lead to the water. Tied to a branch on one of the dead logs was a Jon Boat.

"Okay, let's go." I said and hopped back on the side-by-side. Ham shook his head feeling we wasted his time. Maybe so, but I wanted to see it all for myself. I wanted to see what Smitty saw as he dragged a body down into the water hoping it would give me a clearer picture as to why he had a body to dispose of in the first place.

We disembarked from the side-by-side. Billy nodded to me, and I nodded back. We were done with Ham and neo-naizs for now. We started back for the Jeep when Ham called out.

"Now I, I told you everything. I ain't lying." Ham ran a hand over his beard once more. "Right Russ?" Ham looked over to his partner.

Russ shrugged then mumbled something I couldn't hear but understood to be an agreement.

We waited there in silence. Ham shrugged once more. Billy nodded and I nodded back. Then Ham started to stutter.

"Well, nah, there were sumpt'n else. After Smitty left about two days later we spotted a guy keeping watch on us."

"Damn revenuers." Russ said.

"ATF or FBI you think?" I asked.

Ham nodded he did. "We all lined up along the property line fully loaded and he took off. Ain't been back since."

"Okay, thanks Ham." Billy said.

"Don't know what Smitty is up to, but we ain't want no part of it." Ham turned to his left and cupped a palm alongside his mouth, "We ain't want no part of it!" He shouted into the woods for any Revenuers or government agents to hear.

"Neither do we. That's why we're looking for him," I said. Billy and I both turned to leave.

"Hey, wait up. We ain't got what we wanted." Ham said.

"Sure, you did." Billy said without turning around, "You don't have to look over your shoulder for this guy."

I smiled but they couldn't see it.

Chapter 14

The streets were thinned of cars, commuters had found their destinations as we drove back to town. The only sense of daylight came from a pin hole in heavy dark clouds that let the sun's face show through. Gusts of wind bent the tops of pine trees and flapped against the soft top of the Jeep as we headed back to the shop. Steel grey clouds were heading in from the west.

The thoughts of Smitty dumping a body out at Ham's place didn't make sense. I had never known Smitty to kill anyone. All the mob stories he told of killings and body dumps seemed to be second or third hand. Maybe that was his way of never admitting to it. I did know if we had gone through to the back of Ham's property, we'd be knee high in water covered in lily pads and a dozen or so pairs of eyes telescoping from the black water watching our every move. Gators digest bone.

The two-lane road led us out of the pines and scrub palms into neighborhoods and strip malls. The heavy clouds broke loose, dumping its contents all over the town. Traffic was picking up as we made our way down International Speedway Boulevard. The variety of cars expounded. One that remained the same was a dark sedan behind us.

"Hey, have you been watching our tail?" I said to Billy while looking back through the plastic window of the Jeep soft top that was cascading with water.

Billy leaned his head looking in the side mirror. "I can't see shit out that back window. What's got you spooked?" Billy asked with concern.

My sidemirror didn't show a sedan. I looked out the

back once more and it was too fogged with condensation to see much of anything, just blobs of steel going 45 miles per hour.

"There was a sedan back there, but it's gone now. Maybe it was nothing." I said and turned back in my seat.

"None of Ham's boys own a car." Billy said glancing all around as he drove us on.

"I'm just getting worried about Smitty. He's in over his head. Thanks for taking me out there," I said.

"Didn't mean to put you on the spot like that with the threats and all." Billy said wheeling the Jeep down closer to his shop. The sky remained grey, but the rain was disappearing, turning to a mist.

"It was a good threat. Reminds me I need to hit the gym." What I really wanted was the gym to hit me. I could find pain at Ben's MMA gym.

"I don't know why you like getting sweaty and rolling around on the floor with another dude." Billy flicked out his cigarette and rolled the window up.

I let my answer go as we pulled into the shop. Standing under the small awning at the office door was a suit I had seen yesterday morning.

I climbed out of the Jeep.

"Agent Alvarez," I said. Billy sized him up and down. He nodded to the agent but said nothing. With his back turned to Alvarez he shot me a look with his eyes bouncing quickly before walking off.

"I've been trying to get a hold of you Roger." Alvarez flashed that toothy smile.

"It's loud in the Jeep."

Billy moved on to unlock the office door and went in. I stayed out front with Alvarez.

"Delgado's dead. Throat slashed." Alvarez said.

"Not surprised.

"Want to track down any other contacts you might have? Maybe that Danzig knows something."

"Not today, I got stuff to do." I walked past him for the office door.

"Oh, and an FBI investigation isn't important enough for you?" Alvarez's smile faded into a sneer. He put his hands on his hips pulling open his sport coat exposing the badge and Sig Sauer on his hip.

"Like you said, an FBI investigation. Not mine."

"That's right, Roger Grimes PI, just sits in his car and watches while seven people are murdered and all he does is poke his head in. And doesn't even stick around to talk to police." Alvarez crossed his arms.

I took a long stride and stabbed my right palm out over his crossed arms, pinning them to his chest as I backed him into the closed bay door. It rattled in a wave action as he fell against it. He tried to lower his arms, but I caught them and held him against the wall.

"You think you know better? You think you'd have done better? You think you could have done better!" I shouted hot breath inches from his face.

His eyes narrowed into slits of fire then simmered to the soft amber they were. His body relaxed then his arms dropped out of my grasp, and he stood up straight.

"Cut the shit Roger. You know more than you let on. The FDLE might be fooled but not me." Alvarez said. He shifted into a lean, as if he were going to take a step. His body didn't move, but I wanted him to. It would be easier if he lunged or took a swing, anything but instead attacked me with his eyes, studying that knot I synched tight around my neck that night two years ago. Clues like bubbles rose to the surface to give truth to what I had sunk in a swamp of my own creating. All it would take was one curious investigator like Special Agent Alvarez to take a dive and find me there at the bottom of the swamp.

"You're covering for him." Alvarez said.

A trickle of sweat ran down my back and collected in my waistband. A tingle in my chest caught words in my throat.

"Your friend Erich Schmidt" Alvarez said with pompous conviction.

My brow crinkled as an easy chuckle broke my throat open. I turned around. "Who?"

He took a step towards me, "Come on now Roger. I know you're not really looking for Muncy or stolen guns. I mean if they turn up great, you're a hero. That's not what you're after."

I stood with my eyes fixed on the FBI Agent. His smile faded, covering up his white teeth.

"You really don't know, Erich Schmidt, alias Smith alias Smitty." He shook his head, "Because we have photos going back at least three years of you two," he pointed to the shop door, "And Billy Hroseblood too."

I let a little chuckle out of my mouth. Alvarez's face reddened as he ground his teeth. I hadn't heard that name in so long I questioned if I had *ever* heard it. The old man was always just Smitty.

"I can't help you," I said.

"Grimes, c'mon, let's go find Muncy together. If we find Smitty, we can hear his side of things. Maybe he's not in this that deep." Alvarez flashed his white teeth and nodded like we were going for a beer after a long day at the office.

I stood there for what felt like a long time, too long of time. Alvarez's head tilted as he studied my face, reading me like a billboard sign in the distance. And it told him I never met Erich Schmidt.

"Let me dig up some other suspects we can track down before they're dead too," I said.

"Good, that'll be *real* good." Alvarez started to walk off. I was still standing there.

"Can you recommend a good place to get lunch?" He said turning back.

"Um, Gina's on Ridgewood Avenue." I said without putting too much thought in it.

"Oh, I thought you might recommend something downtown, a place I can get a pint."

There was enough sense left in my head to not recommend Cooper's, but I knew he was already on his way there. Special Agent Alvarez was doing his homework. The place I stopped in to ask questions and answer them was now a place for someone to be asking about me.

I left him standing there and went into the shop.

Chapter 15

Billy stood behind his sales counter with his hands on his hips. He had put on an ash grey sweatshirt and tucked his braid into the back, meaning he was ready to start wrenching.

"What'd the Fed want?"

"Someone named Erich Schmidt." I went to the coffee maker. The pot was cool, and the coffee nearly gone. I poured the remnants into the water reservoir and filled the pot from the shop sink just on the other side of the office door. When I came back in Billy was leaning back in his chair, feet up and braid out.

"You really didn't know?" Billy said in a low tone.

I switched on the coffee and turned to lean against the counter.

"I don't know. Either I didn't know or didn't remember. Alvarez just filled me in," I said. Now that Alvarez was gone, I let my nerves unwind. My hands began to tingle. My stomach twitched as I began to feel like I was at sea as my head filled with questions that were pushed out by memories. Fuzzy memories, images, conversations. Had any of it been real?

"I'm sure you knew." Billy said trying to assure me I wasn't losing my mind. "Them early days we kept everything a secret. Hell, you didn't know where I lived that first year."

"Same." I said nodding with a smile.

Billy smiled wider, "I knew. I followed you that first night we boosted that Caddy."

That awkward chuckle crept out again as I shook my

head. When it faded, I said, "The fed knows something about all three of us, more than he should."

"Like what?"

"The usual, *known associates*."

Billy scoffed. I kept quiet. Alvarez and the FBI kept a file on me, Billy and Smitty. We all had local police files on us. I was locked up in county jail for nine months, long enough to convince me to go straight. Smitty was no foreigner to the criminal justice system. He did time in a federal pen because he wouldn't snitch on the mob. He did his time and walked out more criminal than when he went in. We had heat on us before. An unmarked car down the street from my apartment or out front of Billy's house. The van that showed up whenever the three of us got together. It became old hat, routine and sort of fun. Then it all got old, and the cops got bored. Now this FBI file. How long have they been watching? And how close? And our files were gone. Maybe looking into the into the criminal world for the culprits was looking in the wrong direction.

Sanford's White Knight had been busy the last couple years. Everything wrong or bad or dishonest I had ever done came screaming back into my mind. A sharp pain pierced through my brain as it tried to manage the overload of images, screams and smells of violence. I took a seat and stared at the worn linoleum beneath my feet waiting on it to dissipate.

"Hey brother," Billy said getting me to lift my head. "I've got a few places I can check out; places you don't know about. Maybe Smitty will turn up and we can take care of all this shit."

I nodded but hadn't shaken the weight from my shoulders. I needed to take a step back, distance myself from the whole thing, the poolhall killings, those that followed and Smitty in the mix of it. Now every suspect I sent Newstroms way was turning up dead. I needed to find something I could do to help, something that would help silence my mind, something that would occupy my hands.

There was something therapeutic about going to an MMA gym. Some days it was about honing my skills, the timing, speed needed to take down an opponent. Others it seemed that timing was gone, a block too slow, a hold too loose then reversed on me. A tap out. Days like that I think I just went there to hurt myself.

Upstairs, I changed into basketball shorts, sweatshirt and grabbed a pair of softly worn Asics wrestling shoes. I left Billy's shop in the Camaro and headed to Ben Saadon's MMA gym. In a strip mall off Nova Road held a BBQ place, a generic dollar store and a small bar that advertised pool tables and darts. It was the kind of place that if you blinked, you'd miss it. And if you missed it there would be another strip mall just like it 30 seconds down the road. Tucked back at the end of the strip were a series of black tinted windows that ended in an unmarked door. I opened the door and was hit with a gust of stale air made heavy with old sweat and dried blood. It was a return to the beginning, to the start of all of it. A place where primordial ooze struggles to take shape into a more advanced lifeform. This is where I learned to fight, and I've done it so well ever since.

I caught a few sideways looks from guys already covered in sweat and someone else's blood. I had lost *regular* status here. The older members still offered a nod or a wave. The Nubes laid eyes on me, sizing me and smelling out a challenge. I found a familiar smile to greet me. It was placed in the center of a round face that was getting thinner by the week. He was large with fresh muscle pushing away the fat.

"Yo, Grimes." Terry nodded as he paused hitting the heavy bag. I was glad to see he was making this a regular place. After a hard break-up with a street gang, Terry needed a new family.

"How are things, Terry?"

"Good, man." Terry shook his head as sweat cascaded to the floor. "I'm getting fit and aint nobody bother me no more."

I nodded then moved on to the back of the gym. I knocked on a blue steel door marked private.

The electronic lock buzzed, and I pushed my way in.

"Grimes," said Ben with an Israeli accent. He turned around in his chair then stood. His black hair was growing more silver every day. It meant nothing with regards to his strength as we shook hands. His medium height with a solid frame was dressed in the usual black tee shirt and black sweatpants with a white drawstring hanging down. On the left thigh was the Haganah, the Israeli Defense Force emblem. He had been a member of the Mossad. For how long or what he did, no one knew.

We sat. The office was lit by an array of monitors displaying fighters training in the gym. The rest of the office consisted of an L shaped desk, two chairs, a locked metal cabinet and a mini fridge filled with energy drinks.

"Come to work out?" Ben said returning to his chair. He began looking over the fighters on the screens. He was a master of surveillance and that worked in every fighter's favor. Video of fights was watched over and over again. Every grab, strike and takedown were analyzed. You can learn a lot watching your own mistakes.

"Yeah," I said.

Ben turned slowly from the monitors to look me over. His deep brown eyes rolled over me from my feet to the top of my shaved head. He crossed his chest then planted his other arm on top so that his fingers were pressed against his lips restraining his own voice.

He said, "You cut your hair. That is good, but you did

not shave your face." He tapped a finger against his lips.

I shrugged like I didn't know or care about the point he was making, but I knew what he was getting at. Though I had not consciously recognized it, I was not completely ready to take on whatever tidal wave was forming ahead of me.

"Maybe after I work out, I'll get a shave." I said and turned for the door.

"Perhaps." Ben said and went back to watching the monitors.

Back in the gym, I found an empty corner. The grunts accompanied meaty slaps of flesh as warriors collided with one another filled my ears. My mind was ready to start a warm-up, but my body was too cold to move. Stiffness in my joints couldn't find the muscle to push through some basic exercises. My left shoulder carried a dull ache and was difficult to get over my head. With muscles that refused to work my mind wandered and I felt like giving up.

"Hey, Grimes." An unwanted voice cracked across the gym.

I got up off the mat and stood facing Enrico Salazar. He was tattooed up both arms and his neck and chest were covered too. His twenty-two-year-old dark brown eyes had seen a lot, aging him so he looked over thirty. He wore his black hair shaved around the sides and brushed back on top. At five-nine he tilted his head back to look at me. His gold tooth gleamed as he opened his mouth again.

"What up homie?" He said and put out his hand.

We slapped hands and I said, "Just trying to get a workout in. What's up with you Ricky?"

"Haven't seen you around."

"Keeping different hours," I said.

"I brought in a new fighter. My boy Drex." He said and

nodded to a gaunt pasty white guy with a shaved head, no shirt and no tattoos that I could see. His mouthpiece was in giving his mouth an exaggerated pushed out chimp look, a fellow knuckle dragger. I guess we are all part ape in here and everyone wants to be king of the jungle.

"Ben likes him?" I asked.

"He sees the potential." Ricky said nodding his head to the thin agreement he and Ben were in over Drex. Ricky worked at the gym, mostly cleaning up, a kind of cabin boy to the rest of us. It was the only job he could get after getting out of juvenile detention. I knew his father, Enrico senior. We pulled a few jobs together nearly ten years ago and I remember Ricky back then. A kid eager to start a life of crime and be like his old man. Senior never dissuaded his son and so after a bunch of petty larcenies, young Ricky finally got popped for robbery and assault. At eighteen he got out and hung on to the swinging door of the criminal justice system until two years ago when he put me down as a reference. Ben asked about Ricky and I shrugged, the kid lost his dad while he was locked up and was aimless. Ben took on the challenge to set Ricky straight. Never mind the sob story, I didn't really like Ricky. Senior was a professional, his kid never had the mentality.

"That's good." I said hoping the kid would leave me alone so I could get back to hating myself. Instead, he went on to tell me all the technical details of Drex's fighting abilities. Ricky, himself, wasn't much of a fighter, but he had a good eye for style. For all his talking, he'd make a great announcer and perhaps one day a coach.

After what felt like ten minutes Ricky suggested, if I was ready, I should spar with Drex. I came here to hurt myself not anyone else. I declined.

"Yeah, well," Ricky said backing up, "You got your rep around here you wouldn't want to lose. I get that." Then he smirked and the glint of the gold tooth took me back to the poolhall that night two years ago. Standing there facing several of the Third Street Gang and a few Russians wanting revenge for me killing their comrades. A fire started in my chest, and I could no longer feel my arms like I had been tied up and they went numb from the ropes. It wasn't fear or PTSD, it was judgment raining down, holding me in place and I needed to hear the verdict.

Guilty.

"Yeah, let's do a round and see what happens." The words came out of my mouth on their own.

Ricky pumped his fist and jogged back to Drex. He was rambling on and on feeding his fighter with every bit of information he knew about me, and Ricky had studied me a lot. Things had changed in the last year. My fights were with untrained half scared, half-crazy criminals who knew I'd kill them if they lost.

If anything, Ricky said was true, then Drex would be an altogether different animal. An animal worth challenging, worth losing to.

We stood on the mat in the middle of the room. Both of us shaking out any nerves and making sure the blood was flowing. Walking in here today, I hadn't liked all the gym rats stopping to smile and nod. All the newbies pointing and waving hoping I'd wave back. Had I become some sort of mythic fighter? My fists on a medallion, the saint of fighters? I didn't like it and I didn't want it. Drex can be that guy, he can get the waves and stares next time. It would be his in three minutes.

With mouthguards in we touched gloves in the middle of the crowd that had formed around us. The music was off, and no one talked except Ricky who shouted tips to Drex in a high whisper. My chin was tucked, as we circled each other. The first move was his.

Muscle memory has saved my life every time I nearly

lost it. So, when he threw a quick jab, I leaned back. He never touched me. This went on for nearly a minute. A few jabs, a kick. There was little contact coming from Drex. I had to get my mind out of my body. So, I went back to that poolhall, filling my nose with the smell of warm blood, my eyes fogged by gunpowder. Now I could my body was coming alive.

His 1-3 combination backed me up. Then he shot in, and I got a taste of his ground game. He was fast and stronger than his lanky body looked. He was a young fighter with a dream like everyone else that had come to the gym, like I had when I first started training with Ben. Sweat bubbled from every pore as I tried to grab hold of his arms and block is incoming knees. Each blow radiated pain. Flashes of a blood splattered checkered floor followed each blow. His hammer punch came in, but I did little to stop it. A pop sounded in my skull like the pop of a gun I used to kill a woman so someone else didn't have to. I killed them all so no one else would get hurt. I took the pain they gave and bury it deep. Drex threw more and more. Each punch drove their pain deeper. There had been so many since I took on the mantle of vigilante. Killing the worst offenders in our city, the ones the law could not touch or were not concerned with.

I tried to crawl out from under Drex, but he had me straddled. My forearms covered my face to stop the blows. Teeth gnashing grunts followed each throw of his fist. With pinched tight eyes I saw the bloody faces of the dead. Each face lessened the pain from the blows. I could take it; I could be sustained.

My hips bucked and the hold his legs had around me loosened. A second buck and he lost his hold. He turned as we both scrambled to our feet.

He came at me again, hands up ready to box. Success found him the first time. Now that I knew my place in all of this, he wouldn't get a second chance. His fists missed every time. Back to the ground game, he shot in. His strength got me down but as I found my reserves, getting out of every hold he tried. I became a fortune teller, foreseeing his every move before he made it. I was ready and easily escaped blows and holds.

The bell rang and Ricky shouted. Drex, growing frustrated, was slow to let go.

We got up and slapped hands.

"One more." He said as more of a command than a question.

I nodded. I wasn't done either, just getting warmed up. I was beginning to remember, to remember why I took on Sanford's call for justice. Those faces, each one bloodied and gripped by death meant that I helped someone escape, someone got to live because they died. I took the blow so they wouldn't have to. There were plenty more out there needing me to set them free from others sin. The white knight was not done.

Ben was now in the small crowd, no longer in his eagle eye control room. This was real, not just on some monitor. He crossed his hairy arms over his black shirt, but gave no nod, or attempt to communicate. It was a shame he never played poker because with that face he could bluff every time.

As the round started, I watched Drex dance around, arms held tighter in and feet stepping shorter. His confidence was lower, choosing caution over aggression.

We locked up like bulls. His left hand around the back of my neck and mine around the back of his. Each of us tugging quick snaps to get the other off balance. My right hand was on his elbow. I let go, rolled my right shoulder as my right forearm broke his grip. Quickly I was behind and to his side holding him around the waist. Then jerking my hips up, I lifted him off his feet and slammed him to the mat.

The *splat* silenced the crowd. Drex went limp for a

second. My mind knew to stop but my arm was already swinging down. Ben yelled. His words unrecognizable. Only the tone commanding stopped me cold. Breathing heavy I sat back as Drex rolled to his side then pushed himself up to his knees. He was on all fours when I stood and gave him my hand. He got to his feet, and we bumped fists. The fight was over.

Ricky ran up slapping Drex on the back and rubbing his shoulders while giving him encouraging words.

"You're good, Drex." I said nodding.

"Not as good as you." He nodded back with a half-smile.

"Just not today." I said and extended my fist out for one more bump.

Excitement dispersed with the crowd leaving Ben and I standing alone. My gloves came off and I grabbed a jump rope. The rope tapped on the mat as I bounced. Slow at first, timing my lift with the rope passing under.

"A positive attitude like that will keep Drex a good fighter. He didn't lose his head and he didn't push himself to the limit because he knew this fight wasn't worth it." I said as I found my rhythm with the rope.

Ben nodded, "That's why I stopped you."

"I would have stopped." I said breathing faster with the increasing speed of the rope. For the last two years all of my fights had been to live or die. It was a mentality I thought I could turn off, walk away from, but today proved otherwise. In here fighting is a sport, in the natural world it's life or death. So far, I was still alive.

"Drex will be a good fighter, but why did you let him beat you in the first round?" Ben said as he began circling me, watching my rhythm jumping over the rope each time.

The rope turned faster. Each tap of the mat grew closer and closer. Breathing more and more. My heart thumped.

Images of Drex laying his hands on me blurred into clearer scenes of my own hands choking a pedophile, purple faced with bulging eyes. The rope turned faster.

"I have seen the rope-a-dope, I have seen fighters taking a beating, waiting for their opportunity. I have never seen a man take a beating just to taste his own blood." Ben circled all the way around.

My eyes were on the mat as the rope tapped faster and faster. He moved closer until the wind of the whirling jump rope rustled the thick black and silver hair on his head.

"Except." Ben snatched the blurry rope like a fly in the air. "Except guilty men." Ben searched my eyes.

I looked back at him holding my own poker face. Keeping a wall of bodies stacked like a dam holding every wrong decision back. The terror I inflicted on the criminals in this town had ended. The objectives had shifted to helping people solve their problems instead of avenging the wrong perpetrated on them. I could walk away knowing there were less dirtbags and dead beats leaching on society, but I could not get them off my back. The weight had given me a stoop in my posture and put my mind in a crawl. Forward progress seemed impossible for me as all I ever did was look back at their dying faces covered in their own filth.

"I am guilty," I said. I let go of the rope and dropped to do push-ups.

"What did you come here for, today?" Ben said clasping his hands behind him.

"I needed a workout."

Ben's foot pressed down on my back. My arms couldn't hold up against the weight and my chest smashed against the mat.

"That is *why* you came here. What do you need Grimes?"

"I don't know." The words wheezed from my chest as the pressure grew more intense.

"Yes, I think you do."

"To find Smitty."

"No, that is what he needs. What do you need?"

I pushed as hard as I could but wasn't strong enough. He pushed down with more force.

"To clear my head."

"Of what?"

"Stuff." Each breath was harder to take in as less was coming out.

His foot came off and air sucked deep into my lungs.

"Get up." Ben said extending his hand. I grabbed it and together I stood. I felt every eye in the gym on me, but no one dare look.

"Now, are you ready to tell me what you came for."

I nodded and we went back to his office.

Ben sat in his desk chair. To his right on the floor was a mini fridge. He opened it and grabbed two energy drinks. They were the expensive kind in colorful cans, packed full of vitamins you mostly piss away in the first five minutes. The guy lived on them. His kidneys must be limestone.

"Start with the details you want me to know." Ben said staring at me with deep set black eyes. The man didn't want the novel, just the foot notes.

"Smitty is involved in gun running and it's tied up in that first bloody case I had."

His lower lip curled giving him a bulldog face. He began tapping on a laptop, navigating into a thread on some dark web site. Once I took a job through the site. I preferred the old ways, knowing a guy who knows a guy. Anyone could be sitting on the other end of that keyboard.

"There's chatter." Ben said as he turned the screen towards me. I skimmed the thread but there were to many acronyms and other initialed words to put it together without starting from the top.

"So, what is it?"

"There is a gun deal about to go down."

"Any of that chatter say where Smitty is?"

Ben shook his head, "No, there's more. Someone in town has hired a professional killer. The kill is here, in the Daytona Beach area."

"That explains a couple of recent murders. Am I supposed to find him or something?"

"No, I believe he's supposed to find you."

My temples imploded as a new headache came on. The pile of sand I had been scrambling up just got bigger.

"How do you know I'm the target?"

Ben exhaled heavily through his nose, "This town isn't that big."

"I can't deal with this right now. I've got to find my friend Smitty. He's in trouble and I want to help him." I sipped the drink, berry flavor and heavily carbonated.

"Yes." He frowned, "And his troubles cause you to take a beating?"

"No. I'm frustrated. I had an old case rear its head. It was an ugly case. I saw things I can't unsee, that kind of stuff. I want it to go away."

Ben nodded. He knew what I was going through. He had done things while in the Israeli Defenses that I will, nor anyone else, ever know about. The difference between us was that he did it for his country. I went out there because, as

Sanford put it, I was *picked to do it*. His *White Knight*, as if there would be sagas told about me long after I died. The truth is when I die, there will be no folded flag for loved ones or gun salutes. Just the trail of dead I left behind and they will be waiting to welcome me to hell.

"Accept what has happened and stop living there. Then go on living Grimes." Ben leaned forward as he spoke. "Don't let your guilt stop you from what you still need to do, or the things you have done and witnessed will be for nothing. Find your meaning, accept your place in it all and keep moving."

We sat silently. Fighters moved on the monitors with no sound. Slowly Ben turned and clicked around on the computer.

"I'll tell you more on the hitman as it unravels."

"Thank you. What about the FBI? What do they have on me?"

"I'll look into that as well."

We sipped our energy drinks. I got the work out I came for.

Chapter 16

The sky had completely broken open as I walked to my car. Each drop felt like ice on my skin as it collected and ran down my back. I sat in the Camaro without starting it. My life since the poolhall case had been either coasting on autopilot with orders from Sanford or failing when I tried to strike out on my own. There was no way out. As I passed judgement on the guilty, I waited for someone to pass it on me.

There was a text from Alysa that she was working at Coopers tonight. I stared at it, choosing not to respond. I still had the drug dealers at Coopers to deal with.

Ben was right, moving forward, inch by bloody inch, was all I could do now. Living in the present meant keeping my friends. Billy had gone out of his way giving me a place to live, helping me on cases and lending me cars whenever I needed one. I couldn't have done half the work on the Scout without him.

It was still early for dinner but after the workout I was hunger. I swung into a fast-food joint and called Billy to see if he wanted anything to eat. There's nothing better than food to share with a friend to smooth things over. He didn't answer. I waited but hunger got the better of me and I got into the drive thru.

As I drove off with my sack of Krystals, Sanford called.

"Any news on Smitty?" Sanford fired off in his usual speedy cadence.

"No." I said steering into the parking lot of a closed

cellphone business. I wanted to eat and my Chiks were getting cold. I picked one out and took a bite.

"Are you eating?"

"Hhmm, Krystal Chiks."

"Grab me a two piece from that chicken place on the corner and come on up." Sanford clicked off, not giving me a chance to say no.

"Damn it." I said to myself and my Chiks.

Thirty minutes later I was on the seventh floor of the CBR building holding two grease-stained bags of fast food. The line at the chicken place was into the street blocking traffic along Ridgewood Avenue.

Monique was at her desk, clicking away with the mouse then typing then clicking. She looked up when I came in.

"That kinda food will kill you, Grimes."

"So, all the criminals in this town need to do is come after me with fried chicken." I laughed.

She raised an eyebrow but refused to indulge in the joke. So, it goes with Monique. The ever stoic one in the office.

"Find anything on that name I gave you?" I didn't get an answer as Sanford came out sniffing like a bloodhound on the trail of escaped convicts.

"Is that for you Willis?" Monique shot Sanford an evil eye.

"Just what the doctor ordered." He said taking the bag.

"The coroner you mean." She replied then shook her head disapproving of our dinner choices.

Sanford shrugged then said to me, "C'mon in Grimes my chicken is getting cold."

Inside Sanford's office, I had my last Chik in the microwave. As it counted down Sanford sat at his desk, white napkin tucked in his collar chowing down on fried chicken.

"What's this *sort of* news?" Sanford asked.

"Nothing much, I found out, his name is Erich Schmidt." I touched my Chik and it bit me with heat. I'd have to wait some more for it to cool.

Sanford nodded; it wasn't the kind of news he was hoping for. I told him I had nothing, that I had asked everyone I know that knows Smitty and they all came back with nothing except Kurt. Kurt knew something, but I would never get it out of him.

"And who is this Kurt?" Sanford asked.

"Just another old timer." I said, not wanting to get into how I know Kurt or use his services.

"I've been doing some digging of my own. This Muncy character is a pretty bad dude. He was sentenced five years at Hardee State Prison. I know a prosecutor in Hardee County, made a call. Guy did eighteen months. Supposedly the easiest months anyone ever saw." Sanford said then sat back in his chair sucking sweet tea through a straw.

"Guardian angel?"

"State house rep kinda guardian."

"Shit. Who?"

"Trevor Brooks. A couple years ago he ran for governor, failed, then got busted texting with cops posing as kids."

"Fits nicely. Where is he now?"

"Starting an exploratory campaign. Rumor is he plans to run for Senator."

"He loses a bid for governor and now he's running for senator. Can't these people take a hint?"

Sanford laughed with a mouth full of chicken. After he swallowed half he said, "Brooks is a puppet for the power elite. Muncy was used for opposition research. Hired by Brooks' backers anyway. One of these political packs. Muncy's job was to steal dirt on opponents, allegedly."

"Wish I had a gig like that back when I was a thief."

"I'd hope you wouldn't have the stomach for it." Sanford laughed. I smiled too.

"With our files stolen, Monique had to go back over what little we had on associates of Hines. Monique is doing a quick check on them, see where they are now."

"She can scratch two."

"Delgado and Lumino."

I nodded as I finished my last Chik.

"Do you think Muncy crossed over from being a thief to a killer?" Sanford said. His eyes darted from mine searching for a place on the desk. *Killer*. The word sent a chill up my spin. Thief to a killer. It was like reading my own tombstone.

"It's possible. A very reliable source told me there's a hitman here in our sleepy little beach community. Luminos and Delgado were on his list and so am I."

Sanford dropped his chicken leg. His fingers crumpled a napkin. For the first time ever, I saw his mouth open but he wasn't speaking.

After a needed breath he said, "Grimes, I'm truly worried. Maybe we all need to get out town for a while, long while. We can –"

"No. I can get you and Monique somewhere safe, somewhere I wont even know about, but I'm staying."

Before Sanford could argue, Billy called me back.

"Where you at?" was all Billy said.

"The office. You want me to pick you up some food?" I said hoping to make good on my idea food would help smooth things over.

"Nah man get over here when you're done." Billy hung up.

His tone was soft like he was tired. It was only five o'clock. He usually worked until eight most days. Though he didn't sound urgent, simply asking me to get there was putting pressure on me to get moving.

Sanford didn't ask questions, just said okay as I walked out the door. Monique was typing away and said nothing to me as I hurried out. I doubt she even lifted her head from the screen.

I made it to the shop in eight minutes. The bays and the office door were closed. I parked the car close to the office door and went in.

Billy was in his desk chair with a shop rag full of ice pressed against the back of his head. His braid was out, leaving his black hair to spread out like crow's wings over his shoulders.

"What the hell happened?" I said with ease thinking he just bumped his head on the car lift or dropped a wrench on it. It happens.

"Fucking got jumped."

"Who?"

"Dunno. One guy, maybe five, I was hit from behind. I saw stars and woke up on the garage floor after they left."

"What'd they take?" My thoughts went directly to the pistol I left on the nightstand.

"Nothing that I know of." He swiveled in the chair and winced as he turned. "When I came to, I looked around and it seems they were interested only in your apartment. I went up there but, shit, I don't know what you have or don't have." He cracked a faint smile that quickly faded.

"Let me take you to the hospital, get checked out." I said waving him up.

"Nah," He said waving me off. "I'm fine. Go check your stuff."

I leaned on the counter to insist but stopped when I saw the .357 on his lap.

"They won't catch me a second time." Billy smiled.

I took each wooden stair with the expectation of someone waiting there to shoot me with my own pistol. With a flat palm, I pushed against the door. The room was empty of people. Everything was turned inside out, like all my furniture decided to throw up on itself. My favorite old velvet couch was cut to shreds, mattress too. The nightstand drawer was on the floor. Even my toothpaste tube was squeezed out. Someone did a thorough job searching the place. Sifting through the ruble, the only thing missing was the pistol I left on the nightstand.

Downstairs, Billy had his head tilted back and his eyes closed. I sat in the metal framed chair.

"What'd they take?" Billy grumbled with eyes closed.

"My gun."

"Only one?"

"The only one I had left."

"Shit. Sorry brother."

"It's not your fault." I said taking a seat.

"No shit." He said back. Maybe it was the bump on his head or the deadline to get that Mach 1 out in time that he was suddenly in a bad mood. Either way, the air became heavy, and the fluorescent light brightened making my seat all the more uncomfortable. This wasn't how I thought things would go. A sack of Krystals and some beers were supposed to get us a good time.

"It's not tracible." I said for comfort.

"Listen brother, this just isn't working out." Billy took the ice from his head and set it on the counter as he sat up in the desk chair.

Apologies didn't mean anything, so I kept quiet. He had something to say, and it was best to let him have his words.

"I've made a change; I've stopped being a thief. I've helped you out on cases, but tonight, here in the shop, nearly getting beat to death, and the shop getting torn apart, I just can't keep doing it and run a car restoration business. You paid me the rent you owed, now I think it's time you find a place to do your business that isn't directly connected to mine." Billy reached out and opened the shop rag that held the ice. He mixed them around then wrapped up the rag and put it back on his head.

My knee bounced. He was right, I was leaching off his friendship long enough. Maybe he saw me as he saw Smitty, just a business associate. I didn't see him that way, but I hadn't treated him any different. He had my back so many times and now where was I when he needed me?

I stood up, "No worries. It's time I got my own place." I pulled the keys from my pocket, both the Camaro and the office keys. "Maybe I can finally get a dog." I smiled.

Billy nodded.

I went upstairs, took a shower, and dressed in jeans and a fresh t-shirt. I put on my jacket and stuffed all my clothes into an old olive-green seabag. Since what little furniture I had was carved up, I'd be traveling light.

Billy was sitting at the desk. A bottle of Scotch and a cup with ice were out, just the one.

"I'll be back tomorrow to take care of that mess up there." I said standing at the counter knowing I should go but waiting to patch things up, even a little.

"There's no rush man." Billy said pouring three fingers worth of the Scotch. He sipped and grinned a little.

"I haven't seen you drink Scotch since the old days, the bank job days." I said with a grin of my own. Usually, we celebrated with Miller High Life, but on occasion, if the score warranted it, Billy would bust out some Johny Walker or Glen something and sip it slow all night. I never cared for it.

"I bought it when I got the lease to this shop." He raised a glass to toast the whole place then sipped. When he was done, he continued, "The place was a mess, and I went to work so fast I never got to celebrate. I figured I better do it now."

Salt in my wound. I remembered that day. I was sleeping off a night of violence and booze, while he was moving in tool chests and tire machines. By the time I came to, he had it all done. He hadn't even called me to ask for help.

"Congrats man." I smiled and nodded. He sipped some more. "When this shit with Smitty is all over, what do you think about me coming to work for you?"

"As a tech?" If Billy had ears that moved, they'd have perked.

"Yeah, I mean, I'm not as good as Jose, never will be, but what if we start flipping cars like we always talked about. You know I'm good at finding deals."

Billy smiled and slapped the counter. His hand went out and we shook.

"I didn't mean to snap at you earlier."

"You're right to," I said. It was his apartment, his dream to live there and I was stopping it all up. Several months back I had a mysterious tale. When I closed the case on the bent cop acting as the vigilante the tale went away and so did my paranoia. Lieutenant Gibson had warned me about it but if it wasn't in my face, my line of sight, I buried it in the sand, hoping it would go away. Ben's words returned and I was living in the now, keeping my only family safe was priority one.

"I was pissed because someone got me good when I wasn't looking, wasn't ready." Billy's voice trailed off. He stood up and leaned over the desk with his arms outstretched to the higher counter above. The Scotch working its way through his veins, he was feeling loose, letting emotions rise, trying not to log jam them.

"Somewhere along the way, I lost control of my life. I'm getting it back and just have this last thing to finish. After that, we start flipping cars, just like we've always wanted," I said.

I left Billy's shop in my Scout. Recognizable or not, it was who I was and if anyone wanted to find me, they could. I drove to see Kurt because I was not going to be left without a pistol. On the way I called Sanford and filled him in on the burglary. All he could come up with was what I had already been thinking. Someone out there wants to silence us and destroy any evidence we may still have on the human trafficking.

I had to force my mind to cycle back through the events of that night two years ago, through the faces and the blood that covered them. Several minor players came and went. Low level drug dealers like T-Bag trying to make a name for himself. The three Russians I left to burn in their house of torture were investigated. Later we found out all of them were illegal immigrants with fake ID's and things went cold. Lastly Chloe and her father. Gregg Hines's connections were broad. He was a failed politician turned lobbyist with contacts in all sorts of government contracting as well as big pharma. The list of people whose lives were threatened by what I exposed that night was endless. Any number of high-powered political elites could be putting a bullseye on my back. The hardest of all to fight would be if the FBI, itself, had broken into Sanford's office and made off with our list. Gregg Hines's reach was endless.

Chapter 17

Duke was standing out front of his shop talking with a customer when I pulled in. His smile faded as he watched me park.

"I need to see your dad again." I said interrupting the conversation he was having with the customer.

Duke nodded. The customer left.

"Grimes, we're closing up. Come back tomorrow." Duke said not moving from his spot.

He was a large man with strong hands, and I did not want to have to go through him.

"I'm in some trouble and I know he can help." I said hoping our history would turn something loose in Duke and he'd let me pass.

"Lem'me go see." Duke said slowly then took his time walking off to find his pop. As he got into the bay he looked back, "Now don't you go nowhere."

I nodded.

A few minutes later Kurt came out. His gate was stiff as if walking on stilts and with the sheer size of the man he might have been.

"What is it you want?" Kurt said with no pleasantries of a friend.

"Maybe we can go talk in your shop."

"Not a chance in hell, if you's in trouble I just assume keep it off my doorstep." Kurt shoved his hands into his overall pocket.

Out of habit I looked around at nothing really, just buying time to choose my words.

"I need tools."

"Uh-hu." Kurt muttered without moving.

"I need one right away." I said and pulled a top of the cash roll from my pocket.

Kurt grumbled then waved me back.

Once inside Kurt's gunsmith shop, he leaned on a stool. I stood without saying anything while the old gunsmith looked me over through thick eyeglasses and silvery smoke coming from his nose. I didn't have to tell Kurt what happened to the last pistol I bought from him. If I was here needing a new one, then it was gone. He shook his head then got off the stool. A wash of failure came over me like a child handing over a poor report card.

From a box he grabbed a pair of blue latex gloves and slipped them on, snapping them like a surgeon on TV. Stacked on the large work bench were rectangular metal drawers. Kurt pulled open a drawer, removed a slide and laid it on a pad on the table. After he went through four drawers, I saw a spring, barrel, and polymer grip to a Glock. I didn't know the model or caliber yet.

"I know your preference for a Glock in forty-five caliber, but all I got at the moment is this nine mil. Unless you want a Smith." Kurt said as he switched out his glasses for some bifocals. The cigarette, now half gone, burned as he worked.

"The Glock will be fine."

"I ain't doing this for you, it's for Smitty." He said. Then with a click the Glock was assembled.

I held the Glock 43 in my hand. A single stack 9mm. It felt light and small in my hand compared to the .45 caliber I normally carried. Kurt handed me the empty magazine. He nodded to a shelf stacked with varying caliber bullets. I plucked a box of 9mm, putting it in my jacket pocket. I fit the

9 in my back pocket.

"You talked to Smitty?"

Kurt nodded he had. "You mean a lot to him. He just wants to keep you safe." Kurt took the last drag from his cigarette then smashed it out on the blackened corner of the work bench.

"I'm trying to do the same for him. He's mixed up in gun sales to skin heads and 3rd street."

Kurt chuckled, "I didn't see it before, but I see it now. Both of y'all running around Daytona doing this and that, trying to just get out of it all."

"What did he say? Where is he?" I asked not knowing or caring whatever it was Kurt was getting at. I needed answers not a folksy recap of the last few days.

"He told me not to tell ya, but I think he's just being stubborn." The smile faded as he lit another cigarette. "I've seen stubborn, I've lost friends to it. Ain't got many left."

We stood in silence as he puffed on the cigarette. His words sunk in as the smoke glazed everything under the single yellow drop light hanging over the work bench. Billy was right, Smitty and I were tighter than he had been with the old gangster. And all this time I had been burning through friend credits with Billy. When this was over, I'd have to make it up to him.

"So where do I find him?"

"You ain't gonna like this." Kurt said flicking the ash from his cigarette. "He's been doing business with Azad Aziz."

My eyes nearly shut as I wanted to facepalm myself. Azad Aziz was an Armenian gangster wannabe I had the misfortune of owing a lot of money to last year. He tried to kill me for it and he lost a lot of soldiers trying. Smitty knew him which is how I ended up in the card game that cost me a lot. Why the old gangster was mixed up with Aziz again troubled me.

"No, I don't like it either." Kurt said reading my face.

"Can you get a hold of him? I need to find him right away," I said.

"Probably at Aziz's right now."

Chapter 18

I took Oakridge Avenue over the river all the way to A1A. There were quicker ways to Aziz's beachfront home, but I wanted to ride along the ocean. Something about the vastness of the ocean bubbled up feelings of magical possibilities. The ever-lapping waves and white sand always felt good on my sun kissed skin. Sometimes, in the late evening just as the sun was going down, I'd stand in the still warm sand as a cool breeze whipped off the ocean. That was a time I wanted back. Simple and clear to me then, now everything I did carried the weight of everyone else with it.

A sex trafficking ring had been busted up, in the vacuum Aziz tried to swoop in and carve out a criminal empire for himself. I took him down and pressed on to squash any other criminal from establishing a foot hold in my town. It wasn't just my town. It was Billy, Sanford's and Detective Camp's town too. We all lived here and tried to carve out an existence here. Wayne had Coopers and Alysa had her gym. If I were to get through any of this, it would be for all of us.

As the memories mixed between good and bad my eyes caught sight of a Chevy sedan a few car lengths behind. The sun was gone now. With headlights in my mirror, there was no way to see the driver.

Paranoia or good instincts got the gas going on the Scout as I pushed well over the speed limit along A1A. I zigged and zagged around cars with out of state plates. Each time looking up to see the Chevy in the distance. I slowed; the Chevy slowed. Paranoia turned to fact.

A hard right chirped the 33-inch tires on the Scout as I rounded the corner onto a residential street filled with single story concrete block homes. The Chevy remained south on A1A. I exhaled and mumbled a few cuss words of relief until

I stopped at the stop sign.

This tale could be who broke into the shop and hit Billy on the head. My blood began to boil. I wanted that bastard, cop or crook, he was going to get the vengeance I had been dealing all over this town.

Looking both ways, the Chevy sat a block south waiting. This time the cuss words I chose were out of anger. I made the left and chirped the tires once more heading his direction. The rear tires on the Chevy began to smoke as the sedan lunged into the street heading south on Peninsula Drive, a narrow winding two lane residential street that runs parallel to the river and A1A on the other side.

Despite over 300-foot pounds of torque the 345 in my Scout just wasn't fast. As I began to watch the Chevy fade into the distance Billy's voice echoed in my head, *We can shoehorn a new Hemi in there*.

Slapping the steering wheel, I conceded to the Chevy as it rounded a small bend. At 50 MPH the road was too much for the leaf-sprung suspension and I was forced to slow down. To calm myself I blamed it on Gibson, deciding it was a state trooper assigned to tale me. My gut was screaming at me otherwise. I was on the tale of my own and Smitty was close this time. There was no changing course now.

Before I got to Aziz's oceanfront mansion, I text Sanford asking him to relay a message to Newstrom and Gibson to back off. I needed to know if they had the tale on me, next time I wouldn't try and run, I'd charge.

Off A1A, sandstone pavers cut between a dip in the dune. I stopped at a pair of tall turquoise gates. Both sides of the drive ahead were covered in palmettos and sea grape trees, beyond, just the apex of the terracotta roof was visible. I pressed the buzzer at the gate and waited. It had been a year since my run in with Aziz and I hadn't kept tabs on the robust bearded Armenian since. The only thing I knew was that he wouldn't be happy to see me.

I sat with the engine idling waiting to push the button on the gate. My arm wasn't moving, I wasn't moving except for my chest taking deep breathes.

"Yes." Came a long boring voice.

"Roger Grimes here to see Azad."

"Mr. Aziz is not taking visitors."

I slapped the button down, "You can either open the gate or I'm coming through the gate." I said and looked up at the little camera above the buzzer.

I counted down on my fingers until I made a fist. Then I shrugged. I did a K-turn and backed up. Under the back seat was a tow strap that I hooked to my bumper. I wrapped the other end around the gate and waved once more at the camera.

As I climbed back in the truck, I heard the once boring voice cry out with urgency.

"Stop! Please sir, this is uncalled for."

After locking the front hubs, I slapped the transfer case shifter into 4-low. Then I let the low-end torque and gears do the work. It took a couple yanks, but the metal couldn't hold to the concrete pillars and came off.

I swung around taking out shrubs and digging ruts along the driveway and headed for the house, dragging the gate like a plow over the block drive as I went. Aziz was standing on the front steps of the beachside mansion with his hands on his hips, glaring at me through bushy eyebrows and those amber colored eyes. He didn't say a word as I parked and got out.

"Howdy." I said as I passed by him. "I'll put that gate back when I go."

"I sue. I sue you, your boss Willis Sanford. I make you pay for all of it." Aziz said trailing behind me. Once inside he barked some orders at a man with olive skin and curly black hair. The man nodded and ran out.

I had been to Aziz's house before. It was on his back porch that I lost my shirt in one of Aziz's notorious high stakes poker games and spent a few weeks of hell trying to pay him back. Back then Aziz had the power and influence to make me pay. In the end I proved that to be a lie. If Smitty where here, he'd be sitting at that felt table shuffling cards and sipping a cold drink.

"Your house looks a little sparse." I said as I passed through an empty living room once filled with leather and porcelain. I grabbed ahold of the sliding glass door. "I guess crime isn't paying what it used to. At least you've managed to keep the house."

I pulled back on the door and was hit with a rush of salty air that drowned out the cuss words coming from Aziz. The moon was bright enough to show the white caps on a choppy ocean. I stepped out onto the patio. To my left was a pool and to my right was a tiki bar with thatch roof under the roof was a poker table and a man sitting at it.

"Hey kid." Smitty said sitting in a dark blue sport coat and flowered shirt half unbuttoned, sipping from a fake bamboo cup. His hair was all white and that gold tooth still gleamed when he smiled. "Pour a drink and have a seat." The old man said.

Since there was no bar tender, like Aziz had in the past, I went behind the bar and found a mini fridge stocked with beer. I grabbed a bottle and looked up at the horse race on the television. It was a harness race up north with snow on the track. I took my seat next to Smitty. Aziz joined across from me.

The old gangster shuffled the cards then started to deal them. When the fifth card came my way, I said, "I don't have any money."

"Neither do we." Aziz said with a smile that turned to more of a sneer.

Smitty nodded to me.

I flipped the corner back on my cards, wasn't much. I kept the three, seven and Jack of clubs. "I'll take two."

Smitty tossed me two cards. Ten of clubs and a King of clubs.

Aziz took one card and Smitty delt himself three. We flipped and I won easily with a flush. Smitty delt again, again I won with three sevens. Smitty started to deal a third time.

"Enough with the cards." I said tossing back the card.

"C'mon kid, one more hand." Smitty tried to smile but it looked more like hurt him than joy.

"No more games. Where the hell have you been and what the –"

Smitty put his hands up. Once I stopped talking, he said, "I've got it under control." He dealt another card my way.

"Whatever *it* is you think you have under control, you don't. The FDLE is looking for you because you're hanging around with the criminals I have been trying to put away. Whatever you're into has ties all the way to the top and the cops are coming for them, all of them. I've put my neck out trying to find you." I slapped the table.

He tossed another card at me. I flipped the corner to see another ace. Ace of spades and ace of diamonds.

"Just stay in the game." Smitty smiled, this time without the humor in the corners of that broad grin.

He looked to Aziz. "One." Aziz said and Smitty delt him one card. He looked at his own two cards and said, "Dealer takes three." He dropped three cards then looked at me.

"I fold," I said.

He tossed the other two cards in my direction. I would have had four aces.

"So, you're a cheat. What's your point, Smitty?" I was letting him hold all the cards.

Smitty stood up, "Poker never was your game. Maybe you should try chess." The old man looked to Aziz, "C'mon, let's take a drive."

When I didn't move, he grunted, "I'm not asking, kid. Get up." His eyes narrowed. His face plastered over in a hard shell that I couldn't crack. The unfamiliarity spooked me enough to get me to my feet.

Aziz was up now too. All three of us went back through the house and got into Smitty's black Lincoln Continental.

"Where are we going?" I asked from the back seat.

"You've got a lot to learn about the way the world works." Smitty said looking at me from the rearview mirror.

A text came through on my phone from Alysa asking if I could talk. I replied, no. When I looked up to see Smitty still watching me in the mirror I turned the phone on silent and shoved it in my pocket.

Aziz mumbled directions a couple times as we went back to the mainland traveling west then took Clyde Morris Boulevard until we neared the airport. A left turn took us back around a winding road behind the airport. To the right was the wide empty expanse of concrete marked with lights and wind flags. To the left was nothing but a few warehouses and overgrown Florida jungle. We turned left down a dirt road.

The road was heavily rutted with fresh tracks from large trucks. The combination of vine wrapped oaks and tall palms created blocked out any ambient light from the airport across the road. Up ahead a flashlight blinked on then off two times. We pulled up to see a man with slicked black hair and black button-down shirt tucked into black denim jeans holding his left hand out. In his right hand was a bullpup shotgun. Smitty's window went down, and the guard's head leaned in. He shined the light over all three of us over. Aziz said who we were, and the radio chirped in the man's ear.

"Go ahead." He said with a heavy Spanish accent.

One of those dual axle trucks pulled up behind us with the lights beaming into the car.

My pocket lit up in the dark backseat. I slipped out he phone to see Sanford's name across the screen.

"Leave your phone in the car." Smitty said. He looked back over his shoulder, "And your piece." Smitty waited until I complied. The Glock came out of the holster. I didn't like any of this. I kept my mouth shut and relied on the trust I had for built in Smitty over countless burglaries. The jobs came through him and so did the plan. That was a long time ago and that trust was thinning but wasn't gone.

"Where's the Colt? The 1911 Colt you always carry?"

"I had to stop carrying that."

"You love that gun."

"It's a nail driver." We said in unison. "I used it a few times too many. It's safe, relax."

"I'm cool. I just thought you preferred it to those *imports*." He said like carrying an Austrian handgun was unpatriotic, costing American jobs.

"It's an heirloom piece. I don't like to use it in my work anymore."

I tucked my pistol and phone under the seat and got out of the car. Aziz led the way with Smitty in front of me. The truck lights cast black shadows across most of the men's' faces and the various weapons they held. They were all dressed normal enough, no camouflage, cigars or fedoras. These looked like everyday people except a few had machineguns pointed at us.

A man with a pistol sticking from his waste came over and patted us down.

A man with short-cut black hair wearing a pastel blue V-neck sweater tucked into white linen pants made his way over. A typical south Florida look that no one in Daytona copied. He finished off his look with his hands on his hips.

"And who are they?" He said pointing a finger close enough to my face I could have bitten it off.

"Sorry Emel. Change of plans, but I vouch for him." Smitty said.

"Where is Muncy, huh? He is the plan of this." Emel looked both Aziz and I over. Aziz's face was covered in beads of sweat holding in place.

"Muncy wasn't the right guy for this job, so he's out. Aziz knows the drill. Be cool."

Emel walked off the distrust then said, "You have what I want?"

Smitty nodded and Aziz reached in his pocket. Under careful eye over every man with a gun, the Armenian gangster slowly took out a flash drive.

Emel's man retrieved it, handing it to Emel.

"You can check it." Aziz said like the amateur he was.

"If it is not what they want, you'll be dead, all of you." Emel said coolly with any emotion absent from his face. He waved a hand, signaling to the gun toting men to open the cargo truck. The door rolled up and inside were stacks of boxes sitting on a pallet, wrapped in cellophane. Each box was stamped with familiar names of major gun manufacturers. American guns being sold back to Americans.

Where they came from or how these out of towners got them, I didn't know. Newstrom and Gibson would want answers. All those eyes and all those barrels kept me silent. This was Smitty's game now.

Smitty stepped up, "What about our deal?" he said to the gun runner. The man pulled a white envelope out and handed it over to the old mobster. Smitty opened it, thumbed what was inside and stuffed it in his pocket.

Whatever was on that drive and in that envelope was worth more than cash. Information, blackmail, security codes, I had no idea. Then two links in a chain fused and I couldn't separate them. Sanford had a flash drive stolen from his office the other night. Smitty, the greatest thief I ever knew was trading a flash drive to a cartel for guns. My heart lept into my throat, choking me off from screaming. Billy was wrong, Smitty was never my friend. He used me to make money and he was still using me long after I quit.

I stood there motionless as people moved around me. The cartel loaded up into the other box truck. Emel tossed Aziz the keys to the truck with the guns. Smitty got into the Lincoln and Aziz drove the truck. I stood there.

"C'mon kid let's hustle." Smitty yelled then shut the car door.

I looked around contemplating running off into the brush and start my disappearing act right away. I still had my locker at the marina with cash, credit cards and ID for someone named Charlie Wolfe. As I planned it all out, the Lincoln roared and stopped short of taking me out at the knees.

Smitty had to answer for what he did before I went anywhere.

Chapter 19

We rode along in silence for several minutes, turning this way and that. Aziz was on the road somewhere in the box truck with the guns and the cartel was headed in another direction with a flash drive that would send me to death row or worse. Questions raced through my mind, but I sat without raising one of them. We were on our way to deliver the guns or stash them somewhere and if I had any hope of getting out of this it would be to ride along and gather as much as I could for the guys at FDLE.

"Feels like the old days." Smitty grinned as opposing car headlights spot lit his face.

I nodded. It did feel like the old days, days I left behind me. I quit stealing for a reason. Years later, after becoming a private investigator then vigilante, I was full circle back. I hadn't stolen anything, I didn't arrange the deal and I wasn't going to fence those guns, but I was part of it. There was no separating me from Smitty or the life.

"Do you feel as laser focused as I do? I'm running on sheer adrenaline, and it feels fantastic!" Smitty laughed.

"Sure." I said not laughing. A sinking feeling that took me to a colder place deeper and deeper took over and I wanted to just cut and run. Finally get away from him, Sanford and this town that has brought me nothing but grief. I had a fresh start waiting for me in a locker. Maybe Alysa would come with me. She was mixed up with me on a case of her own. Right now, working undercover at Coopers. I couldn't just disappear without saying goodbye.

"Lighten up. You're always so serious. Don't you ever just enjoy being alive?" Smitty said taking a hard turn, faster than we needed to be going. He was always speeding. Even now, in the middle of a huge deal, he smashed the peddle down taking a chance we'd be stopped by police. Besides the federal stint Smitty took for not ratting, he had never been pinched for a real crime. Neither had I. I did nine months in county jail because the judge got tired of seeing me walk all the times before. I was cautious now and to the end of this. Whatever this was.

"So, who lined up the gun buy, Muncy?"

Smitty looked at me from the corner of his eye. "C'mon kid, the less you know the better."

"Yeah, well I know about the flash drive. I know what's on it."

"You do?" Smitty asked continuing to wheel the car like we just robbed a bank.

"It's my fucking death sentence and you just traded it, so I want to know who I have to kill to get it back!" I yelled. My cool was long gone. Fear attacks you in different ways. I could have run; I could have hidden. I decided with that statement I was going to fight and kill. This time it would be for my own life, not that of another faceless victim. I didn't kill Aziz last year when I had the chance. I didn't kill the motorcycle gang that had killed a young reporter. And I didn't finish the job of killing every one of the pedophiles involved in the sex trafficking. All those bricks I stacked were about to come tumbling down on me. The only way out was to kill them all.

Smitty remained silent.

"If you won't talk, then I'll make Aziz. He knows what I am capable of."

Smitty nodded. He knew all too well what I had done. He cleared the path with 3rd Street for me the night I took out the low-level trafficker. And he knew how I single handedly took apart Aziz's little criminal empire.

"You don't know what you're into here. Muncy is the least of your problems. There're bigger things at play." Smitty twisted his grip on the wheel of the Lincoln.

"Bigger than my life?" I said wanting to punch something to drive the point he seemed not concerned with at the moment.

I continued, "I need Muncy to testify in the human trafficking case. If he doesn't then it all falls apart and everyone walks. And you know they'll walk right for me. They want me dead. The only things keeping them from a full-frontal assault is the state investigation." I finally admitted out loud what had been in every dark corner of my mind for nearly three years.

"I won't let that happen, kid." Smitty said checking all three mirrors, looking everywhere except at me.

His words didn't make me feel any better. His actions made me feel even worse.

We turned on to Carswell Avenue and went north then a quick turn on a side street that dead ended into a metal building with three bay doors. The building was a faded cream color and the asphalt had tall weeds growing from the cracks. The other side of the street was a cement wall with razor wire around it. At the end of the short road a sign that said No Dumping was covered in trash. He shut the car off and got out. I followed.

Smitty jiggled a key in a lock then rolled up the middle bay door. Aziz pulled up and into the bay. Smitty waved me in and shut the door behind us.

Aziz climbed out of the truck leaving the lights on. I charged him, grabbing his shirt with both hands.

"Where'd you get that flash drive?" I demanded.

His amber eyes grew large and darted every which way except into my eyes. He saw what I did to his top security man Boghos last year and all the rest of his hired thugs in that bar. It had been a rainy day when I went into Baldy's to pay back the debt I racked up. That should have been the end of it, but Boghos didn't like challengers. I don't remember their faces, only sound of bones breaking and screams. Up until then, I had kept telling myself I wasn't a violent man. They wouldn't let me be anything different. After I left there, I chose to become numb to what I did and used violence as a mechanic uses a wrench.

"I,I…" Aziz stammered.

Smitty grabbed hold of my thumb and bent it back at an angle. The rage in me would have let him break it before I let go, but there was more to do with my hands, and I wanted a thumb that worked.

I let go of Aziz and Smitty let go of my thumb.

"Cut the shit." Smitty said. He shuffled in the dim light to the wall. Above us, fluorescent bulbs hummed then flicked on.

"You said he would be cool." Aziz said backing away from me as he straightened out his shirt then he ran a hand over his greasy black hair.

"He doesn't know everything." Smitty said with a sneer. The grandpa diminished; he was turning gangster.

"Then maybe you should tell me. Or maybe I'll just walk out of here and go straight to FDLE and tell them everything I know. Hell, they probably already know everything. They've had you under surveillance for a while," I said.

Aziz started mumbling to himself in his native tongue.

"Listen, kid, I got you in to this, I can get you out." Smitty said. His eyes were soft, and he struggled to hold a grin.

"You got me into this fifteen years ago. Back when I actually was a kid. You got me into this life, and I've spent years trying to get out of it. I don't want it. Looking over my shoulder, never settling in one place. I can't even go to the damn grocery store without worrying I'll run in to someone who knows what I did. It's over Smitty. Give Muncy up and then stay the hell outta my life," I said.

Smitty shook his head, "I can't."

He might as well of hit me square in the gut the way acid rose in my throat. I knew what he meant, he didn't have to say it and would never say it. Muncy was dead, gator food or shark bait, either way he'd never be found, not by me or any one at FDLE.

"I needed him." I said with all the breath in my lungs. Smitty didn't say anything or move a muscle. "I'm done here." I said and started walking towards the door.

That's when I heard Aziz say, "No you don't." He had a pistol in his hand, shaking the business end at me.

Chapter 20

It was silent in the warehouse except for the sound of Aziz's heavy breathing. Nearly wheezing as he shook a pistol at me, daring me to make good on my statement of leaving to rat them all out to the cops. Aziz had tried to kill me once before but was too afraid, sending goons instead of taking care of it himself. This time was different. Fear of prison was greater than pulling that trigger.

I threw up my hands and said, "Go ahead Aziz. Either way I'm done with all this."

Aziz glanced at Smitty then back to me. "You've ruined me once, Grimes, not a second time."

I forced his decision by taking a step. Aziz leveled the pistol. The cocking of a second pistol flicked his eyes away from mine. We both turned to see Smitty holding a snub-nosed thirty-eight revolver.

"Hold it, the both of you." Smitty's eyes were slits and the corners of his mouth hung low. The old man was on the job once more and he didn't like screw-ups. Screw-ups make loose ends, and all loose ends have to get tied.

"You wanna go, then get the hell out." Smitty said to me then turned to Aziz, "And you, put that thing away. You'll blow the whole deal if you shoot that off in here."

Anger spilled from Aziz's amber colored eyes. The pistol began to shake in his hand then he shoved it in his waistband.

I looked over at Smitty and started to say something.

"Just go kid." He said and waved. Not in a good-bye way but in a he *was through with me* way.

I walked out of that warehouse in worse shape than

when I went in. The list of failures rattled in my head like a marble in a tin can. I walked along Ridgewood Avenue; a busy four lane road lined with the walking dead of Daytona Beach. Druggy there and a prostitute over there. The same ones I saw last week after breakfast with Newstrom and Gibson. The same ones that will be here tomorrow and when they're gone someone will take their place. The best of the down-n-outs this town had to offer. What was I even fighting for?

The night air had dried, cooling the air as it pushed through my jacket and into my bones, making the walk that much less enjoyable. I was about to cross over into 3rd Street territory. My pants were noticeably lighter and looser having left my pistol in Smitty's car. There was no way I was going back, so I had to walk. I could have called Billy. He would answer and drop what he was doing to come get me and take me all the way to Aziz's to get my Scout. Or would he? What would I say if he turned me down? I didn't want to open that box, so I walked on. I still had a few miles to go to get the Scout but along the way was a watering hole, my favorite watering hole, Coopers.

The miles of pavement faded behind me and Smitty. The rotating thoughts did not. All this time I had been searching for him, to keep him out of trouble, I was thinking I owed it to him. That somehow, he had been there for me, and I was going to be there for him.

No honor among thieves.

The smirk I had faded as I spit onto the sidewalk. A million dollars' worth of stolen cash and property had passed through my hands over the years. My bank account was empty, and all my possessions fit into a locker at the marina. Smitty taking me under his wing got me nowhere. Billy might be struggling with his shop, but he has something, something real he can be proud of. Everything I did, I did in secret. My only legacy from Smitty was the training, to steal, fight and kill. I used it all right and was used by it in

Sanford's one-man war on crime. I traded one bad mentor for another.

The long walk eased my anger and let me think. This is where it all folds in, the house of cards collapses, and everything falls on me. With Muncy dead, there's no testimony and human traffickers go free. They'll come for me. I thought Smitty had my back all he did was get me started. Sanford finished me. All his files stolen were going out on the street. Every bad guy with a brother will be coming for revenge if Newstrom and Gibson don't arrest me first.

I needed a drink.

Chapter 21

It was close to 9 pm when I passed through the back door of Coopers. My feet were screaming at me for elevation and sweat left a salty glisten to my skin. I went down the long hallway lit by neon beer signs and found a decent crowd for the hour. To my left were tables, mostly booths only half occupied. At the bar were several open seats in the middle, both ends were full.

Charlie was my bartender. I knew his name, but he didn't know mine. He was about 30 and had a goatee. His Tampa Bay Rays hat was turned backwards, and he wore a Kelly-green Coopers polo. He swung a bar rag over his shoulder and leaned in on the bar.

"Miller Lite and a shot," I said.

Charlie stepped aside so I could see the rows of liquor.

"Elijah Craig bourbon." I pointed for no reason.

"Sounds good." Charlie said and went about pouring my shot.

I held it to my lips and heard a familiar voice.

"Go easy Grimes, we need to talk." Alysa said running a finger along my shoulders as she passed by. She was in her Coopers uniform, Kelly-green polo and tight khaki shorts. Tagging along behind her like a blonde shadow was a young waitress in training. She was probably 19 with a thin frame. My eyes were on Alysa, just the sight of her and I poured the bourbon down my throat to chase away certain biological urges.

"Another." I said to Charlie as he dropped my beer off.

"Roger Grimes?" Charlie asked pouring my shot.

I nodded, then drank my shot.

"The two shots are on me. Chastity told me about what you did to those two wanna be gangsters." Charlie smiled and wiped the bar top then took the shot glass. Wayne was right about Chastity's loose mouth. I was glad I had kept a lid on my feelings about Alysa or a whole other worry would be swimming in my gut.

Busting those two up seemed so long ago. Walking in here tonight I forgot about Wayne and his drug dealing problems.

I sipped my beer and looked up at the TVs on the wall without watching any of them.

"Those guys are assholes." Charlie said as he mixed two drinks.

I nodded.

"I've seen them in before. I never thought much about them." He said.

"Do you know who they work for?" I couldn't help asking the question. Maybe looking into this would somehow take me away from the hole I was sinking in with Smitty.

"I think one them drives a delivery truck." Charlie said pouring out the shaker then placing the drinks at the server's station.

"Not their day jobs. Their other job." I clarified.

"What's that?" Charlie asked not looking up from the bar.

"You know." I said then tapped my finger to the inside of my arm like a junky ready to shoot up.

Charlie looked down at the other end of the bar and nodded to no one in particular then mumbled something and walked to the other end.

He didn't come back to my end of the bar until Alysa

walked over with some Irish eggrolls; corned beef and cabbage fried in a roll.

"Eat if you're going to drink." She said and winked at me as she walked around the bar and poured a pint. She walked off to one of her tables. Once she was done with them, she cocked her head and rolled her eyes at me. I looked behind me, making her laugh as she pointed towards the hall.

The egg rolls were still too hot to eat so I slid off my stool and followed her down the hall.

"I've been asking around." Alysa whispered through her smile.

"Good."

"I saw one of my old regulars, Dillon, he runs the paddle board store a few doors down. Well, he did until he had to close it a couple months back. I started asking about closing and he didn't want to talk so I fed him some drinks and soon he was beat red and ready to spill it.

"He said *they* wanted him closed because he wouldn't play ball." Alysa had a broad smile on her face and her hands on her hips, hips I wanted to wrap my hands around. Maybe drinking to forget her was having the opposite effect.

"And?"

Her smile faded, "*They*!"

"Who's they?"

"Isn't that what we're trying to find out? Dillon's brother Ryan was there and he kinda shushed him before he started spouting off." She shrugged. "That's all I got for now. What about you?"

I frowned and shook my head. I hated seeing the disappointment in her eyes. I let her down like I let Billy down. *Could this night get any worse?*

Her blonde shadow popped up and they walked off. I

went back to the egg rolls and found them cool enough to eat. I grabbed one and heard a familiar voice and knew it *could* get worse.

"Roger, can I join you?" Alvarez pulled the bar stool out next to me.

"I guess you found me." I said and bit into grease and cabbage. Alysa was right, this would cancel any drunk I tried to tie on.

"I wasn't looking for you." Alvarez said sitting down.

"That wasn't you in the Impala?" It was a possibility Alvarez was sniffing around.

"Nope, they still got me in a Crown Vic." Alvarez smiled with gleaming white teeth made brighter by his light brown skin and black hair. The rest of his body was covered in a royal blue button down tucked neatly into grey slacks. His Glock and badge on one hip.

He waved over Charlie the bar tender and ordered a coke. I passed on Charlie's offer for a third shot. The first two had me calm and a third would slow me down. I had a decision to make. Smitty could go down in all this and I would just have to live with it. If I separated him, like Billy had, from my life and forced the idea we were just ever business partners than maybe I could. What if he got in my way of Muncy? A giant black hole opened up in my mind, sucking in all my thoughts. It was a chance I would have to take.

"Say, that blond you were talking to is hot." Alvarez followed Alysa around Coopers with his eyes glued to the same parts mine usually were. I hated him.

"She's a good friend."

Alvarez shrugged. My tone shut down any ideas about Alysa, but then I didn't think he was really asking about her for those reasons. The FBI agent was like a cockroach, infiltrating everything and everywhere in my life. I had to stop him infiltrating everyone in my life too.

"Are you familiar with 3rd Street gang?" I said offering up anything that might change the subject.

"Nothing beyond what was in the file. The poolhall was a known hang out for the gang but after the shootout they all went quiet. Typical street gang behavior." Alvarez said then thanked Charlie as he dropped off the coke and took my empty beer.

"I spoke to one of the higher ups in the gang."

"The same one from the night of the shooting?" Alvarez said. He had read the report thoroughly and put it to memory thoroughly.

I nodded, "He confirmed what we already know. Smitty is part of the gun deal."

"And?"

"And that's it. He didn't know anything more about it. Who was selling who was buying, none of it?" I wasn't going to tell a Fed everything, just enough to let him think I was working on it, and I was working on it over time. Smitty was in this deeper than I thought, and he was dragging me down with him. All the years I had known the guy he looked out for me, he made sure the jobs I was on were smooth. Now he was selling information about me to someone. What they wanted with it, I had no idea, but my gut decided they wanted to kill me.

"We should go back, maybe the two of us could shake something loose."

"I doubt it."

"Hey, this badge is like a magic wand. I wave it and people's mouths just open right up."

"Now you tell me something. Any leads on the two

murders?"

Alvarez shook his head. "A real pro. Got in, got out. Interesting though, he didn't use the same method. At Lumino's home there was no sign of a break in. It's as though she let the killer in. Delgado is a different story. A back window was cut, and the alarm wire jumped." Alvarez sipped his coke watching my reaction.

"Strange. My guess is she knew the killer. Delgado either didn't or maybe he didn't hear the doorbell ring."

We sat at the bar, neither talking. I watched Alvarez as he watched everyone else in the bar. His eyes found their way to Alysa and especially her young trainee. She was an attractive girl. Too young for me. That wouldn't stop most men, men like Alvarez. His face was smooth, no lines around the eyes. His hair thick and black, not a single strand of grey. To guess his age, twenty-five to thirty-five. I really couldn't say.

"So, your friend there, is hot," Alvarez nodded to Alysa who was across the room holding a tray. The trainee was taking plates off and handing to a group crammed in a booth. "But that young one is cute. Can you put in a good word for me?"

"Why don't you just use that magic badge."

"Hey, if you're not going to help me out with Muncy and Schmidt, at least help me with this."

I didn't have time for his fun. My mind was churning with thoughts about Smitty and the gun deal that just went down. The more I thought about how little he cared about me the harder I fought to not spill it all to the FBI agent next to me. I had to choose one of two realities for the myth of Erik Schmidt, AKA Smitty. Either he is nothing but a lifelong crook looking out for number one, or he's seeing a bigger picture and is working to keep me safe once again. I wasn't sure of either but the one truth I did know was Alverez wasn't getting shit out of me.

"How long has it been?" Alvarez flipped open a menu.

"How long what?"

"Since you got laid. Or been in love with Alysa?"

"I wouldn't say —"

"Lemme guess, you two hooked up the first night you met and since then you've carried a torch and she calls when she needs advice or needs you to chase off any of her other mistakes." He put other mistakes in air quotes. I didn't remember inviting him to Coopers and I know I didn't invite him to take the seat next to me at the bar.

"The last two women I slept with died shortly after."

Alvarez burst into laughter, "Tell me that's not your pickup line."

When I didn't laugh, he quickly recovered with a frown.

"How about we focus on Muncy?" I said getting that bright smile on Alvarez's face once more.

"We suspect he's still in town. Where or what he is up to, is anyone's guess."

"Any chatter out there? Anything about gun buys or anything we could use?"

Alvarez broke his stare of the young server and met my eyes. He held them there a few seconds, then blinked. "Ah, no." he said. I stared at him. He smiled, "Nothing, no chatter."

I wanted to speak but stopped. It was best to let him do the talking if he had anything at all to say.

I pulled my wallet and pulled some cash. Alvarez said not to worry, that he would get my tab. Since I find it a waste of time to argue with people who want to pay your tab in a useless back and forth of, *I got it, no I got it*, I said sure and made for the back door.

Alysa caught up to me in the hallway of colorful neon beer signs.

"Heading out so soon?"

"I've had a long day and need a dark, quiet cave to crawl into, maybe hibernate until all this shit blows over." I said looking down at my Vans. Her silence brought my head up and looking into her green eyes, round and large.

"Wow, sleepy little baby needs his baby sleep." She laughed and touched my arm.

"That was weak." I said then laugh quietly.

"Weak is going home before ten."

Home. Shit, I had forgot about Billy and the mess I left at the shop. I didn't even help him clean up the apartment. I had no home, nowhere to go and sleep off this emotional hangover.

"Alright, Grimes, get some sleep. We have a lot to go over tomorrow, Boss." Alysa said with a wink. Then she walked off and I was too tired to even watch her body go.

I stood in the hall, looking at the door to the back-parking lot but didn't move. I had keys but no truck.

"What's the matter, forgot where you parked?" Alvarez said coming up behind me.

We stepped out into the cool night together. He seemed less affected by the fifty-degree weather than I was. Florida had thinned my blood.

"I walked." I said and waited for him to depart for his car. He waited too, probably to see which direction I went. A few more seconds and I decided to just head north.

"I can give you a ride." He said dangling the keys to his Crown Vic.

"I'll be okay."

"Have it your way." He smiled and walked off.

Chapter 22

I left Alvarez standing in front of Coopers. Amber eyes tracked me north, once satisfied, he went back inside. For a man that doesn't drink it was an odd place to be this time of night. Maybe he just didn't like his drinking company. I would have to work with him eventually. Muncy was their key figure for prosecuting these elites. They were safe behind mansion walls and the guns of their security for now. Then it would be a race to get the fanciest lawyer and make it all go away.

Acid churned in my belly, rising in my throat with the memories of what I did that night in the pool hall. There were arrests, prosecutions. Those were the low rung soldiers, not the generals calling the shots. Guilty predators were still out there with debts unpaid.

I turned into the next alley and circled south. I made it over the Silver Beach Bridge and east to A1A. I continued south over a sand sprinkled sidewalk going south. The road was nearly empty. Right now, the city had shrunk to its official census population. All the Christmas vacationers were long gone but it was too early for spring breakers to invade. Every year it started with the Canadians first. Easy enough to spot in shorts and tank tops while the rest of us wore jeans and jackets. I liked this time of year in Daytona Beach.

The cold was biting, and my face stung. I pressed on to Aziz's and my Scout.

My feet crossed over the block driveway drawing closer to the dark mansion nestled in the dunes. Not a single light was on. The front door was locked. I stood with my nose dripping and any bone I broke recently aching. Warmth and sleep were all I could think about. I wanted the night over.

Giving the V8 a moment to warm up, I stared blankly with no direction. A shiver crept up my spine and I blasted the heat. The motor was too cold to help me. I pulled out of Aziz's and made it two blocks before looking at the lineup of hotels along A1A. For every two nice white hotels with glass walled lobbies, there was a rundown two-story job with chipping concrete and few cars. I kept driving before giving up and pulling into the lobby of a hotel.

The backlit sign was in French. The three-story hotel was smaller than its neighbors by a few flights, but it looked to be recently renovated with fresh paint and windows. What they lacked in size was probably made up for in service. All the lobby furniture was grey and rectangular. The floors looked like long strips of petrified wood, but really just painted concrete molds. The lights were dim except around the empty lobby desk.

I stood looking at my phone. On the screen was a map with a blue circle telling me where I was. I guessed Azad's house was only a mile more down the road. My feet hurt and my nose continued running from the cold salty air blowing off the ocean. My brain was in a fog, tapped out of anger I was left with only confusion. I wanted a hot shower and comfortable bed for the night.

Finally, a slender young woman with olive skin and well-placed moles on her face came out from a hidden door in the fancy wood trim behind the desk. She was pulling her curly black hair up into a bun. She had on a long white sleeve shirt tucked into black pants.

"How may I help you?" She said softly adding a smile at the end.

I told her I needed a room for two nights. With nowhere else to go and feeling like a coma was coming on I decided to go ahead with the second night.

She gave me the receipt to sign, and I handed over cash.

"Sorry, I'll still need a card to keep on file."

The only credit card I had was in a locker at the marina for a guy named Charlie Wolfe. I stood contemplating driving out there and getting it, but she already saw my real ID. I dropped my seabag and dug in until I found a fanny bag. Inside that I pulled a company card Sanford had given me once to buy some surveillance equipment. I conveniently forgot to give it back. I gave her the company credit card, and she gave me two key cards.

"Do you have security on site?" I asked not realizing I had until I heard the words come out of my mouth.

"Yes, every night from ten to seven."

My eyes surveyed the lobby spotting cameras in every corner. I sighed, "Okay thanks."

"Do you need me to radio him?" She reached out and grabbed a two-way radio.

"No, thanks. I was just checking." I smiled. Something eased in my shoulders. Even if the rent-a-cop was just an illusion of safety, it worked.

"How about a parking pass?"

"No need in the off season." She said with a smile and stood still waiting for me to walk away before she went back to whatever it was, she was doing.

The room was on the third floor at the end of a hallway Drew Brees couldn't throw a football to the end of. Inside the curtains were open but all I saw was my reflection in the black glass. I pulled them shut, sunk my ass into the bed and kicked off my shoes. The carpet felt like little brushes on my feet. The modern furnishings of square metal and raw wood furniture made the room feel sterile like a hospital room trying to feel warm. A chair in the corner and a small table next to it. The TV was on a three-drawer dresser.

In the shower, hot water pushed steam over my worn-out

body. Thoughts like racecars lapped in my mind, coming around the turn, screeching their tires only to fade as they went around the track then the next one came in just as fast and just as loud.

Everything I thought I knew was disintegrating. Piece by piece, breaking off like clumps of sand in the surf, washing out as the tide grew stronger and stronger. Smitty really was a crook and Billy wasn't the friend I thought he was. Maybe I hadn't been the friend he thought I was. All of it, the jobs from Sanford, the nights I never slept and the days I just stared off into an abyss void of light washed over me like the hot water from the shower head.

I clenched my hands into fists and felt the strain on my knuckles. The hot water soothed the pains in my shoulder and lower back, injuries from a war no one knew I fought. The soap was foaming, cleansing but it didn't go deep enough. I turned it hotter until my skin was pink, and my entire body burned.

I toweled off then switched the towel for a dry one. I sat on the edge of the soft bed. Sleep was my escape; sleep was my cure, but the screams of the dead crept up my spine and smothered my face. I was too weak to push them down, phase them out, put them back in their box. They grew louder, angrier, refusing to be ignored. I screamed out against them, thrashing fists into pillows that never did anything to me but would never tell a soul.

Naked and breathing heavy I stared at a king mattress turned on its side and blankets and pillows scatter over carpet. The hotel phone wrang.

"Hello." I said trying to slow my breathing.

"Good evening, sir. Is everything alright? There was a… noise complaint." Said the soft voice of the hotel clerk.

"Yeah, sorry, just had the TV up too loud." I hung up.

The fear subsided allowing the anger in me to drain

through damp skin. I got dressed and left the room.

The girl wasn't at the desk as I walked by. Outside I looked up and down A1A, spotted a 7-11 and made way towards it.

Twenty minutes later I was back in the bed, under a sheet and comforter with a plastic bag of snack food, soda, beer, water, and a sleep aid. It was nearing midnight, my body ground down, but my mind wouldn't shut off. I needed to force it closed. I had the TV on showing a black and white movie. A beer was open, and half gone. I flipped through my phone looking at anything that could distract me; a new shop to lease for Billy and me, used cars, classic trucks, puppies up for adoption. The dogs with pointed ears, wolfish features captured my attention. The wolf hybrids were too big, but something mixed with a coyote seemed like it would be a good fit for me. Half domesticated, half wild, appealed to me. I read articles on coydogs until my eyelids grew heavy and my phone dropped on my chest.

I managed to plug the phone in with the charger I bought and rolled over focusing on getting a place of my own, something with a yard for my coydog to chase squirrels.

A soft light cracked the black sleep of my eyelids. One lid opened. The comforter was up over my neck. I peered out into a room filled with sunlight. The sun had risen fully above the ocean and found the sliver between curtains screaming at me to get up with the rest of the world. I breathed deep then pulled the comforter over my head.

With no sense of time, I opened my eyes and felt my hot breath reverberating back on my face. It was stuffy under the comforter, I needed air.

The sun was still up, a little higher now taking the direct beams with it. I sat up, rubbed my eyes, then grabbed my phone. It was just after eight. Alysa had called and texted a couple times, so had Sanford, so had Billy. Turning off my ringer granted me uninterrupted sleep for the first time in years, I didn't care about missing a call or text. I tossed the phone into the comforter and went into the bathroom.

After a shower and shave, I was more awake than ever but still needed caffeine. There was a pot in the room, but I wanted to move around.

Before I left the room for the lobby and my complimentary continental breakfast, I looked at my phone and the messages waiting to be read.

My finger hovered over the text icon and the red number 5 telling me there were five texts to read. Three were from Alysa and one from Sanford and one from Billy. I didn't read them. I just replied to each of them a simple "I'll get back to you." I thought I was slick, I thought I was making time for solitude then Alysa called.

"Yeah," I said.

"Good morning to you too." She let out a little laugh, but it wasn't enough to cover how pissed she was at me.

I said nothing.

"Hello, you still there?"

"Yep,"

"What's the problem Grimes?"

Being short with her was stabbing me in the chest but getting involved in the drug dealing case right now would be stabbing me in the back. I had twelve hours of solitude, no cases, no bad guys, no rage, and it was fantastic.

"Sorry, I'm just tired." I said but didn't mean the apology. I closed the metal hotel door shut as I went into the hall.

"Where are you?"

"A hotel, long story." I said getting on the elevator.

"Oooh."

I said hello to the housekeeper pushing a cart out of the elevator.

"Ooooh, and you're not alone. Good for you Grimes." She forced smiled through the phone, with a hint of disappointment. Any other day a corkscrew would twist in my chest thinking she was jealous or was lying about congratulating me, but today I just didn't care.

"Just the housekeeper." I said ending the confusion for her and for my guts. "I'm headed down to the lobby for breakfast."

"What hotel?"

The elevator doors opened. Across the lobby I saw the black letters back lit in blue against a stone wall. "Chateau Plage."

"Is that the fancy one just south of Silver Beach? With all the hanging curtains outside?" she said in an excited hurry.

"Yeah, I guess," I said. There were two clerks now behind the desk.

"I'm like two minutes from there. Get me a waffle started, I'll be right there." She hung up before I could even tell her where or what was on the menu.

The breakfast room was small to encourage people to get their food and leave. There were four four-seat tables and a two top against a window that was blacked out with tint. On my left was the buffet of eggs, sausage patties, fruit salad and a tray of muffins. Next along the counter were cereal dispensers, three kinds of juice fountains and at the end, the waffle maker.

I studied the maker, reading over the directions, then went about pouring some premixed batter into a paper cup then pouring that onto the griddle then closed it. I stepped back expecting something to happen.

"You gotta turn the handle." Said a female voice.

One of the front desk employees, dressed like the one last night in white shirt and black pants, stepped around me, twisted the handle flipping the maker over. A red countdown began. Alysa had three minutes to get there if she wanted her waffle hot.

"Thanks." I smiled. She smiled back then cleaned one of the tables of Styrofoam bowels and a plate with used napkins on it. She went out of the room.

I fixed a plate of eggs and sausage and sat with my face to the open double doors and my back to a TV tuned to cable news. Another political scandal, another accusation of wrongdoing followed by a denial. Either way it never seemed to be investigated thoroughly enough to send anyone to jail. The worst they got was a forced resignation. Money and power buys top lawyers. The kind of legal team that can twist facts until up means down. The accused just waits out the news cycle, then it's the next guy in hot water.

When Billy, Smitty and I would travel out of town for work, I always liked to watch the local news channels in other towns. It was a glimpse into the local life, things that mattered to them. Most of the motels were dives that didn't have complimentary breakfast. Those places were the 'L' shaped strips you find off highways or down back country roads. Places we wanted to lay low and not be noticed. Those mornings I was lucky to grab a Danish or piece of fruit. Smitty never ate breakfast. The earliest I ever saw him eat was a banana around ten thirty in the morning. We had been up late that night driving after a jewelry heist in Atlanta.

I was clouded in a memory of a job well planned, well executed when Alysa breezed in. Her blond hair was free, strands flowing in different directions. She had zero makeup on and didn't need any. Being early spring, her usual tan had faded allowing her cheeks to show pink and a nose dotted with freckles.

She stood looking at me with a half-smile while I was frozen holding a chunk of boxed eggs on a plastic fork.

DING. I snapped out of my trance and turned to the waffle maker. She had done it!

"Is that mine? Did I make it?" She said and skipped to the maker. Flipping it open like an experienced pro, she plucked the waffle out and dropped it on a plate. She went about getting single serving butter and syrup, set it on the counter then poured some juice and joined me at the table.

"Sooo," She said. I shoveled eggs in my mouth. "C'mon, man what gives with the hotel room?"

I swallowed, "Just needed a quiet place for the night."

"Is Billy working late?" She asked knowing my apartment was above Billy's auto shop.

I was silent for a moment, narrowing down how much of the story I wanted to tell her. "Someone sacked my place and sapped Billy pretty good yesterday."

"Oh my gosh!" Alysa had a little piece of waffle stuck to her lip. She licked it away then said, "Is he okay?"

I nodded, "Hard head. Anyway, they slit open every pillow on my couch and my mattress. The place is a mess."

"Was it the drug dealers?"

"I have no idea." The thought had never crossed my mind. Up until now I assumed it had to do with my mystery tail the other day outside Aziz's beachfront mansion.

"None? Not a single idea? Grimes, come on." She smirked and cut into the last piece of waffle.

I got up and shoveled more eggs and another piece of sausage on my plate. I sat down and she jammed her fork into my plate taking half my eggs. We chewed in silence.

"How well do you remember Chloe Hines?" I said with a smirk. She returned the smile with a shrug then set her fork down.

"Wasn't that the lady who was shot in the poolhall?"

I nodded, "And the one you warned me about that night, but I was too drunk to listen."

A half smile curled the corner of her mouth. She needed to hear the rest of the story. The version of events I relayed to her was the same edited version the police got about the night in the poolhall. And about the young kids being sex trafficked here in town that lead me there.

Her jaw was slack, and she pushed a paper cup back and forth between two hands as wrapped up the story. I pushed my plate away; I hadn't taken a bite since I started my story.

"Ah, Grimes that must have been an awful thing to see." Alysa said.

I said nothing. Just sat there looking at my plate, listening to the news anchor talk about politics.

"I didn't really know her. I just, I'd seen her in the bar a lot, always with a different guy and I thought, well you didn't seem like her type." Her eyes looked down at hands folded in her lap.

"I appreciate it, but I already knew who she was. I used to babysit her kid those nights she was out."

"Oh, dang she had a kid." She shook with a shiver.

"Anyway, some pretty powerful people were implicated, and the case is ongoing," I said. So ongoing in fact, someone has been tailing me for a while. The powerful will do anything to keep power, including sending a killer after me. It's possible Luminos and Delgado were messages. Warnings or just names on a list and mine was next. Hitmen were not the kind of criminal I hung around. Sure, there were guys who had killed rivals or for money, but a genuine professional I never met. Was he taking his time? Daytona Beach could be growing on him. I figured a pro hired to kill me would do a better job of going unnoticed or have taken care of me by now.

Something on my face changed because Alysa asked, "What? What is it?" She waited once more for me to speak.

"Nothing, tell me about the drug dealers." I said, but it was something. A light, a path, a direction into what was happening around me appeared. They were scared, whoever was unmasked the night I shot up the pool hall and whoever had dealing with the dark side of Gregg Hines was scared and I scared them.

Alysa got up and poured two cups of coffee and came back to the table. She added cream but no sugar, I added both. Her hair was pulled back behind each ear as she started her story of working two nights at Coopers.

She went with a list of employees and their drug habits. All seemed severe to me, but she said it was normal restaurant fare. With all those drugs freely traded in restaurants, I wondered how much cocaine ended up in my food. Maybe it's why I always went back. Her list included who they bought from, with the majority buying from the two I slapped around the other day. The two stopped returning calls from the employees making them cagey as the withdrawals quickly set in.

"I think some of the employees are pissed at you. Careful who you order a drink from." She smiled. I soaked it in.

"So, who is supplying the two I beat up?" My eyes caught the same front desk clerk as before coming into the room pressing pause on our little intel session. The clerk had on plastic gloves and held a spray bottle in one and a roll of brown paper towels in the other. The towels and spray were set on the counter then she went to work tossing the food under the hot lamps into a trashcan. The complimentary breakfast was over.

Alysa looked over her shoulder. When she looked back at me, she was ready to say something but took a deep breath, then said, "Maybe we should go back to your room?"

My room was left with scattered towels, shavings in the sink and empty beer cans. First impressions had always been impressed on me. Two sides of my brain started a fight over having Alysa alone in a hotel room or her impression of me after seeing how messy it was.

When I hesitated, she flushed.

"It's warm out we could just walk the beach." She said before I could formulate words in my waring brain and then force air through my vocal cords making sounds that resemble them. The opportunity sailed off over the Atlantic

"Sure."

We went out through the east side of the lobby, past the automated double doors and onto the pool deck were the sun blinded us for a few seconds. The water sparkled as did the white plastic chairs lining along the pool. The mini-Tiki hut that served as the pool deck bar, had its metal shutter down and secured. There wasn't a soul out on the deck as we came to a low metal railing then followed down wooden steps to the sand. We kicked off our shoes and left them under the stairs.

Back in the early 2000's, a multitude of hurricanes took out most of the dunes that separated the beach from the hotel sea walls. Beach restoration and lack of hard-hitting hurricanes allowed for small dunes to return. Our bare feet slipped through the soft white sandy path between two small sand dunes crawling with Beach Morning Glory stretching out in long green vines. The waves rolled in knee high, curling against an outgoing tide. We walked along the harder packed sand left by the retreating waves.

"So, the two you gave a beating to, are Chad and Wes." She paused waiting for my question of who was who, but I said nothing. "Chad drives a moving van most days. Wes is the one with the connection. He gets the drugs, divides or cuts it or whatever dealers do, then sells it. Chad's just the muscle."

I laughed, "I'm sure there's *some* muscle under that blubber."

"I guess he's managed to scare a few people, because they own Beach Street."

"People like Wayne?"

"That one perplexes me." She said then touched a finger to her lips like Sherlock or something. Alysa was really taking on this investigator gig well.

"I couldn't tell if he was more pissed at them for showing up or me for throwing them out."

"I've seen him get mad; he can be a scary dude too. It was easy to get info on the dealers, addicts talk, but what's hanging over Wayne's head and who holds it was a challenge. Since Wayne won't talk about it, I had to be really careful who I asked about it." Alysa said. The sun was directly over us now. She turned to me with a hand acting like a visor pressed against her brow and smiled. The smile was soft, showing little of her teeth but stretched the corners of her face. She was enjoying this, the job I had given her, the walk on the beach and the cool Florida winter temperatures.

I smiled back and she went on with what she had found out and how she found it. Alysa convinced one of the cooks, Manny, to hook her up with weed. Manny was suspicious, because everyone knew Alysa and I were friends, so she explained it was for pain from working out at her gym. He suggested prescription pain pills and said Wes sells those too. It took some flirting, and Manny said he'd make the call.

Wes responded this time and she him to stop by. Alysa managed to go along for the ride. Wes lived in a pink single story block house off one of the numbered streets in Holly Hill, the small town between Daytona Beach and Ormond Beach. It's a working-class town with scrap yards, building contractors, and small manufactures lining the railroad tracks.

Alysa said they backed in the driveway and Manny honked the horn, three quick beeps. A chubby girl with long stale brown hair came out all smiles until she saw Alysa. That sparked some loud questioning, but when she saw the cash in her hand she shut up.

"Oxycontin." Alysa pulled a baggy of four pills from her pocket.

"You kept it?"

"Yeah, it cost me forty bucks." She laughed then said, "I dunno, thought we might need it."

I shrugged. She was probably right. Tracking down drug dealers to expose them instead of burning them out was new to me, so was working with a partner.

"When do you work at Coopers next?"

"Thursday."

"What's today?"

"Tuesday."

"Great. Feel like coffee and donuts?"

"Stake out!"

■■

Ten minutes later the guy behind the register at the 7-11 told me the total.

"What?"

"37.58." His stare hung on his face like a coat on a hook.

Alysa grabbed the two plastic bags full of stakeout supplies, as she called them, and headed out. I paid and left.

We took her car and headed towards Holly Hill and Wes's house.

"I've never spent that much at 7-11."

Her frown lasted a second then curled into a smile, "Ah, we bill it all to Wayne anyway, right?" One hand was on the wheel of her Subaru and the other searched inside a grocery bag like a squirrel looking for nut.

I swatted at it. "Not until we get there." My laugh brought her hand back to the bag.

Wayne had never agreed to pay me at all. This was supposed to be a legitimate case, with paperwork, billing and results. Those damn results. Even when I got to who was behind the dealing, Wayne was hesitant to do anything about it. They had him by the beer taps and if he tried to buck their system, Coopers would close, or worse. There was no plan of action, no direction. My focus had been on Smitty and this just landed in my lap.

Wayne could have broken it all down for me, but I needed to know all the players, find out who they were and what they were capable of, and they needed to know what I was capable of.

We made a pass of the pink house. The neighborhood was lower middle class, single story, mostly block construction. All the yards were cut and maintained but didn't have that edged look by lawn pros. Some yards were wrapped in chain link fence that extended to the sidewalk. The palm trees were tall and the oaks round. The street was built around the 1960's.

Alysa circled the block and parked four houses down

along the road. She asked a couple questions about properly positioning the car and what to say if someone asks what we're doing. I told her we'd figure it out. I put the seat back, rolled my jacket up and tucked it behind my head the slurped on my Slurpee. The sun was out, so was a soft breeze keeping it comfortable in the car. We had the windows about half down. The Slurpee was a good choice as I sucked it down waiting for something to happen. Alysa had a bag of beef jerky open and a bite out of a protein bar already. She sipped a bottle of water and kept her eyes straight ahead at the house.

Neither of us spoke for twenty minutes. From a built-in plastic box in the dash Alysa's phone dinged. She reached for it then looking at me, retracted her hand.

"It's okay," I said.

She nodded along in agreement. Her hand went back in her lap. Then a second text came through and that was more than she could stand. She read the texts, typed out a reply, flipped it to silent and put the phone back.

"I'm working." She smiled.

The stakeout continued, boring as they usually are. As a thief it was casing a place, learning the goings on of the store or house I was about to burgle. As a PI, I tailed a guy on a disability case for three days with about two minutes of action when I finally got the photographs, I needed of him as he went up a ladder to clean his gutters.

An apple shaped woman in an unzipped hoodie and wearing black yoga pants, walked along the sidewalk with a little hairy rat on a leash. The dog growled at every blade of grass swaying in the wind. I could feel her eyes on me as we waited in the car. Alysa did a great job of not looking right at her.

Apple lady and her rat were the only action for another twenty minutes. Alysa's knee began bouncing. Then her hands searched the plastic bag some more, looking but not finding. She slid her seat back and tried crossing her legs. I noticed the bottle of water was empty.

"Gotta pee?"

"No, I'm good."

"You sure?"

"Well." Her lip curled at the corner making a half frown and smile simultaneously.

"Got a toolbox in the car?"

"Are you going to make me pee in the car?"

I shook my head.

"In the trunk." She said and pushed the button to pop it. I got out and went around back. The bag was a mess with loose sockets and wrenches. I grabbed a flat head screwdriver then went to the driver's window.

"That house across the street looks vacant. I'll wait it out there. You go find a bathroom. Call Manny and see about setting up a big buy. Maybe that will get us some action. Wait for me at Coopers or some other place so we aren't seen together. When something happens, I'll text you. Pick me up there." I pointed to the next block.

Alysa agreed and started the car. I walked in the opposite direction of the house. I heard her say something, but I ignored it and she pulled away. A block up then one over, I came to the house that sat directly behind the house that was across the street from Wes's house. It was a white house with black shutters, single story with a row of bushes along both sides of the house. I went up and rang the bell.

When no one came to the door, I stepped back off the porch and stood in the driveway still in the line of sight of the front door incase whoever lived there was late answering. I pulled my phone and pretended to check notes on the phone, looked up and down the street searching and then took pictures of the roof line with the phone.

"Can I help you?" A round man, bald and blotchy from a lifetime of sun burns stepped out of his doorway.

"I'm with Sun Roofers and just out canvassing the neighborhood checking on roof damage. Did you know-"

"The roof's fine." He said taking a glance back at this roof.

"I won't know until I get up there." I pulled the screwdriver and pointed at the roof, "See those divots? Could be hail damage and your insurance might pay to fix it."

"No need. Thanks anyway." He turned and headed for the door.

"I was talking to your neighbor behind you," I said trailing him to make sure he heard me.

"No, you weren't."

I paused and he paused, "That house is empty."

"Right, the one next to it. Anyway, thanks for your time."

He waved over his head as he went back in the house. I darted into the back yard and cleared the fence into the vacant house behind.

After fighting through ten yards of vines wrapped in bushes and small trees, I came into the back yard. The white block was mildewed at the corners and the wooden porch sagged with rotten planks. The large sliding glass door had no blinds, and I could see in the room was empty. I walked to the edge of the house and up to the grey wooden fence. The jungle covering continued along this side, blocking out the sun and kept me out of sight of any neighbors. I found a plastic milk crate and slid it over. Sitting on it I pulled the screwdriver and pried loose the moist fence board. I had a clear view of Wes's front door.

Nothing was happening. If the front door of Wes's house hadn't been open, I wouldn't think he was home. The brunette Alysa described came out with a bag of trash and tossed in the can near the garage. She knelt and petted an orange cat then went back in the house.

Wes came out, smoked a cigarette then went back in. I sat and looked at my phone. Wes was just a frog in a small pond with a big fish. It was the fish I was after; the frog was bait.

The battery in my cell was below fifty percent, the sun was dipping changing the sky from deep blue to light blue with soft pink outlining the clouds. Stuck between the block wall of the house and a line of jungle, the light was disappearing, and the cold was seeping in. I checked my phone twice a minute and turned the ringer up so I wouldn't miss a text then decide it was too loud and turn it down. This routine went on for another half hour until I finally got a text from Alysa.

Done – Alysa

Time and place? – Me

He wants 1,000. On my way to get it. Will I get this back? – Alysa. She added an emoji face with a hand on the chin looking up in wonder.

Time and place? – I text back, skipping over the question. I could bill Wayne if I didn't get it back, but I didn't expect to lose it either.

He said he would need an hour, my gym. – Alysa

I texted back for her to meet me at the intersection a block away. Wes needed time which meant he needed to go get the drugs or have someone deliver them. As I thought up plans and contingency plans, a car pulled in.

A late model, silver Nissan Maxima with black rims and

blacked out tint pulled along the front of Wes's house then backed in the driveway slowly. I didn't know it was Chad until a lumpy guy with a blackeye got out, pulled up his grey sweatpants and walked up to the door.

He pounded three times on the metal screen door then let himself in. There was some loud talking, not angry, not joyous, just loud. Then a horse cough, the kind that caught something in the throat and spit it out. Wes and Chad walked out of the house, heads on swivels as they approached the car. Their eyes scanned, searching things that didn't belong, things like me. I knew they couldn't see me in the shadow of the house from behind the fence. My eyes tracked the pair. Chad halted at the car. He looked over at the house, at the side yard where I was standing then he yanked open the door and got in behind the wheel. The car pulled out, headed west.

I scaled the fence and walked casually to the sidewalk. Wes's sweeter half stood in the haze of the black mesh of the screen door. She snorted then hacked something up. Silver white smoke permeated through the screen then she slammed the door shut. I picked up my pace and found Alysa parked at the corner.

"That way." I said pointing west.

Chapter 23

I opened the rear passenger door, pushed some yoga pants off the seat and leaned forward, keeping my eyes just above the dash.

"That way, silver Nissan Altima."

"Roger that." Alysa slapped the shifter into first and took off, fast at first but quickly letting the transmission slow the car to below the speed limit.

At our first four-way stop we saw the silver car with two drug dealers pull to a red stop light several blocks ahead.

"You're gonna have to time this just right. Slow enough so we're not right up on them but fast enough to make that light." I said staying in my low position.

The RPMs jumped, letting off the gas we coasted until the light changed and she gassed it some more. The Altima went straight through the intersection crossing Ridgewood Avenue and disappeared over the small rise in the road as it dipped down towards the Halifax River.

Coming over the ridge, two blocks ahead, the Altima turned right going south along Riverside Drive. We made the right and rode along with the brackish waters to our left and large homes to our right.

"I know we're tailing them, but what exactly are we doing?"

"I want to know who they buy from. Then we go after them and so on up the drug chain until we get to the head of the local market."

Alysa's face was still, her mouth slightly open. I caught my heart beating in my throat and lowered a hand I had raised along with my voice. In her large eyes I saw my own reflection of the beast. I had started down that path, one I had taken so many times in the past going after criminals. My only goal with her was to never show her that beast again.

I cleared my throat of the thumping heartbeat, "I'm not concerned with anything beyond that. If we have a name, I'll pass it along to Detective Camp or an FBI agent I know."

Alysa nodded, her eyes shifted back on the road and the car ahead. That was all the plan I had when I told Wayne I would investigate the drugs. Investigate, find evidence and kick it over to the police. But that's not what I was feeling as we followed the two dealers. Slight perspiration, a tingle at the base of my neck as hair stood on end, I was looking for more.

The Nissan slowed and turned into two looming white towers built on the very edge of the river. The condos had been built years ago and everyone laughed because they seemed out of place. Sixteen stories tall on the mainland side of the river, towering over blocks of residential homes. The condos went on sale just as the housing market crashed. For years there was never more than three lights on in the entire building. With Florida filling with 10,000 Yankees a day, the condos eventually filled.

Alysa slowed the car.

"Keep straight. There's no point in trying to get in." I said pointing at the active guard shack. "Take that next left."

We passed the condo parking garage and entered a small drive that led to a river front park flanked with large palmettos obscuring most of the coquina rock with the sign bolted to it, giving the impression it was part of the towers' property. I knew it because I had fished off the dock there several times.

The Subaru stopped in the one of the few parking spaces. Alysa started to get out, but I told her to wait. If they spot me, it could be coincidence, if they see her, it's a set up. I jogged a short but windy sidewalk to an aluminum gate and fence that ran the length of the property all the way to the sea wall at the river. I grabbed the top of the fence and hoisted myself over, flipping my legs as I went.

Upon landing I looked up to see a little white fluff ball with four legs in a squat as a little old lady with a white fluff ball head bent in a squat of her own. A blue plastic bag covered her hand in anticipation. The dog yelped as my feet hit the lush grass with a thud. The woman straightened up.

"Just wanted to see if I still got it." I said with a smile and continued my jog down the sidewalk.

I was between the southern tower and the parking garage. The garage had three floors. I scanned the first floor. The Nissan didn't stand out. There were plenty of open spaces, so I doubted they parked above. I exited and headed for the front of the building.

Past the towers, I stood at the brick lined drive from the front gate. It opened to a large circular drive with three fountains in the middle. Parked along that brick lined drive was the Nissan, yellow flashers pulsating. The thin silhouette of Wes was in the passenger seat, his white arm hung from the window pinching a cigarette.

My neck was bent back as I looked up at the two towers, each sixteen floors high. There must be 300 possible condos Chad went into.

"That's him, that's the man." A voice with conviction said behind me. I turned and saw the old white-haired woman, leach in hand, standing next to a security guard. He was short with dark hair wearing black slacks and a white button with a badge pinned to it. He nodded to the woman and then started walking towards me, as he did, he waved me over with the authority of a cop directing traffic.

I dipped my head, keeping as much of my face away from him as I walked slowly towards him. Now wasn't the time to cause a scene, but any official report with my name was out of the question.

"I was just leaving." I said with my palms out chest high. My direction changed, I was heading to the guards left, towards the parking garage and pedestrian exit on the other side.

His eyes pinched as he barked a command about staying put, then yanked his radio from his belt. He was law and order through and through. Determination to get me brought out his teeth as he barked again. Not something I wanted to entangle myself with, my only option was escape. I launched into a full sprint. My long legs pumped as my Vans struggled to grab concrete.

Inside the garage, my feet slapped smooth pavement echoing through the concrete cave. The light was dim, the setting sun pushed orange rays around the large pillars. I had entered the northeast corner of the garage and ran towards the middle, assuming there was a southwest exit closer to where I left Alysa. I saw the green exit sign above the door on the other corner of the garage. The jingle of keys was getting closer as I turned to my right to correct my course. If the guard were quick, he would catch me.

I ducked behind a car and crab walked. The jingle slowed then stopped. The radio cracked, he mumbled back. The soles of his boots squeaked with each step. I laid with my chest to the ground and saw his boots thirty feet away. A yellow beam of his flashlight came down as he started pointing it low trying to see under the other cars.

I popped my feet up and under me in a hunched over squat position. I tried walking with my knees thumping my chest to keep below car. The exit was nearing as I heard the keys begin to jingle my way. I broke into a sprint and exploded through the exit.

On the other side of the door was a large sidewalk to my left that was lined with glass windows of empty store fronts except one. That one was the managing office for the condo. A couple of flags fluttered out front of the office, one said *open* the other *for sale*. I walked quickly but not as too, catch the attention to whoever was inside.

Someone was coming out, but I had to just keep moving. The door opened behind me, then the door to the parking garage opened. The jingling keys collided with whoever was coming out.

I dipped behind a pillar.

Apologies came from the young guard. The man exiting was not so cordial. He began berating the guard, belittling the man's profession. The guard apologized once more then got on his radio. The guard's jurisdiction ended; he went back through the garage.

The man began to walk off as well. There was a familiarity in his voice, I had to risk being seen to confirm it.

The low-hanging grey sweatpants confirmed it. Chad clutched the front of his sweatpants as he walked around the corner of the garage, heading back to the waiting Nissan.

I sprinted off towards Alysa. We needed to get to the gym for the deal.

■■

When Alysa had told me the name of her gym was *Beach Body Fitness*, I laughed. When I saw she wasn't, my laugh turned into me clearing my throat then I told her it made sense. She wasn't fond of the name either, but her clients kept telling her they wanted to be beach body ready, she went with the name. The gym was on the second floor of a two-story strip mall along A1A in Ormond Beach. On the first floor was a Vape shop, an accountant, a reality firm, and a surf shop on the end. The best part was the Dunkin Donuts next door.

The building was white with black metal accents. Palm trees with manicured hedges were spaced evenly across the front. She parked the car around back. She started up the stairs while I stopped. She looked back.

"What?"

"I'll watch from next door." I nodded with my head as my hands were shoved in my pockets. It was now dark, and the temperature had dropped ten degrees. I wanted a coffee.

"Oh, right." She smiled and cocked her head to the side, "Enjoy your coffee while I bust the drug dealers." She took two steps at once then looked back, "Alone." She was smiling so I smiled back.

"They'll probably text you to come down and meet them here. I'll be sitting right there watching."

Her smile eased, "I'll leave my phone recording in my pocket. Maybe get them on audio."

"Good idea. Ask about setting up another buy. A steady customer might lower their paranoia."

I sat with my hot cream and sugar coffee at a small table in the window. I could just see the rear deck of Alysa's car, but not the stairwell she would be coming from. Before I could pull my chocolate glazed donut from the bag, the silver Nissan rolled in with bass thumping from the trunk. They backed into the space directly behind the Subaru, which was perfect for me.

The driver's window went down a few inches as smoke bellowed out. My coffee was too hot to sip, so I went to work on the donut. My knee started bouncing with every flash of what could go wrong. *This is what Alysa wanted to be a part of and I wanted her here too.* I repeated a few times.

I finished my donut as Alysa walked across the parking lot to meet them. The sun was totally gone now and there was only one streetlamp to show me what was happening. If I hadn't already known what all the players looked like, I would have had trouble piecing together what I was seeing now.

Alysa leaned near the window but kept her distance. She shook her head a couple times and nodded yes as well. The bass softened then she grabbed the rear door handle. As she got in there was the vaguest of glances to the Dunkin' Donuts.

I stood. The Nissan began to roll forward, the bass thumping once more. Then the Nissan launched. The coffee was still on the table as I blasted out the side door.

It was fifty yards to the parking lot, but by the time I got there the Nissan with Alysa in it was heading south down A1A. I grabbed the handle to the Subaru, locked. I bolted up the stairs to the gym. That door was locked too. Alysa had the keys.

Images of that night Alysa was kidnapped played back in my head as I stood looking south on A1A. Just as before, I was helpless in a parking lot and Alysa was leaving with criminals.

My phone chimed. A text. I pulled it from my pocket. Alysa.

They're taking me to see the king pin!! – Alysa

I held the phone, staring at the text. Who was the King Pin and why had I never heard of him?

Can you escape jump out at the next light. I'll find you. – I text back.

LOL no its cool – Alysa

It wasn't cool with me. Had Alysa become such an adrenaline junky that taking a ride with drug dealers was exciting? I started to text back that she needed to get out of that car when a video came in through our thread. I hit play.

The screen was blurry. Alysa must have held the phone down by her side as she walked up to the Nissan. Then the screen went black as she stuffed the phone in her pocket. The audio was muffled but clear enough.

"Hey girlie." Said a male voice.

"Hey Wes." Alysa said back.

"This is my ride or die boy, Chad."

"Thanks for helping me out on such short notice."

"It's *i-et*. Lucky we had some. The state's been cracking down, easier to get you crack than d'em pills, girlie."

"You think you could get more, like double that on a regular basis?"

The two in the car laughed. Their gangst'a accent was creeping up my spine. I had slapped it out of them the other day in the bar.

The video played on, "Oh damn, girlie, you going into business for yourself?"

"I run a gym; people get hurt." She said.

"Get in, we'll set it up."

Then the video ended. No indication who the king pin was. I had busted a few drug dealers in town over the last two years. A couple of meth cookers who were intentionally mixed it wrong and killed several people across the county. Detective Camp told me later in her round about 'here about this one' way that a meth lab had exploded. The sheriff's department and DEA had been working on the case. I guess they were a little late.

My phone chimed, *Wait there for me. I'll be back soon.* – Alysa

I sent back an 'Ok' and went back into the Dunkin. My coffee was still on the table, but I ordered a fresh one. I sat at the same table with a clear view of Alysa's return. I got my phone out with intentions of texting Billy but stopped before I typed anything. I laid the phone on the table. My fingers drummed along the tabletop, then I started spinning the phone in circles. I opened it to the web browser and started looking at used cars. If I was going to make things right with Billy, it would have to be through actions. If I brought Billy a clunker to restore or an easy flip, he would know I was serious about working together. The right car wouldn't be easy to find. No flooded-out cars, no bent frames and salvage titles. Something with a bad transmission or blown motor would work.

There wasn't much time to hunt for a car. My work with Sanford was far from over. Smitty was still out there and those that were a part of the sex trafficking had not been brought to justice yet. Justice had become a relative term. Finding them and turning them over to the cops meant nothing to me, it was going through motions, doing for doing's sake. The form of justice I was after came with a permeance.

What are you up to? - I typed out the text and stared at it, deleted it then typed it again and sent it to Monique. My knee bounced. Too much caffeine can make me itch from the inside out, problem was I only sipped a little from my cup. Alysa was with drug dealers setting up a big buy and I had to keep my mind occupied.

Binge watching my shows. Why? – Monique was even sweeter after hours than she was during working hours.

Alysa's out busting drug dealers and I'm at Dunkin' waiting for her to get back. - Me

Gotcha. You at the one next to her gym? – Monique

Yeah? – Me

… - the three dots when someone is typing a paragraph or deleting and typing something else and deleting that. It wasn't helping my current nervous condition.

I can be there in five minutes. – Monique. I sent an Ok back and continued bouncing my knee as I watched out the window for a silver Nissan and my new partner.

A blue BMW M3, no less than two years old, pulled up on the other side of the Dunkin'. Monique got out. She stood there, her eyes gazing at the parking lot, then she came in. She was wearing blue jeans and a Brown University sweatshirt. Her shiny black hair was styled in large curls, with no earrings or necklace that I could see.

At the counter she ordered then took a seat across from me.

"You got here fast," I said.

"I live down the street."

"Oh," It seemed I should know that, but I had no memory of ever being told that's where she lived.

"How's the case going?" she said folding her arms under the curves of her breasts. Even her sweatshirt wasn't enough to hide them.

"Well, she's out with a couple drug dealers setting up a big buy. I don't know where they went or how long they'll be." I sipped my coffee thinking I should have got something without caffeine.

An employee stood holding a large iced creamy drink. She looked twelve but was probably nearing the end of high school. "Here you go." She dropped off the drink and walked off. Monique thanked her calling her *hon*.

She wasn't wearing make-up; she didn't need to. Her skin was smooth brown porcelain free of cracks or blemishes. All the facets of her face were rounded, the tip of her nose, cheeks, and chin. She put the straw in her mouth and tasted her drink. She put the drink down and stared at me. Reminding me I was the one that texted her, asked what she was doing, interrupting her evening.

"So, hopefully she'll be back soon." Reasons for texting her weren't registering. Just an urge, something to kill the time while I waited. Something to take my mind off Smitty and Alysa. I didn't expect physical company.

"I thought maybe you text to see if I found him." She said taking a quick sip.

I took a beat. My fingers drummed along the tabletop. I wasn't sure why I had text her. So much had happened this week, I lost track of what day it was. He had been on my mind, always there in a far corner, when I saw a similar face or similar age.

"What have you got?"

"Not much. Actually, I just started searching when you texted." Her soft brown eyes wouldn't break from mine. "Are you sure you want to know?"

I said nothing, remained still. Lost in the week of trying to find Smitty, Muncy and whoever stole our files, I had forgotten about the name I gave her.

"He isn't easy to find." She said filling in my silence. "I've sent a couple of requests and should hear back soon."

"Thanks." Was all I said. Her head was turned slightly to the window, but her eyes were still on me loaded with questions. I didn't offer any answers. I wasn't completely sure why I had asked her to find him. I was a capable PI. There was something to having a buffer, something about having someone else do the digging and getting the results first made her the fire wall to keep my mind guarded from the reality of what I might find at the end of the search.

Monique turned to face me completely, moving her drink to the side of the small table and leaned in. "When I saw the name, I figured it was part of the case, but he's not is he?"

I shrugged.

"You've got to give me more than that, Grimes. Its sealed, I have to call in favors, hell, I have to do favors just to unlock one door only to find another locked door." She leaned back and crossed her arms again, higher this time covering her upper chest.

I sat, heart increasing beats, breath coming from deeper in my belly. Fractured thoughts fell into an empty chasm in my mind, draining all thoughts to a bottom I couldn't find.

Her slender fingers spread out on the table, "I've looked at that file Grimes, I've seen those pictures. I wasn't there like you were. I didn't…" Her face hung over the table once again. I leaned in as she lost the words.

I sat back. My breath held, pricking the inside of my throat. I wanted to clear it, take a breather, and say something but the dam held. The softness retreated from Monique's face as she read the furrowing lines of mine. The wall I continued to build was going up. She wasn't going to make me say it.

My shoulders eased, so did my jaw. I wanted the wall torn down, "All of this must mean something. I need it to be about more than chess moves and photos in a police file. I hope…one day…"

Her hand flipped, palm up, fingers spread. With my eyes, I traced every dark line in her palm reading them as a psychic would. Gravity eased around my arm as my hand floated over the table. It was hovering over hers, awaiting orders to descend.

"I just want to know if he's happy."

She withdrew her hand all the way to her lap. Her eyes twitched until finding a home at the large pane of glass looking out at the dark parking lot.

"I didn't think you cared." She said looking more into the reflection of us together at the table than the glass.

I sipped my coffee. My objective, my feelings on it were

my own.

Monique's brown eyes slowly found mine and held them for a second. "You're a cool one, Grimes. So cold that I'm not sure what to think when you drop something like this in my lap."

"I have feelings in here somewhere." I said with a half a grin as my palm spread out over my chest. She wasn't smiling. Her eyes narrowed.

"I transcribe every one of your after-action reports. And every morning there you are as if the night before never happened. I don't know how you do it."

I exhaled, "Comes with the job." This forced soul searching was not something I was up to doing. I looked away and sipped my coffee.

"You're the coolest man I ever met, and it scares me, Grimes. Sometimes you scare the living shit out of me."

I'm cool? She's the ice queen, or had I misinterpreted it all along. Her lack of eye contact, the quick responses, never smiling, all this time it was because she was afraid of me.

"When Alysa showed interest in you, I warned her, I told her to back off."

"What? Why would you do that?"

Monique held up her hand, "But now I say otherwise. Grimes, you've shown me you are the stable one in all of this justice crusade Willis has us on. I'll find him for you, Grimes. I swear." Monique said.

Headlights flashed in the parking lot. We both turned to watch the Nissan back into the spot it occupied earlier. My hand recoiled and stuffed into my coat pocket. My other hand grabbed my coffee as I stood. She stood as well, and we watched.

Alysa got out, crossed the parking lot, and bounced up

the stairs to the gym. Before she disappeared from sight, the Nissan pulled away.

Monique and I went over together.

Chapter 24

Alysa was standing at the top of the stairs, rolling up on the balls of her feet, suppressing the urge to bounce.

We took the stairs two at a time, getting to the top as Alysa opened the door to the gym. Darkness covered everything. She flipped a few switches bringing fluorescent light down on us and all around us due to the mirrored walls. Along the north wall were one of every machine you needed to work your entire body. In the middle were tractor tires, ship ropes, chains, a kind of adult jungle gym and to the south wall a rack filled with free weights. Up front were six tread mills and stationary bikes. Everything felt evenly spaced out. If a client wanted to lift, they could without the distractions of tires being smashed with sledgehammers.

The three of us walked to the front counter. Alysa opened the tall cooler and grabbed a drink promising to be packed with everything your body needs. I sipped my coffee.

She dropped a Ziploc bag containing two brown pill bottles on the counter. Took a swig then wiped her mouth, "Too easy."

"What have you two gotten into?" Monique poked at the bag, pushing the bottle around watching the pills rolls in the bottle. The fact that she was still with us meant she wanted to know more. Her friendship with Alysa had grown rapidly in the weeks following the April Ward case. Another beautiful face I saw dead next to me. She wasn't murdered by me but because of me, because of the war on crime I waged.

Alysa filled us in on the drive she took. They went to a house off Peninsula Drive in Daytona Beach. It was an average sized house but what made it expensive was that it sat on the river. She didn't catch the house number but knew she could find it from memory. They pulled up and went in. There wasn't much furniture, a couple of black leather couches and a large TV, *very* large, she said. Then Pete introduced himself.

Pete was maybe 5'10'' and thin, but with recently packed on muscle. Being a fitness instructor and gym owner, Alysa knew what she was talking about. She also said he was maybe twenty-five with longish hair cropped short on the sides. His hair was slicked back, not long enough to be a ponytail, so he had a clip holding the short ends.

Alysa didn't mention his clothes, only his looks. Pete wanted to meet her because he ran a hands-on operation. I'm sure he wanted a *very* hands-on operation with Alysa. Before I let it piss me off, I remembered I wanted to be hands-on as well.

"He offered me wine, I declined, but the rest of the conversation was all very professional." She said. I scoffed. "More than you were with me when you hired me as a PI."

I looked down instead of looking at Monique. I could hear Monique's smile.

"He wanted to know what my plan was, how to sell, how to approach clients."

"Clients? So, drug addicts are clients now?" I said.

They both stared at me, upset with my interruption. She went to explain his business model and how much she should charge and expect to make. Then he said if she wanted more, they'll work out better pricing.

"Does he offer a 401K, medical, dental?" I leaned against the counter disgusted with how enamored she seemed with Pete.

Alysa sucked her teeth, "We're gonna bust the guy, Grimes. Wayne needs our help to keep him out of Coopers before someone O.D.'s or worse." She frowned. Her eyes forced a childish shame in my gut.

Pretending to be friends with a girl I wanted to date was dumb. Hiring her to be my partner was dumber.

I stood straight, "Right, for Wayne. I think we have enough here to kick it over to the Sheriff's department. I'll call Camp and see what she recommends."

"Enough for what? There isn't enough here for the cops to go pounding on Pete's door with a warrant. The only thing you have evidence of is that you all bought drugs with intent to sell." Monique shrugged. Alysa looked at me waiting for my counter, my proof that we had proof. Monique was right, all we had was a bag of pills and a muffled recording that never confirmed it was a drug buy.

"Let's take a drive out to Pete's," I said.

"Grimes, this isn't one of those cases." Monique pleaded.

"And get his address. So, we can look him up, find out if he owns the house or who may be funding this operation." I said, as my eyes pinched, and I bit my lip. Monique jabbed the straw in her mouth to keep it occupied.

Alysa jingled her keys. Monique declined, "This isn't the Three Musketeers kind of ride."

"C'mon Moe." Alysa complained.

Moe? In three years, I had never called her Moe, nor had it ever occurred to me.

"When y'all get some real evidence, I'll help you."

We all walked out into the parking lot. Monique said her goodbyes and walked back for the Dunkin' where she left her car. We got into Alysa's Subaru. She put the car in reverse, but held the brake, looking ahead instead of behind her.

"What did she mean, 'not one of those cases'?" She didn't look at me.

Alysa knew what she was asking, she just wanted me to say it. I had come close to spilling it all to her last year when evidence came to light that I had been taking the law into my own bloody hands. A year before that she saw my rath after she had been kidnapped. She had floated the two together for a theory of who I was, but never pressed me to disprove it. Maybe she didn't want to know the truth, maybe she didn't care. I clung to the idea she suppressed it because knowing the truth would drive us apart forever.

Facts were facts, admitting to them or not did not erase them. Burying them only bought me time until the day they were dug up. I was hoping to be dead by then or at least have that marina locker cleaned out and sailing to South America. Tonight, Alysa grabbed a shovel.

I kept my eyes forward, "Sanford has a client list. She was referring to that." I looked behind us, nonverbally telling her to move the car.

She nodded, then drove us out of there without pressing it further.

We took A1A south, past all the big hotels, boardwalk and bandshell. Then cut across through a quiet neighborhood of single-story block homes to Peninsula Drive and continued south. The houses along the river grew in size and style. She slowed the car as we passed Pete's riverfront home. It was unlike the modern mansions on either side with it's single story, 1970's in design with dark wood trim, tan brick façade and a two-car garage. The house number was on the mailbox. I typed it in my phone.

She made a second pass then drove on to the next side street and pulled over.

"What do you think?"

"You sure that's the place?"

She nodded. My mind and my direction weren't made up. The house was simultaneously boring and expensive. For the same price Petey could have a penthouse in tower on the beach. To his credit this was unassuming and out of the way. A young guy dealing drugs and living here on the river was different than any other dealer I had met thus far. I had moved up a few rungs on the ladder with this one. No longer busting up meth labs in trailers or kicking doors of dilapidated houses. To afford this house took moving a lot of product. Taking him out might put a sizable dent in the drug trafficking in this town.

"I think I've had enough stakeouts for the day. Tomorrow I'll go into the office and work up a profile on this guy, see who owns the house. Maybe that will get us somewhere."

"Well, since your shift as a PI is over, how about Coopers for a drink?" Alysa said waggling her eyebrows.

"Don't you ever get sick of that place?" I smiled through the question but was asking sincerely.

"Not when employees get thirty percent off." Alysa started the car and pulled out into the street. My silence meant my acceptance. As much as I wanted to go back to the hotel, crawl under the comforter and watch TV, I couldn't say no when I saw those arched green eyes, and that smile of hers waiting for me to say yes.

Chapter 25

It had been a slow night at Coopers, as most weeknights were. That was part of the reason I liked it there. Charlie was behind the bar. I had three beers and a burger. The beers only made me sleepy; the bar seat was hard with all sharp edges and my burger was over cooked. Conversation was light, Alysa joked with Charlie most of the time, while I watched a rugby game on a TV over the bar. We couldn't talk about the case in the open there and all our other chitchat had been gone through during the stakeout.

When we were done, she hugged me goodbye, hanging on a second longer.

I was in the hotel bed alone by 9:30 pm. Sleep quickly overtook me.

Blades of orange sun sliced through the room. One cut my face in half, ripping me from the dream I was in. Instead of feeling jarred and bitter for being awake, a warm calm wrapped around me softer than the hotel sheets. My dream faded, bits remained, I was in a little banquet hall with wood paneling and a large corkboard with green paper pinned to it. Friendly people with smiles surrounded me, friends, though now awake, their faces were unfamiliar. In the dream they were friends. I drank from a Styrofoam cup and laughed. That was all I needed to feel happy.

I rolled over, on to the opened folder for Smitty, crinkling the few papers it held. Beside the folder, a spiral notebook. Scribbled notes on the stake out covered the page. Lots of arrows crisscross the page and things were circled. My vision was still a little blurry and the room dark enough to keep me from reading any of the notes. I grabbed the TV remote and flipped on a show about two guys who find junk and try to sell it. Then I sat up with a pillow behind me and just watched, stared into the forty-six inches of LED lights.

The faces from the day before scrolled through my mind like the credits at the end of an 80's TV show. Freeze framing on the stars, running their name across the bottom of the screen in *order of appearance*. Tweedledee and Tweedledum as played by Chad and Wes. The Bar Owner, Wayne. Mo played by Monique. Willis Sanford guest starring. Co-starring Alysa and starring Roger Grimes. My character wore a mustache.

After I fleshed out the rest of the characters, I focused on the plot and the plot needed a villain. Smitty was playing the villain. The one-time friend of the star now turned bad. For greed or just to be evil? I stopped writing my little script because it didn't make sense. Smitty in reality had been my friend when he wasn't to Billy. He supported me when I quit being a thief and tried to go straight. He didn't argue and even showed up when I needed him on several occasions putting his reputation and his life on the line, that's more than a friend, that's family. Before that he was there when my mom faded away. As a man I grew to resent that, blaming him for a youth wasted on crime, but again he was there giving me structure even if it was the wrong kind of structure. Now I've cast him as my villain, the arch enemy to the star of my show. I couldn't accept that.

High thread count sheets, memory foam mattress and the soft hum of cold A/C kept me laying thought less, enjoying the best Sanford's money could buy. My stomach growled in rebellion. There was no rush to get to the office, but lying-in bed felt wasteful.

I dressed in jeans and a black pocket tee shirt. After slipping my feet into a pair of Vans, I left the room for another waffle and powered eggs.

An hour later I was showering after working-out in the hotel gym. There wasn't a lot of equipment but enough to work the major muscle groups. I wiped the fog from the large mirror. Water droplets beaded on my skin as I examined the body in the mirror. This mirror was much larger than the small one in my apartment. From ceiling to the vanity with bright lights above revealing a history of pain on my skin.

Puffy pink scar tissue mixed with dull white scar tissue like the brush strokes of a painter across my arms and chest. I was thinner, lighter, than in the past but my muscles looked taught. I rotated my left arm, warming up to throw a pitch, and felt pain. Doctors ask to assign the pain a number. My scale with 1 barely noticeable, 10 being passed out. As the doctor worked on it, I nearly passed out. Last week rotating was an eight. Today, a five.

Old wounds were beginning to heal. What changed? A good night's sleep two days in a row in a comfortable bed. Consistent breakfast. A workout in a gym that wasn't fighting back. And complete silence when I wanted it. I was getting used to hotel life. I extended my stay two more nights.

The emotional upswing was more than the contents of a hotel room. I was alive. Many people had tried to kill me, snub me out, over the last two years and all of them failed. Some are still out there, somewhere someone may come for me but for now I was alive. Yesterday proved that. The subtle nuance of a routine case. Spending the day with Alysa investigating drug dealers for a friend meant something. That desire to work returned, the desire to keep going and bring about the change in this town and in me that I needed was not extinguished yet. No matter if Smitty was in my corner or across the matt in another.

■ ■

The sun was gleaming off the southeast side of the CBR building as I pulled up. The air cool but yellow beams warmed my skin.

Sanford's inner office door was open. I passed the zebra hide and Zulu spears on the wall and walked in to find Monique standing at an open filing cabinet. She wore purple blouse and black slacks. Sanford, dressed in a white shirt and silver vest, sat behind his desk in the burgundy chair slightly rocking staring up out the window. He swiveled to align with me as I entered.

"Good morning, Roger, good morning." Sanford was usually upbeat. So much so, that I usually avoided the office in the mornings. Never going in until I had plenty of coffee in me.

This time I returned a big smile, "Good morning boss." I turned, "And good morning, *Mo*."

Mo shot me a smile with no teeth then shut the cabinet and went back to her desk.

Sanford's smile curved into wonder then returned brighter. "Good to see you so chipper. Solved the crime, caught the crook and got the girl?" He said intertwining his fingers, anticipating a story behind my entrance.

I shrugged in usual form, "I think it's just this weather." Low 70's, dry and sunny was the best feeling in Florida. The kind of day you take a deep breath and let out with a smile. A time of year all natives long for and love to talk about.

Sanford nodded in agreement. "It's just one of those days, isn't it? Feels like everything is alright, alright." He dragged out that last *alright*.

I dropped Smitty's file on the desk and went into detail about what happened. His smile was gone but he said, "We're close. Do you think Smitty will return to Aziz's or has that location been compromised?"

"He's got a plan and he's in the middle of executing it. I have no idea what it is or how we tie into it. I told him FDLE tasked me with finding him. If going back to Aziz's was part of the plan, he more than likely is now on to a contingency plan." I didn't go into examples of jobs I pulled with Smitty. He didn't care to hear about those days.

Monique walked into the room with her cell stuck to her ear and holding a finger in the air, "Huh, yes. Okay go ahead and authorize it. Thank you for the call." She clicked off, then lowered that finger and pointed it at me. She said, "Why are you living at a hotel and billing the company card?"

"I was getting to that." I said then proceeded to tell them what happened to Billy.

After their questions on his health, Sanford said, "Son you've got to check in more."

I agreed and told him that's why I was here.

Monique dropped three files on the desk and pulled up a chair. Sanford poured us all coffees and we dug into the background work Monique performed.

The list was broad. Lobbyists, as Hines was, had hundreds of contacts and dealings across the state and across the country. What we knew from the FDLE investigation narrowed it down to financial ties. Three familiar names kept showing up as officers or board members of companies that fell under a shell company. Sanford made some calls, asked favors. We kept connecting dots, then arguing why they didn't connect until his calls were returned. The shell moved money places we couldn't trace but guessed it was used to finance the human trafficking and the *parties*. Pure evil on display. The most innocent among us conscripted and then used in ways that are unnatural. I saw it firsthand; I saw those in power subjugate the weak. I took their power, showed them what fear was and ended them. There were more out there, and they knew I was coming for them.

Now the wagons were circled. They were trying to end me because they were still scared.

I wasn't going to let that happen and neither were Sanford and Monique.

"Ricardo 'Ricky' Delgado. Peter Danzig and Barbara Lumino." Monique said, laying the paper down. "Two of them murdered, one attempted. The rest I've dug up, the other *players*, have more or less faded away."

"There's no doubt a few more on this list we could check out, but I'm confident these three are the center of power. I've been digging into their financials, and well, they are doing quite well. Maybe not now." Sanford said.

"There has to be one more player, someone we missed. First Muncy, then Delgado, Luminos, and Danzig. Now me," I said.

"What do you mean, you?" Monique crinkled her brow.

"Nothing, don't worry about it. The point is he's calling in markers and eliminating anything in his past," I said. The cloak and dagger game we had been playing with evil was closing in. We were taking out his legs but he was far from dead. Now those closest to him were the targets.

"Why did FDLE drop the ball on this? We handed them over and Newstrom just dragged his feet." I said growing impatient with this late discovery of key figures in this case. For months all we heard was that Florida Department of Law Enforcement was building a case and they had their leads and suspects and this and that and lawyer talk that amounted to smoke and mirrors as far as I could see. It didn't take us long to put together the trail.

Sanford put up a hand to calm my rising rant. "These things take time, and these are very important people."

I started in on a rant once more. "But" Sanford spoke over me. "This *is* unacceptable. They should be way ahead on this. They want us going after this thief Muncy who only *may* have seen some things. It's paper thin, I don't like it."

Monique looked at her watch. "I have to get to court. You boys have fun," She said.

Sanford said nothing as Monique left. I looked at the names while he stared out the window, facing east towards the ocean. The main office door closed behind her. He turned to me.

"I'm sorry Roger."

"What?" He called me Roger and that threw me. I looked up from the file. Sanford's face was long, his hands gripping the back of his leather chair.

"I'm sorry. I want you to know that."

"What are you talking about?"

"On some level we all knew these people were involved. I passed it off, thinking what we did was light a fuse, one that would explode. We'd sit back and watch Delgado, Luminos and Danzig walkout in chains with media microphones in their face and flashbulbs in their eyes.

"Instead, the media is silent, and we're sent on this wild goose chase for an old crook. Maybe Muncy's involved, maybe he's the mastermind." Sanford threw up his hands doubting his own speculation.

I raised an objection, and he raised a palm. "What I'm saying is, I'm sorry for taking my eye off the goal. After all this went down, our next move was meth cookers and rapists. A couple of child molesters in there too, but this," Sanford jabbed a long brown finger into the manila folder, "this is what we should have been focusing on." He swung the chair out from the desk and sat hard.

I sat quietly for a moment. "This isn't over. Not for me, not for you and certainly not for them. You have nothing to apologize for, because what I'm going to do to them will hurt."

Sanford interlocked his fingers, keeping his hands atop the desk, sitting like the President addressing the country from the Oval Office.

"Okay, let's get to work." He said softly.

Computers lined up on the desk. Coke cans and water bottles did too. My spiral notebook was filling up with names and places from the first investigation. Names like Delroy and Milo were circled then circled again with lines extending out to locations like the break-house to the pool hall. Arrows began connecting things. Squiggly lines broke up arrows that didn't follow through. Each line drawn seemed to go to a dead end. Sometimes literally dead. Each person we identified as being connected to the *poker games* either was out of the country, working in the federal government or dead. Sanford ordered food. We ate in silence.

Sanford broke out the Remy cognac. He paced, swirling the drink but not sipping from the glass.

"We're going in circles. Every trail we go down ends with someone dead or so far removed now we can't touch them. What are we missing? Who is calling the shots?"

"When I questioned Danzig he said something about being big and powerful. That brings enemies."

"Or he's just a liar," I said.

Triton Holdings, INC., was at the center. A search of Peter Danzig's address in the tax collector's website showed his house was owned by a holdings group. Digging further, cross checking the multitude of properties owned by Triton, revealed another address. I checked the notes in my phone. It matched that of another Pete I had been looking into. I sifted through my notes, skimming over scribbles, doodles and things scratched out or circled and wished I kept a better system.

Peter Danzig with his dyed brown hair and trimmed eyebrows was an old man. The guy Alysa described was barely twenty-five. The connection between Pete 'DeeZee' and Peter Danzig was easy.

"Peter Danzig's security never thwarted an assassin," I

said.

Sanford looked up from his laptop. "Explain."

I recapped the drug dealers and the stake out for him.

"So, you think he's consolidating power and bankrolling his kid in the drug trade?"

"I think he's following in his father's footsteps. DeeZee, as he wants to be called, is not only selling drugs but he's trying to extort business owners on Beach Street. Coopers, along with a couple others are leasing buildings from this Trident Group. Daddy Danzig has to know about some of this."

"With Delgado and Luminos out of the way, Danzig gets it all." Sanford said sitting up in his plush chair.

"More than that, he eliminates loose ends."

"We get this to Newstrom and they can shift their focus, bring in lil' Pete, get him to spill his guts on dear old daddy." Sanford was smiling again.

"Newstrom might back off Muncy, which will ease things for Smitty. Then I'll walk Muncy in, if he's still alive."

"Grimes, my boy, I think you're shaping up to be one hell of an investigator. I'll call Newstrom." Sanford said and got on the phone.

My phone chimed with a text from Billy checking in on me. I texted back I was good and reminded him I would follow through with my promise to get back into flipping cars and restoration work. He sent back a thumbs up.

"I left a message. We'll see what he says when he calls back." Sanford said.

"I think I should go pay this Pete DeeZee a visit."

"Deezee?"

The voice came from behind me. I spun to find Agent Alvarez standing there, big grin, "Sounds like some kinda rapper." He walked into the office paying no attention to the view or the fancy marble bar, more like he had been there several times before. He stood in between me and the chair next to me. His hands on his hips pulling open his light grey sport coat. No tie, just a tight-fitting cobalt blue button down tucked into grey slacks and that gun and badge on his hip.

His smile faded in the silent reception. He took a seat. Three pairs of eyes darted from one to the other.

Finally, Sanford broke the standoff, "Any luck with Muncy?"

"I was going to ask you two the same thing." He looked around at the mess of coke cans and scribbled notes.

"No clue. He's probably skipped town. Took a boat to the Virgin Islands or someplace," I said.

That toothy smile broke across the agent's smooth complected face. His finger wagged at me, "No, no, no. He's still in town."

"What makes you so sure? Have you seen him?" Sanford asked.

"Cut the shit you two. Erich Schmidt has Muncy hidden some place."

Sanford's eyebrows flexed as he connected the name. I wasn't used to hearing Smitty called Schmidt either. How a kid with German lineage got mixed up with an Italian mob must be a good story. Dutch Schultz came to mind, but he was no friend to the Italians, and it didn't end well for the gangster.

"I only know where he was. He isn't there now and probably won't be back."

"What makes you so sure?" Alvarez leaned forward resting his elbows on knees turned towards me.

"Because he isn't stupid."

"Right," He leaned back in his chair, running the palms of his hands over his slacks. The two of us playing stupid with each other wasn't working for him. The young agent was sharp and that I in F-B-I was something I might suck at, but he didn't. I wasn't a complete ghost in this town. No one in Smitty's old crew, those of the round table at Tully's, would say a word to Alvarez but if he found the right local cop, he might get some place. My friend, Detective Rhoshanda Camp, doesn't know the whole story with Smitty and I but she suspects enough to not say anything. Assuming our friendship was as tight as I hoped. It was time to give the agent a bone or he would go dig up one of his own.

I got up and went to the bar. I grabbed a can of coke, offered the two men a beverage, which they declined, then I sat. "I saw Smitty the other day, Wednesday I guess it was. He wasn't with Muncy and wouldn't tell me where or *if*, he knew where Muncy is." I popped the can and sucked back the soda.

"And what, you just walked away?"

I laughed at the accuracy of what he just said. "Pretty much. The guy is no snitch. He did ten years in a hard prison because he refused to rat."

"What is this *Goodfellas*?" He looked like he wanted to spit. I wanted to slap his face then throw him out of the seventh-floor window. "He tells you to get lost and you do nothing?"

"He pulled a gun on me."

"I have a few problems with your story. One, you should have called me right away. Two, you're not someone to give up just because you're told no. You're a lot harder man than this old timer. I've read the file. You saw a gun fight go down. Then chased the guy but lost him. That's what happened, right? The story makes you sound pretty sure of yourself. I've done my own digging, you see a lot of violent things happen, don't you Grimes."

I sipped my coke. Sanford leaned back and interlocked his fingers, his chin tucked, waiting for him to finish.

He continued, "You're always there just *after* someone dies. You're either the world's worst superhero or a liar."

"Back off, Alvarez." Sanford said coolly from across the desk.

"You don't fool me, Grimes. Maybe the local cops look the other way because you help close cases, but I know. I know who you truly are."

The coke bubbled in my stomach. My throat closed and I couldn't take another sip. I set it on the desk avoiding eye contact with Alvarez. He wanted a reaction, he wanted anger. He wanted to see something in me.

"Eight men dead and one woman, shot point blank while she was on her back. That's one sick son-of-a-bitch. And you chased him. Get a good look?"

"No. What does this have—"

"Really? You didn't look into his eyes, see the rage, or were they icy, sending a chill through you when you saw them? I think maybe you froze."

"No—"

"I think you did; I think you see those ice-cold eyes every time you look in the mirror, Grimes."

"I said back off, now back off damn it!" Sanford cussed, he never cussed. "Are you going someplace with this monologue Agent Alvarez? Is Roger Grimes under investigation? Last I checked with FDLE, they didn't suspect Mr. Grimes of anything."

"No sir." Alvarez settled back in the chair. "I just wanted to know if Grimes knew a killer when he saw one."

I looked at Alvarez then. His upper lip bubbled with perspiration. He ran a hand over the lock of black hair that had fallen in his eyes. That's when I saw it. A flash of darkness, complete blackness covered his eyes. Fire danced around them but at the center an open void. He was right, I had seen the eyes of a killer in so many of the ones I killed. I never saw that in me.

I took my coke and sipped it, then let out an exaggerated *aahhh.* I wasn't going to let this Fed get to me.

"I apologize." Alvarez turned to me, "We're in this deep and it's only going to get deeper. I just wanted to know who I was dealing with." He smiled and straightened out his suit coat.

"Okay," Sanford said, trying to read my mind. "Where were we?"

"I still think Smitty, as you call him, is our best bet. Maybe the two if us can take another run at him? This badge opens more than doors, it opens mouths too." He smiled.

I couldn't look at Sanford, our eyes would do too much talking if Alvarez, a self-proclaimed expert at reading eyes, saw us. He would know we thought he was a little crazy. At this point I was running out of options. We made progress with the Triton Group, but Muncy was still the key to all of it. His testimony seemed the only sure thing to get anyone to prison.

"How about we use that badge and go talk to anyone at the last of the Trident Group? Maybe Muncy isn't running from them but being hidden by them."

"I like your thinking, Grimes. If that's true, Muncy could be long gone." Sanford said.

"We'll just have to find out."

Sanford pulled up the information on Trident and started making calls. He made three calls pretending to be three different people with their own reasons for calling. The best he got was a meeting scheduled for two weeks from now. He sat back with his fingers interlocked. Then he popped up and made one more call. When he clicked off, he said, "Sorry, no meeting." He took his glasses off to rub his eyes. "My guy said Danzig onsite all day."

"The new building off Beach Street?"

Sanford nodded, "Glad I got the southeast facing office, so I don't have to look at that giant tsunami every day."

Up until they broke ground last year, the CBR office we were in was the tallest building on the mainland. Taller hotels lined the beach across the river, but around here this was unobstructed views. Sanford came back disgusted from a city hall meeting one night after seeing the plans. All he said was a monstrous eyesore was going up a few blocks away.

Alvarez stood up, "Well, let's just go down there and push our way in."

"Don't you have rules and procedures for that?"

"You heard the man," he pointed to Sanford, "Two weeks out for an appointment. Muncy, if he's still in town, won't be in two weeks. We don't have the time."

I looked to Sanford and shrugged, it worked for me. I was never one to set appointments. I preferred just dropping by and kicking in a door or two if needed.

Chapter 26

I convinced Alvarez to take his Crown Vic. There was no need to direct Alvarez the few blocks to the new Trident building. He simply had to look up at a large blue mirrored building, reaching up ten stories in a curve that looked like a giant wave about to crash on downtown.

"Easy enough." He said as the asphalt gave way to sand and gravel of the construction site. A few guys in hard hats gave us the eye but being in a white Crown Vic with black steel wheels told everyone who we were.

With the car parked along a couple of pickup trucks, we made our way to the closest worker. A squat guy in an orange vest and yellow hardhat. He was carrying a stack of 2x4's over one shoulder.

"Donde el jeffe?" Alvarez said like a gringo on vacation in Mexico.

The guy paused. He looked us both over then said, "What?"

"El jeffe, your boss." Alvarez waved his hands hoping the extra movement would cross the language barrier.

"Speak English, dude, this is America." He laughed then shouted, "Andele, andele arriba." And kicked his legs like he was about to run off. His laughter wheezed in his throat, and he almost lost the lumber load over his shoulder.

I couldn't hold back my laughter. Alvarez wasn't laughing. His eyes narrowed, "Tell us where we can find the guy in charge."

The worker slowed his laughing, "He's over there," Pointing to the small beige trailer. "Big black dude. Onija." As the worker walked off, he shouted in Spanish to a few other workers, and they all laughed.

Alvarez didn't say a word until we were in the trailer. The10x20 trailer was cramped with a drafting table taking up most of the middle of the room. Then a series of metal lockers and finally two desks filled in the back corners. Every flat surface was covered in large white rolls of plans.

Onija was tall and muscular with a shaved head and well-shaped beard. He wore a plaid shirt tucked into khakis. An air-conditioner hummed above his head.

"Can I help you?" He said with a continental African accent. He didn't look up from the plans laid out on the table.

"Mr. Onija," I said. "Are you the man in charge here?"

"Yes, I am the lead engineer."

"We'd like a word with Danzig and Delgado." Alvarez said with his badge out.

Onija looked up, studied the badge then rolled up the plans. "I was just headed up to see them. You'll need a hard hat, no exceptions." He grabbed a yellow hat for himself then walked to a tall locker and pulled two more for us.

Behind all the blue glass, the interior was still just an iron skeleton. Electrical and plumbing were being run as the interior wall framing was just beginning. Tradesmen moved about carrying the tools and materials to identify their trade.

We took a freight elevator all the way to the top floor. The wind carried a low whirl along with echoes of metal clanging below. The framing was complete on the top floor leaving a maze of aluminum jail cells. We came to a clearing and found more tables with more plans on them.

"Mr. Danzig," Onija said as we approached.

Danizg looked up from under a gold mirrored hard hat. He wore a silvery grey suit, baby blue tie loosened and tucked between the third and fourth button on his white shirt.

The red colored pencil he held was tucked behind his ear. Behind him stood Mr. Security we met the other night, dressed in the same black unzippered jacket with a tight-fitting black tee shirt under it. Shorter than I was and husky from years of working out. The typical professional security type. I had trained with several of them at some of the schools Smitty sent Billy and I to.

Mr. Security did a quick analysist of both of us. Alvarez in a suit minus the tie and me in a tee shirt and jeans, Vans, not work boots. His eyes darted between us, trying to figure us out before we got within twenty feet of Danzig. I caught most of the glare.

"These men would like to see you. I have the updates," Onija held out a rolled-up set of plans, "And will take them to the foreman." He nodded and walked off.

Danzig didn't move, instead he looked calmly at us both as if we were waiting together at a bus stop.

"Mr. Danzig," Alvarez said.

It took him a moment to reply, "Yes, what can I do for you Agent Alvarez?" His voice held no accent and was soft, not librarian soft, more museum tour guide.

"Good memory," he said lowering the badge he had at the ready, "And this is Roger Grimes."

Danzig's eyes continued a steady hold on us both, no change, no flash, no flick of his shaved brows. Our introduction meant nothing to him. According to Newstrom, Danzig been questioned two years ago. I assumed my name would come up. Evidently it didn't.

"Yes." Was all he said. Mr. Security perked up, stepping a little closer.

Danzig paid the man no attention. "How can I be of assistance?"

"We're looking for a man named Harold Muncy," I said.

The old man's blank stare held. "We know he was connected to a former employee of yours, Chloe Hines." Her name echoed in my ears as I said it.

He pressed a finger to his lips and nodded. "Yes, I remember when she worked here, but that was years ago. Tragic how she turned out." He tapped his finger against his lip, "Grimes? Yes, I believe you found her. Am I right?"

I nodded. He knew I had; he probably knew I killed her. Men like him never let details escape him.

"If it's employee files you're looking for, you'll have to call someone in human resources. I don't handle those matters." Danzig held his hands together, draping them at his waist.

"Could you make that call? We've tried and no one returns ours." I smiled.

His eyes narrowed then, a slight arch that smoothed out. Enough to keep pressure on him.

"Maybe just tell us what you remember of Chloe?" Alvarez said.

Danzig folded his arms across his chest. "She was a nice girl. Because of whom her father is, was, I hired her as part of my real estate team. Soon, I heard rumors, but those were just rumors." He waved an open hand past his face as if shoeing a fly.

"No, they weren't just rumors," I said. "How well did you know Gregg Hines?"

"Gregg," he said.

"Was that a question?" I said with a slight grin trying to form.

"No, no it wasn't." Danzig's pale brown eyes swayed from mine. When they came back, his fingers pulled his tie from between the buttons on his shirt. He smoothed it and said, "I knew Gregg. We ran in the same circles."

"Just what kind of circles, Danzig?" Alvarez said.

"Gregg was the kind of guy who knew a guy and so one and that's how buildings like this get approved." He fanned his hands at the wonder of his own making.

"You gotta do better than that, Danzig." Alvarez pressed him as he stepped closer to the businessman.

"Actually, I don't."

Mr. Security stepped in between us, blocking all we could see of Danzig. Danzig did not stay hidden long. He stepped to the side of his hired protection and said, "Let's not dance around the grit. Gregg Hines knew how to throw a party. It's how he got his *business* done.

"And you didn't mind how he did his business, maybe you even enjoyed it," I said.

"I leveraged it. I'm not proud of it and I'm not morally superior, I just know how to pull levers to get things done." Danzig's lip curled at the corners as it beaded with tiny crystals of sweat. A glint in his eye gave away too much.

"Got rid of anyone in the way you is getting things done," I said.

"Roger Grimes, the PI. The PI that cracked the sex trafficking ring right here in Daytona Beach. What have you done since?" Danzig said backing up behind his hired help.

"You know exactly what I've been doing, and I've been doing a good job of it. And I'm not done."

"Though there has been *limited* press, I've kept up with the case. Seems like those associated with it are dropping like flies." Danzig's frown started to curl up.

"It *seems*, no one is safe."

Mr. Security stepped forward with a hand raised. "You can go."

"Out of my way." Alverez stepped up.

"Jacobs is head of my security."

Alvarez pressed, Jacobs shoved, "Close enough." Still Alvarez advanced. Jacobs grabbed Alvarez's shoulder. Alvarez twisted his arm locking it with Jacobs. Alvarez threw a wide right that Jacobs easily grabbed. Then the FBI agent flipped his head back causing the hard hat to fall off as he head-butted Jacobs in the face just below the guard's eye. Jacobs staggard back seeing stars.

Alvarez was quick to compose himself. Danzig, however, lost his cool. "Enough!"

Two more men in black tee shirts appeared.

Jacobs shook his head and touched the puffy pink lump under his right eye. The skin was split, and a trickle of blood descended his cheek.

"Assaulting a federal agent is a pretty serious charge." Alvarez said.

Danzig's eyes ignited. His face reddened as he exclaimed, "My lawyer will reign fire down on your department head and I think you know how that will go for you. Next time you need to speak with me go through my lawyer or get a warrant."

"Three o'clock works for us," I said.

"What?" Danzig crinkled his brow.

"The next time we need to speak to you will be at three o'clock."

"Get out of my building." Danzig shouted.

We backed out of there all the way to the elevator. As the doors closed, I said to Alvarez, "Looked like a lot of security for a businessman."

"Depends on what your business is," he said.

I nodded. I punched out a text to Ben asking him to check into the security firm Danzig hired.

Back on the ground, Alvarez said he was hungry and wanted to go to Coopers. It was only a few blocks away and by the time we got there Sanford was on the phone. He said Newstrom had called him and barked about harassing Danzig. He said Danzig and the rest of Trident had been cleared. Also, Danzig's lawyer said the afternoon meeting was off.

"I didn't know *Newsome* could get so loud. Tell Alvarez to expect a call too from his superiors." Sanford laughed and hung up. He didn't care about the heated State Attorney. He liked the direction we were taking and the more high-ups it rattled the better position we were in.

I told Alvarez. He pulled his cell and there was a missed call. He listened. Then said, "Same here."

"We rattled Danzig. Now we get Muncy and Danzig's dirty laundry is getting aired."

Alvarez nodded say, "We can. Or we can have a drink." Then he grabbed the worn brass handle on the large wooden door to Coopers.

Inside, Alysa and her trainee were both tying on black aprons over tight khaki shorts. The lunch rush hadn't arrived yet leaving us the whole place to ourselves for now. Not even the bartender had come on shift yet.

The trainee looked over and said, "Hi Daniel."

Alvarez hurried past me and said something to her in a low tone. She giggled and Alysa rolled her eyes. I didn't hear it, but body language was enough to tell me what he said.

"Sit in my section." Alysa said, guiding me away from the bar.

"I guess I know what he did the other night I left him here." I said as I scooted into a booth.

She sat next to me and put her feet up on the bench seat across. "Yeah, made quite the impression on our oh so young impressionable Emma."

"And how old is Emma?"

"Nineteen. Old enough to make her own mistakes."

"I don't know. Alvarez seems like an alright guy and hard to top being an FBI Agent."

"Maybe, but he's still too old. What is he thirty-five?"

I looked over at the door where we left the two love birds chirping at each other. "Nah, thirty tops."

"I don't know about that. He dyes his hair for starters."

I rubbed my temple where I had seen a couple of my own silvery hairs the other day before I buzzed my head for the week. "Premature grey happens."

"Not to every guy." Alysa smiled and asked what I was drinking. I ordered a Cigar City Jai Alai and called over to Alvarez for his order. He said coke.

Alvarez came to the table when Alysa dropped off the drinks.

"You've got some quick moves." I said taking a sip of my beer.

"Emma's a hottie." he said more with his eyebrows than his words.

"I meant the security guard back there, but her too."

"I don't wait two years to get what I want, Grimes." Alvarez jammed an elbow in my side.

"Shit, everyone's on my back about that." I laughed as my eyes drifted over to the server's station and Alyssa as she punched an order into the computer. Had it been two years that we formally introduced ourselves? It was the start of a case, one by my own choosing. My friend was sick with drugs, and I thought I had the cure. Believing in second chances got him dead. I stopped giving second chances that day.

Alvarez ordered food and talked about what we needed to do next. He liked the idea of going after the assassin, convinced he would strike again. I didn't tell him I knew the assassin's next target. I was bait in my own trap.

"Isn't there something you can do in an official capacity to go around Newstrom and put some heat on Danzig," I said.

"I could go up to the Jacksonville office and see about getting some kind of warrant. That takes a lot of time. Have you ever worked with the FBI on any other cases?" He stuck a French fry in his mouth.

"No."

"Yeah, nothing like in the movies. Shit takes time, a lot of time. I think we're close though. Muncy is still in town and us rattling Danzig like that might shake something loose."

Alvarez exchanged smiles with Emma. He was more interested in talking about her than the case. After one beer, I was ready to head back to the hotel for a nap. Alysa was too busy to make time for me. The more time we spent in friend land the more likely we were to be trapped there. I left Alvarez to flirt with Emma and walked the two blocks to my Scout. Sitting, letting the Scout warm, I decided instead to go by Billy's and see if he wanted me to haul out furniture that had been trashed the other night.

Two days of silence between us felt like weeks. As I drove over, I tried to picture my life in the future we laid out. I meant what I said to Billy about flipping cars again. Distancing myself from Sanford, and eventually quitting being a PI altogether seemed like the best strategy to keep those around me safe and to keep myself alive. He was the best mechanic in town, but not the best at running a business. I probably wasn't either but together we'd fumble our way through.

At the shop all the bay doors were down, and the office door locked. Only the Camaro I had borrowed days earlier was in the lot. The rest were empty spots with nothing but oil stains to let anyone know this was a garage. I let myself in. The office lights were out. My voice echoed in the shop bays. I went upstairs and found the room just as bare as the day I moved in. I sat with my back against the unpainted drywall. My phone was in my hand. The words weren't there so I didn't call him. I skimmed a couple used car apps to see what was on the market. Buying a good project would prove I was ready to work with him. Nothing caught my eye, an '80 El Camino was the best option. Rusted bed, blown stock 305 ci motor wasn't much to get excited about.

The game I used to play with Tab was still on my phone and I opened it. My high score was still there. It was Tab's high score. He said the way I played; I'd never unlock new levels, so he beat some levels for me. I tapped the screen and gave it a go. The silly wonky saxophone music instantly took me back to us sitting on the couch, one hand on the phone, the other in a Pringles can. Those nights started with a text from Chloe asking if she could ask me a question and finished with never-ending YouTube fail videos. In between Tab and I would have a set menu of chicken nuggets, Pringles and Dr. Pepper. To wind down, I'd turn off the TV and let him play the game on my phone.

I smiled as my character wiped out. The music played on, but I didn't start a new game. Tab was out there somewhere, playing whatever new game came out to replace the old one. My life had changed since those days on the couch. At times during those nights, I couldn't wait for him, his constant questions, and the continuous video game music to go away. Quiet, solace was all I wanted. Sitting in the empty apartment with all the alone time I needed, I didn't want any of it.

Billy's house was a quick drive from the shop. He lived in Holly Hill near the twin condo towers I had followed the drug dealers to. The house was from the early 1920's in a Mediterranean Revival meets bungalow style with thick white plaster walls and a red tiled roof. The neighborhood had been a little rougher twenty years ago when he bought. It wasn't that much better but signs of regentrification were all around. Nicer, newer cars in driveways. Kids riding bikes. Trimmed trees and watered lawns now lined the street.

The garage door was down and the house looked dark as I pulled in over the cracked concrete drive. I knocked on the heavy wooden front door. There was no answer. At the back of the house, it was one of a dozen homes in the Daytona area with basements.

I stood at the top of red painted concrete stairs with grey gouges and scratches from the last 100 years. At the bottom, a thin horizontal beam of light pushed from the seams of the basement door.

The drums kicked and the guitar shredded on the other side of the door. He had a Metallica album playing, original vinyl. I didn't know the song name, but it was probably from an earlier album, something that took Billy back to high school. He would be three beers in by now.

After I knocked the music went down. I knocked again and he swung the door open. A beer in one hand and a .357 in the other. His black braid was out, and he wore a white undershirt with appropriate stains. His belly was a little more swollen than usual and his jeans needed a belt. When he saw it was me, he lowered the pistol.

"Howdy." he said and shuffled into the room. He went to the mini fridge and grabbed a can of High Life.

I took a sip of beer and a seat on the gold velvet couch. The dehumidifier wasn't on and with the cooler weather lately neither was the A/C. It felt like I was breathing through a sweaty sock.

Billy mouthed the lyrics along with lead singer James Hetfield then flopped down beside me. I looked around for all the empty beer cans but there weren't any.

"Delivered the Mustang today," He said.

"That's awesome."

"Fuck yeah, made thirteen grand on that build. I figured I'd take the rest of the day off. Tomorrow too, maybe."

"You earned it." I raised the gold can then drank the golden liquid.

He did the same, drinking the can to a finish and got up for another. He sat back down, popped the can and said, "Thanks brother."

I nodded, though wasn't sure why.

"If you hadn't helped me out with the 'stang the other night, wouldn't 've been able to deliver it early. That made the customer super happy. So, cheers man." He clanked his can into mine.

"I should thank you. I remembered how much I like wrenching. And how good we are when we work together." I drank back the beer letting the carbonation fill my insides as the alcohol filled my blood. Just like old times except we were doing it legally. I still had a little grime under my nails and a few nicks on my forearms from wrenching. These were bruises I to be proud of, not hide and regret.

"You find that Muncy asshole yet?"

His question took me out of my contentment and brought be down to my current reality.

"Not yet. What a mess this week has been."

"Hey, if you need to crash at the shop, it's cool."

"No, thanks. It's good for me to get out of there. I need to find my own place, some place I can have a dog." I finished the can and helped myself to another. The sense of time and space since we last drank cheap beer in the basement, compressed. Inside, I was warm with a little bit of excitement. That knot in my chest was gone and I didn't want to let any of the things that tie it up back in.

"You should totally get a dog. Hell, bring him by the shop and make him a real shop dog." Billy went over to the record player and turned up the volume, "This guy's the greatest." He said as he air-guitared alongside lead guitarist, Kirk Hammett.

When the guitar solo was done, the song soon switched to a slower tempo. The mood dulled and I didn't help by bringing up what Smitty did to me.

"He pulled a gun on you?" Billy's eyes were large as his jaw slacked.

"Yep. I don't know what to do. After that, I'm ready to just turn him over to the cops. I know Ruben and De Carlo know where he is."

"Shit. Shit man, that sucks. You think you know somebody." He slurped his beer.

"I guess I don't know Erich Schmidt as well as I thought."

"Ruben, De Carlo and Smitty. The knights of the sons-of-bitches table. Man, screw them and their old tough guy bullshit. You ought'ta go in there, to that booth, and burn that bitch down." Billy was on a roll, feeling twice as good as me and wasn't going to let my problems bring him down. I didn't want that either.

"Special Agent Alvarez seems like an all-right guy. I think he'll find Muncy, and I can put all this behind me. I'm ready. Ready to get on with my life, ready to start flipping cars."

"Yeah," Billy said. His energy was waning. He pulled his long hair back then forward over his shoulders. "It doesn't make a lick ah sense. Smitty's a good guy." He looked at me, "If he says he's got it under control you can rely on that." He stood up with a wobble.

"So I shouldn't burn the booth down?" I laughed.

Billy nodded then said, "Feel free to stay, crash here if you need to, but I'm going up stairs, turning on the Mecum Auto Auction and taking a well-deserved siesta."

He left me sitting on the couch listening to Metallica. I turned off the record player and headed for my hotel.

As I pulled in the parking lot of the hotel, my phone wrang, drowning out the sound of my growling stomach. The number was blocked. I held it trying to decide if I wanted to answer it or wait until after I ate.

The call ended and started immediately again.

"Yeah,"

"Grimes?"

"Yep,"

"This is Sargent Gibson, FDLE." He said like I had never met him or was previously clueless to his title. "We need to talk."

I waited.

"Can you hear me?" He said sincerely wondering if the connection was bad.

"I can, what do you want to talk about?"

"Let's cut the shit. Time to get serious here."

I didn't say anything. This had never been a joke to me. My life has been in everyone else's hands except mine since all this started. Every day there is a battle of evils, those in the outside world and the ones that remain with me.

Monique's words laid heavily on me. I was on the verge of becoming a monster. Gibson thinks I hold out to get one up on him, staying ahead of the law. It was time for another way, I had to take it.

"Grimes, I've been a cop a long time. As a detective my job is to put clues together, add them up. Some things about this case, all of this dumpster fire of a case just aren't adding up. Now, look, you've seen more of this from the inside, things I just aren't putting together." Gibson let out a breath. He was on the move, to his car or down a hallway getting away from open ears.

"Gibson, I'm ready to do what needs to be done to put all this behind me," I said. He started to speak but I cut him off. "Believe it or not, I've been working on this. As it turns out, people I thought I trusted, and had my back, are actively working against me."

"That's why I'm calling. I've been warning you for months about your *shadow*." There was static on his end. I pictured him covering the phone.

"You were right. I think whoever has been shadowing me is also who killed Delgado and Luminos."

"There are things going on that don't add up, Grimes. One plus one aint two anymore. I can't talk here. Where can we meet?"

Pressure built in my head as my stomach churned acid in search of digestible material. I wanted to order some wings or a sub or both and on a full belly take a nap.

"I'll meet you in the lobby of the Chateau La Page." I said thinking of the peanut butter crackers still in the room.

"Okay, what the hell is that French?"

"A hotel on A1A."

"Gotcha."

Chapter 27

I stepped off the elevator into the long hotel hallway. Special Agent Alvarez was leaning against the door to my room. The elevator doors shut behind me, trapping me in the hall with the FBI.

He waved and even from thirty yards I could see his white teeth. We met halfway to my room.

"I think I might have something on Muncy. He's still in the area alright." Alvarez was still dressed in his light grey suit but had switched to a black button-down shirt.

"Gibson is on his way over with information on our assassin." I turned back towards the elevator.

"Gibson? Where are you headed?" His smile was broad as he pounded a fist into his palm.

"There's fresh coffee in the lobby. We can discuss it there."

"What if someone overhears us? We should meet in your room." He said catching up behind me. "I'll text him to meet us in the room." Gibson said already on it with his phone.

"I'm not worried about it." I said getting on the elevator.

We sat on curved grey cloth chairs with a small end table between us. I had a hot coffee with cream and sugar in a paper cup. Alvarez bought a coke from the vending machine. Gibson was late. Alvarez sat cross legged, bouncing the top leg on the bottom playing on his phone. I said nothing, sipping my coffee and watching his eyes. He looked over his shoulder a couple times and then at all four of the security cameras in the lobby.

"So, where's Muncy," I said.

"Are you familiar with any of Smitty's old crew," he said. His legs uncrossed and he sat with his elbows on his knees.

I nodded, no point in lying. I was ready to come clean on all of it.

"I think they're actively hiding Muncy. Probably worried he will implicate them."

"And who is them?"

Alvarez smirked, "C'mon Grimes, the crew, the old guys. You're gonna make me name names? Roman De Carlo, Ruben Rothstein, and your pal Smitty."

"You know this how?"

"I talked to the local PD and they put me in touch with a snitch. He said –"

"Who's the snitch?"

"C'mon Grimes. You're a little too close to this one."

We sat saying nothing for a couple minutes. Pressed now with a choice, I wasn't ready to completely cut Smitty loose. Billy renewed trust in the old gangster I had lost after watching him throw my life away. I played back what I saw and what Smitty had said to me. There was a plan in motion, and I had fumbled my way into it. There was still a thread of hope he knew what he was doing. I would have to hold onto that thread and hope it didn't completely unravel for me.

Alvarez stood up, "Tell Gibson hello, but I want to follow this lead. Call when it's over and catch me up. Maybe we can meet at Coopers." He smiled.

I laughed, "The waitress." I shook my head. His finger and thumb came out like a gun, and he fired it.

"Nailed it." He laughed as he strutted off.

The coffee only made my angry stomach angrier. I went to the desk and asked if they had food. The clerk pointed at some cookies in a basket. It would have to do.

The cookies made me nauseous enough to keep the hunger away as I waited. After half an hour, I tried calling Gibson's phone. No answer. I used my phone to go through a food delivery app and ordered ten Teriyaki garlic wings, half a rack of ribs and fries from a restaurant five minutes away. *Damn that Gibson.*

Back up to the front desk, I told the clerk a police detective was supposed to meet me. She said she would ring the room. I told her if I didn't answer it was okay to send him up. I wanted that nap.

Three hours later, my head was buried under a pillow as muffled voices talked about paint samples. *Was Billy having the apartment painted? The whole shop? Why not do it himself?*

I sat confused, rubbing my eyes. As the blurry waves smoothed across the TV, some guy in a flannel shirt was hosting a home makeover show. Tacky fingers skidded over my face. Imbedded under my nails was maroon sauce. A foam food container filled with bird bones crunched under my elbow as I rolled reaching for my phone on the nightstand. A dozen missed calls. It was just after seven pm.

After a shower, my fingers were clean enough to dial some of the numbers back. The only one I recognized was Sanford.

"Tell me you got one hell of an alibi." Sanford's words dragged compared to his usual machinegun volley.

"Um, what?" Maybe I was still asleep. In fact, I better still be dreaming. Why would I need an alibi?

"Uh-oh. You haven't spoken to anyone? Not a single person?" He said picking up speed.

"Not since Agent Alvarez left here, I don't know, four hours ago, I guess."

"Agent Alvarez, your hotel about three."

I didn't know if that was a question or if he was just saying so we were both clear.

"Yeah," I put him on speaker and looked back through my missed calls. Most were blocked numbers. A couple were from an area code I recognized as the Tallahassee area.

"They found him," I said.

"Yes, behind a Publix on beachside."

"Shit." That meant Muncy was dead and the evil sick sons-of-bitches that partook in the rape of children would be free not just from prison but worry, shame and fear. Newstrom warned me my testimony wouldn't be enough to take them all down. They won, they got Muncy before he got them. A war I wanted to put behind me was catching fire again. The elite had shown their power and escaped justice, but they couldn't escape me.

"Without Muncy this whole case falls apart. I won't let them walk away," I said.

"Muncy? No, no, no Grimes. Lieutenant Gibson's been murdered, and they found a gun."

The phone slipped from my hand and disappeared into the comforter. My eyes held focus, but I couldn't see. Gibson murdered. Gibson murdered and they found a gun. My *stolen* gun? Or the gun I left in the back of Smitty's car? I hadn't carried a gun in months and now I've lost two of them. The thoughts cycled a few times, his words repeating, *Gibson's been murdered, Gibson's been murdered.* Gibson wanted to meet with me. I was going to fully cooperate; I was going to give up Smitty and end a lifelong relationship with the only family I had left. It was too late for that now. The frame was set. Was Alvarez right and they were all working against me?

The tail, the talk of an assassin, I was the target, but not for murder, for a frame up. Like attracts like and I had attracted a killer. Someone who studied my movements and knew my past. To kill me outright, to shoot me in the street, would be too easy. This killer wanted me to suffer, to fry like an ant under a magnify glass. Either by his hands or the State. That's why my gun had been stolen. It wasn't random, all of this had been planned from the beginning. As soon as Sanford and I pointed a finger at Danzig he pointed back, but his with a hand holding all the cards.

Sanford's voice squeaked from the comforter.

I picked up the phone, "Yeah, I'm still here. I just don't get it. What the hell happened?"

"Newstrom wants to talk to you bad. Real bad. You better get to my office ASAP before they pick you up without me present."

"I don't understand. Why are they looking at me?" I said as I stood and started looking for my shoes. Sanford was right, I needed to get to his office. PD had probably already been to Billy's and the last three of my known addresses. It wouldn't be long before they found me here.

"Newstrom is convinced. It was no secret Gibson had an eye on you."

I had my shoes on but no pants. Damn it. I kicked them off and found my pants. "Yeah, I guess. Gibson called, said he had important information he didn't want to discuss on the phone. I told him to meet me here. If he GPS'd my hotel they should know by now that's where he was headed."

"Hurry your ass up Grimes."

"Walking out now." I said and closed the hotel door behind me.

My phone wrang the entire drive to Sanford's office. Newstrom was already there when I walked in. The State Attorney wasn't alone. He had two plain clothes detectives and two State Troopers with him. All four cops looked like they wanted to beat me in ways only retired cops from forty years ago knew how to do. All that meat I had eaten earlier was pounding my stomach like the surf over rocks. I wanted the hunger back over this sloshing lump of gurgling protein.

"Look, that don't mean squat." Sanford said as I entered. Everything went silent. Five pairs of state funded eyes raked over me.

"Cuff him and bag those hands." Newstrom said pointing a long finger at me.

All seven of us erupted into shouting. The cops yelled *Hands behind your back* and *don't resist*. Sanford shouted for them to back off. And that they didn't have enough to arrest me. Two uniformed troopers grabbed me at the bicep and forearm. I held my wrists together, as one of the plain clothes came at me with a zip tie. The troopers tried to pry my arms apart but each of my single arms was stronger than both theirs. The fifth cop, plain clothes advanced, he came up behind me trying for a choke hold, but I tucked my chin. Everyone's feet were planted, we swayed this way and that, but I refused to budge.

Sanford tried to block the detective with the zip tie. He shoved Sanford aside. The trooper to my left cleared his taser. The other two let go and stepped back. The orders came to get on the floor.

At that point Sanford shouted, "Delayed justice, Grimes, Delayed justice." He was telling me to comply, we would have our say before a judge. He was right. These cops were so fired up at the death of one of their own, killing me was a very real option. Right or wrong, with evidence or not, they wanted their justice. And I couldn't argue with that. I was no hypocrite.

My thumbs were bent back as my wrists were bound. Thick plastic bags went over my hands. They left me on the floor, one trooper kept a knee on my upper back.

Sanford and Newstrom argued a little more, then a Trooper corralled Sanford back to the corner of the office. Newsom got in close to my face. I struggled to control my breathing. I needed to be the calm little center of the universe.

"What'd Gibson tell you? Why was he coming to meet you?" Newstrom was gritting his teeth. His face twisted, beet red with rage.

"He wanted to meet. All he said was it runs too deep and that's why he wanted to talk in person. You've got a rat with a badge or worse." I said feeling the anger rise with my heaving chest. The knee on my back pressed down.

"Bullshit. We're making the arrest Sanford." Newstrom said.

Sanford juked and side stepped the Trooper, getting up close to Newstrom, "Listen here for a second, just think on this. Grimes was with Agent Alvarez and told him he was meeting Gibson. If that isn't enough, Grimes's testimony is all you have in the biggest case of your life right now. Muncy? Where is he? No one knows. Do you really want to throw all that away? You pin this on Grimes, and you lose the child trafficking case and worst of all the guilty go free while an innocent man, one who has put his life on the line to bust them, rots in prison." Sanford was using his preacher voice, starting soft and growing louder. "This man here can find the truth, find the rat."

Newstrom threw up his hands, "Alright, alright, let's hear it, Grimes."

I still had the bags over my hands and the Trooper on my back as I told them about Gibson's call and where I was staying. One of the plain clothes called the hotel to verify. I told him to question the clerk I spoke with and mentioned all the cameras the hotel had. It would be easy to verify I never left.

Newstrom never had the suspicious eye of me Gibson had. Gibson was a law man through and through, from his black shoes to his ugly haircut, he was a cop. I was never anything more than a criminal to him. The state attorney told the Trooper to cut me loose. Relief and circulation rushed over me as the zip ties came off. Newstrom still ordered one detective to scrape under my fingernails and they checked the contents of my pockets.

"We're going to check your story out and then check it again. If anything, anything at all doesn't add up I'm busting your ass. I don't care if it costs me every case for the rest of my life. Remember, cop killers get a very special kind of justice in this state." Newstrom pointed a finger in the air and twirled it. All the cops understood and obeyed, leaving Sanford and I in the office.

"Whoooah," Sanford said as he staggered like a punch-drunk fighter to the marble topped bar. After loosening his tie, he splashed three fingers of golden bourbon into two tumblers and handed one to me.

My fingers were still tingling, and I nearly lost hold of the glass. I set it down, shook them out then kicked back a large gulp of bourbon.

Sanford bit back the burn, "Shame though about Gibson. I hate to see the good ones go down like that."

I nodded. We lifted our glasses in memory. The bourbon fought the tightness in my chest. The frame-up had failed for now. That meant death would follow, but that wasn't why I had the knot. Gibson died trying to warn me. He had since he first saw my *shadow*, as he called it, earlier this year. He warned me then and I didn't listen. I sat in the chair as my knees just didn't want to hold my weight.

"Gibson always distrusted me. I was never more than a dirty crook to him."

"Don't beat yourself up about it."

"I didn't trust him either, super cop. Johnny Law. When the time came, he risked his life to save mine. He upheld his oath." I brought my hands up to hold my head now. Each breath went in a little faster only to go out faster still.

"Hey, son." Sanford sat on the edge of his desk, one leg dangling just over the thick carpet. "He knew what he was doing and accepted the risk. You above anyone should know—"

"No," I was looking at Sanford now, "No, I don't compare to Gibson. The man knew the difference between wrong and right, law and order."

No one said anything then I said, "Gibson was killed with my gun."

The office was silent. Sanford stopped swinging his leg. "Can they match your prints?"

I held up my hands, palms out for him to see. My fingertips were smooth. After my conviction years ago, I had Billy take a grinder to them.

"They could still match up a palm print or maybe find some DNA on it," I said.

"I'll do whatever it takes, Grimes. We're going to get ahead of this."

"Maybe," I said, "Or maybe after tonight, you and Monique begin to separate yourselves from me."

Sanford stood tugging at the bottom of his vest, "Just what are you saying, Roger?"

"When this is over, finally over, I'm quitting." I headed for the door.

"Hey now, where are you going?" Sanford said.

"It's best you don't know."

Chapter 28

My die was cast, I couldn't change what I had done or who I became. The straight and narrow was anything but that. A vast expanse of squiggly lines with no direction was my path. It led back to me and those that preyed on the innocent, those that used power and influence to escape justice. I couldn't let that stand. I had to be Roger Grimes, White Knight, one last time.

My last chance was to get Muncy and turn him over to the same law that failed so many. It was the only way to change course and alter the outcome for me and those who stood against me. At the center was Danzig, hiding behind his money and reputation. He crossed a line, threw his hat in the ring and challenged me to a fight. His son was a nothing but halfwit drug dealer and would provide the link to taking poppa down.

The law wouldn't be able to keep me safe fast enough. It's why Sanford created the White Knight, to do what they couldn't. Would it be enough?

I did what I always did when everything in my life was collapsing. I went to Coopers for a drink. On the way I called Billy to explain what was happening in case cops came looking for me. He said he would swear to whatever story I needed. I thanked him but didn't think it would come to that.

In my rearview mirror was the black and tan Trooper mobile. If whoever followed me wanted to take a run at me, it wouldn't be with that cop behind me. Being bait didn't bother me. I welcomed the confrontation. A physical confrontation would be easy. The thing about the shadow that circled around my mind was that there was lack of physical confrontation on his side. Several times I'd tried to chase him down. I know now, confrontation wasn't what he was after.

Half a dozen people sat at the bar. A group of college age kids had two tables pushed together and were sitting around them. No one was sitting in any booths. I grabbed a booth and looked around for a server.

Emma, from the other night came up to the table, slinging her blonde ponytail as she walked. "Whatch'ah drinking?" she said like she had been at this game years instead of days.

"Breakfast stout. Are you still shadowing Alysa or are you on your own?"

She twisted her tiny head on a pencil neck trying to figure out how I knew that. Obviously, I was forgotten about already.

"Sorta," she said recovering quickly. "Alysa is still here to check on me. Want me to get her for you?"

"No rush. I'll be here awhile."

The creamy foam head was gone as half the breakfast stout was in my belly. The light oat flavor was crisp, and the hint of cinnamon was just enough to make me think it was cold outside. My thoughts drifted to finding an all-night diner for eggs and French toast when Agent Alvarez strutted in from the back hall. He paused to take in the clientele, looking around like he was expecting to see friends. Instead, he saw me. Before he got to the table, he was intercepted by Emma. She threw an arm around him, and he leaned in close to her ear whispering something that brought a chuckle. Then he pointed over to me. She nodded and went about her job.

"For a man who doesn't drink, you sure like to hang out at bars," I said.

He took off his suit coat before sitting. There was no badge or gun. "I drink, just not when I'm working."

"I find it helps me work."

Alysa breezed by flashing a smile as she went. Emma

brought Alvarez his coke. They chatted, he gently grazed his fingertips over her hand, then held it for a moment. I shook my empty pint glass until the two love birds broke their intertwining gaze.

"Another?" She took the glass and left.

Alvarez watched her go.

"So, you're working now?" I said pointing to the fizzing coke.

"Working on her." he said with a growl as a tremor passed through his body. Aggressively hitting on women was never my style. When it came to flirting and picking up women, I was my worst enemy. I found chitchat difficult with the inevitable 'what do you do' question that starts all chitchat. As a thief I said nothing. As a PI, I said nothing. *Not employed* isn't exactly the kind of thing a woman over the age of twenty-five wants to hear.

If Alvarez was here to talk about Gibson, he'd have to go first. Newstrom suspected me of killing him, and if Gibson were alive, he would too, never mind the obvious issue with that statement. Alvarez should have something to say about it. I knew his game plan; work in a series of sly questions about our meeting or come at me with a timeline. Newstrom may have updated him, let him know he was cutting me loose.

He sat with his arms spread, gripping the back of the booth. A plastic straw poked from his lips, bouncing as he chewed on it. His smile didn't stop.

"Alright," Alvarez said.

"Alright, what?" I said, thinking how he was coming right out with it.

"You got me, nailed it as soon as I sat down." Alvarez took the straw from his mouth and jabbed it into the ice at the bottom of his glass. "Shots!" Alvarez slid out of the booth and went up to the bar.

Alysa brought me my beer and took a seat next to me. She smelled like old fryer oil and ammonia.

"We have been in the weeds all day. This is the first time I've sat down in how many hours. I dunno, since three. What time is it now?" She said in a hurry and then stole a sip of my beer. Her mouth soured, "I don't know why you drink that."

"It tastes good. You do know you don't really work here, right?"

An aggravated rumble crept from her throat. "I know. I know. I haven't even checked in with the gym since we were there."

"Any drug dealer visits?"

"Not that I noticed." She rubbed her eyes and then ran a fingernail along her tightly pulled back hair.

I didn't want to talk about how the drug dealers played a bigger role, or dead cops or friends who betrayed me. I wanted out of all of it. I wanted normal, a dog, a girlfriend and a place to sleep that was mine. Alysa owned a gym, she was attractive in more than looks, which were plenty good, but also in the way she was selfless. Giving up time from her own business to help me and to help Wayne. That was a loyal friend. That was what I needed to bring stability into my life for once.

"I really liked your gym. I can't believe how big it is." I said going with the flow of alcohol I now had in my system. These stouts are 8% alcohol by volume. Compared to the 5% of your average lite beer.

"Really? Thanks Grimes. It needs some work still, paint, and a new carpet. Stuff like that."

"I can help. I'm good with my hands."

She smiled, "Oh really? You'll just have to prove that

some time."

My face flushed, "Ah, I meant, but I can, use them for whatever." I was losing it, her and my mind.

"I know what you meant. That would be great." Her smile lit up the room then quickly faded as pink hued cheeks took over. She looked down at the table. "I could really use the help. That's sweet of you." Her hand slid across the heavy resin of the table. A finger uncurled and hooked the side of my palm. Then more fingers joined as we held hands. Only the corners of her eyes would dare look at me and wouldn't look long. A soft giggle emanated from her chest.

I didn't move, I didn't speak. I barely breathed.

"Hey, I got us shots." Alvarez was back and the hand that I had held after waiting so long retreated.

Alvarez put down four shots and slid into the booth with Emma following.

"We're still on the clock." Alysa scooted to the edge of the booth.

"It's dead and we've worked a double." Emma pouted.

"Less talk, it gets in the way of drinking." Alvarez held up the shot glass. We all followed. Alysa held hers towards me and we cheered then sucked back the cinnamon flavored whiskey.

As we all breathed fire with our eyes pinched tight, I felt Alysa get up from the booth.

"We still have to empty all the trash, then I'll see if I can get you cut early." Alysa said to Emma. She looked back to me, "We'll talk more later, okay?"

I smiled. They both walked off to their closing duties, each with a lighter step than when they sat down and both for different reasons.

Alvarez started in about Emma again and I cut him off,

"Are you really not going to say anything about Gibson?"

His smile dropped. "A real shame. I hear he was a good cop." He cleared his throat, "Did you two ever meet up?"

"No. Did Newstrom fill you in?"

"Yeah, he went over everything. Asked me a lot of questions about you and what time I left your hotel." His big brown eyes dropped to the table.

Both my elbows were on the table holding my head just over the pint glass. A highly respected police officer was gunned down, in a case Agent Alvarez was working. All the agent had was a cold stare. There was no fire, no pent-up rage like the Troopers who met me at Sanford's had. They wanted blood. Years back when a gunman walked into an airport and TSA took him down, a couple of them were killed. Police responded as if they were one of their own. I've heard that with security guards too. The bond between those who wear a badge is tight and this Fed just wanted to get laid.

Maybe wearing a badge doesn't make you right, just, or noble. There were cops who secretly praised the work I did, I did the things they wanted to do and operated how they wanted to operate. Every day while they towed the blue line, I blurred it.

"How about another shot?" Alvarez slid out of the booth and stood waiting on my reply.

The case blurred before my eyes. Alvarez was off the clock, why shouldn't I be?

"I'll get this round."

When I returned to the table with only two shots Alvarez frowned. He looked over at Emma.

"What about the girls?"

Alvarez was right. What about the girls? Gibson's sudden death reminded me no one was untouchable. Tonight, could be my last. There was an assassin hunting me, toying with me, wanting me to mess up so he could take his shot.

Alysa was standing at the Point of Sale. Her knee was up against a lower shelf outlining the curve of her butt. She was nibbling on the end of a pen and one golden lock drooped down into her face. She huffed and it went sideways.

The whiskey went down, and my body was in motion. I was a hunter, winding through the slalom of tables, pulled-out chairs and standing bar patrons, I stalked up behind Alysa. Deaf to the clatter, blind to the eyes on us. I spun her around.

"Oh, Grimes. I –"

Hesitation was for losers. Our lips met softly. My hand slid up to her neck. She leaned in, turning slightly, moving her mouth with mine, a little firmer, a little more open. I breathed her in, taking her essence to the subatomic level transcending into the 4th dimension where time and space became irrelevant. The years and the tragedy ceased. Then I pulled back. My eyes opened to her smiling face. She was blind now too to the eyes on us having met me on the other side.

"No matter what happens tomorrow, I had to know what that was like tonight," I said.

"Don't worry, you'll know tomorrow, and the next, Grimes." She touched her lips and smiled.

My hearing returned as Alvarez stood on his chair and whistled then cheered. Emma cheered and so did most of the bar.

Alysa flushed as she looked at the cheering crowd. They simmered, returning to their drinks and conversations. With her ponytail straightened and fixed she cleared her throat.

We smiled together. I went back to my table a little lighter, a little dizzier than when I left. She avoided my eye contact for a few minutes, trying to focus on what she was doing, but it wasn't helping. A few more smiles were exchanged as she went about her busy night.

Alvarez offered more shots. I waved him off and leaned back in the booth, my neck tilted, my head resting on the wood. Heavy eyelids closed like drapes as I drifted in a warm sea of blackness, searching deeper into my own body. Instead of escape from my shell, an electric light emanated from my entire being. I was fusing with myself, accepting the way things had gone, accepting the order that brought me to this moment. I wanted to live here in this moment forever, perfectly preserving it in a glass bubble, like a snow globe moment I could take out and shake and relive over and over. And I knew tomorrow would be okay.

A scream kicked my lids open and brought my head up.

Like pausing a movie, every conversation, every sip, and every thought was frozen still. One collective thought raced through all our minds; we digested the high-pitched screech. In that second of doubt all eyes made connections with other eyes throughout the bar. While their brains caught up, I was out of the booth clearing a path to the back door.

Tires spun on pavement. Someone shouted. A car door slammed. More tires squealed. Metal impacted metal. I ran down the wooden walkway into the parking lot. A Chevy Astro van cut right out of the parking lot.

Then I saw a pair of black nonskid shoes tied to feet with tan legs ending in tight khaki shorts. A soft constant ring went through my ears, barely audible but my brain said it was real. My legs scrambled, my arms pumped, but I wasn't breathing until I cleared the last car in the lot and looked at blond hair matted down with heavy crimson blood.

Breath held for too long finally escaped like a dropkick to my chest. I stared at the Kelly-green polo, the khaki shorts with legs twisted and covered in road-rash. Then my lungs exploded in faster, tighter breaths, my lungs wanted more. I couldn't gulp enough air with each heave.

A hundred opportunities to tell her, to hold her, to show her all that I had inside of me faded to red. Snow globe moments now lost in a past I could never go back to. Things I had never shown anyone, and had never wanted to until I met her, were gone. The things we were to do and time we were to spend together drained away like the blood from her skull. No more tomorrows, gone in an instant.

A tremor started in my hand as I stretched out, preparing to roll her over for a final look at her face.

A hand touched my arm and I spun.

"Is she okay?" Alysa said.

A silent eruption of feelings poured hot and thick over my heart as I scooped Alysa up, cradling her head into my shoulder. Three steps later I set her down. Voices behind us shouted, mostly confused, some calling to us for direction. Someone said they were calling the police.

I didn't let Alysa look back.

"Go call 911. Dark green Chevy Astro van." I squeezed her hand, taking in the flesh then let it go. I ran back to the body to check for a pulse. Alvarez was standing over my right shoulder as I knelt. Her skin was warm as my fingers pressed into the soft side of her wrist.

"Don't." His voice jagged, pinned my movement.

We had both seen death; knew the difference between light and darkness. The body was just a shell now. Whoever was Emma, was gone.

Alvarez turned, shoulders squared, eyes narrowed with dark focus. He walked with purpose, not back to Coopers but towards a white Crown Vic.

"Grimes," Alysa yelled from the wooden walkway behind Coopers. "Grimes is she breathing? Is there a pulse?"

She held a phone to her ear, repeating the questions the 911 operator had for her.

I called to Alvarez. If he heard me, he didn't acknowledge it. The Crown Vic fired up, then he drove in a half circle and headed right towards me. Hitting the brakes hard. His window was down.

"Get in or get outta my way." He barked.

Alysa watched me go around to the passenger seat, then began pleading with me to let the cops handle it. I remembered her hand I held as I opened the car door. Our kiss was still on my lips. All of it crushed by the hopelessness of seeing her dead body.

"Wait." I said to Alvarez.

I ran up to Alysa. My hand went through her blond hair as my other went around her waist. I pulled her in and held her tight. "That was supposed to be you, and it was because of me. You'll be safer if I go."

Her arm held me tight, "I'll be safer with you by my side." she said as I pulled away.

Alvarez hit the gas before I got the car door closed.

Chapter 29

"Where are we headed?" Alvarez pulled out of the parking lot and onto Palmetto Avenue. We caught the red light, but he didn't let that stop us.

"We should let the cops handle it. The heat is already on me because of Gibson's murder."

His eyes glowed; his knuckles whitened over the wheel. "Then get out."

The brakes pulled me forward into the dash.

I sat back in the seat, "Turn right and then make another right." A chill rippled through my body, every pour on my skin opened to take a breath. *That's not what I do.* I told Wayne that when he asked if I was going to kill them. I wanted to keep that promise to myself to stifle my growing reputation, and let it be forgotten. Too often I lay awake trying to circle back to that first kill, further back to the first bank robbery, all the way back to the first car I stole. I try to stop myself; I try to figure out a way to change my past and escape my present. The only thing I can do is work to make my future better. Avoid those violent mistakes. This ride felt like one of those mistakes.

"Make a left. The house is on the right, The pink one." Fire built in my belly and a knot synched around my chest. A headache was coming on. It always does when I'm ready for the kill.

He crawled the car around the block and parked in the same spot Alysa and I had parked before. I was sixteen, it was a Ford Mustang 5.0 rag top. A screwdriver broke the ignition. Billy had me practice every day that week on one of his old cars. The point in my life I wanted to change more than anything. Here I was again, believing Alvarez was here to make an arrest; he could call local PD and have the drug dealers arrested. When Alvarez got out of the car, I knew none of that was going to happen.

Alvarez popped the trunk and started clanking things around. When came back around his suit coat and dress shirt were off. He wore a white undershirt and blue latex gloves. The badge and pistol that were normally on his hip, were in his hand. He stashed them in the center console.

"No guns," he said.

"I don't have one." I pulled tarnished knuckles out. He nodded.

The street was vacant of people. Low hanging oak branches blocked out most of the light from the streetlamps above. The last few jobs, I had started wearing a mask. Without one I felt exposed. Alvarez wasn't wearing one, erasing any doubt these drug dealers would be left alive.

By pointing his finger, he told me to circle left around the house. He went right. We met in the backyard. The detached garage was closed. Looking through the window of the side door, I saw a square vehicle covered with a blue tarp. There was no question it was the same van we saw speed away.

From a kitchen window, light spilled onto the small block patio. The window was open and hurried voices were muffled by the walls of interior rooms. Neither voice sounded happy. The voices traveled, going room to room and back again. No one came into the kitchen.

"We both go in through the back." He grabbed the knob. It wasn't locked. He slipped in silently. I followed.

At the end of the galley kitchen was a dinette table and three chairs. The table held digital scales, baggies, and foil, but no drugs. The voices were in the hall around the corner from the dining room. A female was asking a lot of questions while a man told her to shut up. The man was Wes. The woman was the same one I saw the day before.

"Get off me." Wes shouted. Sounds of a light struggle in the hall ended in a door slamming shut.

The brunette emerged from the hall. Alvarez moved swiftly. His gloved hand was up. Her eyes were large, and her mouth opened. Then the hand palmed her face and drove her back into the wall. She crashed over an end table, breaking the glass top. Her head left a dent in the wall.

"Don't be fucking up my house." Wes charged out of the room and down the hall. He stopped short of exiting when he saw me then saw Alvarez standing near his girlfriend. His long arms went out as he stumbled back trying to turn but also not wanting to take his eyes from us.

I snatched his belt. An elbow came back and impacting above my right eye. I held, but Alvarez was already picking up the slack. His charge smashed Wes into the wall. Their arms tangled, ending in Alvarez having complete control of the lanky dealer.

Wes's head hit the wall three times.

"Where's the other one?"

Wes blinked a few times as his eyes tracked stars circling his vision. Alvarez shook him.

"I don't know, man. Get off me." Wes struggled. Alvarez smashed his head once more.

Wes grunted as blood began seeping from cracked skin on his face. His knees weren't holding the weight. Alvarez hoisted him up. "Why the girl?"

Wes looked at me then Alvarez. He closed his eyes tight knowing talking would bring pain, "To send a message. To get him to back off." His eyes shifted to me.

"But I didn't know that girl," I said.

"Chad said it was her. When I grabbed her, I realized it

was the wrong girl. Chad sped up so fast I let go of her and oh shit man, it was all so fucked up. I'm sorry, I'm so sorry." Tears squeezed from the corners of his eyes as he pinched them tighter. He sucked quick breaths then let out a long high-pitched groan.

"Is she okay?" He said through sniffles.

I didn't see the blade but heard it pop open. Wes squealed and tried clawing at Alvarez. His fingers racked across Alvarez's face but did no damage. Wes staggered back and fell to the musty carpet. Blood came out of his lower back, kidney region. He reached around, trying to cover the wound but he couldn't stop the blood.

The metal spring on the screen door zinged as it was pulled back. The door opened. I stepped back into the kitchen and Alvarez stepped into the hall.

"What the fuck did you do Wes?" Chad called from the living room. "Sabrina, get up. C'mon girl, get up. Wes, you idiot. We don't have time for this shit."

Two shuffled steps neared the hall then stopped. He whispered something as he peered into the hall. A struggle broke out, louder than before. Chad held a pistol; Alvarez held his wrist. His knee came up into Chad's groin. Then again. Chad slid to the floor. Alvarez bent Chad's wrist past ninety degrees. The chubby dealer grunted. He was losing, and he knew it. Heavy breathing didn't help hold the gun as it slipped from his grasp. Alvarez drove his shoulder into Chad's face. Then he grabbed the pistol and shot him three times.

Without hesitation, Alvarez wiped the pistol then put in Wes's hand, holding it tight with the finger on the trigger. Then he put the stiletto switchblade into Chad's hand. He came out of the hall. Sweat beaded along his forehead. His styled black hair was now scattered.

Sabrina started to come to. Alvarez had forgotten about

her, I hadn't but was keeping my mouth shut, secretly rooting for her to survive. Her questioning of Wes was proof to me she knew nothing of the kidnapping. She didn't have to die.

Alvarez knelt. He slapped her fully awake then cupped her chin, pinching the sides of her face, he said, "They killed each other over a botched kidnapping. Got it?" He rocked her head in a 'yes' motion. "One girl already died tonight. I can make it two. Got it?" He rocked her head again.

We left her there on the floor, bleeding, crying, not knowing what the hell just happened or how different her life will be forever more.

Chapter 30

We drove in silence. I could see my phone light up with calls and text messages but didn't look at who they were from. I didn't know where we were going, just a direction, west.

We crossed under Interstate 95 and swung into a gas station. He parked on the side near a dumpster out of the reach of flood lights and cameras.

"Grab us a couple drinks, Red Bulls." Alvarez said looking straight ahead instead of at me.

"Why don't you go," I said.

He pulled on his white tee shirt, showing the blood splatter.

"Gotcha." I went into the store and bought a few energy drinks. When I came back to the car Alvarez was wearing his button up with no undershirt.

"We should head back to Coopers, give our statements to the cops." I was texting Alysa back to say we were okay and don't know where Wes and Chad had gone. She *might* have believed that last part and was more excited to hear I was okay.

"No way. If they want to talk to me, they can call me in the morning. Our night isn't over."

"It is for me. Look, I'm sorry about Emma. She was a sweet girl, but I can't go on a vengeance ride with you."

"Come off it, Grimes. Back there you wussed out, just stood there like a fucking spectator at a ball game, but I know you've done a lot worse than that for a lot less of a reason. Yeah, I know you. I know what you did, the pool hall and probably a few more," he said.

The pool hall was all in the file. Everyone in law enforcement thought I was lying, thought Sanford was lying, but no one could or bothered to link me to actually pulling the trigger on anyone. "I think we should just cool it for tonight." I said avoiding any confirmation of Alvarez's theory. He was an FBI Agent who I just watched murder two drug dealers. That didn't make us the same. He still wore a badge and as far as I knew a wire.

"Oh, don't clam up now. You took part in a double homicide, friend. We're glued together now." That toothy smile returned. He looked up in the rearview then used his fingers to straighten out his hair.

I hated him. I hated myself more. Agent Alvarez, FBI, had me on a leash. He said he could spot a killer and I know that to be true. Every time he looked in a mirror there was a killer looking back. His smooth angled face had gone undetected as a killer. He was nothing but an easy talking, arrogant federal agent until tonight. Those moves with the knife and the quick frame up with the pistol were not panicked actions of an amateur.

"Why the hell did you just waste those two back there?"

"Kneejerk reaction. I was pissed, they killed Emma simply because they're fucking idiots. No one is gonna miss them. If it wasn't me, they'd mess up again and get dead." He said it so casual, like avenging a dead girl was so normal.

He looked at me with eyes like scanners detecting subtle changes in temperature or movement. "You took out all of Azad Aziz's crew over what, a gambling debt. Twenty grand, was it?"

"That wasn't me –"

"Who are you fooling? Cause it ain't me." He had that smile back.

I sipped the energy drink to keep my mouth shut. Arguments, denials, and the official statements I gave to the police crossed my mind, but he had seen through those. How he came to know the truth, I wasn't sure, but he knew it all.

This time I scanned him. His square jaw, shiny black hair that was always perfectly out of place possibly dyed if Alysa was right. Amber eyes that slowed you down and a white toothy grin that trapped you in place. That Glock 22, something only law enforcement could have, was openly clipped next to a polished brass badge. It was all out there in the open, who he was and what he wanted. Yet somehow, he managed to hide another side, a dark side, he kept buried deep. Something I knew too well.

Then a question crept into my ear and into my head, *was Alvarez me?* Was he real, had I thought him up as some kind of super me? The perfect hair, styled hair instead of a buzz cut. The FBI badge instead of a PI ticket and hooking up with the hot waitress at Coopers. His suits fit better than my t shirts. That had been the life I wanted, that had been the life I was trying to build. It all made sense now. Alvarez was nothing more than a mental break, an escape into what life could have been. Did I watch my better self, kill two drug dealers because my mind just couldn't handle another death? Was I living a waking nightmare? I wanted to call Sanford to confirm he had met Alvarez too. *That would be crazy, I would sound crazy.* How would that conversation go? Not well.

A lack of sleep over prolonged periods of time can have strange effects on the brain. Catching up on sleep isn't possible, the damage is done. A few nights at the hotel weren't enough to repair all the damage done to my mine and all the concussions to my brain. Was I still asleep? Could this be a dream?

I poked him in the arm. "I didn't kill the drug dealers. You killed those two drug dealers." My finger came back uncertain it had touched him.

His smile faded as he leaned back into the door. "Are

you wearing a wire?" He jabbed a hand at my chest. I deflected it ensuring I was awake. "Are you, Grimes?"

"No, I'm just, sorta losing my mind, I think." I rubbed the side of my temples. He knew all about me, everything I had hidden and suppressed. The things that ate me up during the day and spit me out at night. Here was a guy just like me. I wanted to lay back on a couch and spill my guts to him, I wanted to confess every graphic detail because he would understand. Now the dam I held could break and what a relief. There was one other thing I needed to do to survive, I needed to confess.

"You're right about all that," I said.

Alvarez glanced over at me with a raised eyebrow.

"The poolhall, Aziz's crew. I did it. I did it all alone. Me, just me." Feelings of pride mixed with a release of guilt.

Alvarez was silent longer than I would have liked. "You think because you saw me take out a couple of shit-bag dealers I'll keep your secrets?"

It wasn't the response I expected. The high of my confession began repacking into the box I kept it in.

"I'm just fucking with you Grimes." Alvarez said and slapped me in the chest. "I knew I liked you the day we met. Don't worry. Everything I said was just my own theory. No one is looking at you for those killings and no one will."

The sigh I let out had been held for years. It's the kind of breath you don't know your holding until its expelled. Sanford never let me talk about it. Attorney client privilege wasn't an issue. If my recount of what happened became too detailed, his eyes would lose contact. He would stare more out the window; out over the town he grew up in. I knew he just didn't want to hear it. Monique hadn't either. She told me so back at Dunkin and all this time she had been afraid of me, of the way I went back to normal after all I had seen and done.

Alvarez relaxed into his seat. "Anyway, we're going to get Muncy, and we're done. You and me, this night, we put it all behind us." He said and patted my arm.

No confessions, no relief, the dam held, I kept silent about my past. "You're right about Tully's. He's there, I'm sure of it," I said. I didn't want to give Smitty up, but I saw no other way out. What I wanted was to retreat through a time portal and start over. But unlike Alvarez that wasn't real.

Alvarez drove without asking directions. He knew where he was going. His window was down, and the radio was on a Latin station but turned low. With his left hand he would touch his lips every now and then, the fantom pain of a smoker who recently quit.

Excitement built inside me. Not for a coming confrontation but to put all this behind me. It started with Smitty and would end with him. When I quit being a thief, there were only two people on this planet I trusted, Billy Horse Blood and Smitty. Ever since then it proved to be a false positive. I saw with my own eyes Smitty sell me out. He asked me to trust him. Billy and Kurt expected me to do the same. They didn't see what I saw, they don't live under the same threat I do. Turning Muncy over to the FBI was what I needed to do to survive.

Alvarez took us across the Granada Bridge. The moon hung silver and full overhead, lighting a pathway to the dark Atlantic down the road. It was something I had seen dozens of times before and never grew tired of it. We cut north onto John Anderson Drive, past million-dollar mansions, then turned up a street to Halifax Drive and circled back towards Granada Avenue. A moment later we were sitting in the parking lot of the Post Office, across the street from Tully's.

"He's been here all along." Alvarez said pointing at a second-floor window. The shade was drawn. Soft yellow light leaked from the edges. "They have him stashed up there."

"Tavolo"

"What? It's nothing but old guys watching him. Should be a piece of cake." Alvarez slapped my arm then got out of the car.

My guts were as twisted as my thoughts. Those *old guys* were no piece of cake. I grew up with the stories. I sat at the meetings. Assuming they were past their prime was a mistake. Assuming I could pull the trigger on any of them was a mistake too.

Alvarez walked a dozen yards away from the car and made call. He kept walking when whoever he called answered. I couldn't hear what he said.

I sent a text to Billy: *Muncy is at Tully's. Confronting Smitty now. Head over if you can.*

Billy was a few beers in when I left him this afternoon. It wasn't like him to sober up and be at the ready to respond to text messages in the middle of the night. He was all I had. Smitty was across the street knowing I'd show up eventually. He couldn't hide Muncy forever. I had a Fed with me. The badge might not be worth much to the old timers, but everyone behind that badge might show up in force.

"All set." Alvarez said, holstering his Glock and clipping on the badge.

"I feel a little naked without a gun. You got a spare?"

"Sure, I do." He patted his lower back, "Now let's go." He said as he walked past me down to the sidewalk.

We stood shoulder to shoulder looking across the street at the tap room. Four large windows with Tully's Tap Room painted in yellow letter by letter of each separated pane of glass. A string of white lights framed the dark wood trim. The overhead lights of the main dinning were out leaving only a dim yellow from the rear of the restaurant. I knew that light, it was over the booth. A booth I told Roman De Carlo earlier I had earned a right to sit at. Walking in a Fed would end all that. I'd never be able to show my face at Tully's ever again. I would be cutting half my life out the second I crossed through that door. Like a surgeon I would be cutting out the infection to save the patient. It had to be done.

"The front door is locked. There's one in the back that probably isn't. The employees use it and I'm guessing they didn't lock up for the night." I told Alvarez.

We went around back. The dumpster smelled of rotting meat. The constant drip of decomp made the black top alley slick. There was almost no light as we neared the door. I knew its placement from memory. I felt the handle, unlocked. I pulled it open.

We crossed greasy kitchen tile to the double doors that opened into the dining room. A sliver of light showed the tips of our shoes. Alvarez put his hand on his gun but didn't draw it.

"I can talk them in to giving Muncy up," I said.

"In case you can't." He said looking down at his side.

I swallowed and pushed open the final doors.

Smitty was sitting at the booth. His elbows were up on the table, a sweaty glass of amber liquid was in his hand. His chin led his eyes towards our entrance. De Carlo's hand was in a bowl of nuts. Ruben was sitting at a table next to the booth. His beefy bodyguard was standing behind him, back against the wall.

"Be cool." I said hoping a familiar voice would hold them off long enough to register what was happening.

"FBI," Alvarez said loud enough to be heard upstairs. I

grabbed his arm and shook my head. He shrugged me off. "Nobody move, keep your hands up."

No one complied. Smitty sipped his drink like nothing happened. De Carlo went on snacking from the bowl and Ruben just blinked through his thick lensed glasses. The bodyguard shifted his weight a little and unclasped his hands.

"Relax." I said more to Alvarez but wanted the group to hear it as well. "This is Agent Alvarez. We're here for Muncy. I know you've got him upstairs."

Smitty put his drink down. "Yeah, and now, he knows it too, dumb ass. Watch what you say, the guy's a little jumpy." Smitty got up and moved away from the booth into the middle of the dining room. To his right, past the bar was a hall ending in the stairwell that went to the second floor. Smitty looked to it and took a breath then sighed.

I moved past him. A familiar waft of aftershave filled my nose. An instant of memories stopped with the realization this might be the last time I smell it. At the bar was a narrow hallway decorated with a hundred years of photos of Tully's past. To the right were two doors for restrooms and straight ahead was the staircase for the second floor.

"Harry Muncy, get down here." I shouted up the stairwell. It was silent for a while.

BAM! A single gunshot echoed between my ears.

I spun on my heels and looked across the restaurant. No one had moved as if the shot had never happened, except Agent Alvarez. He was flat on his back. A pistol was in his hand. He was dead.

"What the hell!" I knelt to inspect the gunshot wound. A single shot under his left eye had traveled at an upward angle and exited through the top back of his skull. I looked at the badge on his hip. Killing an FBI Agent would bring heat none of us could escape, not even to Uruguay.

The bar tender from earlier came out from some place I had never seen. In a building this old there were rooms and then there were back rooms. He took one look at Alvarez then went away again. I heard the hollow sound of water filling a bucket.

Smitty stood holding his drink in one hand and a revolver in the other. I wanted to choke him. He lowered the revolver, his shoulders with it and stood ready for the punishment. I stopped short. I shut my eyes and placed the heels of my palms over them. My mind sparked like a rim without a tire racing along the highway.

"What the fuck is going on?" I said in a whine. It wasn't my most stoic moment, but this downward spiral hadn't stopped. I was nearing a cliff, where 'hold it together' wasn't going to stop me from going over thc edge. Breathing exercises, mental training, or anything else could no longer hold me back. Only moments ago, I had seriously considered the possibility Alvarez was in fact me. An image projected by a brain that had been over worked and over medicated for far too long.

"What FBI agent carries a pistol with a threaded barrel?" Smitty pointed with the revolver. Then he walked over and felt the dead man's front pockets. Reaching around the small of the dead man's back, he pulled a suppressor. Holding it pinched in his fingers he set the suppressor and pistol on the bar. He went back and pulled the pistol from Alvarez's hand. He put it on the bar. Two glasses joined the small cache of weapons as he poured bourbon straight. He pulled a barstool out and said to sit. At this point I had nothing left. Bottom was just something you talk about but never reach. I hit it hard. All the crimes, coverups, and vengeance had put me there. I did what I was told and sat with my eyes fixated on the suppressor.

"You're getting sloppy kid."

I sat not blinking. Smitty was right. It wasn't the issued

Glock 22. This was a Berretta with a threaded barrel. A simple cylinder shape in the man's back pocket was enough for Smitty to draw and shoot Alvarez dead.

"You still with me, kid?" Smitty was staring at me like I stared at the dead FBI Agent on the floor.

"Shit, where do I begin?" Smitty crossed his arms over a broad chest. His chin was up, ready to begin a story with the missing pieces I had been running around Daytona Beach trying to find.

The bar tender came out pushing a yellow bucket on wheels and wooden mop handle. Tucked under his arm was thick plastic sheeting, like you'd put down to paint a room. The mop bucket had bottles of spray cleaner hanging from the side.

"You got the bar tender helping now too."

He looked over at me, plunged the mop then said, "Name's Sloan and I'm the owner."

Ruben chuckled, "On paper, only on paper."

Sloan shot him a sneer but mopped the blood anyway.

"I did what I did to protect you, Roger."

Those words had been used many times before. First from Billy then Sanford. None of it seemed to be protecting me, just making it worse. Walking into Tully's I was angry at Smitty for working with criminals, for siding with them and not me.

Smitty looked over to Sloan, "You know where to take him."

Sloan nodded as he mopped.

"That's why you were out at the compound, the swamp," I said.

Smitty rubbed at his jaw, "There was another one. I had to get rid of him."

"Yeah, Roger. Look at the guy, he's a mess, ain't slept all week." De Carlo added his account for the week.

"Tell him the rest, Erich." Ruben said from his seat.

"I'm getting to it." Smitty snapped. His blue-grey eyes kept steady on the bar. "Word came to me you were in trouble, there's a contract out for you."

"I'm aware of that. And so, what? Your solution was to kill an FBI Agent I'm working with?" A pit opened in my stomach, the kind when in an instant you want to take back the last two minutes, make all the changes and then go on with your life avoiding the giant screw up you were now in. But that pit told you it couldn't happen.

Smitty rolled the suppressor along the bar.

"Are you telling me he was going to kill me?" Things started to add up as I said it out loud. The drug dealers he killed so seamlessly; the dyed hair Alysa noticed. His overall lack of professionalism. Things I should have noticed. I watched the man skillfully carve up a drug dealer with a stiletto switchblade. After the botched kidnapping of Alysa, Chad and Wes were loose ends. It wasn't a killing of revenge but of anger for failing. The same man used his skill on Delgado and Lumino to silence them. Silence was something Alvarez worked with. When he didn't have the blade to slash a throat, he switched to a suppressor to carry out the hit.

"He's not Agent Alvarez. The real Agent Alvarez was discovered yesterday morning behind a rest stop on 95, just south of Jacksonville. He'd been dead nearly a week." Smitty looked back at the body now being rolled in plastic.

"See kid, Muncy and I go back, along with these fellas here. He'd lost touch over the years. Then he turns up in Florida, working for the people you put down. They wanted him to break into Sanford's office, get the evidence on them. He called me looking for a crew, wanting to hire you actually, not realizing you were the damn target. I found out who hired him and decided I better get involved. While we planned the heist, I convinced Muncy to cooperate as a witness. Muncy agreed to go into protective custody."

"So that was you that broke into the office?" I rubbed my temples. Relief seeped from my pours, but it wasn't over. Smitty had still sold the evidence. "Why did you trade it to the gun runners?"

Smitty slammed his hand on the bar. As withdrew it, I saw the flash drives. "I tracked the currier down after the swap." Smitty sipped his bourbon. "We figure this guy was hired to kill you and Muncy too when those files didn't show."

"He had plenty of chances to kill me this week. And why would he want to kill Muncy if Muncy pulled the job?"

"Roger Grimes is not an easy man to kill." Ruben said.

"Besides that," De Carlo said, "The Tavolo still hold sway. Word was you are protected. After that other hitter disappeared, this scum bag had to be cautious. I think time was running out on his cover, cause he got greedy and tried to take us all out." De Carlo shoved some snack mix in his mouth and chewed loudly.

"He needed a way in here to get to Muncy and probably figured you'd find him and make it a two for one job."

A shout from upstairs drew all our attention, "What the hell's going on down there?"

"Harry, get your ass down here." Smitty shouted back. Shoes scuffed along floorboards over our head then the stairs creaked. He stooped, trying to get a better look at the men in the room below him. Then clopped down the steps and into the dinning.

Harry looked like his photo, about 5'9'', potbellied with a couple of tattoos on his forearms. He had a tight navy-blue pocket tee shirt on and jeans a little baggy. His blue eyes were wide with hanging jowls covered in white whiskers. A rough hued hand rubbed his face.

"Hey, Sloan, can I get a drink?" Muncy said paying no attention to the dead FBI Agent.

Sloan looked up from mopping the floor and nodded. Muncy slipped behind the bar and grabbed a canned beer and came back around the bar. Once it was opened, he slurped the top and said, "Hey Grimes."

I sighed, then looked at Smitty for answers.

"Something's wrong. Alvarez or whoever he was, was acting on orders. And those orders included killing Gibson," I said.

"The state cop?"

"Gibson called me with information. He was found shot and a pistol was next to him, probably the one that was stolen from my apartment."

"With Muncy gone, and if you go down, the case against the pedophiles goes away." Smitty said.

De Carlo walked over to the bar. "What do you bet when they failed to arrest you, this fella' here figures it's his lucky day. Well, that went to shit for him." He chuckled.

My eyes floated down to the body of a hired killer. Sloan had him wrapped in a large sheet of plastic. The night I took on some drug dealers and ended up bringing down a child trafficking ring opened the gates of hell. Professionals were sent in. It had been two years and they were still after me, unable but very willing to kill me.

"They thought the Tavolo was done, that we'd just roll over and let them take Daytona Beach. They thought wrong." Rueben pounded on the table.

"Peter Danzig and his tag alongs." Smitty said.

"This hitman took out his 'tag-alongs' a couple nights

ago. Danzig is sitting on top," I said.

"Danzig is scared, getting paranoid someone will flip." Smitty said.

De Carlo moved to bar with an empty glass. He leaned on his forearms like someone was about to take his order. "Tavolo aint goin' nowhere." A toothy smile stretched across his sagging face.

"Danzig's been moving in on the Tavolo for years now. It was time we fought back." Ruben pointed at me with a crooked finger.

All three of the old men had a chuckle. The light heartedness of the old timers eased my tension. Then as it faded De Carlo pointed to Smitty's revolver, "When'd you start carrying a revolver? What happened to that Colt 1911? You love that gun." The rock bottom of my life suddenly turned to sand and had a hold of my feet. What lay beneath, I didn't want to know.

"I gave it away." Smitty said looking at De Carlo and shook his head at some previous conversation De Carlo obviously forgot about. Then all eyes fell on me, waiting for me to fill in the blanks. I didn't want to, no more digging. Some lies are what we want them to be in the construction of our own truths. I was fine with that.

"Tell him, it's time he knew." Ruben called out from behind me.

Smitty looked back at him. He refused to look me in the eye. That's when I saw his eyes were red and ringed. He ran a hand through long slivery hair that needed a trim. And he needed a shave as well. Years ago, on a long job he went without shaving and none of us got much sleep then. That was the only time I'd seen stubble on his face.

Ruben motioned his bodyguard to the bar. He pulled up a can of ginger ale and opened it and walked it back to his boss. "Tell him the whole damn thing, Erich." Ruben said before taking a sip.

De Carlo rubbed his bald head, "The kid's a detective. Let him figure it out." He laughed and waved a dismissive hand.

Life is looked at linearly, the points plotted along it make up events worth remembering in your life. Born, live, die. These events happen in a line, along an amount of time we recognize from seconds up to a century if you're lucky. Only in our mind we can jump back and forth, time only exists as a marker, a landing point for the mind to replay events. Alvarez's timeline was over. As Sloan relocated the body of a hitman sent to kill me, I traveled back to the time my dad handed me the Colt. Still a few inches away from the six-foot-one I am now and about fifty pounds lighter, I came home that night around eleven. Like normal I dropped my skateboard and went straight to the refrigerator. I grabbed a Styrofoam container, probably from Tully's, and tossed it in the microwave. I turned around to find Steve sitting at the dinette. The Colt on the table.

He was gone often as a Merchant Marine, so seeing him was a happy surprise. Usually when he came home, he had money and we had fun. This time was different. He was sitting at the table, beer in hand, staring at the Colt. He looked over at me and stood up. "This is for you." He dropped the pistol into my hands.

The timer on the microwave dinged but I ignored it. I stood looking down at the pistol.

Before I said anything, he said, "I'll be gone more and more. Maybe for a while. You'll be the man of the house." He took it back and proceeded to show me the action, pulling the slide, dropping the magazine. Then slid it back in and released the slide. He made me repeat it twice. Neither of us spoke. Then he walked out of the room. We didn't discuss it and I never told my mom I had it. That was the last time I ever spoke to him. I saw him briefly one day then he was gone for good. The Colt was all I had and became to me, an heirloom piece.

Jumping time and space to the present, I sat at the same bar my mom had worked back when I got that gun. Beside me was Smitty, someone I regarded as the only family I had left. And I was ready to throw it away tonight when I brought an FBI agent here.

"Was it yours?" I said looking to the mirror behind the bar. In the reflection he nodded without looking me in the eye.

His silence made me ask, "So, what are you, my grandfather?"

All the old guys chuckled, this time I didn't join in. Smitty finished the bourbon in one gulp, his gold bracelet dinging the side of the glass as he put it down.

"I met your mom—"

"Oh shit," I stumbled off the stool, knocking it over.

"Listen, sit down and listen to me." He picked up the stool and tried guiding me back to it.

"This isn't the fucking time or place." I brushed off his hands.

Ruben coughed, "Right place alright." Then he looked at De Carlo with a grin. I marched over ready to slap it off him. His goon got in my way, and we squared off. I needed to punch someone, I needed to be punched. Just like at Ben's gym, just like in the hotel room, I needed to swing my fist.

We didn't fight, because at that moment the back door opened slowly. Cowboy boots scuffed over the kitchen floor. Then the double doors parted. Billy stood there holding them. He looked around at all of us, including the body wrapped in plastic.

"I don't know what the fuck is going on in here but

there's a carload of dudes in black outside watching this place." He had the .357 in his waist band.

"Time to go." I said and waved him in.

"Harry," Smitty said, "It's time to go."

Though unrehearsed, everyone moved in sync. Ruben motioned for his gorilla to grab the corpse. Billy questioned nothing as we backed him up into the kitchen. Smitty went into the narrow pantry and pulled the shelving unit back. De Carlo went first, then Ruben then Harry. The gorilla went followed by Smitty. Billy waved me on.

I stopped at the tunnel entrance. It was just over five feet high, leaving me to stoop as we moved, and three feet across. The construction was brick with the floor wet sand. A wire strung along the side once held electric lights, but they had long since corroded, the copper wire now green and all the bulbs were broken. The tunnel ran to John D Rockefeller's house two hundred yards away. Over 100 years ago Rockefeller moved to Ormond Beach for the weather, at a time when it was fashionable for tycoons to winter here. Something that still hasn't fallen completely out of fashion, it's just not as exclusive. His house was built facing the Halifax River and next to it sat the Ormond Hotel. Long torn down, it was a destination spot for many of his friends. Wanting to avoid what passed for paparazzi of the day, Rockefeller had tunnels built to the hotel, Tully's and even a boat ramp. This way friends and lovers could pass underground to and from the hotel or drinking establishments unseen.

During prohibition Tully used the tunnels often even with Bill McCoy to run rum. Yes, the real McCoy. Now we were running in the tunnels, but it wasn't rum, it was for our lives. Living here, I had heard rumors but didn't know they really existed. Slipping on each slimy brick, the old men's hands went out, fingers stabbing at the tunnels walls to steady themselves. One man with a semi-auto rifle could take us all out.

"No, you go man." I said pointing to the tunnel.

Billy started but when he saw me close the shelves behind him, he stopped. "Get in here, we'll close it together."

"I'm not going."

"C'mon."

"I'm staying and fighting, it's what I do."

"Staying does nothing. You can't stop them all, Grimes. Now get your ass moving."

Sloan appeared in the pantry. "I'll close it behind you."

"What about you?"

"There are other ways out of here." He grabbed the shelves. My hand went up, blocking him from closing us in.

Smitty looked back. He turned shakily then started back towards us. Smitty said, "You both are crazy. Now get in here." He started to turn then turned back when I didn't move.

"Knock this shit off, there are too many of them." He reached out and grabbed my shoulder, "You don't have to do this. Muncy will be in the Marshals hands soon enough."

I pulled the secret door shut.

Billy and I came out of the pantry and went across the kitchen to the dining room door. I slipped through and crawled to the bar where my hand came up and fished around for Alvarez's pistol and suppressor. I heard the rubber soled boots cross the old wooden floor. Billy was waving me back to the kitchen, his pistol out, his braid pulled tight and tucked into the back of his shirt. I rewrapped my fingers around Alvarez's Berretta and screwed on the suppressor.

My palm planted on the swing door. I took a breath and before I exhaled a shotgun exploded on the other side. Bam!

Bam! Bam!

I flinched then pushed the door open to see Sloan standing in the same stairwell Muncy had descended earlier. He held a semi-auto shotgun with a drum magazine. It was belching fire and sending steel shot across the bar into the men standing on the other side clad in black holding AR-15 pistols.

Some dropped for cover, others dropped dead as Sloan kept firing. I fired the magazine until empty.

As the smoke cleared and the moaning subsided, three of the five-man team ran to the front door. They took positions and returned fire. I ducked back into the kitchen as the glass window exploded.

Tires screeched in the street and another volley of fire concentrated on the three men in the doorway. Dropping all three.

A car door slammed outside as I crouch-walked from the kitchen. Sloan took up behind the bar, shotgun at the ready. Billy covered me from the doorway.

"Roger!" Smitty called.

"Smitty, all clear in here." I shouted back.

His large frame filled the doorway. "Everyone okay?"

I looked back at Sloan who lowered his shotgun. "I think so. Sloan here took care of it."

"It's my taproom." Sloan said. He laid the shotgun down and came around the other side of the bar stopping to inspect yellow pock marks in the deeply stained pine boards. "Where the hell am I going to find hundred-year-old southern pine to replace this?"

"We don't have much time." Smitty said stepping over a dead man in the doorway. "The other two got away in a black SUV."

"Thanks."

"I've got your back kid." Smitty brushed the white-blond hair from over his grey-blue eyes.

"It's best if none of you were around when the cops come." Sloan said stooping to grab a Merc by the shoulder and began dragging him back to the kitchen.

"I'd offer you a ride, but. Anyway, no time for words." Smitty nodded, I nodded back.

"Billy and I will get another ride," I said. The smart thing to do was ride with Smitty and keep as close to Muncy as possible until he is handed over to the US Marshals. I *knew* that. Smitty did just cut off my hand back there like Vader and Luke, with his story of the Colt .45, but I needed space, a breathe, away from him.

"Suit yourself kid." Smitty said. He dragged the body in from the doorway then shut the door behind him. I watched him through the window as De Carlo stood in the street with a sawed-off pump. He fanned it around until Smitty was in the SUV. De Carlo climbed in, and they sped away.

Having my back was more than words to my father. Coming to terms with calling Smitty father or dad was going to take time but trusting him without knowing was not. He proved it time and time again. He wasn't there when I was a skate rat getting into trouble, or stealing my first car, but he took me in and made sure I had the best training and safe jobs that always provided me my fair cut. Guiding me through early adulthood the best he could and having my back even when I wasn't looking.

"The Camaro is across the street." Billy said peeking around the corner of the building, looking east to red and blue flashing lights closing in.

Sloan had his hand out for the pistol I held. "It would be easier to explain without you here."

I handed it over and we took the tunnel back to the Rockefeller's house. A silver wispy fog had rolled in off the beach. Every streetlight was haloed. The top of the condos across the street were barely visible. We walked the long way around and came up a side street to find two squad cars blocking the Camaro in. Billy shook his head, he was right. Too risky to ask the cops to move their cars so we could leave. This side of town is very quiet this time of night. Two guys walking up would be too obvious not to ask questions.

We turned back, walking west towards the river. We went down a flight of steps to a park with a large gazebo, water wheel and a couple of bronze dolphins spitting water. We kept on, going under the Granada Bridge, to a park on the other side. There I called Sanford.

Sanford only slept four hours a night and I just woke him short of three hours. It took a few times to convince him I was okay and where I was before cobwebs of sleep cleared from his brain. Fifteen minutes later his Cadillac circled the small park.

"What in the hell is going on?" Sanford said wide eyed as his head swiveled searching for potential threats.

"Don't worry, they're gone." I said sitting in the front seat. "I found Muncy."

"Uh-hah," he said looking in the rearview to just Billy in the back seat.

"Found Smitty too." Billy said.

"Seeing is believing." Sanford said pulling out of there and taking John Anderson Avenue north.

I filled him in on what happened and who Alvarez really was. He wanted to call Newstrom right away, but I told him to wait on that.

Sanford circled back and took us over the Granda Bridge and turned north onto Beach Street. Large homes lined the street looking out across the Halifax River. Wooden docks dotted the water's edge with soft pale white light reflecting off the dark water. Traffic at this hour was nonexistent. So, when Sanford saw the headlights gaining on us, he said, "We got a tail."

I checked the mirror and Billy looked over his shoulder, "Maybe you should let Billy drive."

"I got this, don't worry, might be nothing." Though Sanford's words were dismissive, his heavy foot on the accelerator was not.

The houses turned to blurs as we sped north. "If you cut left, we may lose them in the neighborhood." I said grabbing the door handle anticipating the hard turn.

"No, no, no. We're too far north now. All these roads come back to this one. We have a better chance losing them in the Loop." Sanford gritted his teeth as he gripped the wheel. The lights kept gaining. I knew the Cadillac could go faster and it would have with Billy driving. Beach Street was a single lane road with lots of divots and dips from settling sand beneath the asphalt. At 35 miles per hour, you hardly notice but at 70 they drop your tonsils into your stomach.

The Loop, as it's known to locals and the thousands of motorcyclists that come every year to ride the road through Tomoka State Park. A long straightaway disappears under a mossy oak canopy road that twists along the marshy shores of the Halifax and Tomoka rivers.

The road opened from under the leafy canopy and faded into a fog that settled in along the river. The lights behind us grew fuzzy but they did not disappear.

"What's the plan?" Billy said being a justified backseat driver.

"Cut off on one of them park service roads." Sanford licked his lips.

Sanford hit the brakes but didn't skid as we rounded to corner then cut back straightening us out in time to hit the bridge over the Tomoka River. We caught a little air, and the Cadillac suspension cushioned the landing as much as it could.

"Up ahead, where the road splits, take the left." Billy said.

"No," I looked over to Sanford. "Take them deeper into the park. We can trap them down in Bulow."

"Grimes we should get someplace safe." Sanford said.

"No, these are pros, there is nowhere safe anymore. They want us dead. If not tonight, then tomorrow or the next and so on."

Sanford nodded and kept the heading. The road snaked and he did his best to keep up our speed. The car behind us was evenly paced accelerating when we braked and braked while we accelerated. We hit some ripples in the asphalt bouncing us like a boat cutting another's wake. The SUV behind us took the bumps better and gained on the straightaway.

The bright lights disappeared as the tall bumper smashed out the taillights of the Cadillac. We lurched forward, Sanford fighting the wheel. The second hit put us into a spin. We went off the road taking small pine saplings with us as we bounced around like a pinball into the thicker tree line. The SUV wobbled; the driver hit the brakes, but it was too late. They hit the sloping end of the guard rail of a bridge spanning a tributary and launched into the air. The SUV smacked on the driver's side and slid another fifty feet.

As we all shook consciousness back into hour brains, I thought back to Newstrom saying the Troopers would be my shadow now. I wished they had been there.

The Cadillac was still running. Sanford gave it some gas, but it was useless in the muck of the swamp we settled in.

My door was caved in, so I slipped across and got out on Sanford's side. Billy was already out with his .357 in hand. He pointed to the SUV.

With my hand I motioned for Sanford to stay back. Billy and I spread apart as we crept up to the SUV.

The road was dark except for the one headlight still beaming out of the front of the SUV. Tiny Tetris shaped bits of glass covered the road. I wished for a gun.

The rear hatch window erupted in gun fire. We both dove. Billy scrambled along the ditch and leveled his aim and fired three shots. It was silent for a moment then something began moving in the SUV. Glass crackled, metal on metal clanged. After long moments of silence, I motioned to Billy. We stayed low but came out of the ditch and back onto the road. Keeping apart we proceeded once more.

I shouted at the SUV, "Come out and we won't shoot."

There was no response, so I shouted again. Without a response I went around to the front. The windshield was busted out. The driver's body was still belted in the seat. His head was missing. I looked through the back seat and to Billy standing on the other end of the sideways SUV. He waved.

"I see some blood on the seat but no other body than the driver." I said and looked off down the road lit by one headlight. Whoever the shooter was he got out through the front windshield and ran off into the marsh.

The headless driver wore a black button-down shirt with black cargo pants. A typical Merc. If I'd have found his head, he'd have a crew-cut and trimmed goatee. Along his right leg, I found a holstered Sig Sauer. I took that and the two magazines on his other hip.

"He turned the airbag switch off when he rammed us." Billy said half hanging down from the passenger's window. He opened the glove box and rummaged around.

"Even without the head, I recognize this guy. He was keeping guard of Peter Danzig. We need to get out of here," I said. Billy slipped back up through the window and crawled out of the back.

Sanford was on his knees, jamming sticks under his rear tire. "Damn thing is half sunk," he said.

"Fire it up and let's try and bounce it out." Billy said. Sanford got in behind the wheel. Billy and I positioned ourselves over the trunk.

Sanford gave it a little gas while Billy and I found our rhythm pushing down and letting up on the trunk of the car. As we pushed down a little traction was found but not enough. We kept at it until finally the tires grabbed, spitting dirt back at us as Sanford spun around up to the road.

Chapter 31

I clenched my jaw to keep my teeth from rattling as Sanford topped the Caddy out at thirty miles per hour. Billy said it was a bent tie rod. My guess was ball joint. Our debate didn't last long. The shuddering sedan forced Sanford to shout his rapid-fire questions. The lawyer wanted details, to know exactly, word for word, what Smitty said, Ruben, De Carlo, Sloan and even the gorilla said.

"So just that fast, boom. Smitty saw the threaded barrel and shot a man dead. Cold, cold, cold." Sanford shook his head while saying it.

I said nothing, playing the scene over in my mind and that heavy rock returned to my gut. A man dead on the floor twenty minutes after I watched him murder two other men. They laid on the floor in a similar form; arms out wide, legs twisted in a vine. Death has a certain unmistakable look about it; I had seen it so often there was no shock, no awe. Nothing. Where had my reaction gone? Fear, excitement, that tightening in the gut, did I ever have it? It's what made me so good at killing. Then there were Smitty's cold steel eyes, with a steady hand full of a hot barreled .38 as he poured himself a drink with the other. That's where I got it, the ability to kill, I got it from my own father.

"If the fake FBI agent is dead, then who was driving that truck back there?"

"Top security for Peter Danzig." I waited for Sanford to say something. He kept quiet.

"Who is this guy?" Billy said from the back seat.

"He's rich and powerful. Comes from a line of rich and powerful. Doesn't make much sense, does it? A man with everything and anything, and he abuses kids, allegedly. At the very least covers it up for other rich and powerful. I think it's best we all lay low, let Newstrom do his thing with Muncy's testimony." Sanford said.

The rest of the lumpy car ride was silent until we pulled into Sanford's garage.

"Don't worry about the car. Billy and I will take it to the shop and rebuild it. In the meantime, keep your garage door shut," I said.

Sanford nodded. He motioned for us to get into his other Cadillac, a 2022 CT5-V.

"I haven't even made a payment yet on this, so please Lord, no more car chases."

As we once again drove south down Beach Street a line of Volusia County Deputies raced north past us responding to a crash in the Loop. I wondered if Camp would get a call and be lead detective on the case.

Sanford dropped us off at the shop.

We sat in the first bay of the shop. The door down, one fluorescent light on above a long work bench with tool cabinets underneath and a double stacked chest at the end. Billy sat on a stool smoking a cigarette. I was on the middle seat of a minivan that had been pulled out. I held a bottle of water but didn't drink it. We stared, we thought, we said nothing for some time.

After his second cigarette Billy said, "Hell, I need a drink."

He disappeared into the blackness of the office and came back holding a bottle of Scotch. The bottle poured into a coffee mug, stained brown around the lip. He sipped it then said, "What now, you still want to run?"

I shook my head.

"Hell, I didn't think so." He lit a cigarette.

"Those will kill you."

"So will a bullet."

I shrugged, "Peter Danzig is behind this."

"Where do we find him?"

"We Kemosabe?"

"Yes, fucking we." Billy pulled at the top two snaps on his western shirt to expose a black class three Kevlar vest.

"I've always trusted you with my life, but this time we'll need more than just us." I scrolled through my cell.

"Yes."

"You were right. I need help. Can I text you an address?"

"Yes."

The text dinged through the receiver.

"When?"

"Right away."

"Done."

I clicked off. Billy stood adjusting the vest.

"Who was that?"

"Guardian angle."

"Okay, where to now?"

"We start back at Coopers."

Chapter 32

Only a few cars dotted the parking lot behind Coopers. Sagging yellow tape twisted in the offshore breeze, the only marker of a crime. The back entrance was locked. The lights were still on, so I banged on the door.

Charlie's face filled in the frosty rectangular window of the door. The lock clicked back as he opened the door, "Hey Roger. Alysa went to the hospital to help with Emma. She said to tell you to call or stop by her place."

"Thanks Charlie. Is Wayne still here?"

He pointed to the office as I passed him by. Billy went up to the bar and pulled a chair out.

The door to the office was open, I let myself in. Wayne was leaning back in an office chair. Beside him on the desk was a nearly empty bottle of Patron and no glass.

I sat in the other desk chair.

"Did you do it?" Wayne slurred.

"Do what?"

He pointed to a monitor. A small box on the screen held the security video of a van slowing down and a man grabbing the young server as she hauled trash out to the dumpster.

Wayne waved an open palm, dropping it on the desk. "Probably best I don't know right. What's it gonna cost me, Grimes." He said my name in a hiss. That could have been the booze or just what he really thought of me.

"I haven't done anything."

His bloodshot eyes rolled from the monitor to meet my eyes. He pinched at the tip of his nose and his eyes shut. "Well damn, what am I paying you for?"

"So far you haven't paid me anything. Tell me exactly what is going on between you and Danzig."

Wayne swayed in the chair, spinning in little quarter turns, rocking with the spinning room. "The guy's an asshole who likes to crush the little people of this town." He grabbed the bottle leaving less in it.

"He owns half of downtown and other properties. Why would he risk that to pressure a money-making business-like Coopers?"

"The thrill, because he can. Hell, I dunno." Wayne shrugged. His head went back as he looked up at the ceiling. Then it snapped forward like that was a bad idea. I thought he might puke, but he held it together.

"His office is in the Kress building. Let's go down there and ask him." Wayne grabbed the desk to stop the spinning in his head. It didn't work and he flopped back in the chair.

"You're not going anywhere."

"C'mon man. Let's go down there and waste him. You can shoot him or whatever. Got your gun? Let me see it." He said with his hand out.

"You're drunk and going nowhere. Also, I'm not carrying a gun because I don't kill people for money." I said getting to my feet. This reputation was beginning to piss me off.

Wayne put his head down on the desk. Muffled by his arm, he said, "They're gonna kill me if…"

I waited several seconds for him to finish his sentence. When he said nothing, I thought he passed out. Tapping on the desk he shot up. His head turning side to side as his saturated brain connected cells to tell him where he was.

"Why?" I asked not believing Wayne was really threatened. The guy had always come across to me as tough. A natural toughness that isn't taught, it's in his DNA. Danzig really had him spooked and I didn't like it.

"Him and his group." Wayne's eyes were watery and red. "Trident, Tri…whatever. Hell," He shrugged convinced there was no avoiding his death sentence.

"Why would he want you dead?" I was losing him to alcohol with no clue what he was saying.

"Nah, you know the I know something. They made it look like a suicide. You know the one guy. He tried to get out, him and his daughter." Wayne's face was now pressed against the desk. His lips were loose and curvy as he breathed through his mouth.

That churning in my gut weakened my knees and I sat back down. A rumor the man *suicided* by this local town kabbala had to be Gregg Hines. I alone knew the truth because I was there. I watched him put the gun in his mouth. Once a coward, the pedophile had grown into a mythical hero fighting against the dark machine pulling the strings of this town. A fire burnt in my chest. I went there to kill him, put him down so he could never hurt a child again and now in death he was venerated. I should have stopped him, grabbed the gun, shot him in the leg, something to keep him alive so he would have to confess his evil deeds in a court of law. Then everyone would know the kind of person he was, and we would all know who his allies were.

"Are you talking about Gregg Hines?"

"That's him, he was gonna confess it all man." Wayne sat up. "The cops knew there was someone else in the house but could never prove it." He stretched out his arm and opened a mini fridge. His arm came back holding a Red Bull. After sucking down half the can he came up for air with a burp. Then another burp. Only this time he grabbed the small plastic trash can and hurled up the Red Bull and the Patron still in his stomach. One of the Cooper's company shirts was on the desk, and he wiped his mouth with it then sipped a little Red Bull.

"Shit I feel better." Wayne rested his head on the back of the chair as he stared up at the ceiling.

"Good because we're leaving."

"Are we really going to kill Danzig?" He said standing too fast and waving his arms like he just caught a wave.

"Not what I do." I said and nudged him back into his seat.

I went back out into the bar leaving a drunken Wayne to sober up. Billy was leaning against the bar, choosing to stand than sit. Before him was an empty shot glass and he held a Miller Lite bottle. His head was down, long black hair out of the braid and covering his neck and face.

Charlie came over and I ordered two waters.

I sat on the stool next to Billy.

"What's the plan?" Billy said without looking up.

"You should ditch the piece and go home."

His head lifted; hair parted to the sides of his high red cheeks. "We ain't done yet, brother."

"You are."

"Like hell." He sipped his beer. "We're family Grimes."

My phone buzzed in my pocket. "More family." I said as I answered.

"Hello."

"Are you safe?" Spoken like a worried father, I guessed, since that wasn't something, I ever had.

"Sure."

"Are you alone?"

"Just get on with it Smitty." I regretted dismissing his cautious behavior, but we were both professionals.

"I thought you should know we're on our way to meet the Marshals."

"What time?"

"Thirty minutes."

"Okay. Be safe."

"You too kid. Listen when this is all over," He left it there for me to say something. I didn't. "Well, listen, don't go looking to settle a score. Let the law take care of it."

"Is that what you would have done?"

"No, no it ain't. But it is now."

"I gotta go. We'll talk later." I hung up before he could say anything more. A tremor in my gut radiated out to the tips of my fingers. The man I looked up to all this time, the man I subconsciously wanted to be my father was actually my father and all I could do was be rude.

We stepped out the back door into the parking lot of Coopers. Alysa was getting out of a white Ford sedan and on the other side was Detective Camp from the Sheriff's department. Camp was about 5'5" with black hair pulled tight behind her head. She had on a grey suit coat and grey slacks with a red button-down shirt. Her eyes, normally large and brown, were thinner now as she stared at me.

Alysa jogged a few steps to cut our distance. As she neared me, Camp called out, she wanted to talk with me.

"They said Emma died pretty quick." Alysa said as we closed the gap between us.

"Oh,"

"Detective Camp met me at the hospital and gave me a lift back. I can't believe it. I mean, she was right there, and I turned my back for just… just a minute to… I don't even know what I was doing." Her voice trailed off. Those green eyes, glassy, scanned over the parking lot where everything happened. I'd wished she had kept talking, saying anything to fill the silence. A silence I was expected to fill.

"I…" I was just trying to do my part in the conversation and failing. So I remained quiet.

"Anyway, I'm headed home now, but I don't think I'll be sleeping any time soon." Fingertips touched at building tears in the corners of her eyes. "I'm not scared or anything. Camp's escorting me home then putting an officer outside my place."

"That's good."

"Just a precaution. She asked why I thought anyone would try and," she took a deep breath and let it out slowly. "Try and kidnap Emma, or me. I didn't mention the dealers. It's your case, if you want to tell them, that's up to you.

"I'm really sorry you're in the middle again. I never thought it was connected…" I had to offer up something. Letting her do all the talking was making me feel worse.

"I volunteered this time, remember." She smiled. Tension eased just enough to let hope back in.

"And I'm sorry about earlier, the kiss in the middle of the bar." This was it, my last shot to get it all out and on the line. In case I didn't survive the night, I needed her to know some things about me.

"Oh," Her eyes faded as she looked to the ground.

"I mean, only if it made you uncomfortable."

Her hand came up, wrapping around my neck as she brought my face down to hers. Our lips embraced as I pulled her body in and up into mine. Her feet barely scraped asphalt.

"Don't ever be sorry for that Grimes."

I smiled. A sphere of normalcy covered me like the protective dome of that snow globe life I pictured for us. A dog, a house with a garage for my Scout. It was there, a life I wanted to live was waiting for me. I just had to survive my enemies and in order to do that, I had to leave the loving arms of a girl I longed for.

"So, if you want to come over, I'll be awake. Just make sure and let the cop know." She forced a laugh meant to ease things.

"I can't right now."

"Oh, okay. Yeah, I'll be fine with a cop outside." Her hips turned in a half step past me.

"You don't have to worry about them coming after you." As the words came out pressure built in my head and neck. My hand went out, grazing hers, checking to see where we were at.

The nothingness of her silence told me more than her words could. In that moment a void pulled open I had been working to close. Things had been good; they had been close. The trauma from last year had faded with Alysa joining me on an investigation and we were headed in a new direction. She had convinced me her fear was gone, replaced with the high of chasing dreams and saying yes to a life she knew could be fragile but worth the risk.

"That's why you can't come over." She said with her eyes down.

"I've got to finish this. When it's over, but right now—"

"Yeah, Grimes. I'm familiar with the routine." Her hand went through blond strands of her hair, "You're still the same. You surprised me tonight. In a good way, in a way I have wanted. But now I see Roger Grimes." Alysa's arms dropped to her sides, hands slapping the bare flesh of her thighs. She was done, out before whatever we had officially started.

Billy was doing his best to keep Detective Camp entertained. It wasn't enough. That bulldog scowl was coming my way. A natural detective, great at reading body language, she was reading our little scene like a billboard.

"Alysa, we better get you home." Camp said walking away from Billy and whatever he was bullshitting her about.

"Okay," Alysa said with a wave. She stepped in close to me, close enough to fill my nose with the sweet fresh citrus of her shampoo still there under the fryer grease and alcohol of the bar. "When this is over, when it's finally finished, you come home to me or don't come home at all." Her hand was on my chest, fingers spread, connected but also kept us divided.

I understood what she meant and said nothing so no promises would be broken.

"Hold it, Grimes."

I turned around. Detective Rhoshanda Camp was standing there with a thumb in her belt between her badge and service pistol.

"Camp." I nodded and started to move towards the pickup.

"Not today." Metal clanked from behind her back as she pulled a pair of shiny chrome cuffs. "An arrest warrant went out. Every cop in the county is looking for you."

"On what charge?" Billy said with a cigarette dangling between his lips.

"Murder of a police officer."

"Camp, you know I didn't do it."

"They have a palm print, Roger. It may not be yours, but Newstrom thinks it's enough to arrest you. Please, let me bring you in." Her face softened around the hard edges. Camp had trusted me in the past and I had proven myself worthy of it. The trust paid off for her too, that detective badge was proof.

"No, listen, I'm this close to blowing open the child trafficking case. I can get the proof, we're on our way now if you want to come."

"Not tonight. Don't make this hard on yourself."

"Camp you know it's bullshit. Gibson was protecting me. He was trying to warn me when he got killed."

"Please, I'm asking as your friend here Roger. If any other unit catches you, they won't ask. They think you killed a cop. You won't make it to the station alive."

"Trust me. After this I'm done for good." I said and couldn't stop my eyes from catching Alysa as she slipped into her Subaru.

Camp slid the cuffs back into their case. "Check in with me in fifteen minutes."

The drive out to Danzig's house would take thirty minutes. We had a stop to make, business between us to settle.

Our first stop was the marina and a locker.

Under bug infested fluorescent lights stood a bank of yellow metal faced lockers. Each locker was two feet cubed. I slid my key into locker 131. A small red and black canvas tool bag was the only thing in there. Inside the bag was a passport and credit card for Charlie Wolfe. A fake identity I set up years ago. Under that a stack of U.S. currency totaling ten thousand. Beside it a soft sided zippered case. I pulled the 1911 Colt from its nest and slipped it in my waist band.

I held the door open so Billy could look inside.

"There's ten thousand in cash. If shit goes wrong and I die, it's yours. Locker 131. Remember that."

He scoffed and looked off to the large white yachts lining the marina.

"If they kill me, just run."

"I ain't runn'n."

"I mean it, Billy. These guys aren't going to stop. Remember this, locker 131 at the marina."

"Yeah," he said keeping his eyes on his worn boots.

"Locker 131. There's cash for you. It's not enough to retire, but you could move back to South Carolina and start a new shop."

"Why are you talking like this, Roger? We got nothing to worry about." Billy smiled.

"This is different than any job we've ever done. Back there in the Loop you shot out of instinct, self-defense. It's what those elite security schools were all about. Killing a man when he doesn't know it's coming is totally different."

"Don't worry about me." He wiped the corners of his mouth taking the smile with it. He nodded and I knew he would have my back until I died. After that he was on his own.

The next stop to make was Billy's basement where he grabbed his tool bag from the hidden compartment in the false basement wall. Inside the bag we had electronics as well as an old-fashioned prybar. Tools of a trade we had long put away, but never forgot about.

Another tool was a Kevlar vest. He tried to get me to wear it, knowing I would be out front takin the heat, but I told him it was his. Then he tried to leave it behind, but I asked him to wear it. I said, I could think quicker not having to worry about his old ass. He put it on.

From there he made me drive so he could re braid his hair. The mansion we were looking for was tucked back on the outskirts of Ormond Beach, just past the small private airport. An unmanned security gate left open greeted us. We passed easily and wound through black-top streets nearing

Danzig's mansion. The deeper into the neighborhood we went the larger the homes grew. The size of the home correlated to the amount of vegetation surrounding the driveway. Until each drive disappeared behind low hanging oaks and big leafy green tropical plants.

Salmon colored sand pavers disappeared into the blackness of the tropical overgrowth. This was the house. We went in on foot under a three-quarter moon bright enough to cast shadows. The moon disappeared once under the green enclosure of the tree canopy above. About 200 yards ahead the bright moonlight guided us to the exit. Emerging from the Florida jungle path we saw a clearing of lush grass. Closer to the house a well-maintained island of palms and other tropical plants were lit up from the ground. More small lights in the ground threw up white semi-circles of light all the way to the apex of the large glass double doors. A six-car garage was to the left with a metal roof and two dormer windows jutting out. To the left smaller, Apex roofs marking each wing of the house. There was nothing modest about the house for the real estate mogul.

A white Lexus sedan sat parked next to a long Buick sedan sitting high on twenty-inch rims. The third vehicle was a black SUV, just like the one that flipped in the Loop. We crouched along a small hedge line bringing us 500 feet from the main entry to the house.

"How we gonna play this?" Billy said softly looking around at the lay of the house.

"We can split up and circle the house."

"What about Ben? Thought he was coming."

"He's here somewhere."

Billy nodded. Just as we turned our backs to make the split the front door opened. We lay flat with our heads up enough to see Newstrom walk out. He paused looking back at a black silhouette in the doorway.

"You better hope it's his print." Newstrom said.

"You just take care of Muncy like you were supposed to and everything will be fine." The silhouette shouted back.

"Your goons aren't making it any easier for me." Newstrom waved dismissingly as he slipped into the Lexus. The headlights came on. We buried our heads in the plush grass as he rounded the drive and sped off the property.

The door closed. Through the glass I could see two blurry silhouettes. He wasn't alone.

I mumbled a string of cuss words. The missing pieces fell into place. Danzig's power ran as deep as his pockets and at the bottom was, Newstrom, a state attorney and lead prosecutor for the trafficking case. From those pockets came payment to Alvarez. Gibson must have found evidence or decided to clear his conscience. Too bad he didn't get a chance. As I lay in the lawn, I had zero evidence to prove any of it.

"I wish I had that on video," I said.

"Maybe we can get his copy." He pointed to a corner of the doorway. Tucked high up in the corner was a little black cylinder with a glass lens.

"We're better off dismantling those."

"Leave no trace." Billy said, an old motto we used. Only this time there would be plenty left behind, starting with Danzig's corpse. It was time to shift gears, shift out of first and the idea I could change my ways. I had all the justifiers I needed to proceed, the law had failed, innocent's life was lost, and the rest of the high ground values hammered out from a dog-eat-dog world, but the simple fact was, I was backed into a corner. Danzig seemed invincible with a reach I couldn't see the end of. He wanted me dead. That comes with consequences he could not imagine, but I was about to show him.

Billy opened his tool bag. He handed me a mask; the kind motorcyclists use. He put one on and tucked his long braid into the back of his shirt. He pulled a radio frequency transmitter from the tool bag. Identifying the brand of security system, he could find the frequency and jam the signal effectively rendering it useless.

"They'll get an alert one of the cameras is jammed as soon as I hit *go*. Won't jam'em all though."

"At least it will keep them busy once we're in."

We scrambled to the porch and stood on either side of the front door. I looked out where we were and around the property hoping Ben was out there. Or that he was already inside and everyone in there was dead. It might be an over assumption of Ben's skills. Knowing the man as long as I did and never hearing him talk about what he did in the IDF or any kind of bragging about doing anything, lead to believe he was capable.

Easily enough, the door was unlocked. Once inside we had a look around. To the right past a staircase was a large white stone fireplace with fresh stacked logs but zero signs of soot or ash. Two white over-stuffed couches held too many pillows to sit. To the left was a dining room with a table setting for eight, beyond that a wet bar with two glass shelves lined with crystal glasses. Bottles of liquor filled the marble top and a mini fridge sat below. On the right of the bar was a short hall to the kitchen. To the left, another short hall where a flickering light emanated from a dark room.

Billy went to the right through the living room.

I neared the kitchen and paused at the sound of two mumbling male voices and glass clinked on marble countertops.

"Hey you two." Called a voice from the room with the TV. The mumbling stopped. "The front door camera is reporting an error. Go check it out."

A couple of 'I, sir' came from the pair as they started out.

I ducked into an open door that was for a bathroom. Two men walked out the front door. Radio chatter came from the TV room.

"Do a perimeter sweep and come back." he said. I recognized him as Jacobs, from Danzig's security. I stood behind him as he was sunk into a couch facing a giant bright TV showing a NASCAR race on mute. The cars circled in left turns around and around, as numbers scrolled along the bottom. A light blue strap went over the top of his shoulder leaving the left arm in a sling a square white bandage dotted with pink was taped to the top of his head. I found the missing shooter from the SUV. A laptop was open in his lap. His fingers stopped typing.

I didn't hesitate. My fingers slipped through the brass in my pocket and came out with such force that Jacobs's head snapped to the side then swung back taking his whole torso with it down into a decorative throw pillow to his side.

I undid his boot laces and bound his hands with them. His side arm was an H&K. With the slide off, I took the recoil spring and put it in my pocket. Then put the pistol back in the holster rendering it useless. I searched him, taking a four-inch blade from his pocket and took the radio.

Billy was looking up the staircase when I came around the corner. We both flinched then settled quickly.

"It's all clear brother."

"I found the head of security. Where the hell is Danzig?" I whispered as I joined him at the base of the stairs.

Billy shrugged as looked up the stairs once more. There was still a lot of house left to search. At the back of the upstairs hall, we found a spiral staircase that lead us down to the laundry room. Just as my feet touched down from the last rung to the tile floor white light washed over me. From the window the two guards stood, one shining a flashlight on me. I dropped but it was too late, the radio I held exploded with chatter.

Guard one, with the light, ran for the door. It was locked as he jiggled the handle. The other guard was on the radio as he ran from sight. Billy jumped the last two stairs and hit the tile floor moving. Just as the window exploded in rifle fire.

Glass shattered raining across the floor as we ran for the front door. I got there first and flipped the lock. Then we turned and ran to our left past the dining room and the TV room where Jacobs was now awake, wide eyed and bound as he shouted at us.

We went through a door into the six-car garage. The lights were off but silver moonlight was strong enough to penetrate the small windows in the garage doors. Three cars were evenly spaced across the garage. One Mercedes G-Wagon, one Maybach and at the end was a 1970 Ford Bronco. The Bronco was dark blue with a white top, four-inch suspension lift and thirty-five-inch-tall tires.

From behind us, yellow light from an open door projected long shadows of the cars across the painted garage. A voice called out, "Jacobs?"

We didn't move or breathe.

"What was all that crashing?" The voice said again.

I leaned into Billy's ear. "See if you can hotwire the Bronco. We're taking it with us."

He nodded and crept towards the ancient Detroit steel.

The stairs were wood, and there were a lot of them to the top of the long narrow stairwell. The first step was light, toe to heal as I ascended with the Colt 1911 outstretched. Hurried shuffling came from above. Whoever was up there didn't care about stepping lightly.

Twisting metal screeched as the interior door to the

garage ripped off its hinges. I looked out from the stairwell to see Jacobs standing in the doorway of the house with one of the guards behind him. He drew his pistol and squeezed the trigger. Nothing happened. I laughed as I ducted back into the stairwell. The hammer to another pistol cocked above my head, taking the smile off my face. I looked up to see Danzig pointing a revolver at me. He fired and I jumped. I hit the floor and scrambled for the Bronco.

Gun shots popped and bullets whizzed by. The concrete sparked in orange flashes as the bullets ricocheted. Billy slipped out from under the driver's side dash. We each took a spot against the large off-road tires of the Bronco.

We both fired a few rounds to halt the security team advancing. I looked out to see the guard go down, shot through the shin. Jacobs backed up to the door. I jumped up and fired twice more.

Two more shots came down from the stairwell, hitting nothing but concrete. Undeterred I moved forward. The guard on the ground started to crawl and I kicked him in the face on my run for cover behind the Maybach.

"Jacobs!" Danzig shouted from the upstairs room. Jacobs took command and made a break for the hall. The second guard opened up on us with the suppressed AR-15 pistol. After he withdrew to reload, I fired three shots into the wall.

Two seconds ticked by then Billy fired two shots. He wasn't waiting for return fire and charged the door. This time when the AR stuck out, he grabbed it and pulled the guy holding it out as well.

They rolled to the ground, struggling to get the upper hand. Each with a strong grip on the rifle and each other. He reared his head back and tried to headbutt Billy. Billy managed to dodge the blow and he caught it in the shoulder instead.

Jacobs stuck his face out and I fired, a near miss, as the door jamb splintered.

The guard who had been shot began to stir. Billy was still wrestling with the other guard. Jacobs poked a pistol out. I fired again at Jacobs then ran to the wounded guard, shooting him in the head. Next, I grabbed the guard on top of Billy.

He threw an elbow that sank into my stomach. My arm wrapped around his neck going for a choke hold, but his chin pinned down keeping him in the fight. I pulled back nearly locking my knees. He started to turn and pull away. My grip wasn't strong enough.

He squared up and the fight was on. His jabs went as quick as were his feet, slipping back then springing forward. A fist connected over my eye, splitting the skin and sending blood into my vision. He shot in. I spun as he lifted me up. My legs spread and my right planted but his weight was too much, and we collapsed to the concrete floor.

His fists were fast as they pummeled my ribs. My arm was up over the side of my head as his fists made contact. The blow rocked my brain. I rolled to my back. His hammer fist fell but didn't hit my face. My knee came up under his hips. I pushed him back and was able to sit up. From there I slipped my arm under his and clasped down into my other hand. I had him in a head lock as I rolled him to his back. He choked out.

Billy's eyes were calm as they rolled from the head-shot guard to the unconscious one at my feet.

"I need you to get that Bronco started." I said and pulled my mask off.

Billy nodded but didn't move. I pointed to it and repeated myself. Billy scooted back along the floor raising until he was against the Bronco tire.

My head swiveled. Standing with rifles at the ready were

two more guards. There was no time for surrender, no time to fight either. As I awaited death, the first guard's head popped, expelling a cloud of maroon mist all over the second guard. Before he could wipe the blood from his eyes to see what happened, his head popped. They fell together. From the aluminum garage door, two bullet holes cast silvery moon light down on the guards. Ben had an eye on us the whole time.

I turned to see Billy leaning against the wheel, his eyes wide and rolling back and forth. He was breathing heavy but controlled. Then he pulled himself up and duckwalked to the Bronco.

I leaned against the wall to the hallway leading up-stairs. At the top of the stairs was a closed door.

The magazine in my Colt held two rounds and one in the chamber. I went back and grabbed the merc's AR and put in a fresh magazine then charged a round. I took a deep breath then went up the stairs.

Three steps from the top I fired all thirty rounds into the door, shooting out the deadbolt and knob. Shouting came from inside, not death shouts, just fear, as the door swung open.

Two frightened shots splintered the door. Then Jacobs swore. I stepped through and shot him with the Colt. Two rounds hit him in the chest, knocking him back into the wall. He took a step towards me, but his knees gave out and he crashed to the thick cream carpet.

The room was large, almost as big as the garage below and just as dim. Halfway along the opposing wall was a desk with a computer and large monitor flickering blue light into the room. A box was open and filled with a laptop and flash drives. A wrap around leather couch took up the middle and a small bar was at the end of the room. Next to me was an exercise bike and wall mounted television, at least seventy inches.

On the other side of the couch stood a thinly muscled guy I had seen before but didn't know the connection fully until I saw him standing in the same room as his father. DeeZee was dressed in a wife beater and baggy jeans. Beside him was a pimply face Hispanic guy with strands of grey hair that contradicted his acne. They had their hands up.

Danzig was crouched beside the desk.

"Get up." I commanded.

Danzig stood slowly, pausing as he looked at Jacobs on the floor then to the other two. His brow was matted with damp hair. He licked the sweat from his lips and brushed back the hair from his eyes.

Danzig looked down at Jacobs, "A lot of good you did me." He looked to the other two, "I trusted you to take care of him?". Deezee began to explain but Danzig waved him off in disgust. His son had disappointed him again. He turned towards me then, "Look here, Grimes. This bloodshed has to end." His eyes betrayed him for the first time as they glanced to his son.

"It already has." I leveled my pistol. One round to end it all. What happened to the other two was up to them.

Danzig's arms went up, palms out. He crouched as his head shrank into his shoulders. "Just hear me out. Two seconds, then you can kill me." His eyes flashed to his son. All the sons he had destroyed in his life and now he wanted to save his own. Now the father and son stood together to face up to their evil ways.

The computer flickered on the desk. A little blue bar expanded across the screen as files were being deleted. He was erasing evidence. Disc wiping software was deleting everything. I clicked around trying to cancel it. Nothing worked. That evidence had to be preserved, not for the prosecution of Danzig, but the preservation of the crimes he committed against humanity so there would be no doubt justice was carried out tonight.

"That's right, Grimes. Everything you're after, everything you worked so hard for, killed so much for is disappearing. *Poof*." The stubby fingers on his hands danced.

It had been a risk going into that pool hall. A risk going to kill Greg Hines. And a risk every damn day I was alive after leaving so many who weren't. It wasn't enough to kill Peter Danzig. What he and the others did, alive or dead, had to come to light. The kids they ruined had a story to tell. Keeping their secret would allow their kind of cancer to grow as others moved into the shadows. I was ready to die to bring their sins to light.

In one broad step I made it to the wall and bent, reaching for the power plug. It was all the two needed to make their moves. Smashing into me, checking me like a hockey player into the glass, I hit the wall. Two hands went for the Colt as a third impacted my face. Their bodies pressed me with hot exasperated breath filled with half 'Mutha fukka.' 'Gonna keel you.' rhetoric.

A hammer fist came down on top of my head, doing little damage to me. An unseen fist buried into my gut. An elbow pushed up into my neck, cutting the breath from my lungs. The hammer fist closed in on my cheek then my right eye. Four fists pounded on my body in a fury.

My grip on the Colt was sweaty and my fingers could no longer hold it. I fired the last round into the ceiling, avoiding my worst fear of being shot with my own gun. With the slide now open, letting them know I was spent. From one hand I dropped the pistol. The other I tried for my back pocket, to the brass knuckles, but they were too fast. My hips twisted and brought up a knee impacting a thigh then repeated until the leg fell back and pressure on me lightened.

With all that I had; my knee went up once more connecting with one of them in the groin. A pair of hands fell away as Deezee retreated in a hunched stance. My head came off the wall and collided with Zit-face. The pop rang in my ears as my vision blurred but he still got the worst of it.

Zit-face fell to the soft carpet. I raised my foot and began stomping him. His skinny arms were up but couldn't stop the force of my leg thrusting a foot down on his chest. Something cracked.

Deezee recovered and swung on me again. I saw it coming and protected my face then retaliated with a left hook. He fell back out of reach of my right. I stepped through and kicked him. He rolled. Upon sitting up, he drew a small pistol. The pistol barked.

I spun, rolled and sprung up, leaping at him like a tiger. We collided. My head was under his chin, a hand around his wrist. He fired again, only hitting the wall somewhere. My fist pounded his genitals into dust. He wheezed then passed out from the pain.

I picked up the pistol. Zit-face had his hands up. My eye was swelling where his fist had hammered away. I shot him in the face. He wouldn't have given me anything different.

Danzig moved from behind the exercise bike. He stepped around with his hands up, his eyes were on Zit-face's brains oozing into the carpet. He walked with his hands up, stepping carefully towards his son. Danzig tapped him with the toe of his shoe. Deezee moaned as he lay in the fetal position with both hands cupping what was left of his manhood.

"C'mon boy, get up." Danzig nudged his son again. Deezee's eyes remain clenched shut.

"You're one cold bastard, Grimes." Danzig said. He was right. The dead kept piling up and I felt nothing, not sadness, nor accomplishment. Only a die I couldn't break, an MO I couldn't shake. The evil ways of a second-generation criminal. It could go a lot farther back than Smitty. I didn't know. I did know that Colt had seen its fair share of killing.

A family heirloom holding a family curse. Maybe there wasn't a point to hiding my evil ways.

I raised the pistol. Danzig lunged at me, closing the gap quickly. The gun went off, the bullet bit no flesh. Though not large Danzig was strong. Both hands grabbed at the gun. His strength held my gun hand down and close enough in my direction I couldn't fire. I swung him around getting him off his feet. When he landed, he planted, jerking me over. Using the momentum, he tried to break my grip and failed. I went over far enough not to see the knife. Sharp steel slipped through my shirt and my flesh. Instantly I stiffened as my skin split. My breath held through the siring pain then slowly I felt it leak out, not from my nose or mouth but from between my ribs.

"Grimes." My best friend called out to me from the garage below. I couldn't answer. Locked in the death grip with Danzig, my lung wouldn't refill with air. My face felt hot and my throat was tight.

A blade now tipped in my blood, glinted in the flashing computer monitor. I let go of the gun and reached out to catch the wrist before it plunged into my chest. I missed the hold but threw off his swing enough that the blade only nipped my side. Then a downward slash opened my leg, at the thigh. I staggard back, holding both my side and my leg.

"Just who the hell are you anyway?" Danzig was breathing heavy. "A nobody without a past, shows up and tries to dismantle a criminal empire. *My empire!*" Danzig gritted his teeth and smiled, as blood seeped from his gums. Replying was useless, I couldn't keep air in my lungs. The wet blade tip circled, imploring me to make a move. His dyed brown bangs hung in his eyes once again. He brushed them away and I jabbed a left into his square face. His eyes lit up, stunned by my speed, and he took a couple wild swings with the blade.

The computer dinged and a message flashed. The

machine had been wiped. The smile returned to Danzig's face.

"All gone, Grimes. All the evidence you and Muncy thought you would use against me is gone. Same with anyone associated with it. Nothing tying me to Hines or his daughter and all those kids." Danzig waved the knife but kept his distance.

From behind two arms wrapped around my midsection. The blade was a missile flying for my chest. I curled into myself, bending as low as I could. Danzig couldn't stop his momentum as he collided with us. We toppled to the ground. I rolled out into a squat stance.

Deezee screamed as the blade plunged into his neck. Danzig scrambled to push back his sons panicked hands trying to pull out the blade. Danzig screamed as his son pulled the blade and unknowingly ended his own life. Danzig held the wound as he watched the light fade from his son's eyes.

I moved to finish him. I came to kill him; I wasn't going to hesitate. We collided once more.

Rolling apart, he stood, his enlarged eyes narrowed as he played with the knife. The fight continued. The blade danced in the air. I watched his chest, his shoulders, not the blade. My vision was conned and the pain in my chest increased with ever shortening breathes. I was tired and wanted to it over, all of it.

While I was a thief, to get through a job, I convinced myself no one was getting hurt. It was all just material possessions insurance would replace. Then during a routine bank job, the guard got a backbone and drew down on me. My pistol was out and ready to fire until I looked into the round eyes of a little girl clutched tight in her mother's arms. Frozen in complete fear for her life. I stole something from her that day no amount of insurance could ever cover. I couldn't pull another bank job.

Danzig had been taking from children a long time. Tonight, it would stop.

We circled in the large room. Danzig tried maneuvering towards Jacob's body, hoping to make a grab for his gun. I had wanted the same but every time I took my eye from his, he lunged. Then I timed it.

He struck with a downward trajectory. I pivoted to my left and grabbed his wrist with my right hand. My left came up separating his elbow. The blade fell to the carpet. My heel tucked behind his, with my left arm guiding him back and to the floor. Then I was on top of him. With his left he pawed at my face, and I slapped his hand away. My fingers slipped into the brass I carried for so long and used on so many. I began to hammer away. No parting words, no pausing for speeches, no judgements rendered only a sentence carried out.

The images of things I saw over the years, the lives taken, and the living left to deal with their suffering flooded into my mind. All the damage done by all their deadly sins poured out of me as I finished what Sanford started.

The brass filled hand hammered away until it dropped, unable to be lifted.

Willis Sanford's *White Knight* had taken down the king. A little king in a little town. Danzig thought he was above consequences. He only thought in terms of himself. I didn't know what he thought as he took his last breath, and I didn't care.

"Grimes," Billy said standing at the top of the stairs. His pistol leveled in his hand.

I looked up from what I had done. I gulped some air and wiped blood from my face. Once on my feet, Billy was by my side with his hands out ready to steady me, but he didn't touch me.

"Time to go brother." He said guiding me to the door.

He looked back at the four dead men on the floor but said nothing.

******

Billy pulled the F-150 into the hotel parking lot then shut off the engine. My head was held up by the rear glass and my eyes fixated on the sagging headliner of the cab. The sky around us was a deep predawn purple. The sun was crowning, nearing its entrance, ready to burn off the morning haze that surrounded everything. Birds were just beginning their first song of the day that faded in the crash of waves advancing on the beach.

"You gonna be alright if I drop you?" Billy asked looking me over. My skull throbbed, my face felt burnt in spots, but that wasn't the worst of it. The jacket I wore was zipped up keeping him from seeing the severity of my wounds and keeping the shivers of shock at a minimum. His fingers fished in the front pocket of his t-shirt and pulled a pack of cigarettes. The pack shook but nothing came out. He crumpled the pack and tossed it to the cab floor. That's when he noticed all the blood splatter on his t-shirt resembling something like a Jackson Pollock. His eyes bounced around each splattered blot of human fluid.

"Hell," He said and took off the shirt. His eyes glanced over the half dozen hairs on his chest and then down each arm. "Not a scratch." He smiled.

I was too tired to do anything but nod my head. We sat together without talking, Billy with no shirt. I needed a minute to gather what reserves needed to climb out. His fingers tapped the wheel and his head looked off at every noise his ears picked up. He wanted to take me to the hospital or call a doctor, anything to make me better, all I had to do was ask.

"Thanks for everything." I said with eyes closed.

"Yeah, brother." He said then let out a slight chuckle. "Don't worry, we aren't actually brothers." He laughed some more at the expense of my recent family tree revelation.

Pain radiated with every beat of my heart. Laughing made it worse, but my soul needed to.

"It's okay. You'll always be my kemo sabe." I coughed. My side burned as I caught my breath. I smiled through the pain, splitting my crusty lip once more.

He threw his blood-stained tee shirt at me, "Get the hell outta my truck." Then he laughed.

I grabbed the handle and rolled myself out of the truck as he fired the engine.

Billy's window was down, he leaned out, "We start work Monday, seven a.m. sharp."

"What's today?"

"Shit, I don't know."

"See you brother," I whispered as I held my side.

"Later on." Billy said waiting for me to ask for help or collapse. When I didn't, he slapped the shifter in drive and took off.

I stared through the glass doors into the brightly lit hotel lobby. The night auditor was still on duty, brewing complimentary coffee and laying out pastries. I coughed and my head spun as I tried to catch a breath. Breathing was getting harder for me to do. The deep gash in my leg made it hard to walk. I tried to blame it on pure exhaustion, but I knew the wound under my ribcage punctured a lung and loss of blood slowed my heart rate. Death became a real consequence to this life. I was numb to it. All that mattered was that I didn't die in a parking lot or a hotel bed.

The Scout's vinyl seat was cold, or maybe I was just

cold. I couldn't feel the difference between the air temperature and inside my body. I shivered then sipped the last few ounces of an energy drink I had left in the cupholder.

The golden crown of the sun punched its way through a misty Atlantic covering the sand in silver-yellow light. The hotels cast long shadows over A1A as I made my way to the CBR Building. I blasted the heater in the truck and looked out at an empty road. White sand dusted the road, collecting in tiny dunes along the gutters. Birds with long beaks pecked the clumps of grass in empty lots. The air was heavy with moisture and flavored with salt. I drove with my left arm hanging out the window and every so often a glance out over the Atlantic into the rising sun to remind me I was home.

I crossed over the river and descended onto the mainland, the CBR building, once standing tall in the Daytona skyline now dwarfed by the shimmering blue mirrored glass of the Trident building. I made a pass through the baren parking lot behind Coopers. Yellow tape still hung near the dumpster where Emma's body was so casually dumped. It had only been eight hours since I drove off with an FBI agent. Eight hours, the normal working day for most people. They go to an office, clock in, get a coffee and talk about the weekend. Then sit at a desk watching the clock. In those eight hours so much had happened, so many lives lost. Now dawn was approaching it wasn't over for me.

I parked in the first spot at the CBR building. The curly haired guard was back on duty. She waved as I came through the lobby. Then she made a motion with her arm like she was hitting herself on the head and her tongue came out with a giggle like some kind of silent era slapstick. I smiled and straightened out my hobble to hide my pain as I moved past the desk.

She talked to me as I crossed the marble entryway for the elevators. I heard her say the stiches come out at the end of the week. Whether she noticed the bruises on my face or not, she didn't.

I took the elevator to the seventh floor.

I had a key for the main office and let myself in. The place was a dark, quiet tomb. It would be another hour before either Sanford or Monique arrived. Sanford's inner office door was locked. I checked Monique's desk, and it too was locked. I took a couple ballpoint pens off her desk and disassembled them. Using both springs and one ink cylinder I was able to pick the flimsy desk drawer lock.

I didn't find a spare key, but stumbled upon the pharmacy Monique was keeping for me. Percocet, Valium, Xanax and finally good old Ibuprofen. All the drugs needed to keep me going. To forget the past and be content in the now. I lined up the bottles and popped the cap on all of them. I got ready to shovel the contents down my throat and make my pain go away, all of it, inside and out forever. My knees tingled; I plopped down on the floor like a toddler learning to walk. A way out from the constant pain and the violence was on the desk. Alysa was better off without me, Billy too. None of the people I helped or saved even knew my face. Within arm's reach were no more memories, no more criminals, no more me.

A soft, high-pitched voice found its way from a memory to my ear and settled in my head with a giggle.

The difference is, I have time for redemption. The voice had belonged to Jinky, a man-boy caught in a cycle of violence, but the words had been mine, spoken to him after he joined me that night in the poolhall. He died there sitting in a chair, freed from his hate and his pain. I still had time, time to get home to Alysa, to run my fingers through her blond hair and stare into her green eyes. And time to build a new relationship with Smitty and learn about a family I never knew I had. I have finished this. My life wasn't over, I had to live for the living.

I snatched the Ibuprofen from the row of pill bottles. Deeper in the drawer were bandages and first aid ointments. I grabbed a few of them too and set about picking the lock to Sanford's inner office.

Once inside I headed for the mini fridge and stopped. My feet sunk in the thick gold carpet as the sun fully rose from the ocean and bathed the World's Most Famous Beach in the golden light of dawn. A new day began with a row of pelicans flying past the windows at eye level and below cars moved like Hot Wheels in the tiny street. For a few seconds I was pain free, it was mind out of body, kind of free.

It didn't last as my mind collided with my body once more expelling pain from every new hole carved in it tonight. I went to the bar, poured half a tumbler of bourbon, and looked in the fridge for a mixer. My recent stint of moderate sobriety left the fridge empty of soda. I took some ice and dropped it in then fed myself some Ibuprofen.

At the sink, I slipped out of my jacket and set the bandages on the marble counter then washed my hands. I tore open the bandages and laid them on the counter. I pinched the skin around the wound on my side, just below the ribcage and taped it shut. Then compressed a bandage and with one hand struggled to get tape over it. It needed stitches but would have to wait. I was still bleeding from other places on my body and there wasn't enough ice to put on all my bruises.

The soft burgundy leather wrapped around me as I collapsed into Sanford's chair. Comfort faded as each wound pulsated with angry nerves at the damage done. I was bleeding through the bandage, through my shirt and onto his chair. My eyes rolled and I rubbed the sockets to keep awake. The last time I bled in here, I sat on the other side of this large mahogany desk. That chair stared back, reupholstered now, but I knew under the fresh cloth, deep in the wood grain my blood was still there.

That night I transformed into what I am this day. The things I did and saw those few days broke what little conviction I had left of right and wrong. It melted it, twisted it into something that only made sense to Sanford. He saw me as his *White Knight*, battling crime and corruption in his beloved beach town. The city grew to think of me more as a Frankenstein's monster, a vigilante set loose to maim and kill, than a hero. The villagers with modern day torches of protest signs with slogans, marched to end the Vigilante.

But Roger Grimes was forged long before Willis Sanford got a hold of him. Smitty made sure of that. Maybe being a criminal was genetic, maybe it's part of a greater cycle. The dawn, the day, the evening, and the night. I killed a mother of a young boy to break a cycle of violence all the while being trapped in one myself. The sun broke into the office and laid a blanket of warmth over my face. I needed this new day to mean something.

Somewhere between the sun warming my body and the plushness of Sanford's stuffed leather chair I nodded off. Nothing but blackness, quiet, unblemished blackness. Then the click of the outer office door jarred me.

The jingle of keys and the clop of strapless heels moved across the outer office. Then stopped. Quiet. She knew someone was here but didn't know it was me. Sanford's door was open six inches. I watched it open another six then a hand with purple fingernails pointed a Smith & Wesson Bodyguard .380 at me.

"Grimes, I almost shot you, fool." Monique said, taking in a long-awaited breath.

"Sorry." I sent the last of the bourbon down my throat. It stung my lips at the split but was doing a good job numbing everything else.

"Run out of bourbon at home," she said. She wore a black wraparound dress with gold pipping and a thin fabric belt tied in the middle. There was nowhere to put the pistol but to point it down.

Her rich brown eyes released from their narrowed slits as she looked over the condition of my body.

"Grimes, my god, I need to call you a doctor," she said. In four steps she covered the room. Laid the pistol on the desk with her fifth step, then kneeled beside me on the sixth.

I leaned on my good side as she lifted my shirt. Those long-manicured nails now scrapped dried blood as she picked and pealed back the corner of the bandage.

"That's fresh." she said pulling her face away.

"Maybe an hour. Depends what time it is." I said squinting at the rising sun as if it was the face of a clock.

Monique grabbed my glass and went to the wet bar. She washed her fingertips of blood then put ice and bourbon in the glass. It was set in front of me as she made her way out.

"I'm calling Doctor Hammond." She said from the office door.

I could hear her talking on the phone. I stared at bloody finger smudges on my glass of bourbon.

"He's on his way." She said coming back into the office.

"I'll be fine. Just get me some superglue," I said. Every word, every breath stung like the knife that stuck me, stabbing… stabbing… stabbing…

Monique stood beside me, a crease between her eyebrows. She wanted to help but didn't know how. *More pills? More booze?* These last few years have not been easy on any of us. Monique had patched me up before and had worked to keep me out of jail. She was what kept me going. Though we never shared more than a few words and less smiles between us, I knew she would always take care of me, like she was now.

"Did you find him?" I said through the pain.

Her chin cocked to the side as she quickly shifted mental

gears.

"Oh, the boy."

I nodded; it was more of a bob. Despite the brilliant sun, the room was growing dark for me. My neck fought to support my head and my eyelids were losing their battle as well. I shifted some and the pain shot me awake.

She took a step towards me but stopped as I leaned forward on the desk. My breathing was quick and shallow. A punctured lung, tired, beat to hell and half-drunk, I had to find out about the boy before the big out.

"Is he," I pushed up off the desk. She threw up her hands as if magical forces could correct my balance, but there was no magic. I wobbled then steadied myself on the good leg.

"Is he safe?" I wheezed.

"Yes, living in the panhandle with his father."

"Is he hap—" A sharp pain pierced my upper chest cutting off my words. I moved from behind the desk. "Happy?"

She smiled with a nod. "Tab is happy and doing great. His dad works at a university there. He's remarried. Tab has a three-year-old half-brother."

The pain grew sharper. I couldn't speak, my mouth tightened. Fragmented images of a young boy who could smile now, play, and laugh with his half-brother and his father watching crossed the darkness of my mind. The cycle I set out to break was fractured. His destiny was his own.

"I used to baby sit him." I wheezed.

She smiled and took small steps towards me. "I know you did, Grimes. Safe and happy now. I promise."

My neck bent; my head dipped with eyes fused and losing light. Fingertips ran along my arm up to my shoulder. Then a hand grabbed hold. I stutter stepped, from shaky knees. Gravity pulled me down, I fought, she fought too. One hand, then two. Soon she had me wrapped in her arms; fingers interlaced around my back.

"It all means something now." She said holding me up.

I sobbed and she held me.

The end.

9 781942 657132